Dark Magic Series Book 2

Red Lands and Black Flames

J. E. Harter

This is a work of fiction. All of the characters, organizations, and events portrayed in this novel are either products of the author's imagination or are used fictitiously. Any resemblance to actual events, locales, or persons, living or dead, is coincidental.

Copyright © 2023 by J. E. Harter

All rights reserved.

No portion of this book may be reproduced in any form or by any electronic or mechanical means, including information storage and retrieval systems, without written permission from the author, except for the use of brief quotations in a book review, as permitted by U.S. copyright law.

Cover Artwork: Miblart

Editing: Erin Young

Map Design: Alec McK

Paperback ISBN: 979-8-9886106-4-9

Hardcover ISBN: 979-8-9886106-5-6

Ebook ISBN: 979-8-9886106-3-2

AUTHOR'S NOTE

The book contains subject matter that might be difficult for some readers, including extreme fantasy violence, blood, gore, war, decapitation, language, explicit sexual content, depressive & suicidal thoughts, references to rape (consent withdrawn) and sexual abuse.

CONTINENT OF ASTYE

CHAPTER 1

Marai

The cave was a prison. It had no iron bars, no locks, no chains. It was a cramped, dark space; a cage made of rocks and dirt the color of rust, encompassing Marai as she stepped foot inside its mouth. The musty scent reminded her of dungeons' past, and her footsteps ricocheted off the stone walls. Otherwise, it was silent. If it wasn't for the part-fae male in front of her, Marai would have thought her people had abandoned this place.

Raife walked stiffly through the tunnel, grip tight on the bow in his hand, perhaps wary of the person skulking behind him. Marai couldn't place blame—she hadn't seen Raife in eight years. She'd shown up out of the blue, and collapsed in front of him. Sunburnt. Disheveled. She was practically a stranger.

What does he think of me now?

To revive her, Raife had splashed cool water on her face moments earlier. When her eyelids fluttered open, she'd forgotten where she was. Marai's heartbeat had raced as she found herself enclosed in a man's arms. Arms she didn't recognize. Pirates? Bounty hunters? She'd quickly shoved Raife away and got unsteadily to her feet, ready to unsheathe Dimtoir. But then she'd studied his concerned face, his pointed fae ears. Her mind had calmed, and she'd remembered.

"What brings you back here, Marai?" Raife asked her in an apprehensive tone now that they were in the tunnel. He was taller and broader than the last time she'd seen him. Thin, clearly in need of several good meals. More freckles spattered across his cheeks, nose, and forehead.

"I'd rather not discuss it." Marai couldn't meet his vibrant emerald eyes, and the questions swirling around in them.

Raife frowned. "Suit yourself." He must have remembered Marai's moods: her sullen silences and angry outbursts. He knew not to push. He'd always been respectful that way. It was nice to know that, in some ways, he hadn't changed.

Marai glanced down at the black skin on her fingers. The tips had been stained by a magic she wasn't supposed to use; a dark magic that she'd called to in her panic, a power she didn't understand. A permanent reminder of her failure and weakness. The bloodstone jasper ring sat uselessly on her left hand. It hadn't helped her when she'd needed it. If Raife or the others saw her fingers, they'd never let her stay if they guessed she'd called upon dark magic.

Marai removed the ring from her finger and shoved it into her pocket before Raife could see. Then, she yanked on her black gloves, covering the evidence of her guilt.

Decades ago, this tunnel had been the beginnings of a main hallway for a rock dwelling. It was common in the Western Kingdom of Ehle for whole towns to be carved into the canyon walls, complete with window holes, stairs, and towers. Communities made of stone, tucked underneath overhanging cliffs. However, the tradesmen had abandoned this dwelling, most likely due to the horrible drought in the Badlands desert. When Marai was a child, Keshel had discovered the partially constructed cave, and the other young fae outcasts had moved in, happy at the time to have any roof over their heads.

Marai's pulse quickened again as the small tunnel opened into a cavern lit by a roaring central fire that was forever ablaze. An effervescent, ether scent tickled her nose—the first sign of magic.

A few smaller tunnels branched off, forming more private rooms for the inhabitants. While the decor and furnishings were sparse, there was an air of comfort. Woven baskets and clay pots littered the floors. Painted flowers dotted the cavern walls from crushed plant dyes. They'd been there since Marai was a child.

A young woman sat on a smooth rock squashing fragrant herbs with a mortar and pestle. Her long sable hair was braided atop her head; pointed faerie ears peeked out, accentuating the elegant planes of her face. She wore a simple dove gray dress and apron, which contrasted with the rich bronze tones of her skin. She turned at the sound of Marai and Raife's approaching footsteps. Her eyes widened and jaw dropped open.

"*Marai,*" she gasped, setting down her tools. The female crashed into Marai, arms wrapping around in a wave of maternal warmth.

Marai stiffened. Any kind of touch felt wrong, too overwhelming, and it grated against her skin.

Sensing her discomfort, Thora pulled back, tears in her striking ginger eyes. "We never thought we'd see you again."

Marai shimmied loose from her grasp, wincing at the touch to her sensitive sunburnt skin. Her limbs ached with each slight move. Her throat was raw from yelling, and parched from dehydration. Her head pounded–the concussion she'd received a few days prior hadn't healed yet. Everything hurt. Especially the unraveling heart within her breast.

"Come, sit. I'll treat your injuries while you talk," Thora said, wiping away the tears. She gestured Marai over to the rock.

The bundle of churning nerves in Marai's stomach eased.

I expected more of a fight than that . . .

Thora plucked a jar of ointment from a roughly carved shelf as Marai took a seat. Raife thrust a cup of water into her hands, then leaned against the cave wall, still holding his bow, as he watched Thora massage the cooling salve across Marai's pale, thin arms.

"I thought about you every day, you know," said Thora.

Marai had been twelve when she'd stormed out of the cave, without a word or note, leaving her life behind. Young Marai hadn't thought about how her disappearance might affect the others. She'd been selfish and ignorant. When she'd grown wise enough to know better, the fear of their rejection made it nearly impossible for Marai to return.

But she *had* returned, out of absolute desperation and defeat. Now she would have to face the consequences of her actions all those years ago.

"I'm still alive, aren't I?" she said.

Barely. Just a shell.

The green-hued ointment worked wonders on her burning skin. As it seeped in, the salve cooled like jellied ice, and eased away the pain, although it left behind a greenish tint.

Thora's gift was in healing. Whenever Marai had scraped a knee or cut up her palms climbing the cliffs, Thora had passed a gentle hand over the wound and it would vanish. The herbal remedies she collected and prepared were infused with her magic to speed the healing process. It was a rare gift, even amongst pure-blooded fae. With all of them exterminated, Thora was the only fae healer left in the entire world.

Except, perhaps, in the land of Andara . . .

Marai shoved aside the thought of that mysterious country across the sea where she'd once been headed. She downed the cup of water in one gulp. Raife took the cup from her hands and replaced it with his full waterskin.

"We wouldn't have known if you were alive had it not been for Keshel," Thora said. That familiar, stern tone hadn't disappeared, Marai noted.

"Was he keeping tabs on me?" she asked as Thora began spreading the salve across Marai's face and neck, healing cuts and gashes as she passed over them. The small injuries disappeared from Marai's body as if they were never there. Some of the physical pain ebbed away, and Marai loosened her grip on the rock to keep from falling over.

Thora's frown deepened as a look passed between her and Raife. "He didn't have much of a choice. Flashes of you would come every few months. But do you honestly think we wouldn't care? That we wouldn't wait anxiously for Keshel to share a new vision he'd had of you?"

Marai should've guessed the leader of the fae-pack would have received visions of her. Keshel, seven years her senior, had been given the heavy burden of raising a crop of part-fae children after the massacres left their parents dead. Keshel had the gift of foresight, the ability to see the future, present, and sometimes the past.

Thora lifted Marai's arm and attempted to remove her glove.

Marai snatched her hand away and tucked them both behind her back. "I'm fine now."

Questions and concerns flashed across Thora's face. Marai knew if Thora saw her fingers, she'd fall into a panic, worried about their safety. The bloodstone ring seemed to burn a hole of culpability in Marai's pocket. Another secret Marai was determined to hide from her people: Meallán's ring. A faerie queen's curse.

Thora opened her mouth to speak, but Raife leapt in first.

"I should let the others know of your arrival." He gave Marai a weak smile. "So they don't fall over dead from shock."

Raife drifted off down the main tunnel; the crunch of his boots in dust grew distant.

Thora finished dressing Marai's burns and wiped her hands on her apron. "Keshel told us you were on a ship for a while. And then explored the continent—"

"I wouldn't call it *exploring*—"

"What was it, then?" Thora asked, voice rising. "Because you disappeared into the night and couldn't be bothered to visit or send a message—"

"How could I send you a letter? This cave is in the middle of nowhere," Marai said, throwing up her arms in a way that reminded her of someone else she knew. Someone she had left hours ago in the tropical southern port town of Cleaving Tides. She squeezed her eyes shut to erase the memory of him.

"You could've come back." Hurt settled upon Thora's face. "You wouldn't have had to stay, but . . . you could've visited."

Before Marai could reply, a squeal of delight ruptured the tense atmosphere. Dark arms wrapped around her neck, smelling strongly of cactus blossoms and eucalyptus.

"You're here," said a merry voice in her ear. "Raife wasn't joking."

Kadiatu, removing her arms, beamed down with her round face. Her black wiry hair was twisted into long locks and decorated with handmade beads.

"Careful, Kadi, don't want to break fragile Marai, do you?" came a different sniggering male voice. "Arms like twigs, and no taller than the day she left."

At the mouth of the tunnel, Raife stood with his twin, Leif, identical to nearly the last freckle. Both brothers had defined cheekbones and arrow-straight noses, although Leif's sandy hair was shorter, unbound, curlier, than Raife's. That, and Leif's attitude, were the best ways to tell them apart.

A silent shadow lingered behind the brothers. Aresti.

When Marai had left, Aresti had been beautiful at fourteen. Now that she was an adult, Aresti was stunning: straight black hair, as shiny as a raven's wing, cut severely to her chin. Sensuous curves were accentuated by her tight pants and shirt. She had several more piercings in her ears and nose.

"Why are *you* here?" she asked, putting hands on her hips as she stared at Marai with haughty scorn. On her belt hung two short swords, her signature weapons. "I thought we were rid of you."

"That's unkind, Aresti," said Kadiatu, but it wasn't a scolding. No, never from Kadiatu, who radiated kindness and purity unlike anyone Marai had ever met. "We're so glad you're back." She hugged Marai again, and some of the horrible, crushing weight Marai carried lifted. She couldn't bear to lift her arms to embrace Kadiatu back, but she breathed in the comfort, along with the smell of cactus blossom. Kadiatu brushed Marai's wild, white-blonde hair from her face. "You look . . . different."

"You mean *dreadful*," chided Aresti.

Kadiatu rubbed her oily fingers together. "And slimy."

"I covered her in burn salve," Thora explained. "You should have known better than to walk here in broad daylight without coverage."

"I didn't," Marai said.

The others waited for her to go on.

Marai continued. "I didn't walk all the way here."

"Oh, so did you fly?" Leif flapped his arms, shooting Marai that taunting jeer he'd perfected as a child.

None of the part-fae had wings. There wasn't enough faerie in their blood to create those beautiful stained-glass wings that Marai remembered on her own father's back.

All those vivid fae eyes bored into Marai, waiting for answers. Marai's head spun. Too much had happened. She wasn't an innocent child anymore. How could she explain each horrible thing that she'd done?

Footsteps sounded in a tunnel to her left.

He appeared, sweeping into the room with a commanding grace only he possessed. *Keshel.*

His dark, angular eyes met hers, revealing no slight flicker of surprise. He'd already *seen* Marai's return. The others watched with bated breath as he approached Marai on the rock. She adjusted her gloves. She'd always hated the intensity of his gaze on her, how distant and solemn he was. Now, he looked at her in disapproval, as if he already knew each detestable crime she'd committed. He probably did.

"It's good to see you, Marai," he said, but his tone lacked conviction. "We so rarely have visitors who don't wish to cause us harm."

By the wariness in his voice, Marai guessed Keshel wasn't entirely sure she *wasn't* there to cause trouble. Marai squirmed. Had he *seen* her do something?

"Loquacious as always," said Leif under his breath and Aresti sniggered.

Marai shot them both a glare, which spurred on their chuckling.

"Why don't we all give Marai time, and let her explain things when she's ready?" Thora suggested, and Marai melted with appreciation. Thora put a hand on her shoulder and gently squeezed. Her fingers then hovered over Marai's skull, and Thora sucked in a short breath. "Why didn't you tell me you have a concussion?"

Raife stepped forward, his face darkening. "How did you get a concussion?"

Marai averted her eyes. She clamped her mouth shut. Resigned to not getting an answer, Raife sighed through his nose.

Thora went to work, and slowly, the pain ebbed away. Marai's vision sharpened. The ringing in her ears stopped. The fist-like pounding against her skull subsided.

Leif kicked a rock across the cavern floor. "Marai waltzes in here, after years away, and you expect us to *wait* for her to tell us anything? She owes us an explanation."

The silence was deafening as they stared at her. There was no skirting around this, but how could Marai find the words to explain?

"You escaped," Keshel said.

Marai's breath caught, stomach flip-flopping, as her anxiety returned. *How much does he know?*

"Escaped what?" Thora asked, fingers tensing against Marai's skull.

"The Tacorn dungeon and then the pirate ship," continued Keshel.

Marai met his cold gaze. *Everything.* He knew everything. He knew she'd been nearly tortured to death in the Tacornian castle fortress of Dul Tanen by a demented king. And that she'd once again come face-to-face with her worst nightmare in Captain Slate Hemming. The ring she'd stolen from him grew heavier in her pocket. Her fingertips turned numb.

"Why were you in the Tacorn dungeon?" Kadiatu gasped, amber eyes wide. Even Aresti and Leif seemed interested; their heads cocked to the side.

"I killed some soldiers. Tacorn didn't appreciate that."

That was an understatement. In the past few weeks, Marai had killed at least forty soldiers. She hated the shudder she saw from Thora and Kadiatu. She hated to see them come to their own conclusions about her story and why she'd taken those lives. But Marai struggled to find the words to explain. How could she admit all her failings? How could she reveal those demons inside her? If they'd flinched at the deaths of brutish Tacorn soldiers, what would they do if they knew the full length of Marai's tally?

"You . . . you killed people?" Thora asked, stepping back from Marai.

Fear gripped her. If they kicked Marai out, she had no one left. She'd be alone for good.

"She was protecting the Nevandian prince," said Keshel. "He paid for Marai's services."

"Why would he hire *you*?" Aresti asked, peering down at Marai as if she was an insignificant insect.

Marai glared at her. "I didn't come here to tell you *his* story."

No, she wouldn't talk about Ruenen. Not yet. The wounds were still too raw. Her actions in that alley filled her with overwhelming shame. It hadn't been half a day since she'd last seen him through the portal, surrounded by King Rayghast's bounty hunters. And she'd run away, leaving him to their mercy.

Had Keshel seen *that* in his visions? Seen her call upon dark magic?

"I'm here because I . . ." Marai stopped. She didn't know what to say. She couldn't bear to see the horror on Thora's face.

I need you. I need to feel safe.

And then, a deeper chasm cracked wide within her.

I want to be somewhere Ruenen has never been. Here, I won't see the memory of him in every tree, snowflake, or grain of sand.

Instead, she hung her head and stared at her gloved hands. When she looked back up, Keshel's eyes were on her fingers.

"I'm sorry I stayed away so long," she said to him first.

Keshel blinked in acknowledgment of her apology.

Kadiatu knelt in front of Marai and took her hands. "We're all glad you're back."

Marai didn't deserve her kindness. She was a murderer. A deserter. She'd brought danger into their home with the cursed ring and dark magic. Kadiatu might not even forgive her for that.

Aresti scrunched up her nose at Marai. "You need a bath. You smell terrible."

"Let that salve soak in for an hour, then you can go to the river and wash," said Thora, all business again. Whatever shock she'd shown was gone. "And be more careful out in the sun. You're so fair, you'll burn easily."

"You can wear my hat," Kadiatu said, and popped a silly wide-brimmed straw hat across Marai's head. "I weaved it myself from the plants by the river."

"It suits you," said Aresti, grinning.

Marai whipped the hat off as Aresti and Leif exited the cave.

Raife approached, his eyes softening. He, like Keshel, could read Marai's defeated, slumped stance. "How long do you intend to stay?" he asked.

Marai shrugged.

"You can stay as long as you need," Thora said. No one expected Marai to stay forever. They knew she couldn't be held down anymore, jailed like a prisoner in the desolate desert. Not after she'd seen so much of the world outside of the Badlands.

Marai was tired. So, so tired. Her shoulders sagged further as she closed her eyes. When she opened them again, Raife and Thora exchanged glances wrought with worry.

"Come, you should lie down," Thora said, tearing her eyes away from Raife, an ethereal warrior, bow and a quiver of arrows dangling from his back.

Keshel, at the other end of the room, sat on a rock with a book and his personal journal open in his lap, flipping through pages casually as if Marai's arrival meant nothing.

Kadiatu looped her arm through Marai's and lifted her to her feet. "You can sleep in my bed until we make one for you."

"We'll talk more when you're rested," came Keshel's cool voice. A promise that the interrogation was far from over. He didn't glance up from his book as Kadiatu led Marai to the bedroom, which was a small hollowed-out tunnel on the right.

Three cots had been erected next to a petite makeshift dresser made of red shale and wood from desert shrubbery. A lantern with a magical fae flame sat on top of the dresser. Kadiatu turned down the hemp blankets on one of the cots and fluffed up a thin pillow stuffed with feathers and grass. When they were little, Marai and Kadiatu had shared that cot. It was so strange to see them all as adults, to know how many years had passed and how much Marai had missed of their lives.

"Sleep," said Kadiatu. "Come find us when you're ready." She left Marai alone in the tunnel, the soft scuff of her slippers disappearing.

Marai sat on the rickety cot. Exhaustion pulled at every muscle. Her heart ached, her mind whirled, but she shoved it all away.

Walls up, shields up, she told herself, the same chant she'd used throughout her life.

Slowly, pain shooting across her body, Marai lowered herself under the blankets, covering her head. She leaned into the pain. She deserved it. Marai let darkness take her as her weary soul settled down into sheets that smelled familiar and felt like sanctuary.

CHAPTER 2

Marai

"She's clearly been through something harrowing."

"How did she get here? She had no belongings. It takes days to cross that desert."

"Does it matter? She's here now, and she needs us."

The voices were hushed. Marai opened her eyes from under the blankets and continued to listen to Thora and Raife's conversation.

"Those injuries . . ." whispered Raife.

"Nothing more serious than a concussion, though, thank Lirr." Thora sighed. "Being in that dungeon . . . she should've died."

"Don't press her. She's still the same walled-up Marai."

"You cannot blame me for being worried."

"I don't. I know how much you care," Raife said, and Marai was surprised to hear the warmth in his tone. Not about her, but towards Thora. It reminded her of how Ruenen used to speak to her . . .

Marai slammed the door on those intrusive memories.

She didn't want to get up. Every part of her yearned to stay covered in the blankets, to hide away from the world, and sleep forever. But Marai pulled the blankets from her head, startling Thora and Raife standing at the opening of the tunnel. They took a step apart, as if she'd caught them in a precarious position.

"How are you feeling?" Thora asked.

Marai's muscles rebelled at every movement, but at least she felt less awful than before. "How long was I out?"

"Oh, *hours*. I was starting to worry that you'd miss dinner."

Marai got to her feet, wincing. Raife made a move to come to her side, but she stalled him with a gloved hand. She shuffled out of the tunnel and into the main cavern, too tired to lift her feet from the floor. The others sat around the fire as a large bird roasted on a spit. It was a vulture, one of the few creatures that managed to survive in the desolate Badlands of Ehle. Cactus and legumes, usual desert fare for the fae, boiled in a pot at the edge of the fire. Marai's stomach rumbled. She hadn't eaten since the previous evening.

Marai staggered forward and took a seat on a cushion next to Kadiatu. Six sets of eyes watched her every move. "You don't have to stare at me."

"We wouldn't have to if you told us what you are doing here," Leif said from across the fire. His green eyes narrowed as Marai's annoyance bubbled. He'd always given her that superior, judgmental expression as children.

Keshel began to carve the roasted vulture. "Not while we're eating."

That quiet authority managed to stem the fights between Leif and Marai back when they were children. Keshel's eyes flashed at them both, a warning not to cause trouble. Marai was happy to obey this time.

The fae handed Keshel their plates and he doled out dinner. He put a heftier portion on Marai's. He must've heard her stomach growling, or maybe she simply looked that terrible. Leif shoved a piece of cactus in his mouth as he glared at Marai above the flames.

"Reports, please." Keshel served himself last.

"Nothing to report on our end," Raife said, indicating Leif and Aresti with his fork. "All calm in the territory." Since they were children, they'd run daily patrols around the cave in shifts, searching for any signs of danger.

"The garden is doing well," Kadiatu said, then leaned over to Marai. Her face lit up with pride. "I grew these cactuses and legumes, myself."

Most of the part-fae in the room had regular elemental magic, save for Kadiatu. She had little faerie blood, so the magic in her veins was weakest, almost nonexistent. She always had a special way with plants and growing things, but Marai assumed it had more to do with her nurturing personality than magic. Even now, Kadiatu was covered in dirt, including a red smudge across her nose.

When Marai had left, Kadiatu was a little girl, nine years old and gangly. Now, she was a young woman: fresh-faced, lovely, delicate, skin the color of dark cherry wood. Marai might not have recognized her if she'd come across Kadiatu somewhere else. She'd truly been gone for far too long.

"I restocked the herbal remedies," said Thora in between bites. "We're running low on certain items. We'll need to go to Paracaso soon."

Keshel nodded. "I've been taking more notes on fae history."

"Haven't you run out of texts by now?" Marai asked under her breath. What new information could he have found from the same old books he'd been reading for over a decade? What was the point of taking notes when he lived in the middle of the Badlands and would never go back to civilization?

Keshel ignored her. "And I swept the cave."

Marai couldn't tell. It looked exactly the same as it had when she'd arrived. Red dust always collected inside the cave, brought in by the canyon wind.

Everyone set down their plates, and all eyes returned to Marai. Did they expect *her* to make a report?

"I slept," she stated in a bland tone. She intended to do more of the same now that dinner was over.

Aresti scowled. "What's wrong with you?"

Marai stood, aiming to disappear for the rest of the night, but Leif stuck out a long leg, blocking her path to the bedroom.

"Aren't you going to do the dishes? Everyone contributes. That's the rule."

With a groan, Marai collected the dirty plates and forks hand-carved from wood and clay. She carried them outside to the river, noticing that the sun had fully set. She really had slept a long time . . .

Once she stepped foot outside the cave, the canyon cloaked in indigo light, Marai released the tension in her chest, gazing upwards.

The desert sky was as vast and clear as on a southern beach. White flecks of stars littered the open black canvas. A half-moon hovered above Marai's head, guiding her way to the river. On nights when the moon was full, the faeries didn't need to use their magical flames to see. The desert would be illuminated in silver light. It was a comforting feeling that Marai was used to: the sense of smallness, insignificance. Marai didn't mind the desert when she was outside. It was the cave and confinement that had always brought her anxiety and listlessness.

She knelt on the riverbank, removed her gloves, and scrubbed off the plates with her hands in the cool water. The temperature in the desert drastically declined at night, especially in the very early spring. Marai hastened her washing, then set the plates on a rock to dry. She slid off her boots and stepped into the river, fully clothed. Thora's ointment had helped relieve the sunburn, but the crisp water continued to soothe Marai's skin.

The lazy river wasn't deep. Water lapped at Marai's knees. This part wasn't rocky; the riverbed was mostly sand. She lay on her back, letting the water keep her afloat, drifting slowly. She gazed up at that starlit sky and thought of the nights she'd spent with Ruenen. Grief clutched her heart again. Shame climbed the stairs of her spine.

I don't want to feel this anymore. She didn't care where the river took her. She knew further down the canyon were rapids. She wouldn't try to swim to shore. She'd let the river drag her under. She deserved it.

Someone coughed on the shoreline.

Marai shifted her head to see Keshel. The corners of his eyes and mouth were tight. Marai trudged back to the bank, her body now as numb as her soul.

"I needed to bathe," she said, feeling the need to explain herself as he stared at her, unflinching. "You don't have to guard me. I'm not a child." Her tone came across flat, not at all edged and sharp as a blade. Not like it used to be.

"I thought you'd want to talk in private."

The night was still and so was Keshel. He'd wait patiently forever, as long as it took for her to speak. He'd always been that way—steadfast, calm. All the things Marai wasn't.

"I only see pieces in my visions. I know you sailed on a ship. I know something happened onboard that made you wear black and become a killer. And I know you were traveling with a young man who happened to be the Nevandian prince; that you were both brought to the Tacorn dungeon," Keshel said softly.

Marai flinched at each sentence, her armor cracking, crumbling. She couldn't look at him. Her story, her life, whittled down to a few simple points. A sad, harsh reality of what she'd become.

"Permit yourself to be vulnerable, Marai," continued Keshel. "Your humanity is a strength, not a weakness. It's why the prince trusted you."

Marai split open.

Tears cascaded down her cheeks, sobs wracked her body. She covered her face in her hands as shoes scuffed the dirt. Arms wrapped around her, lightly, hesitantly at first, then Keshel pulled her into his chest. She hated it. She hated this physical contact, but she didn't have the energy or will to fight him. The embrace made her cry harder.

"I failed him," she said into his shirt. "I was supposed to protect him."

"Is he dead?"

"I don't know. *I don't know.*"

Keshel placed one hand on her head and gently stroked. It was such an intimate gesture; something people did to those they loved. Keshel never held her before as a child. How could he be so gentle? His visions were limited. He hadn't seen how many lives she'd taken. He hadn't seen every soul-tainting sin. If he had, he wouldn't treat her this way. He would know better than to cradle a monster.

"If he's not dead yet, he will be," Marai said, clinging to him tighter. "And it's my fault. I ran away. I was supposed to protect him."

"If you care about him, why don't you go after him?"

"*Because I can't,*" she shouted and wrenched herself from his embrace. No one should touch her. Deserters and murderers didn't deserve such tenderness. "My magic hasn't recovered enough. I can't summon anything."

Her magic was an empty well, filled with nothing but red dust. She couldn't feel its tingle in her fingers; the awesome power as it once snaked under her skin.

"What does this have to do with magic?" Keshel asked.

Marai lifted up her blackened fingertips to the moonlight. Keshel's eyes snapped wide open as he stared, understanding clicked into place.

"I used it all, and took too much. And now . . . I can't get back to him," Marai said. "I created a portal, a door between places. I stepped through and ended up here. When I turned back to Ruenen, the portal sealed and I couldn't open it again."

Keshel stared at her stained fingers, brows pinched as if he was solving a difficult mathematical equation. Marai couldn't hold back the secrets any longer. She dug around in her pants pocket until she felt the cool metal band. She held out her hand to Keshel, revealing the jasper bloodstone ring, flecked with dots reminiscent of blood. It truly was cursed; the cause of so much of her grief. Keshel's expression darkened and Marai knew he held his tongue, biting back an answer. What did he know about her magic? The ring?

"I'd leave now, go back to him in a heartbeat, if my magic wasn't depleted," she said, pocketing the ring once again. "The hunters will take him to King Rayghast's castle in Dul Tanen. They'll have horses, but I'd be traveling on foot to Tacorn, which would take me at least a month. Even if I left tonight, Ruen would be dead by the time I arrive. I don't know how to help him."

Something else clouded Keshel's face then. A different kind of concern. "He's a human prince, Marai. Perhaps this is for the best."

A bolt of fury shot through her. "I should condemn him to death because he's *human*? *We* have human blood!"

"Yes, and humans killed your mother, one of their own, because she dared fall in love with a faerie. Most humans, especially those in power, do not have your mother's kind heart. Prince Ruenen may not have harmed you, but you could never fully trust him," Keshel replied, staying neutral, staying calm. "His own ancestor began the hunt on our people."

Keshel had always gravitated more to his fae roots. His human father had abandoned his faerie mother when he'd found out she was pregnant. As a child, Keshel had watched his mother be butchered right in front of him by radical Tacornians, men in Rayghast's army. They would have killed him, too, if he hadn't hid with Marai and the others.

"Ruenen deserves to die for his grandfather, King Talen's, crimes?" Marai stepped away from Keshel. She was close to punching that smooth, perfect face of his. "Our fae ancestors kept humans as slaves. That makes them no better than humans. *I've* killed people, Keshel. I'm just as dangerous, as untrustworthy."

Marai didn't miss the flicker of unease in his face. Her words rattled him. At his hesitancy, she stomped back towards the mouth of the cave, still dripping wet.

"I'm only trying to ease your guilt," Keshel called after her.

Guilt? What did he know of her guilt? What did he know about *anything* real? All Keshel knew and experienced were inked words on paper, visions seen through a pane of glass. Marai headed back towards the cave, hoping the distance would allow her anger at Keshel to dissipate.

None of the others had ever spent time amongst humans. While they held deep prejudices against those with any amount of fae blood, Marai knew not all humans were hateful. Not all of them were possessive and greedy like Slate, or as cruel as King Rayghast. Ruenen had taught her that. Against all her held beliefs, Ruenen had shown her compassion and understanding. And she'd repaid him with betrayal. Perhaps humans were right to despise the fae . . .

Marai stalked past Aresti at the tunnel entrance, who said nothing, but raised her eyebrows. Aresti was Keshel's cousin, but they were more like siblings. They both had the same brown angular eyes, jet black hair. Aresti's skin tone was tanner, deeper, whereas Keshel was as pale as paper.

Aresti kept walking, no doubt heading out for her patrol shift. Marai returned to the cavern to find Thora and Raife once again in quiet conversation, side by side, arms touching. Thora's face tilted upwards, and Raife chuckled at something she said.

They both fell silent when they spotted Marai.

"Oh! Marai, um . . ." Thora's voice was high and flustered. She stepped away from Raife and removed her apron, busying herself. "Where are the dishes?"

Raife cleared his throat. He murmured a casual "goodnight," and disappeared down the other tunnel to where he, Leif, and Keshel slept.

The sight of Thora and Raife, so casual, so close, ruffled something in Marai. A longing that left her feeling queasy. And envious.

"Keshel can bring them in," she said tersely.

Thora frowned. "Why are you all wet?"

"I bathed." Before Thora could speak again, Marai jumped in, "Where am I sleeping?"

"Kadi set up a bed for you on the floor. It may not be the most comfortable, but—"

"Perfect."

Marai stalked off into the right tunnel, not trying to be quiet as she collapsed onto the heap of blankets and pillows on the floor. The youngest fae had given Marai all but one of her blankets. Marai's heart clenched at the sight of Kadiatu's brown feet peeking out the bottom of her cot. Kadiatu was always sacrificing so others would be happy and comfortable.

And Marai, being the selfish soul she was, covered herself up in those blankets and refused to move again.

CHAPTER 3
Marai

She slept through breakfast. She slept through lunch. She wanted to sleep through dinner. But at some point in the afternoon, Thora ripped the blankets off of her.

"That's enough," she said, her face set in that stern motherly way.

Marai pulled them back over her head. "Piss off."

She didn't want to see anyone, especially Keshel. She merely wanted to stay in her bundle of blankets for the next several weeks.

"Whatever happened to you out there, you're not going to feel any better by lying here," Thora said, yanking the blankets back again. This time, she threw them onto Kadiatu's cot, leaving Marai uncovered. "Hiding won't solve anything."

"You know *nothing* about what happened to me," Marai hissed at her.

Thora's scowl deepened. "No, I don't, because you won't tell me anything. I'd be happy to listen, Marai, but I'm not here to pry." She put her hands on her hips. "Until then, you need to help with chores. So get up."

Thora didn't leave. She watched as Marai slowly got to her feet with a groan and a grimace. Everything still ached; sorrow had a way of burrowing into bone, never leaving, settling there like an arthritis. Thora had healed Marai's physical wounds, but the scars and shame still remained.

Someone had brought Marai's boots in from the riverbank, so Marai turned her back on Thora and slid them on. Then gloves, hiding those tainted fingers. Thora then led her into the cavern, where Raife stood leaning against the cave wall. Waiting.

Thora thrust a starchy desert vegetable into Marai's hands. "Eat first."

The vegetable had little flavor and became a thick paste in her mouth. Marai wanted to spit it out, but she forced herself to swallow.

"How well can you wield that sword?" Raife gestured to her father's faerie-made blade, Dimtoir, sitting in the corner with the other weapons.

"Better than you," Marai challenged.

Raife's eyes brightened. He grabbed a bow and quiver of arrows, and handed Marai her sword. "Good, then you can help on patrol."

"Wait—" Thora said, stopping Marai. Her hands hovered over Marai's body, and Thora closed her eyes. Cobalt and white magic coursed down her arms and covered Marai in warmth. It smelled of sparkling wine and rich ether, as elemental magic always did. "Now you won't get so sunburned. Be sure to take Kadi's hat with you."

Raife turned on his heel and stopped at the mouth of the tunnel, an invitation to follow. Marai left Kadiatu's straw hat behind.

"Have you had a lot of unwanted visitors?" she asked Raife as they stepped out onto the copper dirt of the canyon. Oppressive, dry heat engulfed her. Marai shielded her eyes from the blazing sun.

Damn, I should've taken the hat.

"Same as always. Wanderers, vagrants, explorers come around every few months. Most of them are deterred by Keshel's shields, but sometimes they cross through and we have to deal with them."

Keshel wasn't only gifted with sight. He also had an affinity for magical barriers, wards against humans who came sniffing. Some invisible shields were impenetrable; those were the strongest and required the most magic, but he couldn't hold those in place for too long. Another type created mirages, concealing the fae and their little home carved into the canyon wall from view.

But every so often, a human would pass through the wards, ignoring the signs of magic. It happened usually when Keshel was tired or asleep. Marai remembered several instances as a child when they all hid in the cave, silently, as they waited for a human to leave their territory.

Once, a man entered their cave, seeing as it was the only shelter from the harsh terrain for miles. The first time any of them took a life was when an escaped Ehle convict had sought safety in the carved out dwelling. Marai still remembered how Leif had charged the man, half his size. It took four of them, Keshel, Leif, Raife, and Aresti, to take the convict down. The man's blood coated the cave floor. Marai and Thora had sopped it up with their own blankets. Keshel, Leif, and Raife buried the body a mile away in the hot sun.

Something had changed in Leif that day. From then on, he'd viewed the world through a pessimistic haze.

Raife had then created patrol shifts to help avoid those types of situations again. They took shifts overseeing the borders of their little valley, in case anyone got past Keshel's wards. Raife, Leif, Aresti, and eventually Marai, took on those duties. They were the best with weapons. Kadiatu cultivated her garden, Thora healed, cleaned, cooked, everything a mother was expected to do. And Keshel read. Hours and hours of endless reading. Books he'd taken during the massacre. Books he'd found along the way.

Raife and Marai followed the snaking river through the narrow ravine. Along the shoreline, Marai trampled over patches of grass and tall reeds. They didn't speak, but the silence didn't feel awkward. Raife had always understood Marai's moods best. He never picked, never scolded, never pulled rank. He never treated Marai like she was a nuisance or about to explode, as his twin did. No, Raife had always let Marai be Marai, and in his presence, she began to settle.

Until the silent walking reminded her of those days with Ruenen in the White Ridge Mountains.

Marai stiffened and sucked in a breath. Raife's eyes snapped to her, but said not a word. Like the clouds dappling the sky, Marai let the memories drift away, and she relaxed again.

They crossed to the other side of the river before the current became too strong up ahead. They'd labeled this area, where the river turned deep, rocky, and hostile, the boundaries of their land. As a child, Marai used to go beyond to explore, climbing over the massive sandstone boulders on the shoreline, and would always come home to a berating from the others.

"It's not safe," Thora used to say.

"If you get lost out there, I'm not coming to find you," Leif would taunt.

"Stop trying to be brave, Marai," Aresti would snap. "You'll end up dead."

Marai hadn't cared. She'd always wanted to see *more*. She'd always wanted to experience *life*. And she had . . . she'd seen and done many things. Things that would cause Thora to gasp, Keshel to shake his head, Leif and Aresti to shut their mouths.

Sweat trickled down her back, chest and neck, but Marai didn't mind. She'd always relished the sun and heat. Once on the other side, Marai and Raife walked back towards the cave. Raife stopped to fill up his waterskin. He took his time, and watched Marai while he gulped down the contents.

"What's the ocean like?" he asked after a moment.

Marai stared down the winding canyon pass. "It's another world. The water can be calm, and the next minute, it crashes upon the beach with such force it can knock you off your feet, or a boat off course. Stronger than the rapids down the river. And it's so vast, you can't see anything but blue. You don't know if you'll ever see land again, like you and your boat are one tiny speck drifting along endlessly."

Marai took a breath, as if trying to summon the briny sea breeze, but all she inhaled was dust.

"I'd always wanted to see it as a boy," Raife said with a wistful sigh. "Were you ever scared out there on the sea? Being so alone?"

Marai hadn't been alone. She'd been a member of Slate's pirate crew, exploring and stealing across the seas. She'd thought, at the time, that she'd found her rightful place. Her home. *Love.* But she'd been wrong about it all. Captain Slate Hemming had never loved her. He'd used her for her body and for her magic. It was a scar that still hadn't faded.

But she didn't say all that to Raife. Instead, Marai shrugged and said, "Sometimes, but that was what made it so exciting."

Raife gave her a wry smile. "You always had a strange sense of adventure."

"And *you've* never strayed from the cave."

"I do miss the trees," said Raife in a voice so distant it sounded like a memory. "The whispering wind through the leaves. The chirp of sparrows. Leif and I used to climb up and return any eggs that fell from their nests. We'd run barefoot in verdant summer grass. True children of the forest. I've been wanting to go back to our ancestral home in the North."

"Why haven't you?" Marai asked. Raife was gritty enough; he could've set out on his own.

Raife stood and picked up his bow again. "I'd feel guilty leaving them all. I don't think I'd make it far before turning back. Besides, Leif would never let me go alone."

She hadn't felt guilty for leaving all those years ago. Eventually, though, guilt always catches up.

Raife handed her the waterskin and she took a sip. "The humans... did they ever discover what you are?"

The waterskin froze at Marai's mouth. "A few times."

"Did they ever hurt you?" Raife's freckled face darkened.

"One of them," Marai said, "but I hurt him more."

A savage smile grew on her lips at the memory of slicing across Captain Slate Hemming's handsome face. His roguish smile was forever ruined, thanks to Marai; if he lived at all after the fire on his beloved *Nightmare*.

But Ruenen, the second human to know her full truth, he'd never hurt her. And Marai knew he never would have, if she'd given him the chance. If she hadn't condemned him to death.

Marai reached for her magic, checking, but she hardly felt a flicker. Not a pulse. She was too drained; her magic hadn't recovered. Or perhaps, like her heart, it had closed itself off.

Raife started walking again. "What else did you see out there in the world?"

"The White Ridge Mountains of Grelta—"

"Snow?" Raife asked, eyes alighting with interest. "Gods, I can barely remember the cold."

Marai snorted. "Oh, I've seen my fair share of snow. And northern blizzards. I've seen the big cities of Fensmuir, Veilheim, Chiojan in Varana, Havenfiord in the Middle Kingdoms." She glanced at Raife. He listened intently, lips parted.

"I think you were right to leave," he said, causing Marai to nearly trip over her own feet. "You were always too curious, too brave. Fae aren't supposed to live in deserts and dusty canyons. I'm glad one of us got to leave. No matter what you experienced out there." Marai gaped at him and Raife smiled. "Don't tell the others I said so."

She'd forgotten how much she always liked him.

Raife and Marai returned to the cave after their patrol shift. The sun began to set, the final rays bursting above the towering canyon cliffs in lush hues of red, orange and gold. Keshel sat outside on a rock, book in his lap, not acknowledging their arrival. His eyes raked across the pages, as if he couldn't read the words fast enough. Raife shot Marai an arched-eyebrow before he entered the cave. Marai hesitated, then went to Keshel's side. Thanks to Raife, her anger had cooled from the previous night.

"What are you reading about?" she asked.

The book in Keshel's lap was old. Its tattered pages were yellowed. He didn't look up, so Marai stepped into the sun's path, casting a shadow down upon him. He finally raised his eyes, brows knit together.

"I'm trying to discover why your fingers turned black and what magic you used."

Interest piqued, Marai asked, "Have you learned anything?"

"You're unusual," he replied, making her scowl. She'd been told that far too many times by him and Nosficio the vampire. "I've always sensed a different power in you, something far greater than the magic the rest of us command. Maybe even more than a full-blooded fae. And it's not done growing. I don't think you've tapped into your full potential yet."

Keshel had said that before when she was younger. He'd *seen* it, that power, and Marai had experienced it first-hand: the lightning in the woods and on the ship with Slate. Then there were the portals, the doors that transported her between two locations. Strange magic that no other part-fae had.

Why *had* these powers suddenly appeared? Was it because she'd finally stopped hating the magic in her veins? Accepted that she was fae? Or was it because she'd started to *feel*. To *care*. To open up.

"Your well goes deeper, but it isn't endless," Keshel went on. "You used up your magic and then reached beyond your capacity." It wasn't a question.

Marai thought back to the day before. *Yesterday. Gods, it feels like years ago.* The other magic had called to her, had wanted her to use it, as if it had been lying in wait.

"I never knew magic could be dark, something truly forbidden. Black smoke clouded my brain. It wanted to control me, but I was able to stop it once I'd reached this side of the portal . . . once I'd calmed down." Marai stared at her fingers. "I could sense the magic tainting me, but it also felt *good* to have that power. It flooded through me and gave me strength."

But it had frightened her. The lack of control. She could have lost herself to the darkness entirely.

She met Keshel's gaze. "Why do you think my powers are different?"

Keshel shook his head. "I don't know. But the moment you came back to us, when you walked into the cave, I *felt* you before I saw. As if your very blood was charged like the sky in a storm." He closed the book in his lap and stood, towering over her. "Magic is similar to a living being. Every living, growing thing on the planet contains a form of life energy or magic. It has no rhyme or reason for what it does, how much power it bestows, and the kind of magic each being possesses. I've studied it for years, curious about why *I* have the gift of foresight and Thora can heal. Oftentimes, it does pass genetically through each fae lineage. Thora is descended from a long line of healers, and I had a great-grandmother who shared my gifts, as well. But you . . . you're entirely new. At least, as far back as four generations."

The hair prickled on Marai's arm. Why was she so different? Why had her magic developed in such a way?

"Then there's this ring." Keshel held out his hand. Marai pulled the bloodstone ring from her pocket and placed it in his palm. He examined it closely from all angles, wonder appearing on his face.

"It called to me," Marai said, "and enhances my powers somehow. Or maybe the ring opens me up to my magic more."

Keshel turned the ring over in his hand. "I can feel the essence of magic in it, but it doesn't call to me. This ring chose you. I can feel it humming with your imprint." He handed her back the ring.

Marai slid it onto her finger; its solid weight belonged there. "What does that mean, though?"

Keshel shook his head again. "I'm not sure. Again, magic does what it wants. It chooses who it wants."

"I was told the ring belonged to Queen Meallán, one of the ancient fae," Marai said.

Keshel stilled and his face went slack. "Are you sure?"

"That's what I was told," Marai said, but she trusted the source of information. Slate had been a rabid collector of magical items. He did his research.

Keshel lapsed into a pondering silence. Marai took that as her cue to leave, and headed for the tunnel.

"I'm sorry about what I said last night," called Keshel, causing Marai to turn back. He did appear apologetic—he frowned and his eyes saddened. "But you must understand that I may never be able to forgive humans for what they did to the fae. To my mother. I was older and I saw it all. Those images still live in here." He tapped against his skull.

Keshel rarely showed much emotion, but he let Marai see his pain then. The weight Keshel had always carried, burdened with raising six younger part-fae children, after witnessing his own mother's death. The strength it must have taken for him to push his own sorrow aside to take care of Marai and the others, and how many other fae children they'd lost along the way.

"I understand," Marai said, and she did. She understood why Keshel and the others hated and feared humans. She, herself, had thought that way for a long time.

"His name is Ruin."

Keshel had gone pale, eyes a distant glaze, and his voice dropped to a strange monotone. Marai knew this expression. He was *seeing*.

"What about Ruen?" she asked. The sound of his name from someone else's lips was a nail to the heart.

"He will be the ruin of the Middle Kingdoms as we know it."

Marai couldn't breathe. She felt as if she'd dove into a frozen lake.

"I see a great battle. I see death and carnage. I see the ruination of our way of life. Kingdoms will crumble. All because of *him*."

Marai grabbed hold of Keshel's arm, tugging, trying to get him to wake up and take the words back. "That can't be true. Ruenen wouldn't do anything to harm us."

Keshel's eyes cleared and he returned to normal, but appeared shaken, disturbed, by what he'd seen. "The prince's death will plunge Astye into utter chaos. It will be the catalyst. Rayghast will destroy everything. But he's already coming for us—he'll be here soon. Because of you, he knows the fae are not extinct."

"These are flashes," Marai said, fear and anger rising inside her. Blood rushed in her ears. "You always said your visions are merely possible outcomes. Did you *see* Ruenen dead?"

Keshel closed his eyes, body sagging under the futures he saw. He covered her hand, still on his arm, with his own. "I saw a terrible, bloody wound, not a soul could survive. His mangled body dangling from a fortress wall." Marai nearly retched at the thought. "Let this serve as a warning, Marai: danger surrounds your prince. Upon his death, this continent will change forever."

I need to find Ruenen.

Marai reached for her magic. She tried to create a portal, but she came up empty, a mere pulse. A tendril of dark magic stroked across her consciousness. Anger and desperation flaring, Marai contemplated reaching for it.

I could use it again to save Ruenen.

"Don't you dare call upon it." Keshel's voice was as sharp as the crack of a whip.

The desert came back into focus. Marai hadn't realized how quickly she'd tunneled into herself, into her empty well of magic. She'd never seen Keshel so concerned.

"I can feel it in the air; the dark magic writhing, a heaving weight. You can do nothing for the prince. He's dead. You cannot use that magic ever again, not for any reason. Not even to save a friend."

"You said it yourself, if Ruenen dies, then we *all* die. I have to do something to save him," Marai said. The ring on her finger vibrated, sensing her pull on the dark magic.

"You'll do more harm if you let that magic consume you. You're stronger than dark magic." Keshel put his hands on her shoulders and stared directly into her eyes. It was unnerving; Marai had always hated direct eye contact. It had always felt too intimate, and Keshel's gaze burned. "The prince wouldn't want that. You need to let him go."

She didn't know what was right anymore. Her resolve crumbled. Keshel pulled her into his arms. He said nothing more. All he did was breathe with her. Big breaths, in and out. He helped steady her. Marai's head cleared, the dark magic receded its pull, and Marai felt empty once again.

She could do nothing for him, not in her weakened state. She couldn't portal. She couldn't stop the chain of events from happening. Ruenen would die, and Astye would be thrown into peril. Marai would never reach him in time, and if she left, she'd abandon her people to fend off Rayghast's forces alone. He would come for the last of the fae. Rayghast would track them down to the Badlands and slaughter them in their cave, and Marai would lose *everyone* she cared about.

She had to make a choice. A gut-wrenching, devastating choice: go after Ruenen, but fail to save him, dooming her people in the process . . . or stay. Stay and fight. Stay and grow stronger; learn to control her magic.

Marai couldn't wallow in despair any longer. With a breaking heart, she made her decision.

I'm so sorry, Ruen.

As Keshel said, she had to let him go.

I can protect my people. At least I can do that much.

She didn't know how skilled Raife, Leif, and Aresti were in fighting. They could help fend off the hunters, but Marai alone knew Rayghast, had felt his twisted faerie magic in his mortal body, the dark magic that snaked under his skin. If her people wouldn't leave the safety of the cave, she'd have to prepare herself, *prepare them all,* to fight him and the legions he would send their way.

War was coming.

Marai stepped back from Keshel. "I won't let us die here. I won't allow Rayghast's men to massacre us, the way he did our parents."

No, she knew what needed to be done. Tomorrow, Marai would need to convince her people to fight back.

CHAPTER 4
Marai

Ruenen plagued Marai at night, as if he knew her decision to stay. He dangled from the ceiling in the Tacorn dungeon as Rayghast whipped him. Strips of leather flayed the skin from Ruenen's back; it peeled away in bloody patches. Chained to the wall, Marai was forced to watch every strike. Flames of black magic consumed Ruenen's wrecked body, melting bones as he screamed. Until he went silent. Until his body hung limp. Until his heart stopped beating . . .

Marai bolted awake, sweat plastering her shirt to her chest.

It had felt real, visceral, as Marai's nightmares always did. She used to dream of Slate's hands on her body. Of how he used to force himself upon her. This time, she'd smelled the tang of Ruenen's blood that coated the floor.

Marai steeled herself for the path she'd chosen. She couldn't save Ruenen, but she could save herself and her people.

The others were surprised to see her at breakfast. A piece of egg dangled from Leif's open mouth. Raife's eyebrows were high on his forehead as he watched Marai sit.

"You seem better today," Kadiatu said with a smile.

Marai had decided to take a step forward. It hurt less than standing still. She shoveled fried lizard eggs into her mouth.

"You no longer look like a lost forlorn child, at least," said Aresti, who received an agreeing murmur from Leif. "What's put you in such a vigorous mood?"

Marai glanced at Keshel, who met her gaze across the fire, but said nothing. "He hasn't told you what he saw last night?"

The others stilled.

Keshel remained silent.

"King Rayghast of Tacorn will soon control the entire Middle Kingdoms. I've had the unfortunate experience of meeting him, so he knows that not everyone with faerie blood was slaughtered when he attacked the camps years ago. He knows we still exist."

"And how is that our problem?" asked Leif.

"You'd be foolish to think Rayghast won't come sniffing around, searching for more of us," Marai said. "He won't believe that I'm the only fae still living. Keshel saw the riders. They're coming."

"Then perhaps you should leave, so you won't draw his attention here?" Leif asked with a dark glare. "He's after you, not us."

Before Marai could retort with something snide, Raife said, "He doesn't mean that."

Marai's fingers tightened on her fork, which she then thrust in Keshel's direction. "He saw the ruin of our way of life."

Thora and Kadiatu gasped. Raife dropped his fork with a clatter onto his clay plate.

"Ruin?" repeated Kadiatu with a wavering lower lip.

Keshel frowned. "This isn't how I wanted to tell you all."

"It doesn't matter how you tell them," Marai said. "What matters is that they *know*. We need to prepare. We need to train, or we need to run."

Aresti rolled her eyes. "Who's to say Rayghast would be able to find us? He's a human. Doesn't he have better things to do as king?"

"Until you hang from a chain in his torture chamber, you can't tell me what Rayghast will or won't do," Marai spat back.

Aresti pressed her lips together, cowed.

"Bounty hunters saw me exit the portal into the Badlands," Marai continued. "They'll put two-and-two together. They'll alert Rayghast, who will send hundreds of soldiers into this desert. When he wants something, he'll go to the ends of the world to find it. To *crush* it."

Marai thought of Ruenen again and shoved the memory of his smiling face aside. *No. I've made my choice.*

"Why do we need to train? We can handle weapons perfectly fine," Leif said, crossing his arms.

"You know *nothing* of battle, Leif," Marai growled at him. "None of you have stepped foot into the outside world. You've never faced down multiple skilled opponents in the chaos of battle."

"And you have?" Leif got to his feet, ready for the challenge.

Marai's hand went to the hilt of Dimtoir at her belt. "I've spent the past eight years killing."

Shame crawled up Marai's throat at the horrified expressions of Thora and Kadiatu. Raife's face became pinched and serious. But they deserved to know the person she'd become, who they'd let back into their lives.

"I was a pirate. A mercenary. You don't want to know how many people I've killed," Marai said this to Leif, who hadn't shied away. She didn't want to look at Thora, Kadiatu, and Raife again, only to see disgust lining their eyes. "I've gone up against Tacornian soldiers multiple times, and defeated them all. I've faced Rayghast and escaped. None of you will last long against them. You're all too soft."

Leif stepped towards Marai, but he didn't get the chance to reach for the knife at his side. Marai unsheathed Dimtoir in a blur and held the blade to his throat. The others leapt to their feet.

"Marai! Put down your sword," Thora squawked.

Leif glared at Marai, and she at him. "See? You were too slow." She glanced at Aresti, who was creeping up behind her. "And with one move, I can gut you too."

Aresti stopped with a huff. All eyes were on Marai, her senses tingling and alert. She felt like her old self. Strong. Hardened against the world. She swept aside the weak, pathetic girl she'd become after leaving Ruenen. She'd never become that girl again. There was no place for her in this world.

"Then we should run," said Thora, grasping desperately at the unspooling threads of her life around her. "We could hide somewhere else, and leave before Rayghast's men come searching."

"Where would we go?" asked Raife, rubbing his forehead. "This was the most remote, unsuspecting place for us to settle. We're at least protected by the canyon here, and Keshel's shields keep most people out. We have access to fresh water, food, shelter . . . if we go on the run again, we may not be so lucky."

Marai was tempted to tell them about Andara, that there were possibly other fae there, but they'd never leave Astye for somewhere entirely unknown. The fae were stubborn, always had been. They were staying, at least for now.

"Then we train. Tomorrow. I'll teach you everything I know," she told them.

Thora sighed, achingly sad. "I always knew this quiet could never last."

"We accept your offer of training, Marai. There's no harm in it," said Keshel and gestured for her to lower her sword. "Teach us, but in return, you must practice your magic. You need to learn to control it."

Marai sheathed Dimtoir, receiving a scathing look from Leif as the blade left a thin line on his skin.

While Keshel hadn't used the words, Marai understood his meaning. She needed to practice so that she'd never again be tempted by dark magic. Keshel understood magic in a way Marai never had. He studied it, and his own magic was strong, complex.

"You need to learn your limits, but also how much farther you can delve into your well. I can help you," he said.

Marai nodded, knowing that Keshel was the only individual alive able to help her now. She'd promised Ruenen in Cleaving Tides that she'd find the answers to her magic. While it wasn't Andara, working with Keshel was the first step.

Marai walked to the mouth of the tunnel. "Let's go."

"All of us?" Kadiatu asked, voice trembling.

"Women especially must learn how to protect themselves," Marai said as Kadiatu fiddled with the fabric of her dress. "You cannot rely on those stronger than you."

Kadiatu nodded timidly, then reached over to grab a sword from the weapons shelf. She held it awkwardly, and looked at the blade with disdain, but she was the first one behind Marai as they exited out into the light.

Keeping to the shadows cast by the canyon cliffs, Marai faced the others.

"This is such a waste of time," Leif hissed to Aresti.

"Marai's right," Raife said with a hand on his brother's shoulder. "We've never had to fight off more than one opponent at a time. If soldiers do come for us, I want to be ready."

Leif shot his twin an annoyed glare, but stopped complaining.

Marai pointed to Raife, Leif, and Aresti. "You three are the closest we have to warriors. I want you to attack me."

Leif smirked. "Gladly."

Thora, Keshel and Kadiatu stepped closer against the cliff wall. Raife dropped his quiver of arrows and his bow, and grasped the curved, elegant fae knife at his side. Raife was more comfortable with a bow in his hand, but he held the knife assuredly.

"Don't hold back," Marai warned them. "Because I won't."

Aresti and Leif attacked first. Leif, grinning arrogantly, swung his sword lazily at Marai. She dodged, and while his back was turned, unsheathed Dimtoir. She stopped before slicing down his spine.

Leif froze.

"Dead," Marai stated.

Leif grumbled as Aresti came up behind Marai, who whirled and fan-kicked both short swords from Aresti's hands.

Marai's own blade came to rest at Aresti's stomach. "Dead."

Raife wasn't as sly in his approach, nor was he direct. He circled Marai, neither of them making a move. Finally, she attacked, and Raife blocked two strikes before his knife spun from his hand and lodged into the red dirt.

"Dead, I know," he said through gritted teeth.

"Try again, this time all at once," said Marai.

Leif snapped, "I don't take orders from you."

"You do in training," Keshel said, resolute.

Leif clamped his lips shut, appearing as if he had plenty more to say.

Keshel raised his own sword, stood by Raife, and said, "Marai has skills and experiences we don't. If we want to survive, we need to let her teach us. The carnage I saw in the vision . . . I won't let that happen to us. Not again."

Marai and Keshel's eyes locked. She knew it wasn't easy for him to relinquish leadership, to admit that there were things he didn't know. His words had an effect on Leif, however. Leif's face slackened, going distant as he stared at the dirt. Marai knew that Leif, deep down, didn't want to be reminded of the fae massacre where his parents and older sister had died.

Thora and Kadiatu came forward, shifting awkwardly on their feet. Raife had taught them how to wield a weapon years ago in case of emergencies, but Marai doubted either females had ever had the occasion.

"Six against one seems hardly fair," Thora said.

"You think Rayghast's soldiers will play fair?" Marai asked dryly.

Thora swallowed down her response.

Aresti struck first, then Leif, then the rest were upon her. Marai dodged and twirled, light as a spring breeze. She blocked and parried each attack, and knocked weapons from hands as she went. Soon, all of the faeries were unarmed.

"That was incredible, Marai," Kadiatu said, as she wiped the beads of sweat from her brow. "Who taught you how to fight like that?"

"The blackest worm of a pirate captain," Marai replied, voice trailing off as she remembered those days on the deck of *The Nightmare*. Slate was a monster, but he and the crew had taught her well. "Again."

The six attacked, and once again, Marai incapacitated them all. She'd struck Leif across the face for good measure, to remove his arrogant expression. Blood dribbled from his nose; he wiped it away with the back of his hand.

"You're all too slow, too fearful," Marai said.

Thora, Kadiatu, and Keshel slumped forward, ready to quit, but Raife, Leif and Aresti shifted into position to go again. If there was one thing Marai knew, it was the fae's inherent desire for perfection. She felt that about her own skills when she was learning. Faeries were adept at overcoming their weaknesses. They practiced until their flaws became strengths.

"I'm not good at this," Thora said, dropping her sword into the dirt and tossing up her hands. "I'm not a fighter."

"You'll think differently when a man comes at you with a dagger and you know how to disarm him," Marai said. "It's not about being a great fighter. It's about defending yourself when necessary."

Thora pondered that for a moment, and then bent to pick up her blade.

The rest of the morning went by quickly. Raife, Leif and Aresti showed substantial progress by the end of the training session. Even Keshel improved. Thora and Kadiatu, however, were far too hesitant to hurt anyone.

"Thora, you have *healing skills*," Aresti pointed out. "If anyone gets hurt, you can fix them up."

"I don't want to be the cause of anyone's injuries," muttered Thora, putting her hands on her hips.

Marai had never seen Thora so untidy. Her hair curled in the humidity, her body dripped with sweat, and she puffed out heavy, uncomfortable breaths.

"Kadi and I are in dresses. It's not easy to move when you're worried about accidentally revealing your undergarments," Thora continued.

"Then wear something more appropriate tomorrow," Raife said, handing Thora his waterskin.

She shot him a look and he smiled. Thora's tension eased.

"Let's go in for lunch," said Kadiatu with a skip inside. "I'm starving."

As the others made their way into the tunnel, Keshel stopped Marai at the entrance. "After we eat, you and I will begin our own separate training."

True to his word, that afternoon, Marai and Keshel stood by the riverbank. The others had returned to their usual duties, although Leif and Raife were using their patrol time to practice their swordsmanship. Their movements were graceful and smooth. They'd repeat the same exercises over and over until they were perfected. Marai felt an uncanny gush of pride as she watched them spar and give each other adjustments.

She focused back on Keshel, who remained as impassive as always.

"How does your magic feel today?" he asked.

A flutter of power skittered down Marai's back as she tried to tap into her magic. "More than yesterday, but not close to recovered."

Marai hated feeling powerless. It was one of her greatest fears. Without magic, a part of her was missing. She could still defend herself physically, but a magical being without the use of its magic often felt lost. Not so long ago, she'd hated her magic, hated being fae.

But more than that, it would be impossible for Marai to defeat Rayghast and his dark magic without her own powers. Her lightning might be the only thing that could take him down.

"I want to learn how to make a shield," Marai said. She could create small bubbles, protective pockets, but nothing as substantial as Keshel's force fields. It would be a useful skill to add to her arsenal.

"Shields require a fair amount of magic, especially the kind I create around our borders."

"I should be able to do it."

"As you said, your magic hasn't yet recovered enough. Today, all you may be able to do is create one the size of your hand."

Marai grimaced. It was better than nothing.

"Have you ever focused on your life energy before?" Keshel asked.

"Is life energy different from elemental magic?"

"It's the root of all magic within you. You cannot fully master your own power until you understand it, *feel* it. Hold your hands together."

Marai cupped her hands together, feeling stupid. She showed Keshel as much in her expression.

"Now, close your eyes. Dig deep within, search for it."

She did as she was told, and searched around inside herself. All Marai sensed was the usual flicker of elemental magic, and the dismal well of drained power. What if she couldn't find it?

But then she sorted past all that, to a glowing orb of light.

Keshel's voice grew quiet, focused, as he said, "Pull from your center, and bring the energy into your hands."

Marai concentrated. Pulled. Warmth traveled up her torso, through her ribcage and arms. She opened an eye. The ball of light floated between her palms, shining, a miniature sun.

"That's your life energy, a physical manifestation of your whole being," Keshel explained. "Fae lore states that Lirr planted a piece of her life energy, a seed, into the ground, and that's where we came from. You must know the difference between *this,* and your magic. Without life energy, you die. Pulling from the wrong source can extinguish it. Make sure you never tap into your life energy. You must always know your limits."

Marai turned the orb of light over in her hands, and then sucked the light back inside her. She felt it settle in her core, winking like a star in the distance.

This time, Keshel closed his eyes, long dark hair draped over his shoulder; a serene ethereal creature so out of place in the Badlands desert. Her people didn't belong there. Fae normally lived in forests, amongst pallets of green, yellow, and brown. Not copper. Not dust. She wished she could move them someplace better. Andara still called to her across the raging waters . . .

"I imagine the shield first in my mind," he said. "I imagine it expanding and shrinking, adjusting over the land. I can mold the shield to my desires before the magic exits my fingertips."

Without the slightest bit of tension, a shield snapped into place around Marai. If she hadn't felt the magic in the air, smelled its bubbly, earthy scent, Marai wouldn't have known. The shield was entirely translucent. It shimmered if Marai cocked her head and peered at it from a certain angle, but a human could walk right past it and not realize there was magic in front of them.

Marai placed her hand on the shield and felt it fluctuate, a zap of magic rushed up her arm. From the other side, Keshel shuddered.

"Can you feel this?" Marai asked as she traced a finger across the shield, seeing how far it stretched around her.

"Yes," he replied, eyes focused on her blackened fingers. "I can feel your magic against mine. It's strange . . . the others have interacted with my shields before, but even with little power, you feel so different."

Marai sent a pulse of her own weak magic against it. The shield stayed strong, but shimmered.

Keshel stared at her with such intensity, a blush staining his cheeks. Marai felt heat on her own face that wasn't at all from the sun. She removed her hand. For some reason, touching the shield suddenly felt like an intimate act.

He cleared his throat. "Now you try."

Marai closed her eyes and did as Keshel instructed. She imagined the shield, formed it in her mind, and raised her hand. Feeble magic wobbled out, creating a barrier in front of her. Marai could instantly see the difference between hers and Keshel's. Hers was more visible, flickering, trying to stay in existence. It was a paltry imitation of Keshel's forcefield. The moment Marai stopped concentrating, the shield disappeared with a *pop*.

"How are you able to control multiple shields at once?" she asked with a scowl.

Keshel had at least three shields up around the boundaries of their territory: walls at each end of the canyon, and a domed ceiling above them across the gorge. Those shields hardly ever dropped.

Strangely, Keshel smiled. It was off-putting. Marai had hardly ever seen that expression on his inscrutable face.

"You have tremendous power, Marai, but so do I. Where yours is offensive, mine is defensive."

"We'd make a good team, then," Marai said.

Keshel's eyes opened wider. He hadn't been expecting that response. His face softened and he continued to smile. "Yes, I think we would."

Keshel had changed. Before, he'd always been the strict older brother, denying Marai of every freedom she desired. Suffocating her with rules. Talking at her like she was trouble, as if she was a hindrance, a bother. Now, he regarded her as an equal. He'd seen her through flashes, watched her from afar.

Or maybe it wasn't Keshel who'd changed. Perhaps it was Marai who had grown up. And she knew why . . . she knew why she'd softened. She understood why she'd changed.

Because a human prince deemed her worthy of his friendship and his trust.

Ruenen slipped through the cracks again. The chink in her armor. Ruenen brought down the walls, even if he wasn't there.

Even if he would soon be dead.

"You have great control over your magic, Marai," Keshel said, bringing her back to the valley, away from the dusty devils on her conscience. He was no longer smiling. He'd watched her go to that dark place within her soul. "I've always seen that. Your basic elemental magic is strong, but the power you've inherited from *somewhere* is stronger than regular magic. It will take more strength to control. Right now, you don't have the energy to light a fire. Until your magic recovers, practice your focus. Practice breathing. Imagine your power in your mind. Flex it. Shape it. Wield it. That's how I learned."

Keshel left her alone outside, contemplating his words and the gentle way in which he'd said them.

Marai seemed to have a knack for walking in on conversations between Thora and Raife. Before dinner, Thora had asked Marai to pick cactus fruits from Kadiatu's garden. When she'd returned to the cavern, Raife and Thora were quite close, barely a breath apart. Raife tucked a strand of Thora's brown hair behind her pointed ear and smiled down at her with such genuine affection that Marai's own heart stuttered. Someone had given her that look before.

Light on her feet, Marai entered the cave quietly. Raife and Thora weren't aware of her presence, so she cleared her throat and the two leapt apart. Their faces flushed, and Raife immediately hustled from the cave, mumbling about washing up before dinner.

Thora busied herself with stirring the pot of stew boiling over the fire. Marai deposited the cactus fruit onto the wooden table and faced Thora, crossing her arms.

"What?" Thora snapped, worrying her lower lip. "You can stop looking at me that way, and cut up those fruits."

Marai took her knife and started slicing the fruit into perfectly equal pieces, enough for seven people. "Do you and Raife have feelings for each other?"

Thora dropped the ladle into the pot of stew. Frazzled, she plucked it out with two fingers. "We're all very close here. We're all each other has." Her voice was higher than usual.

Marai popped a piece of fruit into her mouth. "You always told me never to lie."

Thora scowled. "It doesn't matter. Whatever feelings Raife and I have . . . it doesn't matter. And you *shouldn't* lie." Her ginger eyes flashed in that stern, motherly way Marai was used to.

"I should think those feelings matter a great deal," said Marai, having learned that herself recently.

"It's complicated."

Marai stared back blandly.

Thora stopped stirring the stew and sighed. "We can't, Marai. It's not safe."

"What does that mean?"

"Why are you so full of questions tonight?" snapped Thora.

Marai couldn't help it—she gave Thora a knowing smirk.

Thora sighed and tucked that loose strand of hair back again. Her expression changed. Her eyes saddened, lips pouted, making her appear younger, more akin to her age of twenty and four. "We've managed to survive this long because we've stayed hidden, always alert, always ready to run if we need to. There's never a moment when I don't fear that we'll be found. You and Keshel have assured us that *will* happen. And I cannot bring myself to love someone in that way only to have them taken from me."

Marai's heart sunk. Thora wasn't wrong. There was certainly a chance one of them could be killed at any moment. Marai understood that fear. It was one of the reasons why Marai had spent the past four years trying not to feel, untouchable and unattainable. She'd experienced the loss of love once, and she never wanted to feel that powerless again.

But she had. She'd let Ruenen into her heart. Now every part of her ached from the loss of him.

"Do you ever think that maybe it's worth it to have a few days of happiness?" Marai asked her, making Thora pause. "That if death comes for you or him . . . at least you had some time together."

Marai wasn't asking about Raife.

Thora studied her for a moment, as if she could read Marai's thoughts and knew she was struggling. "Sometimes I feel that way, but then I worry about children."

Children? Marai had never thought about children before. No new fae had been born in nearly two decades.

"I know I'd love them more than anything," Thora said, wrapping her arms around herself, "but how could I bring them into this world? It would be selfish of me to want them, when all they'd experience would be fear and pain. Our lives are not fit for a child."

"But *we* were children, and *we* survived," Marai said, coming to Thora's side. "Your children would at least have a mother and father, and all the rest of us to watch out for them. Aunts and uncles at their beck and call."

Thora smiled sadly and shook her head. "What if I die? And Raife dies? Then they'd be orphans, no better off than we were, and I wouldn't wish that life on my flesh and blood." She returned to stirring the pot. "No, Marai, we're all better off trying to live for as long as we can. That must be enough."

Marai's anger rose. It wasn't right. Thora deserved happiness. They all did. Marai wanted to give them a world where they would be safe, yet there was nowhere like that here on the continent of Astye. Perhaps in Andara things would be different, but Marai knew the risk of trying to leave these lands. What boat, what captain, would carry seven penniless faeries across a treacherous ocean leagues and leagues away to an unexplored, potentially dangerous country?

Her stomach knotted. Slate would have. He would've had them steal and kill for him, sure, but Slate was the one captain who would have relished the company of faeries and their magic onboard. She hated discovering those small, decent parts of him. They were the things that had made her fall in love with him. If Slate hadn't been so greedy, if he hadn't become a pirate, Marai thought he might have led a very different life.

"Sometimes, I look across the cavern, and I think how much it hurts to love him," Thora said in a quiet, distant voice, full of a pain Marai recognized. "It's almost unbearable. It's not the feeling that hurts, though. It's the thought of anything happening to him."

The memory of Ruenen's dimpled smile and gold-flecked eyes swam into Marai's brain. But then his smile disappeared and became an expression of shock and betrayal. The image was too clear. Too vivid. Too recent. It tore through her heart.

"Have you ever told Raife how you feel?"

"Dinner's ready," Thora said, her voice high-pitched again. "Please go get the others."

Marai left Thora to ladle the stew into bowls, her lungs unable to contract. Outside, she gulped down fresh air, and forced her mind to go blank again. Forced Ruenen out of the chambers of her heart.

She found Raife by the river, staring at the moon. Kadiatu, Aresti, and Leif were farther away, laughing at something as they gathered firewood.

"Thora says to come in for dinner," Marai called to them all.

Raife gave Marai a halfhearted, melancholy smile, before beginning to head into the cave with the others.

"I wish you didn't have to hide your feelings," she said, making him stop. "I wish you could feel free to live the way you want and deserve."

Raife blushed and shrugged, a gesture that so reminded Marai of Ruenen. She hated how she kept seeing him in others, hearing his voice in their inflections. Echoes of him dwelled everywhere.

"It's the only way to survive, as you well know," Raife said. "If I could take her somewhere safe, where we could have a home, I would."

"Do you love her?" Marai pressed, and this time, Raife gave her a real smile.

"With every fiber of my being."

CHAPTER 5
Marai

Days passed, and Keshel had a new vision of black armored men riding across a red desert. Rayghast's men would be there soon. Time was running out.

Marai intensified their training, and became used to the routine. Training each morning after breakfast. Afternoons with Keshel, working on her control of magic. Evenings were Marai's patrol shift.

Stay busy.

The activity kept her from spiraling, plunging into a pit of shame so deep it could burrow into the center of the earth.

Focus.

Leif needed to guard his left side. Thora and Kadiatu needed upper-body strengthening.

Stay busy.

Whenever there was a moment of peace, Marai heard Ruenen's laughter echo through the canyon. The wind whispered *Sassafras* as it twirled its invisible fingers around her hair. She saw him splashing in the river, beckoning her to join, trying to get her to look.

She wouldn't look. *No, stay busy.*

He's dead. Ruenen is dead. Keshel said *he's dead.*

Those words she repeated over and over until she accepted that they were reality.

Marai's magic was still recovering. All she'd managed to conjure at her fingertips were her usual fire, a stronger shield, and a spark of lightning.

Focus on your people. Focus on training. This is the path you chose. Repent by protecting them.

Kadiatu swung her sword down, far too slow, far too cautious. As her blade collided with Marai's, she squealed and nearly dropped her sword.

"You're not going to hurt me, Kadi," Marai said with an exasperated huff. "You need to put power behind your swing. Grip the handle tight. Tacorn soldiers aren't going to go easy on you."

"I know, I'm sorry," said Kadiatu. She sniffed as her eyes shimmered with tears. "I'm not good at all this, but I'll keep trying."

Marai sighed, joining Raife in the shade, as Aresti took over with Kadiatu.

Nearby, Keshel, Leif, and Thora were working together. Leif's pride was wounded from Marai beating him so many times. He was the most animated for training every day; first to wake and last to sleep.

"You're not a very understanding instructor," Raife said.

"If you're too soft, people die," said Marai, watching Aresti pivot effortlessly and cut across, forcing Kadiatu to duck and fall onto her tailbone.

Aresti helped her back up. She and Kadiatu laughed at the large red spot of dirt on her rear.

"Like a giant bullseye," Aresti said as Kadiatu brushed off the dirt, giggling.

Raife also chuckled. "Yes, but you can have the same intensity and compliment the *positive* things, Marai."

He'd been teaching everyone how to handle a bow and arrow. Marai had never taken to archery. Raife was skilled; he could shoot a soaring vulture straight through the eye. He'd carried around a bow since he learned to walk. Thora and Kadiatu were more at ease in his presence than they were in Marai's, and preferred the bow and arrow to a sword.

"In the real world, there are no compliments," Marai told him. "There's life or death."

"Then I'm glad to be here for as long as I can," Raife replied, smile fading. "I know danger's coming, but I'll savor every second of peace and laughter I can collect." His gaze tracked Thora's movements with Leif.

Marai didn't want to admit it, but she'd been doing the same. Every smile, every giggle, every normal interaction . . . she clung to those moments. She never knew when they might be her last.

"We should begin combining our weapons training with magic," she said as everyone took a brief water break.

"What do you mean?" asked Aresti, sharpening one of her blades with a smooth wet stone by the river.

"You'll be the most effective if you can utilize both skills at once."

Aresti switched to sharpening her other sword. "I thought the point was *not* to show our magic to humans?"

"They'll already know we're fae," Leif said. He held out his sword before him, arm straight and steady. "Why not show them everything we've got?"

The air shifted slightly. Magic gathered within him, centering in his outstretched arm. Bright vermilion flames burst forth from his fist and skittered down the length of the blade.

Marai couldn't stop herself from grinning. *Brilliant*. A flaming sword, able to slice *and* scorch. She'd done something similar with her lightning and Dimtoir on *The Nightmare*.

Fire had always been Leif's specialty; the eternally burning fire in the cavern was his creation. Leif swung his blazing weapon back and forth, creating a trail of sparks and embers like a shooting star. Marai didn't mind the smug smirk at his lips. It was time the fae stopped fearing their power.

"That's good, Leif," Marai said. "Can you lead the others in this exercise?"

Leif's eyebrows shot up, surprised at the compliment and concession. Marai knelt on the riverbank and dipped her hands in the cool water. Behind her, she heard Leif say, "Alright, children, let's light 'em up."

Flames skittered up Aresti, Raife, and Keshel's swords. Even Thora managed to produce a few tendrils, but Kadiatu had never been able to call forth fire. Her blade remained metal, but she seemed more relieved than disappointed. Kadiatu didn't want to complicate something that was already challenging for her.

Marai's lips twitched into a smile. She quickly turned her head, hoping none of them saw how pleased she was. But that pride disappeared the longer Marai stared at her hands in the water. Keshel alone had seen the black skin of her fingertips. She wore her gloves at all times. Marai didn't want to explain to the others what she'd done, especially since Leif and Aresti had finally begun to trust and respect her.

She enjoyed the company of her fellow fae. Her family. She'd missed them. This way of life was so different than her time away. But how long could this peace last?

Marai knew her time in Ehle was limited. There was only so long she could bear to stay in the desert, so far from civilization. She missed the trees and the grass, the dirt and mud and sand. Her heart ached to hear the chirping crickets, roar of the ocean, the sounds of *life*. She missed ordinary humans sometimes.

But could she leave the others here to fend for themselves? Rayghast would still search for them. They weren't safe here, especially without Marai.

Perhaps we can go to Andara . . .

It was an idea that had been growing in her mind, a flower beginning to bloom. She thought of that part-fae male she'd met on the docks at the Tides. He'd said he was from Andara, the mysterious country far out in the treacherous Northern Sea. No one was allowed past its docks, but the strange faerie with silver eyes had told Marai to come there if she ever wanted to learn more about magic. Perhaps there was a future, a *safe* future, for all of them in Andara . . . answers to questions that sat on the edge of Marai's tongue. Once Marai's magic fully returned, she could go there, and maybe convince the others to come along, the same way Ruenen had for her.

That evening, after training, Marai joined Kadiatu in her garden to harvest food for dinner. Kadiatu had been working on this small stretch of land by the river for years. The garden housed native plants and foods that she'd embellished with her limited magic. Their colors seemed brighter, fragrances stronger, tastes more nectarous.

Marai paced between the rows of plants, mind whirring about Andara and Rayghast. She'd been spending more and more time with Kadiatu in her garden in the past two weeks. Kadiatu's gentle presence eased the anxiety knotted up inside her.

"You're restless," Kadiatu said.

"I've got a lot on my mind," said Marai, "and I've never liked it here."

Kadiatu chuckled. "I know. You used to be worse, though. Gods, you hated being cooped up."

"I still hate it," Marai said, the corners of her mouth lifting. "This place doesn't feel like home."

"I hate it here, too," Kadiatu said with a frown. "It's so empty and lonely. When we travel into town . . . we're outsiders. We have no community, the way humans do."

The town of Paracaso was several hours' walk away. Twice a year, since the fae arrived in Ehle, three of them would traverse the desert to Paracaso to gather supplies and trade goods. The town was entirely carved into the canyon wall, beneath an overhanging cliff. Usually it was Thora who went there with Raife, Leif or Aresti. She was the least conspicuous; her brown skin and hair blended in with the locals. They traded Thora's ointments and medical remedies and Kadiatu's woven baskets and produce in exchange for meats, grains, linens, knives, and books for Keshel. But they never stayed long, for fear of being discovered.

Kadiatu yanked a large bulbous tuber out of the ground and tossed it into her basket. "But home has nothing to do with the place you live. I think home is being with the people you love."

With her fingers laced into the dirt, Kadiatu sent out a pulse of nurturing magic beneath the ground. From that one pulse, the stems of the plants straightened. Flowers turned their heads to the sun. Kadiatu's garden bloomed, and the dirt beneath her hands darkened with fertility.

"You have more power than you let on," Marai stated.

Kadiatu met her gaze and smiled. "It's not exactly a helpful gift. I could never protect anyone with this. I cannot call a flame like Leif or a wind like Aresti. I cannot create shields. But I can help nature grow. I can feed us, and that's enough for me."

She stood and brushed the dirt from her hands onto her apron. "You're strong, Marai. And I don't mean your magic. I mean *you*. You're so much stronger than you think you are, and I've always looked up to you."

"Me? Why?" Marai was probably the least likable person anyone had ever met. A prickly desert cactus. A moody, shrouded vulture. She never wanted to be likable. She'd told that to Ruenen once before.

"Because even when you're afraid, you stand up for what you believe in. Because you make the hard decisions, even if it means others judge you for them. You chose to stay here and protect us. If that doesn't show true strength, I don't know what does."

Marai looked away, down the canyon pass. Her lips became a thin line, biting back the negativity that sprung impulsively up her throat. Was she strong? She certainly hadn't felt that way in a long time. There was a stark difference between true inner strength and erecting walls to keep others out.

"There's more to you than the hurt someone else caused you," said Kadiatu softly.

Marai swallowed, and tried to hide how those words affected her. She'd never thought of herself in that way. She'd never consciously done any of that. But Kadiatu, similar to Ruenen, had watched her, had *seen* something valuable underneath all the garbage.

"The Nevandian prince must've been a very good person to have gained your high opinion," Kadiatu said.

And for the first time in days, Marai smiled when she thought of him. It didn't wrench her heart out. She didn't shed a tear as she said, "He was."

Kadiatu grasped Marai's gloved hand to her chest and smiled as brightly as a sunbeam. "You are so loved, Marai. We love you. Leif and Aresti do, too. We are your family, and I hope you feel safe with us."

Tears stung Marai's eyes. She blinked them away. "I do."

Keshel's collection of faerie books had grown slightly since Marai left, but he seemed to be finding new information within them all the time. Every day he jotted down notes in his personal journal. Marai wondered if perhaps he'd one day write his own book. One of his favorite tomes was entirely dedicated to fae ancestry. It showed the common branches of the faeries, including those who'd bred with humans.

One afternoon, he brought out the enormous green leather volume and reverently placed it on the prep table. Keshel opened the yellowed pages and found the dog-eared sheet he sought. With one long, pale finger, he pointed, and Marai came to his side. The name under his finger was her own, inked in his handwriting.

"Thanks for adding me," she said wryly, unsure what his purpose was.

"Trace the line."

Marai's eyes zigzagged up the line to her own parents. Her mother's line didn't continue, seeing as how she was human and considered insignificant to faerie history. But Marai's father's line continued up and up.

She didn't see what the point was. Nothing about this was interesting.

Until her eyes reached the final name, the first in her line.

Queen Meallán.

Kadiatu and Thora hovered nearby, preparing newly picked medicinal herbs from Kadiatu's garden. They perked up when Marai whispered the name.

"You said your bloodstone ring belonged to her, correct?" asked Keshel, giving Marai that intense stare.

"Is that why it called to me? Because I'm related to Queen Meallán?" Marai could hardly believe that *she* was part of a royal line.

"I believe so. You said your magic manifested as lightning?" Keshel pointed at Meallán's name. It was surrounded by hand painted strands of lightning. A shiver traveled down Marai's spine. "You appear to be her progeny."

Progeny. Nosficio had hinted at it. Her power came from one of the original faerie queens. One of the first fae. And the ring she'd happened upon . . . But Marai didn't believe in fate, that the gods had a plan for her. Is that what Keshel was implying? That she was a piece on a board in a game the gods were playing?

"Marai's the last in a royal line?" asked Thora, coming to Marai's side to peer at the book.

"Humans made sure to eliminate any surviving heirs of faerie royalty. Meallán was a Northern queen, which was why your father's family had never left Grelta, Marai," explained Keshel. "I've read journals that state Meallán was the most powerful of all the old fae."

"And the angriest," Marai said, "since she cursed the ring."

Thora's eyes were as wide as blooming marigolds. "You have a cursed ring?"

Marai reached into her pocket, unfurling her gloved hand to reveal the dark jasper ring flecked with crimson that she'd stolen from Slate.

Thora sucked in a breath. Kadiatu gaped, coming to Marai's other side.

"What kind of curse?" Kadiatu eyed the ring as if it might explode at any moment.

Raife, Leif, and Aresti walked in, drenched in sweat from extra training. They gently set down their weapons and stayed quiet as Marai held up the ring.

"I was told that when the human slaves rebelled against Meallán, she cursed them before they killed her," Marai told the room. "She vowed that whoever wore this ring would have the power to vanquish all human life."

"I've recently had visions of Meallán—" said Keshel.

"Any other visions you want to tell us about?" Marai asked, eyes narrowing. How much more did Keshel see that he never told anyone?

Keshel continued. "I saw her curse the ring. A terrible darkness shrouded her. Then I saw the humans kill her, and bury the ring in a mountain on the White Ridge."

"How did Marai get it?" asked Leif. He stalked forward and took hold of Marai's wrist to examine the ring.

She wrenched herself free from his grasp. "I stole it from a greedy pirate captain." Leif didn't require any more details than that.

"Meallán's magic courses through her veins. She's the rightful owner of this ring," said Keshel.

Everyone towered over her to get a peek at the jewel.

Claustrophobic, Marai stepped away, giving herself space. *But I'm no one. A mere half-fae.*

"This all seems unbelievable to me," Aresti scoffed. "*If* Marai is Meallán's successor, why does that matter? We don't need a faerie queen. There's only seven of us. I don't want Marai *lording* over me."

"Well, it's a sign, isn't it? We could use this ring," said Leif, straightening up, green eyes alighting with an internal flame. "If it truly is cursed to bring about the downfall of man, we should use it."

Marai's heart stuttered.

Thora put her hands on her hips. "We cannot use a cursed ring. In fact, Marai shouldn't be holding it."

"Don't you understand? There's a reason this ring came to us now," Leif continued, ignoring Thora. "The gods or Meallán or fate are telling us that now is the time to take down the humans. You said it yourselves: Rayghast is coming for us."

What a fucking idiot.

"Absolutely not," Marai said. "I'm not wielding this ring to hurt anyone."

"That's what it's for, Marai. You apparently have a queen's power. We're all that's left of the fae. Why else were you given both Meallán's magic and her ring if the gods weren't *begging* you to save us?" A cold fire stoked in Leif's eyes. Marai had never seen him so passionate before.

Kadiatu backed away against the cave wall. Keshel watched impassively, listening. Unhelpful.

"I agree," Aresti chimed in, stepping up beside Leif. "I'm tired of hiding from humans. We can use this ring to protect ourselves against them."

Thora shook her head. "This is a terrible idea."

"Why? They've slaughtered *thousands* of us," Leif shouted. "We're the last of a mighty people. We're nearly extinct!"

"Humans killed us, but we enslaved them centuries ago. We'd killed thousands of humans, too. *Meallán* killed humans. It's a terrible, treacherous cycle," Marai said, blood boiling. She craned her neck to stare into Leif's searing gaze. "You've never stepped foot outside of this territory. You don't know what's out there. You've hardly interacted with humans, other than the people in Paracaso, and the few stragglers that wander here."

"What have humans done to *you*, Marai?" Leif challenged, jeering down at her as if she was a pathetic child. "You came back here, a shell of a being, barely able to stand. You don't think we know what happened? You don't think we guessed? The truth was written all over your face. Keshel told us you were shunned and hurt by humans. Over and over. *You* slaughtered them when you were a mercenary."

Marai whirled around to Keshel and speared him with her nastiest glare. Her fingers itched for her sword, but she kept breathing, kept calming. Thora came to her side, linking her arm through Marai's.

"Easy, Storm Cloud," she whispered.

Marai's anger didn't dissipate, despite those familiar words. She shook Thora off.

"You know nothing about my life," she said to both Keshel and Leif. "You have a one-sided, ignorant opinion."

Leif growled, holding up his clenched fists. "Humans are the enemy. They killed everyone we know. Our parents. Our siblings. An entire race of people. They deserve to be punished!"

"We aren't murderers," whispered Kadiatu.

I am, Marai thought bitterly.

Raife stepped closer to Thora. Marai saw him stop the impulse to put his arm around her.

Thora pleaded, "What about the innocents? The children? We all have human blood in our veins."

"Why not kill the rulers?" Aresti posed. "The nine wicked kings. We don't need to kill innocents. We give them all a choice: fight against us or submit. We don't need to rule over humans. We just want an equal share; our own land where we can live in peace."

"I'm tired of living in this fucking cave as if *I'm* the evil one," Leif said, red rising up his neck. "It's time we take back what's rightfully ours, what the *gods* themselves gave us!"

"*No*," Marai snarled, and a pulse of magic shot through the cavern. Lightning snaked and crackled, creating a stunned silence in the room. Magic sparked in Marai's hands. It was the first true sign of power she'd seen in weeks. The jasper ring vibrated in her clenched fist. "I am Queen Meallán's descendant. The ring presented itself to *me*. I'm the one who can wield it, therefore it's *my* decision what to do with its power."

Raife stepped in front of Thora protectively, but she still peeked around him, gaping. Kadiatu covered her mouth with her hands, eyes wide as saucers. Leif and Aresti lowered into fighting stance, ready to combat Marai if needed. Keshel's face remained blank. He didn't move a muscle. The silence was heavy, saturated with fear and confusion and fury.

Marai didn't want this responsibility. She didn't want to be a descendant of queens. She'd never craved power, but now it was at her fingertips, and the idea frightened her.

"Even if we chose to use the ring," began Raife in his calm tone, "there are only seven of us and thousands of them. Our magic is no match for their numbers. There's no way we could ever succeed. And Marai's right—she's the one with the power here. Not us. It's her choice."

Marai glanced at him and he gave her a nod of support.

"I've done terrible things; things I'm not proud of," she said, her voice a low growl. "As you stated, Leif, I *was* a mercenary and a pirate. I don't regret most of the lives I've taken. Most were crooked, horrible people. I've done my part to rid Astye of those villains, and there are plenty of wicked rulers who deserve death, such as King Rayghast of Tacorn. But not all humans deserve such a fate. Not every human is an enemy."

"But those who don't hate us, fear us. Are you saying that we can merely wipe away hundreds of years of prejudice?" Leif said. "That we can be *friends* with them?"

"No," Marai admitted. "They'd have no qualms about killing us. Their fear and misunderstanding runs deep. As does yours, apparently."

"What about other oppressed magical folk?" asked Aresti. "They'd join us. They have to hate the way things are as much as we do."

"Have you met a werewolf before? A vampire?" Marai asked, causing Aresti to scowl and turn away. Marai's mind briefly flashed to Nosficio, that ancient, deadly vampire. He hadn't seemed too concerned about humans. He was too busy drinking their blood to care. But he *did* seem interested in Marai and her magic. "We don't know what they'd do, what they want. Vampires are loners. They don't often interact with others. And werewolves stick to their packs. They'd all be caught up, as well, if we went to war with humans."

Keshel finally stepped forward. "If we begin this war, the cycle will go on and on, as Marai said. Humans populate quickly. Magical folk don't breed the same way; this was our problem before. Humans outnumber us, and always will. They'll continue breeding and rise up again."

"What will you do with the ring?" came Kadiatu's soft voice from behind Marai.

"Nothing. At least for now."

Leif stomped outside, Aresti at his heels. Thora, visibly shaken, went back to her jars and herbs.

Keshel turned to Marai. "My question isn't about the ring. What will you do with your *own* powers, Marai?"

She stared back at him, trying to keep her face from revealing the turmoil inside. "I don't know how much power I have."

"It's immense, Marai," Keshel said quietly. "I don't foresee you being able to keep it contained forever. You're going to use it . . . you have to decide how and for what reason." He grabbed the green leather-bound volume and disappeared down the tunnel back to his cot.

Marai rushed outside, unable to take the confines of the cave any longer. She ran past Leif and Aresti, who were having a heated conversation. Marai ran to the cliff wall where the long weathered rope hung. She climbed all the way up. It required every ounce of her strength to make it to the top, but her body was resilient once again after days of rigorous training. After she pulled herself up over the ledge, she stood, panting, hands burning from the rough rope through her gloves. Marai wiped the sweat from her brow and paced.

No one would follow her up here.

Marai hated that she'd been put in this situation. She wasn't a leader. She had power, but knew not how to wield it. Why had *she* been given this responsibility?

Whatever I decide will affect them, too . . .

Magic throbbed within her, wanting release along with her frustration.

She let go, feeling the sparks travel down her arms and out through her fingertips. A rightness settled over her. White strands of lightning snapped in the air all around her, unhinged and wild . . . She'd been born with lightning at her heels and in her veins. An agrestal storm cloud bloomed in the sky.

Marai let the magic loose until that pent-up need, anger, and confusion subsided. She took several long, deep breaths, inhaling the bone dryness of the Badlands. There was nothing and no one around for miles and miles. Ehle was the least consequential of the Nine Kingdoms, with the sparsest population. Most of Ehle was covered in the red desert, uninhabitable except for those desperate and resourceful enough to survive. Marai was alone up on that plateau. Alone, even amongst the other fae. Alone, with the weight of responsibility heavy upon her shoulders.

Ruen, she thought, dropping to her knees. Her fingers dug into the copper dirt. *What should I do?*

CHAPTER 6
MARAI

Leif and Aresti didn't say a further word about the ring. Marai supposed Keshel, Raife, or both, spoke to them in private. She was appreciative, but knew it was only a matter of time before someone brought it up again.

Two more weeks passed. The fae celebrated Ostara, the holiday honoring Lirr and the welcoming of spring. As they did each year, the fae lined their entryway with flowers from Kadiatu's garden, mimicking the path of blooms Lirr supposedly left in her wake whenever she stepped foot on soil. They left the goddess offerings of desert fruits and fish in baskets by the river next to blazing candles of green flame, created by Leif. Thora waved incense around the cave and chanted in the language of the gods, cleansing away the dark of winter, ushering in the light.

"Did you know that ancient fae is also the language of the gods?" Keshel asked Marai as they listened to Thora's melodic voice fill the cave.

"No, I didn't," said Marai. She'd been a child the last time she heard ancient fae spoken by her father. The language was lost to her, as it was for the others, except for the few holiday chants.

"Curious, isn't it?" Keshel pondered. "Humans despise us for our magic, but why would Lirr have given her own language to *us* if not out of love?"

Her lessons with Keshel were stressful. Marai's magic didn't want to be controlled. The lightning was feral and yearned to be released, to stretch for miles. Keshel had been correct—her power was immense, but it was dangerous to everyone around her. More than once Marai had almost turned Keshel to ashes, but he'd been quick to put up his shield. Her lightning crashed against it in a bright explosion, ricocheting off, unable to penetrate his barrier.

Keshel had given Marai specific breathing and mind-shaping exercises. He instructed her to imagine her magic as a living thing, part of her physical body, something that must be shaped and honed. She was to visualize her magic flexing and shifting like any normal muscle. It was boring, tedious work. Merely standing there breathing and visualizing was more exhausting than fighting in a battle.

Eventually, though, Marai got the hang of it.

Lightning climbed up the high canyon walls; slunk like a lynx over the water. With a mere thought, Marai directed it, and the strands of white light turned, creating a circle of crackling power around Keshel. Then she reeled it all back inside, as easy as sucking in air.

Trying to catch her off-guard, Keshel threw a ball of blazing fire at Marai. With the flex of her hands, an invisible shield erected around her. The fireball exploded against the barrier, then burnt out, scattering cinders into the red dirt.

"Excellent work," Keshel said, giving Marai one of his rare smiles. "I don't think anyone else could've mastered their magic faster. Including me."

"I still don't have complete control."

"You will," Keshel said in a tone that meant he knew because he'd *seen* it. Keshel was never forthcoming about his visions. Marai guessed there were many things he knew about her that he'd never share. Keshel had told her once years ago that it was often better to let things happen the way they were intended. That sometimes *knowing* something was going to happen made things worse. She couldn't comprehend how much those visions of the future weighed on Keshel. He never showed weakness. Perhaps she'd learned that from him.

Every day, Marai awoke and her heart seemed a little lighter. Every hour, a fissure in her soul healed over, and stitched itself together. She gained sturdiness from the laughter of her people. Resilience in their passion, their dedication to each other. She'd crawled through broken glass to reach this point. To find herself again. Marai's soul was bloodied and torn, but healing.

"I know you miss him," Thora said as they washed bloody bandages at the river. Raife had accidentally sliced his hand on Aresti's sword during training, and the wound had bled a lot before Thora could magically seal the cut. He was fine, but they'd used several strips of cloth to soak up the blood. "Your prince."

"He's not *my* prince," grumbled Marai.

Thora stopped vigorously scrubbing the cloth, and gave Marai her usual knowing look. "No? Then what is he?"

"Nevandia's prince," said Marai.

Thora raised an eyebrow. "It's alright, you know . . . to feel more."

Ivy curled and tightened around Marai's mending heart. They'd saved each other, in a way. Ruenen had shown her possibilities. A future that didn't reside at a blade's edge. He'd opened her eyes to *more.*

"You're one to talk," Marai quipped, letting those feelings of *more* drift away.

"You're not the only one struggling with those feelings," Thora said, face falling. "I know what it's like to care for someone and not be able to be with them." She clutched Raife's wet bandages to her breast.

Marai looked away, staring hard at the water lapping on the pebbles as if the river had personally affronted her. A hollowness took over, encapsulating her heart. "It doesn't matter what I felt once, because he's dead."

"Of course it matters, Marai," Thora said. "Attraction isn't a choice, but *loving* someone is. And choosing to love is a brave, scary thing."

Marai had been brave once; had been willing to cleave her heart in two and share it with another, with Slate. That youthful courage and brashness had been punished. She'd vowed to never let love blind her; that no man would ever hurt or claim her again.

Ruenen had never tried to claim her. He'd *chosen* to care. Marai still didn't know what her feelings for Ruenen were . . . was it more than friendship? Did she *love* him?

But Ruenen was dead. It'd been a month since the day she'd portaled to the Badlands. Rayghast had slain him by now. The cruel king had probably overthrown Nevandia. Keshel hadn't mentioned he'd seen anything about it . . .

Marai briefly considered portaling to Paracaso to see if there was any news about Tacorn and Nevandia, but then she shook the thought from her head.

Do I really want to know? Because then it would be real . . . then there would be confirmation of Ruenen's death, and Marai didn't think she could bear to hear those words spoken aloud.

Aresti's figure appeared, barreling in from the boundaries of the fae territory. She'd been on watch duty all afternoon. Marai stood at once. From a distance, she spotted the frantic expression on Aresti's face.

"What's wrong?" Marai asked.

"Riders," Aresti panted as she neared, sweat plastering hair to her neck and temples. "Twenty–heading this way. Fifteen of them wear black armor."

Tacorn.

Rayghast, the bastard, had arrived.

Marai dashed inside the cave and grabbed Dimtoir and her dagger. It was time to wage war.

The others followed her outside like lost kittens, panic knitting their brows.

"How did they find us?" Thora questioned, biting her lower lip, glancing between Marai and Keshel. "And why so many?"

Twenty wasn't many. Rayghast could have sent dozens more.

"What are you doing, Marai?" asked Keshel. He placed a hand on her shoulder, briefly halting her. "My barriers will protect us. The riders will leave if they can't find us."

"Rayghast ordered those men to find me at all costs. I'd rather kill them now and be done with it." Marai was a threat to him and his plans. She'd killed too many of his men; had humiliated the king by escaping with Ruenen from his dungeon. And more than that, she was fae, and Rayghast wanted to eradicate all traces of faerie blood from Astye.

Marai stalked off in the direction Aresti had come from, ignoring Keshel and Thora's calls from the cave entrance.

She'd make them bleed. The riders weren't Rayghast, but it didn't matter... Marai would make them pay for what the cruel king did to Ruenen.

The riders weren't hard to spot, cantering through the canyon pass, beside the river, to the edge of Keshel's barrier. Fifteen brawny soldiers sat astride their mounts, sporting Tacorn's crossed-sword emblem pins upon their chests. Marai briefly wondered how suffocatingly hot they must be wearing all that black armor. Their five bounty-hunter companions were olive-skinned men of Ehle in lightweight linens and protective turbans. They couldn't proceed through. Their horses reared and neighed at the sensation of magic; their ears twitched. Animals could always sense magic in ways humans couldn't.

"What's going on? Why can't we get through?" one of the soldiers asked.

Hidden behind Keshel's invisible wall, Marai crept closer to the men. *Maybe they'll turn back.*

A bounty hunter pressed his hand up against the invisible shield. "It's magic!"

The soldiers stirred, grabbing for their weapons.

"We found them! The fae are *here,*" one of them said; their commander, based on the red plume on his helmet. "Find a way through this barrier."

The soldiers and hunters began pummeling Keshel's shield with their swords and spears, hoping to break through. Marai wondered if Keshel could feel each strike. Would he weaken? Would his barrier fall?

Feet pounded the earth behind her. Aresti, Leif, and Raife had followed. As reluctant warriors, they lifted their bows and arrows with trembling hands. Twenty against four was frightening odds to them as inexperienced killers.

"Stay back behind the barrier," Marai whispered. "You can shoot from here, and stay out of harm's way."

Aresti, Leif, and Raife didn't move, not forward, or further to safety.

Passing through the shield, Marai leapt onto the nearest rider, pulling him from his saddle. Men swore in surprise. Horses whinnied. Before any of the hunters or soldiers could raise their weapons, arrows flew from behind the barrier.

One of Raife's arrows lodged in the throat of an Ehle man. Blood gurgled from his mouth as he tilted out of his saddle. Leif hit another man in the thigh. He yelped, falling from his horse into the dirt. The bounty hunter was then trampled by hooves in the frenzy.

Bodies tumbled onto the ground. Dimtoir slashed through stomachs and necks, any exposed skin, whistling in the carnage. Eventually, Aresti tired of waiting behind the barrier and joined Marai in the fray. Her two swords became blurred silver in the air as she brought down a rider. His flailing sword sliced through her arm as he fell. Blood spurted, and Aresti gasped at the pain.

Leif and Raife's arrows kept flying, hitting true. Marai cut down a hunter whose spear was aimed at Aresti's heart.

All twenty men were dead in minutes. Their horses galloped away through the gorge.

Leif let out a shuddering breath as he lowered his bow. He was pale, despite the high sun of the afternoon. He'd struck five men with his arrows. Raife had six kills. All shots had gone straight through the eye.

"Is this what you want me to do to all the humans?" Marai asked him and Aresti. "Use the ring to inflict this kind of slaughter on everyone in Astye? I know death. Killing makes you numb. It rips out your soul. I don't want you all to become *me*."

Leif cringed, like he might vomit, but he still managed to lance Marai with a glare. His hands shook as his eyes settled on Marai's cream linen shirt. She'd borrowed it from Thora, and now the shirt was stained with splattered blood. Perhaps Thora wouldn't be cross, what with Marai protecting her, and all. Aresti clung to the wound on her arm with clenched teeth.

Raife approached, staring down at the dead men with a pained expression. "We'll need to bury them right away. They'll rot faster in the sun. And Aresti, make sure you have Thora tend to that wound."

Leif and Aresti went to retrieve their shovels from the cave. While they were gone, Marai knelt to search the dead men's pockets.

"What are you doing?" asked Raife, a twinge of horror in his tone, as Marai pilfered coins, valuables, weapons, and food from the dead men.

"They don't need this. *We* do," Marai replied. She handed Raife two daggers and a long, thin knife. Her hands grasped a piece of paper inside a soldier's breastplate. She unfolded it as Raife loomed over her shoulder. Leif was returning with the shovels.

The note was from Rayghast to his soldiers.

I want the Lady Butcher found. I have reason to believe there are more of her disgusting kind still alive in the Badlands. You have one job: find her, and kill all those associated with her.

Merely seeing the king's signature at the end electrified Marai's blood again. She crumpled the note in her fist, and tossed it into the mass grave Raife and Leif dug behind a boulder.

For you, Ruenen.

Marai dumped a shovel-full of red dirt over the bodies.

Rayghast could send a hundred men, a *thousand* men, after her. She would never let him win.

A week later, Keshel came to her by the river. The sky was brilliantly bright with layers of tangerine and peach. Marai sat on a rock, meditating as usual before training.

"Beautiful morning," he said, and it was. Insects chirped, a frog croaked; there was a gentle, warm breeze, bringing with it the smell of blossoming cactus flowers. Keshel sat on the rock near Marai. He stared at her, taking in every inch, as if truly seeing her for the first time.

He'd been softening, too. Day after day, Marai saw the signs of life in his face, a light in his eyes. He kept finding reasons to be around her, like sitting next to her at meals, or helping her and Kadiatu in the garden. Keshel had his own stone walls inside, and the longer Marai stayed, the more of those walls crumbled.

Unnerved by Keshel's attention, Marai scowled at him. "What?"

"I wasn't sure who you'd be when you came back to us," he said, catching Marai off-guard. "I assumed you would still be that ferocious little girl."

"The demon child?" Marai snorted.

A smile flashed upon Keshel's face, but it was gone quickly. "You were never a demon, just wild. Unhappy. I understand why you were, but it was my duty to protect you, and you never wanted to be controlled. That's why we clashed so often."

"I know that, but it doesn't mean I liked it."

He smiled, this time for real. "I was never surprised you left. Honestly, I'm amazed that you're still here now. But I'm glad you are. You brought a much-needed spark back into our lives."

Marai picked her fingernails, avoiding his gaze. Worms wriggled around in her stomach at the earnest, tender tone of Keshel's voice.

"But there's something you must know." Concern darkened Keshel's expression. Whatever it was he had to say, Keshel struggled. He hesitated, pursed his lips, like he didn't want to say it at all. "Ruenen is alive."

The words hit her like a punch to the gut. A bucket of ice cold water dumped over her head and now she had to gasp for air.

Alive? The word ignited. It shredded through her, leaving her breathless and unraveled.

"How?" Marai managed to croak out.

"He never made it to Tacorn. He escaped the bounty hunters."

Marai's vision went blurry, then white as a thick fog. Magic and rage ripped through her as relief and joy caused her heart to stutter a frantic beat. Lightning crackled at her fingers.

"You told me he was dead. Was it all a lie?"

"No, not a lie. I told you that visions can change. I think because you decided to stay, because you chose the harder path, you changed things. Perhaps Lirr rewarded your sacrifice."

Marai didn't believe in that religious nonsense, but it didn't matter as she imbued her words with venom. "How long have you known?"

Keshel wasn't afraid of her fury. He met her glare, but with sad eyes. "I had a vision the day after we began training. After you decided to stay."

Marai bolted from the rock. "You've known for *weeks?* Why didn't you tell me sooner?"

He's alive. He's alive! Her emotions spiraled, conflicted. Joy and fury entwined, making her hands shake and stomach knot. Her heart hammered, dancing a merry jig.

"You were in no shape to leave here. What would you have done? You couldn't use your magic to portal to him, and you might have been killed in the journey."

"My magic's been recovered for days now, and you know that," she snapped. She'd left her weapons inside the cave. If she had them with her, she would've put her dagger to Keshel's throat.

"Yes, I knew. I know everything, Marai," said Keshel morosely. "His fate is entwined with yours. With all of us. I thought that if I kept you in the dark for as long as possible, I could delay the inevitable. I don't want my people to die, Marai. I fear for our lives."

"You *never* should have kept this from me. It's *my* choice what I do."

"I know, and I'm sorry," Keshel said. He never apologized for anything, because no one believed Keshel ever did anything wrong. The others thought him so wise, so above baseless emotions and petty squabbles, but he was half-human, and no different from them. "I'm afraid of what will happen if you join him. I see us dying on a battlefield bathed in blood. I see you in chains."

Marai didn't care. Ruenen was *alive,* and she finally had the strength to reach him.

"That's one possible outcome. Maybe Ruenen isn't the end for us, but the beginning. Someone who grants us a new life. By staying here, *I* could bring about that downfall. Or maybe joining Ruenen is our death, but I don't care," Marai said, throat burning. Her breath was difficult to catch. "I'd rather die at his side than abandon him again!"

The words rang out, echoing across the canyon. Frogs stopped their croaking at the riverbank.

Keshel finally looked away from her. "I don't want you to go, Marai. I knew the moment I told you about the prince, you'd leave, and I selfishly wanted to keep you here."

Marai strode to the cave, no longer listening to him. She rushed inside, emotions balancing on the tip of a sword. She found a satchel and packed it with a blanket, a loaf of bread, cactus fruit, and a water canteen.

"What's wrong? Where are you going?" Thora asked.

"Ruenen's alive," said Marai, and a hush fell over the room. "Keshel has known for weeks and kept it from me."

"You're leaving us?" asked Kadiatu, voice thick and desperate.

Marai halted her packing. They were all gaping at her.

"I must return to him. I swore to protect him, and I've already failed once. I need to help him escape for good."

"Will you return once you're done?" pressed Thora, coming to Marai's side. Thora handed her a freshly washed black shirt. It was Marai's; Thora had patched up the tears and holes.

"I will, though I don't know when," Marai promised, and she meant it. She drew Thora into a hug, an act she'd never once initiated in her entire life.

Thora tensed in her arms, then squeezed her back tightly, as a sister would.

Kadiatu, tears in her eyes, wrapped her arms around both of them. "Of course, you must go to him."

Once the girls disentangled themselves, Raife came to Marai's side and quickly embraced her, too, in a brotherly hug full of warmth. "One of us should come with you. If you need me, I'll go."

Marai put a hand on his lean arm. "No, you'd be in too much danger. I need you all to remain safe here. But thank you for the offer."

Raife nodded, then stepped away.

"Is your prince really worth this?" asked Aresti. "You're better off staying away from him. He just brings you trouble."

"That may be so, but he's a good man," Marai said, giving both Aresti and Leif a serious look. "Not all humans deserve to die."

Aresti shrugged. "Is he at least handsome?"

Marai's lips twitched. "He's adequate." The lie tasted sour on her tongue.

Aresti sensed it, too, and chuckled with a shake of her head.

Leif studied Marai through narrowed eyes. "You're saying goodbye this time."

Marai sent him a rude gesture. "Goodbye, asshole."

Leif snorted, the smirk on his face didn't disappear.

Marai strapped Dimtoir and her dagger to her belt, then tucked a knife inside her boot. The others followed her outside again where Keshel hadn't moved from the riverbank. She lifted her arms, aware of the six pairs of anxious eyes. Magic tugged and pulled. It raced through her body, electrifying her. Empowering her. Igniting her.

Take me to Ruenen, she demanded.

The portal appeared, a shuddering, open hole of multi-colored light in the desert.

"Amazing," whispered Raife, stepping forward for a closer view. "What is this?"

"A portal. It's how I got here in the first place," Marai said. She heard the whispered questions from the others, but she couldn't answer right now. Every second wasted here was a danger to Ruenen.

The other side of the portal showed a forest in the primary stages of rebirth in spring. Leaves budded on the branches, a few green strands of grass poked through the soil. Marai wasn't sure where this was, but Ruenen had to be close by. She trusted her magic to find him.

Marai turned around one last time. It was harder to leave than she'd thought it would be. They'd brought her back to life. They'd sheltered her, the monster that she was.

"Protect each other. Don't stop training. Don't stray outside of Keshel's barrier. Stay vigilant. There may be more hunters headed this way. I . . . I'll be back as soon as I can," she said through a constricted throat.

"You don't need to remind us," Leif said, and waved her onwards. "Go."

Keshel stood, aloof, behind them all. He returned her goodbye with a curt nod.

Marai stepped through the portal and out of the desert, leaving behind her family and a portion of her heart.

CHAPTER 7
Rayghast

He crumpled the letter in his blackened hand. The bounty hunter's words, etched across the paper, spoke of failure. More and more, piled on to create a mountain of mistakes and inefficiencies, all laid at his feet like bones in a graveyard.

The accursed "lost prince" evaded Rayghast's grasp yet again.

Five of his bounty hunters were dead in Cleaving Tides. They'd been charged with capturing the young Nevandian prince, in order to bring him to Dul Tanen. There, Ruenen would face public execution by Rayghast's own hand. But the hunters had failed. The sixth man in the group succumbed to wounds he'd sustained while on the mission, but not before he'd sent Rayghast the damnable letter.

The King of Tacorn used to have control over his emotions, but the iron cage around them grew brittle, the bars bent and crumbled.

Someone had to pay. But all those responsible for the failures were already dead. Rayghast had to make do with substitutes.

Magic roared in his brain and rushed through his veins. Feral darkness rippled under his muscles. A pounding pushed against his ear drums, throbbing in time with the beat of the organ in his chest. Rayghast tossed the bounty hunter's letter into the pool of blood at his feet. He rolled his shoulders back. Flexed his fingers. Cracked his neck from side to side.

There were two Nevandian knights, fifteen thieves and criminals, and two traitors to the crown in the dungeons below the fortress of Dul Tanen. Rayghast had come down to the dank, filthy cells because he needed to *touch* something, *kill* something. Watch as dark magic consumed and ruined.

The first thief had already been disposed of. His limp body lay on the floor of the cell in a contorted position, eyes wide open from the fear and pain. Blood leaked from his many stab wounds into a large puddle where the bounty hunter's letter now disintegrated.

The second thief was chained to the wall, and still very much alive. He struggled, howled, and begged as Rayghast approached.

"Please, Your Grace, my family is starving—"

Rayghast's fingers twitched. The magic urged. He stabbed the thief through the gut with a dagger. Warm blood poured down Rayghast's arm. The thief emitted an inhuman, pained shriek into Rayghast's ear. The King of Tacorn shoved his other hand into the wound. Magic spilled out of his fingers in smokey tendrils as he injected its necrotic darkness into the thief's body. Rayghast inhaled the acrid smell of blood, sulfur, and charred flesh. Blackness spread through the thief's insides, infesting his organs, across his torso, up his neck—

Footsteps echoed in the stairwell.

Rayghast sucked the darkness back inside himself as the thief's body burst into black flames, covering the signs of magic. By the time Cronhold and his page appeared at the cell door, the man's body was charred and destroyed beyond recognition.

"Your Grace?" Cronhold asked, winded from the descent into the dungeons beneath the Dul Tanen fortress. The wizened and hunched old councilman leaned his full weight on the page, who'd turned a sickly shade of green at the sight of the two bodies and Rayghast's bloody arms. The boy's legs shook. "Lord Silex is here to see you."

Rayghast didn't bother with a rag. He exited the dungeon with his arms still covered in fresh blood.

Silex stood in the arched entryway of the castle, with three men, his personal retainers, behind him. Each man carried a large, ornate wooden chest. Silex grinned, his front incisors crooked, and bowed to Rayghast with an excessive flourish of his wrist.

"Your Grace," he said, "I hate to interrupt you." His eyes darted to the blood, but unlike Cronhold and his page, the sight didn't faze Silex. He was known for similar acts of aggression. "I've brought more funds to assist in the capture of that foul Nevandian prince and the evil creature in his employ."

Word of the Nevandian prince had spread from town to town. All of Tacorn knew. Varana somehow knew. It wouldn't be long before the other six countries knew.

Lord Silex's men opened the lids of the chests, revealing mountains of golden coins. In exchange for his "generosity," Rayghast knew Silex would require recognition: a new title, new lands, a position on the counsel. Whatever it was, Rayghast didn't care. The money was necessary to bankroll the army and bounty hunters, and he'd give Silex whatever he wanted to see this feud finished. Rayghast had raised taxes for all Tacornians to fund the war against Nevandia. The wealthy nobles were as eager as their king to take Nevandian soil; more land, more wealth, for all of them. Lord Silex, the wealthiest of the Tacornian nobles, tried to prove his worth to Rayghast any chance he could take.

A flash of deep blue silk and pale skin caught Rayghast's eye.

Rhia entered the hallway, her cold eyes assessing Rayghast, Cronhold, and Silex, before she bowed her head. A jade and pearl diadem sat upon interwoven gleaming locks of black. Her four Tacornian ladies-in-waiting hovered over her shoulders, as always, wide-eyed and fearful baby birds.

"My King," Rayghast's wife said.

"Queen Rhia, you are absolutely breathtaking, as always," Silex said with a slick sneer, giving her a slow once-over.

Rayghast didn't mind the obvious flirtation. Men were always staring at his wife, and Rhia seemed to enjoy the attention. As long as they didn't *touch* what was his.

"Lord Silex. You honor me." Rhia's voice took on a coy tone she never used with Rayghast. Her eyelids fluttered twice, putting on an act for the lord. Rhia might change her expressions and voice, but the one thing that never changed were her eyes. Those brown eyes betrayed nothing, impassive and always ice cold. She glanced at Rayghast's bloody state, but didn't react to the sight. Her gaze darted demurely back to the floor. Rhia was used to the carnage of his regime. "Still kidnapping Nevandian children?"

"Kidnapping is the wrong term, Your Grace," Silex said. "I'm merely granting the children a better life with proper, devoted Tacornian parents. The children will want for nothing, and grow up to be grateful to King Rayghast for granting them this new life."

Rhia didn't react to such a claim, but Rayghast guessed she didn't appreciate Silex's endeavor. In a year's time, he'd stolen fifty children from villages over the border.

"I've also brought ten of my retainers, Your Grace," Silex said, turning his back on Rhia. She was only a woman, after all. "Strong, loyal, fighting men. I want to help you win in any way I can."

"That is, uh, most generous of you, Lord Silex," Cronhold said, giving the three retainers behind Silex an approving once-over.

"What are you still doing here, Cronhold?" Rayghast asked.

The old man stuttered, nonsensical sounds spitting out of him, before he managed to form a true word. "We should discuss in private—"

"Speak, then get out."

Whatever Cronhold had to say, Silex had earned the right. Rhia, still lingering, probably wouldn't understand, anyways.

"I have, uh, distressing news, Your Grace. There've been reports from some of the towns, from our soldiers, that there have been sightings of animals, uh . . . *creatures*. One of these things killed some peasants in the Boggs—"

"Why is this important?"

"Well, these creatures . . . uh, no one has ever seen the likes of them before."

"What do you mean, my lord?" Rhia asked, interest rising in her voice. Her imploring eyes lifted to Cronhold's face.

"They're not the creatures we know. None of them look the same," the old man said, face paling. His hands trembled with age as he gesticulated. "Our sentries on the road said they battled a monstrous one. A mottled combination of many different animals put together. And it was . . . not easy to kill, Your Grace. The rumors are making people nervous. I, myself, have never heard of anything quite like this. More seem to be appearing all the time. Some of them appear, uh, slightly human—"

"Sounds like Nevandian nonsense to me," Silex said, shaking his head. "It's probably highwaymen dressed up in silly outfits. Nevandians will do anything to survive, including submitting themselves to such embarrassing theatrics."

"Kill them," Rayghast stated. "It doesn't matter what they are. Beasts or Nevandians, dispose of them. Don't bring this matter up again."

"My King, these creatures . . . they sound magical, do they not?" Rhia asked, her tone steely. "More abominations and devils that must be destroyed. Lord Cronhold, please tell our soldiers to be cautious. If they are indeed magical creatures, they must be exterminated. Don't let any survive."

Rhia didn't often voice opinions, especially to councilmen in Rayghast's presence, but this was a subject she never hesitated to speak on. His wife detested magic.

If she knew what lurked in the room with her now.

"Of course, Your Grace," Cronhold said, bowing the best he could with rickety limbs.

Rhia put a hand on his bony arm. "Thank you for bringing this to our attention, Lord Cronhold."

The old man flashed his queen a gap-toothed smile. He never looked at Rayghast that way.

Simpering old fool.

"Lord Silex, allow me to, uh, take those chests off your hands. If you'll follow me, please."

Cronhold hobbled off down the hallway; the boy at his side barely able to hold him up. Silex followed, chin in the air, with his retainers.

Whispered voices caught Rayghast's attention. His head snapped towards the sound down the hallway. Two servant girls stood tittering to each other, staring at Rayghast. The second they noticed his attention, they squawked and dashed away, back to work.

He was used to stares and whispers, but usually people were more secretive than that. Those servants were bold, indeed.

Rayghast turned to his wife.

"Come."

He stalked to his private office near the council chamber. He hardly heard the gentle scuff of his young wife's slippers on the stone floor. Rayghast prowled over to his desk and hastily scratched out a message. He handed the paper, covered in his bloody fingerprints, to Rhia.

"Send this to your father."

The Jade Emperor of Varana, a puppet in Rayghast's pocket. After Tacorn's attack on Chiojan five years ago, Emperor Suli had gifted his daughter to Rayghast in order to curry favor. But he'd been pushing back recently, ignoring Rayghast's letters about establishing Varanese soldiers in Nevandia. Perhaps he wouldn't ignore correspondence from his own daughter.

Rhia stared at the letter, the red stains, dark eyes tearing across the page.

"You ask him to ready his troops," she stated. "Have you decided to strike Nevandia? Is it finally time?"

Rayghast gazed out the window, across the ancient gray-stone city of Dul Tanen and the flourishing moor beyond.

"This war must end. I'm tired of waiting," he said, squinting his eyes as if he could see the city of Kellesar in the distance, the throne of Nevandia in its halls. It was nearly his. Nevandia had once been part of Tacorn, and Rayghast intended to be the king to finally reunite the two kingdoms. He scratched the rough, graying beard at his chin. "We'll rally our troops, prepare for battle, and take down Kellesar, with or without its prince."

Rhia folded up the letter with a nod. "I look forward to the day. What do you require me to add in this request to my father, Husband?"

"Tell him to send your sister."

Rhia froze. Her face, already as pale as snow, grew whiter, still. "Eriu? You want her to come here *now*?"

"She's to be wed. I want her at court immediately so we can get the matter settled."

"Whom will she be marrying?"

"She'll be strengthening ties between Tacorn and Varana. That's all you need to know."

"But why Eriu? Couldn't we arrange a match between nobles? I have a cousin—"

"I'd use my own child if I had one," Rayghast growled at her. "But since you've so far been unable to produce an heir, your sister will act as surrogate."

He would never admit it, but Rhia was not at fault for the lack of a royal heir. Thanks to a wicked old faerie crone, Rayghast had been cursed. He would never sire children. His previous three wives had all died during pregnancy, and while Rhia continued to have her monthly bleeding, the same would eventually happen to her. Rayghast was doomed to go through wives as a peasant might wear out a pair of shoes. All the more reason to conquer Nevandia now. Rayghast had little time to secure his legacy.

"And remind your father that if he doesn't follow through with his end of the deal, the first stop on my conquest will be Varana instead of Nevandia. Tell him to remember Chiojan."

Rhia swallowed, then bowed low. The letter in her hand trembled.

"As you wish." Her gaze stalled on an unfolded letter upon Rayghast's desk. "What is that, Your Grace?"

The letter was written in a foreign language, consisting of sharp lines and circles, a kind of code Rayghast was unable to crack. Everyone on Astye spoke and wrote in the common tongue, as had been established for two hundred years.

"It was intercepted on its way somewhere east of Dul Tanen. We've discovered dozens of these within the past few weeks."

He didn't want to admit that he had no idea what the letters said and who their recipients were, but Rayghast guessed these notes were intended for Nevandia or Varana, and might even have something to do with Emperor Suli's sudden silence.

Rhia took the letter from the desk and examined it. "I've never seen such writing before. Is this, perchance, a Nevandian sabotage tactic?"

Rayghast snatched the letter from her fingers. "Are you suddenly a linguistics expert?"

"Of course not, My King. I would never presume to know more than you." Rhia took a step backwards. "My apologies for intruding."

She glided back out of the office noiselessly, a ghost in deep blue robes.

Rayghast drilled his blackened fingers on his desk. Slender threads of dark magic leached from his hands, igniting the blank sheets of paper beneath them. He watched as the black flames consumed the parchment in an almost hypnotic dance.

He could no longer wait for the capture of the Nevandian prince. He'd take the country *now*. Perhaps that might finally bring the missing prince out of the woodwork. Perhaps then, Rayghast could finally be rid of him.

CHAPTER 8
Marai

Marai stepped into a forest. It had recently rained; a damp, earthy scent overcame her, cleansing away the desert dust. Water droplets glistened on green leaves and buds, but the sun peeked through the canopy above, and blossoms began to unfurl their petals. Marai's elemental magic fluttered in response to all the life brewing around her. It always did in the spring.

The portal sealed shut behind her, disappearing in a wave of effervescent light.

Marai crouched low to the ground, hand on Dimtoir's pommel. *Where am I?*

Many footsteps scuffed and shuffled on dirt close by. Wooden carts rolled and crunched. Horse hooves plodded in rhythm indicating a busy, central road.

What if the portal had sent Marai into Tacornian territory? Could that be Rayghast's soldiers on patrol, searching for Ruenen?

Marai crept towards the sounds, anxiety knotting her stomach. She came to the edge of the forest, and hovered behind the branches of a bush, watching, waiting to get her bearings.

Peasants and tradesmen roamed, but many people were also well-dressed in the height of current fashion: flashy, rich colors, fabrics of silk and velvet, in bold and elaborate patterns. These wealthier women plaited their long hair with ribbons, flowers, and jade pins; dressed themselves in robe-like attire with bell sleeves. The men wore tight fitted trousers and embroidered vests, ebony hair slicked back into tight buns at the nape of their necks.

Marai released her held breath. No black-armored soldiers. Between the forest, the amount and leisurely ease of people on the road, and their fashions, she guessed the portal had brought her East.

Not Tacorn, at least.

There were two kingdoms in the eastern part of the continent of Astye: Varana and Syoto. Varana, allied with Tacorn, was as unsafe as it was in the Middle Kingdoms themselves. Would Ruenen have traveled all the way back to the Northeast? Marai didn't think he could have made it that far on foot from the south in a month. No, this had to be the realm of Syoto.

Marai slid out from the forest and joined the throng of people on the road.

Color was everywhere: lavenders and ruby reds, pinks and royal blues. No one dressed in all black in the East these days. Marai was more conspicuous here than she'd been in the North weeks ago. Marai no longer had her cloak and scarf; her white blonde hair and light eyes stood out amongst the dark-haired inhabitants of Syoto. She no longer cared about hiding her face. Whoever Marai was now, she was no longer a mercenary.

However, people only casually glanced her way, as Syotons were used to fair Northerners visiting their kingdom. The Empire of Syoto was the home to the Nine Kingdoms Library. Scholars from across the continent traveled here, as did merchants and tradesmen. Marai needn't worry about being discovered here.

Across the road stood the entrance to a bustling metropolis. A large stone wall encompassed the city, but the tiers of a castle shot up from the center. Not far away, and just as tall, was the miraculous Nine Kingdoms Library, towering into the sky in the pagoda style.

Keshel would give his left arm to go in there, Marai thought wryly.

The gates to the city were open and inviting. Hundreds of people came in and out, busy with their days, oblivious to the growing threat of Tacorn to their west. Few Syoton soldiers milled about. The country had no conflict with anyone since they'd remained neutral in most matters.

Marai had been here several times. The capital city of Kaishiki was the central hub and power of Syoto. *No wonder everyone is dressed in such fine clothes.* Syoto was the wealthiest kingdom of the nine, and Kaishiki, the cultural epicenter. Most of the powerful lords had homes here, but also grand pagodas in the countryside.

The portal had placed her here for a reason. *Ruenen must be inside the city.*

Marai trudged through the gate, jostled by the throng of people. Kaishiki was the largest city in all of Astye. If Ruenen was indeed here, it could take days for Marai to find him.

First, however, she needed something.

She passed underneath rows of paper lanterns to a street lined with market stalls. Kaishiki was divided into districts. She wandered into the Merchant District, passing vendors of silks, pottery, porcelain, and jewelry. She came across a stall selling cloaks, all hanging from the canopy. Most were luxurious items Nosficio would treasure, lined with furs and sparkling jewels. Marai spotted a simple onyx cloak shoved in the back. It was much too mundane for regular Syotons. Marai knew the merchant would never miss it.

She snatched the cloak from its hanger and disappeared amongst the crowd, latching the cloak around her neck with the silver clasp and drew up the hood. Now she felt more comfortable, more herself.

It was time to find Ruenen.

There were several different options for his location. One, the smartest route, was that he stuck to the shadows and alleys, hiding from everyone. There were many dark, secretive locations in Kaishiki. She could start there.

But Ruenen was reckless.

"Excuse me, where's the nearest tavern?" she asked a merchant selling ornate, painted fans and umbrellas. Marai knew Ruenen well enough to guess that he was most likely performing. His lute had been smashed on the docks of Cleaving Tides, but the prince was resourceful. He'd probably procured a new instrument from somewhere.

The merchant looked her over quickly, deducing she wasn't there to make a purchase. "Two blocks up and make a right." He moved on to the next customer, giving Marai a scowl that suggested she was no more than a mosquito buzzing around his stall.

She followed the man's directions into the Theatre District, and came to the doors of an enormous tiered stone building. This tavern was nothing at all like the ones Ruenen and Marai had been to together. It had two floors: on the first was a long bar and possibly a hundred tables. On the second was a grand balcony where patrons leaned over the edge with their drinks. There was a stage with gauzy curtains, upon which three beautiful women were currently singing and dancing. Attractive young men and women wandered between the tables, serving food and drink.

Despite it being the middle of the day, it was completely packed inside. Marai had to squeeze around people to get to the bar. Three overworked, sweaty men hustled to get beverages to their patrons.

"Are there any performers going by the name Ard the Bard playing here soon?" she shouted to one of the men above the din.

"Ard the Bard?" he asked, his face twisted into a judgmental frown. "Not with a name that terrible. We only book the best musicians here."

Marai scowled. "What about a young male bard with brown hair and eyes? Tall, smiles a lot, good voice..." Her lips twitched when she thought of that dimpled grin. But that description fit so many people. Marai knew there was one thing that set Ruenen apart.

"He wrote the song called 'The Lady Butcher,'" she continued.

The barkeep shook his head and returned to pouring ale from a large barrel.

Marai fought her way back outside and went on to the next tavern down the street. They hadn't seen or heard of Ruenen, either. Five other taverns later, Marai felt disheartened and rather annoyed. Had she been wrong about Ruenen? Was he actually hiding out as he should? Or maybe he wasn't in Kaishiki at all. Maybe he'd been in the woods where the portal had originally dropped Marai. It had never been exactly precise with its locations when she'd used it before . . .

She was about to return to the woods when she overheard a conversation between two women at a table, giggling behind their fans.

"He's been playing at the Three White Cranes for a few days. I love his music. I've already watched him twice. And he's handsome, in that Middle Kingdoms way."

Marai's ears perked up. It was a slim chance. There could've been a dozen bards from the Middle Kingdoms here.

"What's his name?" the second woman asked.

"He goes by the Prince of Bards."

Marai's heart leapt. *Of course* he would call himself the Prince of Bards.

Reckless, as always, but Marai found herself smiling under her hood. She rushed over to the Three White Cranes, on the outskirts of the city, farther from the main gate and castle. It was a smaller building made of stone and wood, not nearly as busy as the other taverns. Before Marai reached the door, she spotted three dark cloaked figures, weapons at their hips, inching towards the tavern from the shadows. They communicated silently using hand gestures and covert glances.

Bounty hunters.

If they were searching for him, they were most likely searching for Marai, as well. They'd recognize her instantly.

She crept around back and found the kitchen door, then skulked in, ignoring the cook shouting, "You can't come in here!"

Marai stepped through the sliding door into the main tavern, which was also quite busy, but with lower-class patrons. The surrounding walls consisted of thick, translucent paper stretched over bamboo frames. The hunters hadn't yet entered, so Marai continued to scan the crowd for him. Perhaps the hunters were waiting for Ruenen to show himself.

"Is the Prince of Bards performing here?" she asked a man sitting at the bar, drinking rice wine.

"He's up next."

Her pulse quickened, hands went clammy. Was she really going to see Ruenen again? What would she say to him? How would he react?

He's alive, and that's all that matters.

Marai took a seat next to the man at the bar and waited, too. Her eyes stayed glued to the door, watching for the hunters. Minutes passed and she heard the audience begin to applaud, her back to the stage. She didn't have the courage to turn around and look at him, but she grinned when she heard his voice.

"Good afternoon, my fine friends. I'm the Prince of Bards!"

Marai's heart pounded in her chest as she heard the rich strummed notes of a lute.

I'll tell you a tale,
One that tore out my heart,
Of betrayal and abandon,
I don't know where to start.

It's not one of love,
Of romance and laughter,
She left me alone,
Won'dring now what comes after?

Marai snorted loudly. Ruenen was pissed.

The man next to her at the bar glowered.

It was marvelous to hear Ruenen's sonorous voice. Giddy with relief, her grin widened in amusement. Perhaps the lyrics should have bothered her, but at that moment, Marai didn't care that he was mad at her. She cared that he was *alive*. She'd take his anger over his death any day.

Stay focused. Her gaze locked on two dark figures entering the room from the main door. Marai spotted a third emerging from the kitchens. She stiffened; her hand went to Dimtoir's hilt.

I'll drink 'way the mem'ries
Rip the dagger from my chest
Curse the good thoughts of her
And burn all the rest.

Gods, he really is *angry,* she thought briefly, tracking the movement of the hunters.

As Ruenen continued to sing his song of ire and revenge, the hunters closed in from three sides. Marai leapt to her feet and caught the attention of the nearest hunter. She pushed her cloak aside to reveal Dimtoir. Her hood fell back, and the man's eyes lit up. The bounty on her head must have been hefty, indeed.

The other two hunters spotted Marai and halted.

Marai looked over her shoulder to make sure the three hunters followed her as she backed into the kitchens, drawing them away from innocent civilians and Ruenen.

"What's going on? You aren't allowed in here," shouted one of the cooks whose apron was covered in brown sauce.

Marai continued to walk towards the far end of the kitchen.

"Get out if you value your lives," she said to the cooks and a young barmaid.

The three hunters slid into the kitchen and the staff froze, glancing between Marai and the large men. The cooks exited out through the back door into the street.

Marai unsheathed Dimtoir.

The men attacked. Marai dodged, blade meeting blade. She cut down the first bounty hunter in two strokes. The second was more skilled, and the third joined in. Marai fought both at the same time, dodging and parrying. She rolled across the prep table, granting space between her and the attackers. She grabbed a metal pan from the hot stove and slammed it into the face of the largest hunter. He screamed as the metal branded his skin and knocked out a tooth. Noodles and vegetables flew in the air and onto the floor.

The other man swung. Marai crouched down, avoiding the blade. She sliced the man across the gut. Warm blood burst forth from the wound, splashing Marai in red. The man fell, and the burned hunter charged again. An angry red welt appeared on his cheek as he furiously stabbed. Marai's fingers latched onto a butcher's cleaver.

She swung both blades, one after the other. The burned man continued to block with his sword. She backed him towards the door. With a mighty swing of Dimtoir, Marai sliced the man across the chest. He fell backwards through the paper sliding door, bursting onto the tavern floor. People screamed and moved aside as the hunter collapsed.

Marai plunged the cleaver into the man's heart. More blood splattered. The hunter's body went limp.

Patrons and staff fled from the tavern in a stampede of screams. The only one left was the bard standing on the stage. Marai's suddenly trembling fingers pushed back her unruly braid as she took in the sight of him.

His chestnut hair was longer; it now fell below his ears. He'd shaved recently. He was clean and tidy, a surprise considering he was on the run. His clothes were new, all leather and soft linen. He certainly appeared the part of a successful bard up on that stage. He had no noticeable injuries.

Marai's eyes stung at the sight of him.

"What are you doing here?" Ruenen asked, voice gruff. A new lute was slung over his shoulder, much nicer than the old one, with its glossy wood. Where had he found the money to buy all these nice new things? He wiped away the emotion on his face by narrowing his eyes and folding arms across his chest, as if she were the last person he wanted to see. "I could've handled them on my own. I saw them enter."

"I came to find you." She could barely speak. The sound of his voice was such a comfort and a heartbreak.

"A little late, don't you think?" he asked, hopping off the stage, making his way to the door. He glanced down at the body of the dead hunter, butcher cleaver lodged in his flesh, and grimaced. "You certainly do enjoy making an entrance."

Marai was covered in blood. She wiped away the wet specks on her cheek. "I didn't know. I thought you were dead."

Ruenen walked right past her, not glancing her way, as he exited out into the street. Marai charged after him. Some of the tavern patrons stood around, speaking hurriedly with each other. They blanched as Marai fought her way after Ruenen. Kaishiki soldiers would arrive soon. It was hazardous for her to linger in the city.

"If I had known you'd escaped, I would've come sooner."

"Really? Didn't seem like you cared what happened to me," Ruenen snapped over his shoulder. He quickened his pace and dodged passersby in the crowded streets.

"Ruen, wait!"

He ignored her. Marai called to him again, but he walked faster, body stiff. She kept him in sight as they weaved through Kaishiki, past markets, stalls, and a knife-juggler performing in the street.

Once out on the road, Marai raced to join him. Travelers caught sight of Marai's ominous appearance and moved to the opposite side, their loud whispers akin to hisses.

"Are you going to ignore me forever?" she asked, catching up.

Ruenen stomped onwards, heading north towards the kingdom of Varana.

Marai scowled. *If he's going to ignore me, brooding in silence, I'll pull a page from his own book.* She'd challenge him.

"Interesting song you wrote about me. I think I prefer 'the Lady Butcher' more, strangely enough. And the Prince of Bards? Better than Ard, but you're not being subtle."

"Leave me be. I'm not playing this game, Marai."

"Then look at me, and let's talk about this."

Ruenen cut into the forest. Marai followed as he stomped over downed sassafras trees. He found a suitable location far enough away from the road, and whirled around. The golden flecks in his eyes blazed.

"You left me."

Taken aback by his glare and injured tone, Marai stopped walking and dropped her challenge. She pushed back her hood, and let him see the apology on her face.

"I never intended to—"

"You *left me* to fend for myself."

"You have no idea how much I regret—"

"I don't want to see you right now."

"I understand, but please—"

Ruenen stepped closer; his movements sharp and rigid. "You ran away, leaving me to wonder what I'd done wrong. Leaving me to wonder what the hell happened to you. I was scared, Marai, for myself. For *you*. For the fear I saw in your face that day. For causing it." Ruenen ran a hand claw-like through his hair. "But more than that, I was embarrassed. And hurt."

The words shot through Marai like a spear. *I deserve his resentment.* She stared at her feet, unable to stand looking into his face. "I know. I didn't mean to run away. I didn't want—"

"Did I misread something? I mean, you kissed me back . . . did you not want to?"

Marai peered up at him. Ruenen was stricken, eyes wide in horror. She realized then what upset him the most . . . it wasn't abandoning him to the hunters.

She shook her head. "No, Ruen, you didn't misread anything. I . . ." Her cheeks were on fire. Marai had never been skilled with words. She'd never properly expressed her feelings to another person before. This moment, saying this apology, was one of the hardest things she'd ever done. "I wanted to kiss you. That . . . that was real. One second, I was in your arms and I *wanted* it more than anything, and then . . . my mind went somewhere else."

Ruenen's face darkened as Marai shifted her weight and picked at her fingernails. She forced herself to keep going, to keep meeting his eyes. Ruenen deserved this explanation.

"I found myself back in my nightmares, to the days when Slate would . . . and all I could think of were his hands on my body, and even though they were *your* hands, it didn't matter. All I felt was Slate. Gods, I could almost smell him." The sweat and sea salt on Slate's skin. Marai nearly gagged. "It was so *real*. So I ran . . . I ran away and didn't realize I was. I was about to go back through when the portal closed, and I didn't have any magic left. I tried and tried, Ruenen, I did, but I couldn't get back to you. I couldn't save you. And then Keshel told me you were dead and I believed him. I'm so sorry."

Marai met his stare again. Ruenen's brown, fawn-eyes were wide, lips pressed tightly together, holding back his thoughts.

"I'm not Slate," he said after a long moment.

"I know."

"I would never hurt you." He'd said the same before, weeks ago in Cleaving Tides. Ruenen's face betrayed a kaleidoscope of emotions, as if he was trying to reign them in, but failing. "I never want to be compared to that monster."

"It wasn't intentional. It wasn't because of *you*, Ruen."

His eyes opened wider in alarm, the anger replaced by something far worse. "If my hands . . . if they remind you of him, then I can never touch you. I never want to cause you pain. It would *kill* me to hurt you."

Marai's heart clenched. Tears welled in her eyes as she watched Ruenen's pained face twist into a hateful grimace staring at his own calloused hands.

She felt the impulse to reach for him, but she grew timid, and instead, clenched her hands into fists at her sides. "You've only ever shown me kindness, and I repaid you in the most treacherous way. I'm ashamed of how I reacted." Marai let out a shuddering breath. "The portal brought me right where I needed to be. It brought me to my family. As much as I hated growing up in that cave, every part of me needed to be there with them."

An ember of strength ignited within her as she thought about Thora, Kadiatu, Raife, and even Keshel. He'd hurt her with his secrecy, but Keshel had given her a purpose. He'd listened to her. He'd trained her. She would be forever grateful to him for pulling her back from the ledge.

"Over the past few weeks, I've been trying to recover. Not just my magic," she continued. "Something in me had to die in order to move on."

The sharp edges, the dirt and grime, the soft spots she was so afraid to reveal . . . Marai couldn't change her past, but she *could* forge a new future. A life of meaning, as Ruenen had once suggested to her.

"The nightmares of Slate don't haunt me anymore. The scene I replay over and over was when I left *you*. The moment I discovered you'd escaped, I left to find you. Please, Ruen, I'm so sorry. I never should have left, and I'm a coward for running. Please forgive me."

Ruenen's face softened a fraction. His cold exterior hadn't broken yet, but he blinked and some of it left. His eyes were open books of dazzling light.

"You went back to the other fae?" he asked in a strained, quiet voice.

Marai nodded, the tension loosening as their gaze held. "I learned how to better summon and control my magic. Keshel, my . . . brother, he's not a fighter, but his magic is complicated and deep, like mine. It manifests differently, but he had to learn to control it, too."

Ruenen looked away. A chill settled across Marai, as if a fire had gone out.

"I'm glad to hear that." Despite being angry, Ruenen was still kinder than anyone else.

Again, Marai stifled the impulse to place her hand on his arm.

The bright sun sank in the sky behind the trees. It had taken hours to get to this moment, this conversation in the woods. Ruenen didn't seem quite so angry now. The stiffness had left his body entirely. Marai knew he was taking all her words in, letting them marinate.

"How did you escape?" she asked.

Surprisingly, he smirked. "Someone helped me."

"Who?"

"A man. A stranger in Cleaving Tides. Didn't give me his name. We were kind of busy with the hunters."

Marai cocked her head, urging him on.

"Right after your portal closed, this man appeared. I think he'd followed the hunters into the alley and knew they were up to no good. He stabbed two of the men who'd bound me from behind. I managed to get my hands on one of their swords and killed the rest, myself. I tried to thank the stranger, but he told me to run. So I did."

Impressed was too small a word for how Marai felt. Ruenen had never needed to hire the Lady Butcher at all. He'd survived five years entirely on his own, and could've gotten himself to the southern ports. But he'd been trying to keep his identity a secret the best he could. It didn't seem like he was trying anymore . . .

"Why didn't you get on a ship?" Marai asked. "You were *right there* on the docks."

"I'm tired of running. While I was being bound and shoved by those hunters, I realized I'd rather stand, fight, and die than run," said Ruenen through clenched teeth, waving his arms in that familiar gesticulation. "I'm forcing Rayghast to come get me himself. Anyone who comes to take me, I stand my ground. None of the hunters he's sent have been able to overpower me yet. I won't be a prisoner. I'd rather be dead."

He held his head high. Shoulders back. There it was: the pose of the Prince of Nevandia.

Marai huffed. *So fucking reckless.*

"If you're willing to die, to stop running, why don't you take up the throne?" Marai asked, temper rising to challenge him.

"Not this again, Marai."

Ruenen started walking. He didn't have a direction—he was trying to create space between them.

She didn't let him get far before she came to his side again. "Become king and fight Rayghast on the battlefield. At least then, if you die, it will have been for something. Because that's the inevitable end with your rash behavior."

Ruenen gave her a withering look.

"Fight and win, Ruen. Be king and live without fear. Have a home, and do something good. Isn't that what you kept telling *me* to do before?"

A flush of anger bloomed on his face and neck. "I don't know how to be king."

Marai grabbed hold of his arm and stopped his movement. "You're scared, I understand. I've been scared for years. I've *run* for years because I was afraid of getting hurt." She took a breath. "Instead, I've hurt myself far more times than I can count by pretending not to feel. You're doing the same. You're running from that life because you're afraid you won't be good at it. I've never met anyone more suitable to be king than you."

"Why?" he asked, but there was something in his eyes. A pleading that said, *show me why I'm worthy.*

Marai nearly scoffed out loud. *How can he not see?*

"Because you're *good*, Ruenen. You care." Marai swallowed as emotion took over. "You have passion and humility. More rulers on this continent should have your genuine kindness. You see people as they could be. In every soul, you see potential."

He blinked and bit his lower lip, letting her words sink in. "What if we lose? What if I make terrible decisions and thousands of innocent people die as a result?"

"They'll die without you. Nevandia shrivels away, and one day, Rayghast will butcher them all. Do you want to see Nevandians at the mercy of Rayghast? He'll torture them, starve them, treat them worse than his own people." She stepped closer to Ruenen, closing all space between them. "Think of those who sacrificed their lives to make sure you lived, so that you could become king. The monks and Chongan. Ruen, their deaths mean nothing if you waste the gift they gave you."

Ruenen stood motionless, lost in thought, eyes shimmering. When he spoke, his voice was so soft; a downy feather stroking her cheek. "I don't know how to do this, Marai."

"You'll have a knowledgeable council, people who know the country and the situation well. They'll guide you, stand firm beside you." She rested a gentle hand on his arm, and felt the corded muscles beneath his sleeve. "And so will I."

His eyes widened for a split second, then narrowed to cynical slits. "You're not going to run away from me again?"

Marai shook her head. It pained her to hear the tightness return to his voice. "No. I'll stay with you, for as long as you will have me."

Ruenen raked a hand through his hair again, but then his eyes snapped open as he grasped her hand. "What in the Unholy Underworld happened to your fingers?"

Marai hastily yanked her hand from his and shoved both in her pockets, cursing herself. She'd forgotten. "It's nothing."

Ruenen stared at her blankly.

She sighed, remembering how unwise it was to withhold information from those she cared about. "The magic, the day I left you . . . I took it from something else."

"What do you mean?"

She avoided his scrutinizing gaze. "I took from magic that doesn't belong to me. In my panic, I pulled magic from a dark place. A place I shouldn't have, and it left a mark."

"Lirr's bones, Marai, it looks like Rayghast's—"

"Arms? Yes. He has magic, too."

Ruenen's jaw dropped as if she'd slapped him. She'd withheld that particular fact from Ruenen after they'd escaped the dungeons. She hadn't wanted him to worry. Marai had always been good at keeping secrets. *I'm no better than Keshel.*

"When we were in the dungeon and Rayghast touched me, I could feel his magic writhing beneath the surface of his skin. But his human body shouldn't have that kind of magic inside. Dark magic is corrupting the drop of fae blood in his veins."

"Rayghast has *faerie blood?*" Ruenen took a step back, the realization hitting him. "But he . . . he *hates* magical folk!"

"It was probably many generations back. I think the percentage of faerie blood in him is miniscule, which is why the magic is too strong for the vessel, and Rayghast doesn't have the ability to use it properly. He's entirely human, otherwise, thus why he's been calling upon dark magic to help him."

Ruenen let out a long, amazed breath. "Dark magic . . . I've never heard of that before."

"No one is supposed to touch dark magic. It taints you. That's why Rayghast's arms are blackened, and it will continue to consume him as long as he pulls from it."

Ruenen looked sharply at Marai. "So you're permanently marked this way?"

"Magic isn't free, and every magical creature has its limits. It was a mistake I won't make again, especially now that I can control my powers better."

Ruenen glanced down to where her hands remained in her pockets.

"I'll put on my gloves if it bothers you."

His face tightened, eyes flecked with fear. "You resorted to pulling magic from somewhere else just to get away from me."

Marai's heart lurched. Her face softened. "Not from you, Ruenen. Never from you."

Ruenen studied her for a moment, pinning her in place, until he bit his lower lip again, and Marai had to turn away. She placed her focus on a mouse scurrying across the forest floor.

"It's getting dark. We should camp here for the night," Ruenen finally said.

They went to work clearing the ground and gathering firewood, as they had so many times before. Ruenen watched her intently as she used magic to light the fire again, but this time, concern was etched into every plane of his face. He glared at her blackened fingertips, and Marai knew he blamed himself.

"Please, think about taking up the throne, Ruen," she said to him across the fire. "I meant what I said. You'd be a great king."

Ruenen's mouth twisted. Flames danced in his eyes. "Go to sleep, Marai." He lay down in his blankets amongst the leaves, cushiony moss, and grass, turning his back to her.

The atmosphere around their campsite wasn't hostility . . . instead, Marai felt the gentle pulse of Ruenen's fear. Fear of becoming king. But more than that, fear for *her*.

He may not have forgiven her yet. That might take days or weeks, but Marai was resolute to continue trying to earn his forgiveness. She'd given up on him once, and she'd never do it again.

Ruenen was alive, and that mattered more than anything.

CHAPTER 9
Ruenen

He never expected to see her again.

Lying in the dark, Marai merely a few feet away, Ruenen couldn't believe she'd found him again. He didn't hear her slow, steady breath of sleep. She was awake, as anxious as he was.

He replayed her words: *I wanted to kiss you. That . . . that was real.*

It *had* felt real. She was the answer to a question he'd been asking himself for years. The boy with a thousand questions . . . now he only had one.

I wanted *it more than anything,* she'd said. But peering at her across the fire, body so rigid, maybe Marai kissed him out of obligation, not affection.

She'd looked so utterly terrified running through the portal that he'd barely been able to breathe. Because it was *him* she'd seemed afraid of. *His* touch she had run from.

Ruenen didn't know what he'd done wrong . . . he'd always tried to be respectful. He wanted *her* to be in charge of when they stepped over that line. But she'd kissed him when he'd least expected it in that alley. He'd forgotten about her boundaries. The second her lips touched his, all common sense left his brain. The clouds around his life had finally parted. Her kiss was a melody swirling around inside him; a song that burst brightly into creation from his heart. He would have held her forever if she hadn't backed away.

But her expression, eyes so wide, skin deathly pale, froze the blood in his veins. A face he would see over and over, in his dreams, out of the corner of his eyes as he wandered. Was *he* the villain? Did he overstep? Did he misunderstand?

Then she'd left him . . . disappeared through the portal as the hunters grabbed him. He wasn't afraid, not when they subdued him, not when they bound his hands behind his back. No, he thought of Marai. He thought of her face. And he hated himself, and her, and the whole messed up situation. He'd been wronged, but had he also wronged her?

When the kind stranger appeared and stabbed the two hunters holding him, Ruenen stopped feeling. A hardness had settled in his core; a heavy stone trampling his emotions. He didn't want to return to Tacorn to become Rayghast's plaything. He wouldn't allow himself to be tortured to death; his mangled body to be paraded around in conquest.

With a knife, the stranger had cut through the ropes binding Ruenen's hands. The silver-eyed, mahogany-skinned man had given Ruenen an opening, and he'd asked himself, *what would Marai do?*

Ruenen had grabbed hold of a sword dropped by a fallen hunter, and then slit the throat of another.

You're too heavy on your feet, Marai's voice critiqued. Ruenen dodged and whirled, maneuvering around the hunter's blade, and stabbed Rayghast's man in the side, angling his blade upwards. The hunter collapsed. Ruenen killed three more, then he was free.

He grumbled now as the darkness lifted and the forest became gray with early morning light. Ruenen hadn't slept a wink. He sat up with a groan and packed up his blankets, snuffed out the campfire embers. It was the first time he'd ever risen before Marai. She stirred on her patch of soil. Like the first time he'd ever seen them, her violet eyes pierced his lungs, stabbed his heart, and froze him solid.

He made sure to keep his face solemn. He hadn't forgiven her yet, but it was becoming increasingly more difficult the longer he stared into those eyes...

"Let's go," he said, although he had no destination. He knew they couldn't linger, not after Marai's incident at the Three White Cranes.

She blinked, surprised by the command. She packed up quickly, and followed him through the woods. "Where are we headed?"

"I don't know," he shot grumpily over his shoulder. He stomped through the dirt, taking out his frustration by snapping twigs and kicking rocks.

A melodious sound drifted up to him. Ruenen spun. Marai strolled behind him, hands in her pockets, surveying the forest.

"Are you humming 'The Lady Butcher?'"

Marai gave him an innocent shrug and kept humming. She didn't exactly have an ear for music; her rhythms were off and the notes were quite pitchy. But she *smiled* at him as she passed by, taking the lead. It was a real, true smile, directed solely at him.

It almost broke him. His anger at her washed away like sand in the tide. Ruenen would do anything for that smile.

"This is north, you know," she said after a few minutes. "Is this really the way you want to go? To Varana? Where Emperor Suli could grab you?"

Ruenen scowled at the back of Marai's black cloak. "No, I don't want to go to Varana. I'm assuming you have an idea, though, of where we should go instead."

"West might be promising..."

To Nevandia.

Ruenen hadn't decided yet. But if they turned and made for the Red Lands, the Middle Kingdoms... that would be a statement to himself. That would mean he accepted, that he was ready to take the throne.

How could he possibly be ready to rule a country? He'd been instructed for a few years as a child, but he'd forgotten all he learned. He would have to lead troops into battle against King Rayghast who had massive forces and *magic*. Tacorn was a military state. Soldiers trained for war beginning at the age of five, becoming diligent and adept killers, who either served *in* the army, or served *for* the army. Women were expected to breed soldiers, as one might breed horses. But the same was not so in Nevandia, a land of mostly farmers and miners. Each Nevandian life taken . . . that blood would be on Ruenen's hands.

"I can hear you thinking," Marai said. "I understand your fear, Ruen, but you've proven many times that you are brave and noble. You're already so much better than Rayghast will ever be."

She said this all matter-of-factly, as if deciding to become king was as simple as picking out a new cloak (black, of course).

"I haven't come to a decision yet."

"Whatever you decide, I vow to fight for you," said Marai, turning back around. "Because we're going to face Rayghast one way or another. I'll help you defeat him, but I'd rather have an army behind us."

She spoke in that same terse, indifferent tone, the one he was used to. The Lady Butcher. She was giving them both a purpose, something to believe in. To fight for.

They walked all day in that silence Ruenen had grown accustomed to in Marai's presence, and over the hours, his anger at her continued to ease, but he still made sure to scowl at her whenever she glanced his way.

Can't let her off too easily.

Ruenen had spent many days walking in silence since escaping the bounty hunters, but it had been oppressively lonely. He learned that there were many types of silences. There was the revenant, hallowed silence of a temple or monastery. The fearful silence of a prison cell. And then there was this silence, easy, not strained. Existing together in space and nature. At peace.

Every damn path turned them West. A collapsed bridge forced them further inland. A trades-worker strike in rural Syoto closed all nearby roads to traffic. Ruenen bitterly suspected that the gods were shoving him in their preferred direction. He wondered if Marai had stoked the strike days ago in advance of reuniting with him. Fate was guiding him towards his destiny.

That night, the forest opened up into a field with rangy, fragrant green grass.

As they set camp, he felt sure that whatever choice he made would be the wrong one. That he was doomed to fail no matter what.

Marai stared up at the night sky. He'd watched her do this many times before, but it felt significant then. A peace washed over her. There was something in the stars, the argent moon, that lit her eyes with possibility. Her gaze then snapped to him from across the campfire. Ruenen quickly looked away and cleared his throat, pretending to tie his boot.

"I believe in you, Ruen," she said.

He met her luminescent eyes, glowing softly in the night, filled with a warmth she hardly ever displayed.

"I believe in your future, and the future of Nevandia," Marai continued.

"What if Nevandia doesn't want me?" Ruenen asked, voicing a fear that had been brewing inside of him for years. "What if people are angry that I stayed away for so long?"

Marai's brows pinched for a moment as she thought. "I abandoned you, but I came back. It wasn't easy to admit my failings, but you listened, and I think you've forgiven me, at least partially."

"I haven't," he said, but couldn't stop the cockeyed smile from reaching his lips.

Marai snorted, and his heart nearly burst at the sound. "You're far more likable and honorable than I am. Nevandia will see your goodness shining through. If *you* can forgive me for leaving, then your people can also forgive you. And I'll be right by your side, for better or worse."

Ruenen had forsaken his people. He'd shunned the responsibility and duty that was his birthright for far too long. Too many people had died protecting him to ensure that he would take the throne.

I need to become worthy of their sacrifice. He could finally set things right.

"Alright, Sassafras, you win," he said. "I'll go to Nevandia. I'll declare myself."

Marai didn't look surprised. Instead, she smiled again as she had earlier in the woods. Smiled with pride, and his whole heart burned bright.

At dawn, Marai held out her hands. In an instant, a portal appeared. She'd summoned it easily; no strain shown on her face. Ruenen smelled the scent of magic, rich and bubbly. He briefly thought that if temptation had a smell, that would be it.

"Where's the portal taking us?"

"The glen on the outskirts of Kellesar, near the river."

Ruenen didn't know where that was. He'd never been anywhere close to Nevandia's capital city of Kellesar. He'd avoided it his entire life.

"It should be a safe spot. You need to go through first."

With a nervous swallow, Ruenen's grip on his lute strap tightened. He stepped into the portal, feeling the tendrils of magic stroke his cheeks and neck. The magic felt more solid this time. As he kept stepping between space and time, he sensed Marai all around him: strong, unwavering, sparkling. It eased his nerves.

His feet touched brown, brittle grass, and he took in his new surroundings. There was the Nydian River in the distance, snaking through the highlands, but its color was oddly muted and sludgy. The nature around him was gray and dull. Trees that should have been budding with spring life remained barren. Even the sky on a sunny day was overcast and glum.

He'd heard that Nevandia's lands were floundering, but it was strange to see it with his own eyes, to feel the emptiness so potently.

Something was wrong.

Marai appeared at his side, the portal gone. "I felt this darkness when we were in the Red Lands before, but now that I've used it, myself... Nevandia reeks of dark magic. I think Rayghast has been using it for years, sucking the life from these lands."

"Do you think it can be reversed?" Ruenen asked. Add that to the long list of things he would soon be in charge of...

"I'm not sure. I don't know enough about dark magic. Once Rayghast is killed, it's possible the magic will be returned to the land."

Once he's killed? Ruenen scoffed. *If* they managed to kill him...

The capital city of Kellesar loomed in the distance, encircled by the Nydian, almost an island in the middle of the highlands. Ruenen didn't want to look. He knew he'd see the castle spires climbing up towards the heavens and the gods-city of Empyra. Kellesar sat on a large hill; the city scaled upwards in a way unlike any other on the continent.

Marai suddenly stiffened and spun around, hand on the hilt of her sword.

Behind them stood a cloaked figure.

A bounty hunter? Ruenen's hand reached for the knife at his belt. But strangely, Marai smirked.

"I should have known you'd be sniffing around here."

The cloaked figure glided towards them and pushed back the velvet hood, revealing crimson eyes and a pointed, gray-hued face.

"I've been trying to track you for weeks." His mouth opened into a dangerous, fanged grin. "I've run up and down these highlands. Dul Tanen is the last place you were before your scents disappeared entirely, so you can imagine my surprise when I caught a whiff of you on the wind moments ago."

Nosficio the vampire.

Ruenen didn't drop his guard. He'd personally staked the vampire through the stomach at Iniquity, a dodgy town full of criminals, a few weeks ago. Since then, the vampire had taken an odd liking to Marai, and had helped them escape Tacorn soldiers. His fangs had grown back, and Ruenen cringed at the way his red eyes shimmered with *want*.

"Why are you tracking us?" he asked the ancient vampire.

Nosficio raised a single, elegantly shaped eyebrow. His dark dreadlocks were draped over his shoulder. "It's lovely to see you, too, Prince," he replied evenly. "A thank you would be nice, since it's due to *my* assistance that the Butcher knew you had been taken by Tacorn."

"We didn't need your help," Ruenen bit back.

The vampire's face lit with interest as he took in Ruenen's outstretched knife. "Then by all means, get captured again, and we'll test your theory, Princeling."

"That branch would make a nice stake, don't you think, Nosficio?" Ruenen asked, letting an edge, a warning, into his tone. "And this time, I'll aim for the kill."

Marai rolled her eyes and removed her hand from Dimtoir.

The vampire smiled in his lethal, smooth way. His nostrils flared. "You've finally come into your powers, Lady Butcher. Have you stopped denying what you are?"

A smirk lengthened across Marai's lips. Then Nosficio's eyes flit to the bloodstone ring on Marai's blackened fingers. It was the first time Ruenen had ever seen the vampire so caught off-guard.

"That ring. Where did you find it? And your fingers . . ."

Marai wiggled her fingers and the ring at Nosficio. "The ring called to me. I've had it for years."

Nosficio's gaze never left the jasper ring. "That ring belonged to Queen Meallán."

"You knew her?"

Nosficio nodded once. The ancient vampire's face shuttered, blocking emotions he didn't want them to see. "She was a powerful queen. A very impressive being."

Ruenen saw it then in Nosficio's face: sorrow. Regret. Years and years of it. An ageless being forever burdened with the loss of one he held dear.

Nosficio's demeanor shifted as his back straightened, chin jutted forward, and the sorrow was washed from his face. "Your voluntary presence in Kellesar can mean one thing: the princeling has decided to claim his throne. Which further means that the war between Nevandia and Tacorn will soon begin escalating."

"Why do you care?" Marai crossed her arms.

"We discussed this before. Rayghast is using magic he shouldn't. He's corrupting this land, and creating creatures of darkness."

Ruenen scowled. "What creatures?"

Nosficio turned crimson eyes to him. "I've seen them. Beasts unlike anything else on this continent, sprouting up like weeds from the ground every time the King of Tacorn uses his magic."

"You've been watching them?" Marai asked.

"I wasn't merely sitting around, waiting for you to return to the Red Lands. I was tracking the scent of one nearby; that's how I was able to find you two so quickly." Nosficio smirked. "This continent has been my home for centuries. I won't let it get destroyed by a human who shouldn't be able to use magic. I want to see Rayghast dead." His eyes blazed with fire on that final word. "He's killed dozens of vampires in his lifetime, and his father was no better. Not to mention all the other magical lives he's taken. He deserves to die for those crimes."

Marai cocked her head in that bird-like way. "I thought you didn't care about what happened to anyone but yourself."

"On the contrary, my dear Butcher," said Nosficio, "I cannot speak for my brethren, but *I* care deeply about Astye."

Ruenen scoffed. "You've killed just as many humans as Rayghast has killed magical folk."

Before Ruenen could blink, Nosficio disappeared, then reappeared in front of Ruenen, as if he'd been a mirage. His face was so close that Ruenen could smell the blood on the vampire's breath.

"There's a difference, boy, between killing by choice and killing from necessity. I was *created* this way. I cannot change what I am, how I feed, and what bloodlust does to me. Don't presume to understand the cravings of a vampire and the complexities of our long lives."

Marai shoved Nosficio backwards. He was far stronger than her, but the vampire let her move him easily. Marai's hand returned to Dimtoir's handle.

"Rayghast *chooses* to take lives, human and creature alike. He chooses to reach into the darkness, like a true monster who doesn't have a heart," said Nosficio. "Forgive me if I still hold on to some human sentiments."

"You want to help us defeat Rayghast?" Marai frowned.

Nosficio gave one slow nod.

"And what help can you possibly provide?"

"The first is obvious: I can fight. I'm far stronger than you and your prince. And you'll need me to help with these creatures of darkness. They're traveling out of the forests and into villages. I also know this continent better than anyone alive. Better than you, Butcher. I know the ins and outs of many kingdoms. I have acquaintances everywhere."

Ruenen waved his hands, suddenly overwhelmed. "Wait, wait, hold on! I haven't even taken the throne yet. We don't know if Nevandia will accept me as their king. It's going to be hard enough to get them to trust *me*, but add on the fact that I'm bringing a half-fae mercenary into their castle, I don't think Nevandians will take too kindly to me waltzing in with a *vampire* on my arm, as well."

"You don't want my help?" Nosficio asked, lifting his chin haughtily. "A foolish decision for a young, inexperienced prince."

"I didn't say I didn't want your aid," said Ruenen, "but I don't think right now is the time. Let me get established first. Let me win their trust. Then, Nosficio, I will grant you your revenge on Rayghast."

"Get in line," Marai murmured.

"I suppose there's logic in that. Fine. I'll wait here until you return, Princeling," said Nosficio with a slight incline of his head to Ruenen. "In the meantime, I shall continue my surveillance on the creatures. I'm looking forward to joining forces with you, Butcher. I cannot *wait* to see what you're capable of." He showed off those fangs again and disappeared with a gust of wind.

Ruenen turned to Marai, feeling weak in the knees and lightheaded. "Things are going too fast for my comfort."

Marai adjusted her hood and clothing, then stepped to Ruenen's side. She tugged at his leather vest, fixing the collar, then brushed a dead leaf from his shoulder. Ruenen blushed at the intimacy.

"Do you trust him? Nosficio?" he asked, following the movements of her hands on his body.

Marai lifted those vibrant eyes to his and Ruenen's face grew hotter.

"I trust his knowledge. I trust his anger at Rayghast. But do I trust *him*? No. We will always need to stay on our guard around him."

Ruenen and Marai observed Kellesar, the once magnificent city that had rivaled Kaishiki, Lirrstrass, and Chiojan. The brown, infertile highlands were so desolate at a time of year when the land should begin bursting with greens and lilacs of the heather. Nearby farmlands were void of crops. The Nydian River, usually so blue, weaved unimpressively through the hilly landscape, carrying mud and clay around the city. Ruenen's heart ached. This was *his* land, his kingdom, and it was dying.

The castle of Kellesar was perched at the top of the hill, surrounded by tall, thick stone walls. Its spires rose like beacons of beauty amongst the floundering land. Monk Nori had told young Ruenen that the Kellesar castle was the most beautiful in all nine kingdoms, with moonstone marble and granite shaped into intricate carvings, engravings, and buttresses. Pristine. A symbol of status. The stone wasn't native to the highlands; it had cost a fortune to transport the materials from elsewhere in Nevandia.

But the white stone, like the highlands, had lost its color. It was dirty, derelict, even from a distance. The castle was intact, but it appeared disappointing to Ruenen, who had the glorious image Nori had told him in his mind.

If I succeed, Nori, I'll return it to its original splendor, Ruenen vowed to the monk.

"Are you ready?" Marai asked.

Ruenen swallowed and nodded. He would never be ready for this moment. "Are we going to walk up to the front door?"

"Oh, yes, and we're not going to be quiet about it," she said, a mischievous glint in her eyes.

Ruenen wasn't sure what that meant, but that expression made him nervous.

She must have seen him waver because she grasped his hand. "You can do this, Ruen. I'll be right here beside you."

Gathering up his courage, he took the first step towards Kellesar. Then another down the sloping hill from glen to highland grass, Marai at his side. They crossed the crunching, brittle grass, step by step.

The city wasn't only what resided behind the protection of the main walls. Thatched cottages spattered the moor, huddled near the water. They passed a few Nevandian sheepherders, who gave suspicious glances; the bells on their livestock tingled as the herders shooed the animals away from Marai and Ruenen. Few others were out on the road. A man in patched clothing passed by with a beat-up old cart, carrying musty hay. His moves were sluggish, back and shoulders curling inwards, haggard and tired.

Step after step until they reached the stone bridge. They crossed over the nearly brackish Nydian, which stank of mold. Marai stepped in front of Ruenen as heavily armored, golden-clad guards came into view. Two approached, crossing spears to block the iron-gated entrance into the city.

"Names and business in Kellesar," one said in a youthful voice.

"I bring Prince Ruenen Avsharian of Nevandia, son and heir of King Vanguarden Avsharian and Queen Larissa, home to you," Marai announced in a clear and strong tone.

Ruenen nearly laughed. *She's so brazen.*

Marai held out her arms, opening her cloak to reveal her weapons; a rare sign of submission from the Lady Butcher. "We've come to meet with the Steward and to announce the return of the rightful king."

Ruenen had to hand it to her, Marai knew how to play courtier. She was, perhaps, as good of a performer as he was. For his part, Ruenen tried to stand straighter, to settle his face into an expression of stoicism and regality, though his chest heaved and palms grew clammy.

The guards and nearby citizens gaped from person to person. Another soldier with a large emerald plume on his helmet approached from behind the stone wall.

"I remember you both," he said, stepping closer. "You were running from Tacorn when they captured you on the road between our two kingdoms in the Red Lands."

Ruenen recognized this man's deep voice. He was the Nevandian commander who'd found them on the moor. Ruenen had barely been conscious at the time, immobile in the dirt. The commander's eyes lingered on Ruenen.

"We appreciate that you tried to protect us from Commander Boone and Tacorn," said Ruenen, hoping to ease the tension.

"You claim to be King Vanguarden's heir?" asked the commander. "What proof do you have?"

Ruenen bit his lower lip. "Other than my own resemblance to the late King and Queen, I also have this birthmark on my left wrist." He lifted the sleeve of his shirt to show the commander the unique brown sunburst mark there. "If you'd let us speak with the Steward, I'm certain he can verify my identity."

The commander narrowed his eyes. "How can we trust you aren't Tacorn spies? You were captured by Rayghast. Perhaps you're here at his behest." Before Ruenen could reply, the commander gave a signal to his men. They grabbed hold of Ruenen and Marai, their grip firm. "Until we can verify that you are indeed not spies or assassins, you will come with us."

Ruenen sighed loudly and glanced at Marai. Her countenance appeared ready to kill, the Butcher's fearsome glare set in place. Her eyes dipped down to the male hands on her arms. She stiffened, but said nothing, and followed the commander through a nearby door.

They entered what appeared to be an office for the guards' station at the gate. The guards quickly tied Ruenen and Marai's wrists, then sat them into chairs. Through his visor, the commander stared them down as his men stood at the door, hands on their weapons.

"Why did Tacorn capture you?"

"Well, that's obvious. I'm heir to the Nevandian throne," Ruenen said with a huff. "Rayghast hoped to kill me so he could end the line and defeat Nevandia for good."

"How did he know there was a lost prince of Nevandia when no one else, including us Nevandians, did not?"

Ruenen scowled. "It's not surprising. Rayghast has many skilled spies and assassins in his employ. He's known about me for twenty-two years."

"You said your name is Ruenen, but who is this?" The commander gestured to Marai, who'd been sitting ram-rod straight in her chair.

"His guard," she replied with a growl. "I'm duty-bound to protect him."

Ruenen's heart thumped. Marai might have felt obligated to protect him when he'd hired her, but she was there now by choice, because she believed in him. Ruenen knew this was difficult for her, to show her face to all these people, to be handled by a group of men.

"A female guard?" asked the commander, genuine surprise in his tone. His attention was fixed on Marai.

Can he tell what she is?

"My premier goal is to defeat Rayghast and return Nevandia to its former glory," Ruenen told him.

"That's a fairly substantial goal," the commander said, a sliver of amusement in his voice. "My men will search you while I go to the castle and speak with the Steward. Any *trouble,* and you'll be brought to the dungeon."

The guards parted to allow the commander to exit the office, then they made Ruenen and Marai stand as they searched. The guards removed Marai's sword and dagger, and Ruenen's knife. They placed the weapons on the office desk and continued to pat down. Marai's eyes closed tightly, face scrunched up in obvious discomfort.

"Stop, please," Ruenen said to the young guard touching Marai's thighs. "She's a lady. She doesn't deserve to be touched in such a brutish way."

The guard, in fact, was being professional about the task. He didn't take advantage of the situation, but it didn't matter because Marai's face was so pained that Ruenen couldn't stand it. The guard glanced up at Marai.

"My apologies, lady—" he stammered.

"Get it over with," Marai said through gritted teeth.

The guard finished the job quickly. He did find Marai's knife in her boot and placed it with the other weapons. She sat down heavily in the chair, crossing both her arms and legs, closing herself off. That distant expression swept across her face.

They sat in silence for a while as the guards stood watch at the door. Marai picked at her magic-stained cuticles. Ruenen could barely keep still. His knees bounced, shifting in his chair. If they allowed him to play his lute, he might be able to keep calm, but the waiting was agonizing. Would the Steward believe him? Would they let Ruenen take the throne? Would they *see* him?

"Are you really the lost prince?" asked the young guard. He'd moved to the small window and had taken off his helmet. He had a round, innocent face, dark eyes of the Middle Kingdoms, which were currently wide as he stared at Ruenen.

"I am."

"We've heard rumors for weeks, but we didn't know it was true . . ." The guard trailed off when an older guard coughed loudly in warning. But Ruenen caught the young man smiling.

Hope. That was what Ruenen had heard in the guard's voice, had seen in that smile. Ruenen's arrival had given the boy hope. Nevandia was a war-ravaged nation that hadn't known safety and security in over forty years. The young guard had grown up fearing Rayghast and Tacorn, waiting for the day when his country would crumble. Ruenen hoped he could give these people peace.

The door opened and the commander returned. "The council will speak with you." He cut the bonds around Marai and Ruenen's wrists. "You'll remain under guard the entire walk to the castle, but we won't let the people see you bound. If you *are* our prince, I don't want to be remembered as the fool who treated you as a prisoner."

Ruenen gave him a true smile. "What's your name, Commander?"

"Avilyard, sir." The man inclined his head. "Head of our military forces, and Captain of the King's Guard."

"Thank you, Commander Avilyard," said Ruenen and followed him from the office.

Ruenen took in the sights and sounds of Kellesar as they walked up the sloping cobblestone streets. Tall, thin buildings crammed together in narrow, winding streets and alleys. Their facades were stone or brick, and plaster accented with timber framing. The wood frames and beams were painted in bright reds, blues, greens, and yellows. Small empty flower boxes perched outside windows. Lanterns and colorful signs dangled above shops, inns, and restaurants, which posted hand-painted menus on their exteriors. They looked inviting, interesting, which surprised Ruenen since Nevandia's lands were so lackluster. The city itself still kept a bit of its spark. He nearly had to be dragged away from a wide open window where a woman sold fragrant, savory hand-pies.

Citizens gawked as they passed. Most people on the main streets lived above their shops. Ruenen spotted heads peering down at him from above. Ruenen assumed it was rare for a group of golden-clad soldiers to accompany strangers through town, especially ones who weren't Tacornian prisoners. First impressions mattered, so Ruenen kept a smile on, stood erect, and walked with confidence.

Up and up the winding streets. They turned a corner and the pale stone wall surrounding the castle came into view. The metal grate was already raised. A bower of dead vines hung limply from the archway. If they'd been blooming, the sight would have been breathtakingly beautiful. They passed through the portcullis and entered the courtyard. It might have once been stunning, with vines and flowers winding up the trellises. Shrubbery and dogwood trees lined the walkways, but all those plants were crumpled, barren, and dead. The clay pots by the castle doors were empty, save for dry dirt.

More golden soldiers stood at the massive entryway. They didn't move, but their eyes tracked him as he entered the castle.

It was truly remarkable inside, despite the gray hue that encircled the city. Colorful tiles in patterns of swirls and shooting stars decorated the floors. Further in, the tiles shifted to the golden Nevandian sunburst. Painted frescoes lined the walls, depicting various scenes of the gods: flowers bursting to life around Lirr, Laimoen charging forward in an epic battle, Lirr playing her lute and singing to children, and Laimoen sitting amongst books in the Nine Kingdoms Library. Nevandian banners hung interspersed between the frescoes.

Ruenen's gaze kept traveling upwards. His jaw dropped.

A large marble staircase twisted up to the second floor. The vast windows brought in streams of natural light, which made the gold paint in the tiles shimmer. Ornate lanterns and chandeliers lined the walls and ceilings. A large stained-glass circular window was the focal point in the entry hall. Its vivid colors created a design upon the walls when the sun shone through. Flying buttresses and beams crisscrossed above his head.

But despite its grandeur, the castle had a stifling atmosphere of emptiness. He saw no one other than guards.

"The throne room is through here, where the Lord Steward awaits you," said Avilyard, indicating a set of large oak doors to his right. There was a matching pair of doors to his left.

Ruenen swallowed, heart pounding, as two guards opened the door and he saw his throne for the first time.

CHAPTER 10
Rayghast

"What is this?"

Rayghast slammed three coded messages down onto the long table. His council, commanders, and spies shifted guiltily in their seats, none of them meeting his black-eyed gaze.

"Why has no one cracked this code yet? Why am I still being brought these letters?" he asked with quiet fury.

"Dozens of these letters are going out each day, Your Grace. The same message, copied over and over again, but it changes daily. We try to intercept all of them, but they seem to be coming from every point in the city: the fortress, taverns, inns, markets, even the army barracks," said Falien, one of Rayghast's best decoders and spies.

"We've questioned the owners of these establishments, everyone within the vicinity, but most are completely oblivious," Commander Shaff, Boone's replacement, said in the council chamber. Shaff was a large man, tall and broad, dark and severe, but had none of Boone's vigor. "We've found messages glued to the bottoms of goblets, in packages, bags of grain, beneath a horse's saddle. It's a whole network."

"And the rumors are certainly not helping," added another commander, new to the position.

"Rumors?" repeated Rayghast.

The young commander flinched. "Yes, Your Grace, rumors are circulating all over the city ... about you ..." He bowed his head as Rayghast stood from his throne.

"And what do these rumors say?"

Rayghast approached, and the man shrunk lower in his seat.

"That you are cursed, Your Grace. That you cannot have a child. That your wives are destined to die."

Cronhold hacked out a cough. "That's preposterous! Our King is virile and beloved by the gods!"

"Yes, of course, you are, Your Grace," stammered the commander, receiving a scathing look from the council, "but the problem is that the people are beginning to believe it. They have *doubts*."

Rayghast remembered the two servants whispering in the hallway the previous day. Since then, he'd certainly garnered more stares than usual, more nervous glances.

"Well, this seems easy enough to solve," Wattling, who was built like a tree stump, said. "The queen must become with-child immediately. All those silly rumors will disappear once we have a healthy male heir."

"The fault clearly lies with Queen Rhia," Dobbs said, caterpillar-brows furrowing. "You've been married for eighteen months now. It's taking far too long, and she has a duty to give you a son, Your Grace. That's all she's here to do. The queen must try harder."

"It didn't take this long with your previous wives. I suggest, Your Grace, that you, uh, visit her rooms tonight, and every night thereafter to ensure she gets, uh, with-child," Cronhold said, receiving several agreeing murmurs from the table. "She must do everything in her power to produce an heir."

"What good is taking over Nevandia if Your Grace cannot pass the territory down to your son? We are building an empire," Wattling stated, giving Rayghast a simpering smile.

Rayghast turned to the young commander, who sheepishly met his gaze. "Is that the only rumor?"

The man hesitated, biting his lip. "Some people say that darkness, an eerie miasma, surrounds the fortress–"

"Yet again, the answer is simple: arrest those circulating the rumors and we'll have them hanged," Wattling said to Shaff and the other commanders at the table.

Shaff stood and bowed low to Rayghast. "Your Grace, I will hunt down all those who wish to stir up discord in our city."

He pulled the young commander to his feet and dragged him from the hall. Rayghast knew the new commander would submit to punishment from Shaff and may even be stripped from his position for the words he spoke at the meeting. But he'd alerted Rayghast to a worsening problem in Dul Tanen. Was his control slipping?

Rayghast found himself outside Rhia's door, listening to the commotion within. He'd decided to come early for their nightly appointment, as he intended to visit the dungeons again all evening.

"You look magnificent, Your Grace," said one of her ladies, rather loudly.

"Aren't you scared of those rumors? That you will also die in childbirth?" another girl asked. "What if he is indeed cursed?"

"Don't you dare speak such treason about my husband," snapped Rhia haughtily. "There's no truth to those rumors. Lirr has blessed our lands. She favors our king."

A loyal wife was hard to find. The rumors were spreading like a festering wound throughout the fortress and city, and Rayghast was surprised to hear her strong support, that she wasn't taken in with the idea, too.

Rayghast slowly opened the door connecting their rooms. Unaware of his presence, Rhia studied herself in the mirror. Her ladies had dressed her in a gauzy robe, so pellucid that it left nothing to the imagination. Rhia's long, straight hair was wet and draped across her shoulders. Rayghast could smell her fragrant bath soaps from the door.

A beautiful woman. A meaningless quality. But *loyalty* . . .

He stepped into the room. Rhia's silent ladies fanned out behind her, darted curtsies, and hustled out past him.

"My King," his wife said in a silky voice, lowering into a grand curtsey. "I wasn't expecting you so early."

She wasn't repulsed by him, the way his other wives had been. They'd always screamed and struggled when he'd visited them. They'd avoided him in the halls, kept to their rooms or the gardens. Rhia, however, understood duty. She understood power. She never complained, never flinched. The magic prowling in his veins was *bored* by her.

If he ever felt affection, Rayghast might have some for her.

He stalked towards her, and undid the buttons of his trousers. Rayghast never removed his clothes. He wouldn't become *intimate* with her.

His blackened hands touched her covered shoulders, shoved her backwards onto the bed, and lifted her nightgown.

It was brief. Perfunctory. He made no sound, showed no pleasure, and neither did she. Rhia sat up and adjusted her nightgown as Rayghast made for the door.

"I hope you find whoever has been spreading those horrible rumors," Rhia said, halting his hand on the doorknob. "Any update from your decoders on those mysterious letters?"

"No."

"How disappointing." She curtsied low, eyes on the floor, then put her dainty hands to her womb. "I pray that today's joining will finally produce results, Husband."

"I won't be at dinner."

Rayghast left then, closing the door behind him, and listened to the faint sound of a drawer opening and closing within, and the soft, contented humming of his wife.

CHAPTER II
Ruenen

He'd spent his whole life running from this throne, but the moment he saw it, Ruenen's emotions swelled. Twenty-two years and so many deaths to make it there. He thought of Amsco and Nori, and Master Chongan. His caregivers. His saviors.

I hope they're watching.

The exquisite throne itself was made of glossy wood, bone, and pure gold with a plush green cushion and upholstered armrests and chair backing. Empty. Waiting for *him*. And there he finally stood, transfixed. The throne beckoned to Ruenen like a siren's song.

The room was not a hall, as Ruenen expected. It was a more intimate space, made from the same white marble and granite as the rest of the castle. Twenty steps, and Ruenen could reach the dais, where the throne was perched. An emerald green rug ran the length of the room from door to dais. Behind the throne stood a wall of floor to ceiling windows. Green and gold drapes and banners hung from the ceiling and columns.

Paintings of past kings and queens paneled the walls. Ruenen's eyes rested on young King Vanguarden and Queen Larissa's portrait nearest the throne. They'd made an attractive couple. Vanguarden and Larissa both had the Middle Kingdoms' dark hair and eyes, sun-kissed skin, but Ruenen only saw himself in Larissa. Vanguarden's face was longer, with softer features than Ruenen's.

A long, polished table sat to the right side of the throne, surrounded by twelve chairs. Three of those seats were taken by men in formal black robes. The man at the far head of the table had a white and green collar over his robe, and a Nevandian broach pinned near his heart. His shoulders slumped forward slightly, lines etched his face, gray hair receding. His mouth sagged, as if the man lived life in a constant frown. Ruenen guessed he was the Steward.

As one, the three men stood when Ruenen entered, several guards still at his sides.

Commander Avilyard bowed to the Witenagemot, the formal title for the Nevandian royal council. "I present Master Ruenen and his personal guard." Avilyard stepped back, but didn't go far. He and his men retreated to the corners of the room, spreading out, watching with hawkish eyes.

Ruenen and Marai bowed to the Witan, who stared, faces impassive. Sweat dripped down the back of Ruenen's neck.

"You've come with quite the declaration, young master," said the Steward, his voice taut as a bow string. He was taller than Ruenen, and thin as a reed. His fingers trailed across an ornate wooden chest, decorated with carvings of the Nevandian sunburst, on the table in front of him. "Forgive us if we find this rather hard to believe. We take these matters seriously, for if there is actually a 'lost prince,' his arrival will affect the entire fate of our country. And we're not deaf to the rumors of what happened recently in Dul Tanen."

"I understand, my Lord Steward," Ruenen said with another slow incline of his head, "and I respect your caution. A wise Steward of the Throne wouldn't trust a stranger so readily. I do not come here with the intention of leading you astray. I'm not a liar. I do not seek fortune or glory. I'm here out of duty to my land and people. To my blood. I promise you, my Lords, that I am the real heir of His Grace King Vanguarden Avsharian."

"Why come forward now?" asked the bald, heavy-set councilman on the right. His round face was all hard lines and judgment. "It's been nine years since King Vanguarden died. If you were truly the heir, why not return at the news of his passing?"

"If I'm being honest, my Lords, I didn't want to become king," Ruenen said, heat creeping up his throat at such a shameful admission. "I admit that it was a cowardly, selfish thing to stay away for so long. Up until quite recently, I didn't believe myself capable of running a country, especially one in a grueling war."

"You believe yourself ready now?" continued the councilman, narrowing his eyes further. "Seems rather opportune."

"Regardless, we are willing to hear your story," said the Steward, giving the man on his right a subtle look. "I'm Lord Steward Koven Holfast." He gestured to the wiry man on his left with long, dark hair pulled back in a plait. "This is Lord Councilman Fenir," then the bald man on his right, "and Lord Councilman Vorae. Please, have a seat."

Ruenen let the Witan members sit first, then he took a hesitant seat in the closest open chair at the table; Marai lingered behind him. Councilman Vorae examined Marai with brown, suspicious eyes.

"You may go, girl," he said with a dismissive gesture.

"She stays," Ruenen said, causing all three men to blink in surprise, then Vorae sneered.

"Very well. Do you not want to sit, then?" he asked, taking in Marai's black cloak, crossed arms, and steely expression.

"I'm here to protect the prince, not to relax," she said.

All three councilmen frowned deeper. Fenir shook his head.

Women of Astye were not employed as guards or knights, or much else, for that matter. They weren't welcome in council chambers or meetings, except in Grelta where Queen Nieve ruled. Ruenen was surprised the Witan allowed Marai to remain inside the throne room.

"What's your name?" asked Steward Holfast, not unkindly, but his wary eyes stared down Marai.

She pursed her lips. Her name was one of her most coveted secrets.

"That doesn't matter—" began Ruenen.

"Marai."

Ruenen glanced back at her. Her hard expression didn't change as she met his gaze, but he hoped she could read the warmth in his face. The apology. The gratefulness.

"Commander Avilyard told us of his encounter with you on the road over a month ago," Holfast said, moving the wooden chest aside and interlacing his fingers upon the table. "He explained how you were captured by Tacornian forces. The late Commander Boone was quite determined to have you. I'm curious . . . how did you escape the Tacorn dungeon?"

"And with all of your limbs intact?" added Vorae.

Ruenen didn't appreciate this man's sarcastic tone.

"Perhaps it's better to start at the beginning of Prince Ruenen's story," Marai said, her voice edged.

Again, Holfast's eyes lingered on her. "Very well, Master Ruenen. Why do you believe yourself to be the son of our great King Vanguarden?" Holfast gestured towards the painting of Vanguarden and Larissa.

Ruenen took in a breath. How surreal this defining moment was. To build up all these thoughts and assumptions over twenty-two years, to imagine this homecoming, and now here it was. How could he ever put it into words . . .

I can't wait to write a song about this, he briefly thought.

"As a child, I was raised in a monastery by Head Monks Amsco and Nori outside the Nevandian border. They were the ones who told me King Vangaurden and Queen Larissa were my parents, and that I'd been sent to the monastery to stay hidden from King Rayghast. That my birth was a secret."

If anything Ruenen said so far was familiar to the Witenagemot, they didn't show it. They listened politely, faces blank.

"Tacorn soldiers destroyed the monastery when I was eight, killing Monk Amsco and Monk Nori, and I was once again rushed off to safety. I passed hands many times, from stranger to stranger, until I ended up in Chiojan with a blacksmith named Master Tomas Chongan. I lived there for several peaceful years, but Rayghast tracked me down and sacked the city. I escaped once again, and have been on the run ever since."

The Witan exchanged looks.

"You believe King Rayghast knows you're the lost heir?" asked Councilman Fenir. He had round, owlish eyes that openly displayed his anxiety.

"If he didn't believe me to be the prince, why would he tell his people otherwise?" Ruenen posed. "Marai and I were paraded through the streets of Dul Tanen, then strung up in the Tacorn dungeons. Rayghast did not, for one moment, doubt me."

"How did you escape?" pressed Holfast, staring at Marai again.

The hair on Ruenen's arms rose as a prickle of fear spread over him. Did Holfast know what she was? Is that why he kept peering at her so intently?

"Why does it matter?" Ruenen asked. "We escaped, and we're here now."

"It *matters*, Master Ruenen, because no one escapes Rayghast and his dungeon. No one is set free. Unless you were released because you've been turned spy," Holfast said, face darkening.

"I am *not* a spy," said Ruenen, fear turning to frustration. He had to keep Marai's truth a secret. They would attack her instantly if they knew she was fae, and everything would be ruined.

"Why can't you tell us how you escaped?"

Ruenen nearly bolted from his seat. He was about ready to walk out the door and never return. His knuckles turned white on his chair's arm rests. *This was a bad idea...*

"I got us out," came Marai's voice.

A hush fell over the room. The guards didn't shift in their armor.

"A woman? Hah!" Vorae scoffed and rolled his eyes.

"As I'm sure you've already guessed, Lord Steward, I'm half-fae," she said, and the room exploded.

Armor clanked as Avilyard and his guards closed in, weapons unsheathed, surrounding Marai and Ruenen in seconds. Ruenen jumped out of his chair, reaching for her, narrowly avoiding being skewered by a spear.

"I wasn't aware any faeries survived the great purge," Holfast said calmly, betraying nothing.

Marai's words were as shocking as if she'd tossed a glass of wine into the faces of Fenir and Vorae. They blanched, tan faces ashen, leaping to their feet.

Holfast, however, showed no such shock. "Why exactly are you helping a human? Especially one who considers himself a descendent of the very king who started the mass killing of magical folk."

King Talen, Ruenen's grandfather. But it had been Rayghast who'd slaughtered the camp Marai had lived in as a child. It was Rayghast who'd killed Marai's parents.

Marai remained calm and cool, despite the blades pointed at her face. "My goal is for Ruenen, the rightful king of this country, to ascend the throne. I care not what you think of me, but I assure you that I'm not here to hurt anyone."

Marai had no physical weapons, but she didn't need them to kill every single person in the room. Lightning could do more damage than a blade. She could open a portal and disappear with Ruenen in an instant.

"I beg your pardon—" said Fenir, swelling up like a croaking toad.

"I bet you do," Ruenen muttered under his breath.

Fenir ignored him. "This cannot be tolerated. A dangerous creature we deemed *eradicated* is standing freely here in the Witenagemot chambers. We cannot allow it to live, nonetheless continue its presence here!"

Ruenen's blood boiled. "You will not speak about Marai in such a hateful way. She's risked her life countless times protecting *your* prince. She's more trustworthy than any of you, and deserves your respect."

He glanced back at Marai, and saw her regarding him with that usual severe expression. But her violet eyes danced. She was here for *him*. No matter what, she was still standing there for *him*.

Fenir opened his mouth, but Holfast raised his hand, silencing the man. "I'm willing to let the faerie stay, if she can agree to remain civil. We'll require assurance that no magic will be used in this room. Do we have your word that no harm will come to us or our people while you're on Kellesaran soil?"

"But you can't trust them," Vorae said. His face was as round and red as a tomato.

"If she wanted us dead, Lord Vorae, I believe she would've done it already," replied Holfast coolly. His focus hadn't left Marai since the moment she'd declared herself fae.

Marai glared daggers at the humans, but folded her arms across her chest. "As long as Prince Ruenen's not harmed, you have my word that I'll stand by and cause no disturbances."

Holfast's lips tightened, then he said, "Very well. Let us continue."

"My lord—" began Avilyard.

Holfast held up a hand. "Trust goes both ways." He gestured to the guards, who lowered their weapons, and took several steps backwards.

Ruenen was the first to move back to his seat. The Witan settled, although noticeably agitated and disgruntled, and sat back in their chairs. Marai crept closer behind Ruenen, hands casually in her pockets.

Despite the near clash, a seed of hope began to crack open inside Ruenen's chest. The Steward would have either killed or dismissed Marai and Ruenen if he didn't think there was a possibility of truth to Ruenen's claim.

"We'll return to that particular conversation in a moment," Holfast said once everyone seemed relatively calm. "The faerie is right, however, we must see if Master Ruenen is indeed Vanguarden's heir."

Ruenen glared at Holfast's clear stab at Marai's heritage by not addressing her by name.

"The young man does look strikingly similar to our beloved Queen Larissa," Fenir finally said, pointing at the wall to the queen's perfectly painted face. "He has her eyes, her nose, and Avilyard says you have a rather recognizable birthmark."

Ruenen stood and approached Fenir, offering up his left wrist for inspection. Fenir rubbed a finger across the sunburst mark, checking for smudges indicating makeup or paint. The councilman nodded in approval, and Ruenen returned to his seat.

"We know about the destruction of the monastery, and the events that occurred in Chiojan," said Vorae.

Ruenen blinked in surprise. Had Nevandia been tracking him all along?

"We were well aware of whom Rayghast sought," the bald councilman continued. "Not entirely sure how he discovered the lost prince, but his spies are everywhere. Our own spies within Tacorn told us what occurred in the dungeons of Dul Tanen."

"So . . . you believe me?" Ruenen asked, gossamer wings of hope spreading, lifting him up and up into the sky.

Holfast glanced sharply at Commander Avilyard. "Leave us."

For a moment, the commander seemed torn. His eyes flashed to Marai, but he eventually gestured to his guards. They exited the chamber; the clang of their clunky metal armor receding into the hallway. Heavy wooden doors closed with a creak and a thud.

Caution folded Ruenen's hopeful wings. Something was amiss.

After several breaths, Holfast got to his feet and walked up the dais steps to the throne. His fingers gently stroked the armrest. The man suddenly appeared quite tired; his eyes closed as if he wanted to keep them shut forever.

"The truth is, Master Ruenen, it's impossible for you to be the Prince of Nevandia."

Ruenen's anger and shock flared, twisting within his gut. "And why is that?"

Holfast turned to him, his eyes suddenly distant and incredibly sad.

"Because the real lost prince died eight years ago."

CHAPTER 12

Marai

Undiluted shock, like a pouncing wildcat, slammed into Marai. Its claws shredded through her brain, leaving no thoughts behind but silence.

The real prince?

"What do you mean?" Marai whispered.

In his chair, Ruenen sat frozen, color draining rapidly from his skin. All around him, Marai watched his world unmoor and shatter to pieces.

"King Vanguarden and Queen Larissa did indeed have a hidden son," said Holfast, a rich and deep melancholy entwining his words. "Lord Fenir, Lord Vorae, and I were present in the birthing room, as is customary here. It was I who took the newborn Prince Kiernen from the Queen and delivered him to the Priestesses of Lirr in a temple along the Northern coast." Holfast hung his head. "After King Vanguarden was murdered, Lord Fenir and I went to retrieve our prince, but found that he had perished in a terrible fire eight years ago, along with all the priestesses and monks. We believe the fire was an accident, since we never had proof Rayghast knew of Prince Kiernen's existence at the temple."

This can't be . . . breath came up short in Marai's lungs. A tinny ringing began in her ears.

Images of a burned out temple flashed through Marai's memories. Weeks ago when she and Ruenen were traveling through Grelta by the

Northern Sea, they'd come across a temple of Lirr that had extensive fire damage. Ruenen's eyes widened as he, too, connected the dots.

"We lost our king, our queen, *and* our prince within a year," said Fenir with a sad shake of his head. "And with that, we lost all of our hope. The royal line has ended."

"Then . . . who am *I?*" Ruenen asked, voice cracking. His hands shook in his lap. His shoulders caved, his face contorted. This was a man beginning to fall apart. "Why was I placed in the monastery? Why did Amsco and Nori *tell me* I was the prince?"

The Witan members regarded Ruenen with pitiable stares, and Marai bit back a growl of contempt.

"Because that is who I told them you were," stated Holfast. "I know exactly who you are, Ruenen, because *I* placed you in that monastery. The monks were following my orders. They didn't know you weren't the prince. I lied, and they believed me." Holfast walked down the dais stairs and approached Ruenen, hands clasped behind his back. "You are the son of Queen Larissa's younger sister, Lady Morwenna, and her husband Lord Rehan Ashenby. You're the prince's cousin."

Ruenen sagged in his chair. Marai wasn't sure he'd remain upright much longer. She knelt next to him and grasped his hand tightly. It was cold and clammy, limp within her own.

"Lady Morwenna gave birth to you a few months after the prince. Many people thought Morwenna was the queen's twin. They looked nearly identical, though they were only two years apart in age. Your birthmark is rather unusual and I remember it clearly on the day you were born. King Vanguarden and Queen Larissa feared for their son's life, and I regret to say that the king and myself devised a plan to use you as a decoy."

Marai couldn't wrap her head around any of this. She tried to grasp the facts, but like water, they slipped through her fingers. Ruenen wasn't the lost prince. He had no claim to the Nevandian throne. This was more difficult to believe than when Ruenen had first told her he was the lost prince. So many lies and deceptions . . . the game of kings was more complicated than Marai knew.

"Our hope was that if Rayghast ever discovered the birth of Prince Kiernen, he would be drawn to *you*, Ruenen. Your monastery was closer to our lands, and noticeably loyal to Nevandia. We hoped he would go after you instead of the real prince. It seems we were correct in our assumptions."

"How do we know you're telling the truth?" Marai asked.

Holfast lifted the lid of the wooden chest. Its hinges creaked open, revealing yellowed bundles of letters. "I saved all correspondence between myself and the priestesses at the temple, and your Monk Amsco. I wanted to ensure a record, should the need ever arise. You'll find letters in here from Lady Morwenna to me, as well, asking after your well-being, Ruenen. Please feel free to read them."

Ruenen stood on trembling legs. He slowly examined the letters, one at a time, eyes tearing across the parchment, until he couldn't take anymore.

"My whole life has been a lie . . ." he stammered. His breath was shallow and rapid as he met Holfast's gaze. "I've been running from Rayghast *my entire life*. So many innocent people *died* because of *you!*" He pounded his fist on the table, crumpling the letter in his grasp. "You sacrificed another child to protect a prince? You took a baby from his mother, the queen's *sister*, knowing he might be killed?"

"It was no easy decision, Ruenen," Holfast said. "One of the worst days of my life was when I stood in Morwenna's chambers, and took you from her arms minutes after your birth. Many people knew she'd been pregnant, so we devised a lie that her child had died. Only our deceased king and queen, and your parents were aware of this scheme. All of us are to blame for the suffering you have endured. I'm sorry on all of our behalf."

"Apologies can *never* fix what you have done," roared Ruenen, moving away from the chest and table. "Apologies cannot bring back Monks Nori and Amsco, Master Chongan, and his family."

"You're a brave young man, Ruenen, to have survived all these years. Your parents would be very proud—"

Ruenen's eyes flared. "Where are they? My real parents?"

For a moment, Marai's heart lifted. Some good might come of this meeting, after all, if Ruenen could be reunited with his parents, if he had a family waiting for him . . .

Holfast stared down at the floor, the shame on his face deepening. "I'm sad to say that both Lady Morwenna and Lord Rehan are dead."

Ruenen stumbled to the floor, grasping his head. He wore a tormented, grief-stricken expression beneath his arms.

Holfast put a hand to his heart. "I'm sorry to bring you such distress. We never expected to ever meet you—"

"You expected me to *die*," Ruenen said.

"If it's any consolation, your mother was the kindest soul I have ever known," Holfast said, and Ruenen flinched, shoulders quivering.

"How did they die?" he whispered, arms still covering his head. Marai could barely hear him at all.

"Morwenna died during a second pregnancy from a wasting disease that tore through this area years ago. And your father, Rehan, was a valiant man, a great soldier, best friend to the king. He fought by his side in every battle. He lost his life during a skirmish with Tacorn a few years after King Vanguarden was murdered."

Tears streamed down Ruenen's face, and Marai didn't know how to comfort him. Perhaps there wasn't a way at all to remove the pain around his heart, not when every truth he'd ever known had been a lie. "I'm sorry" was weak and fragile. "Are you alright?" was an idiotic, near insulting, question.

Magic flickered at Marai's fingertips. She could unleash lightning in that room and destroy the Nevandian Witenagemot. But would that help heal Ruenen's wounds? No, such wild violence would add to his pain. Magic tugged at her, but Marai kept her composure and doused the sparks. She knew these next moments mattered more than anything. She wouldn't take away Ruenen's choice.

He stopped shaking and slowly got to his feet. Ruenen wiped the tears from his cheeks with the sleeve of his tunic and headed for the door.

"Let's go, Marai," he said, weak and distant.

This was wrong. Everything was *all wrong.* She couldn't let Ruenen walk out that door. Everything they'd worked towards, all his years of running in fear, all the lives that had been taken . . . she couldn't let it end this way. Ruenen deserved more. The people of Nevandia deserved more.

"*Wait,*" Marai shouted.

Ruenen halted, but didn't turn. His legs trembled. His fists remained clenched at his sides.

"There must be a way to make this work," she said.

"What do you mean, *faerie*?" asked Fenir, biting out that last word.

Marai shot him a glower and addressed Holfast, the only civilized one of the Witan. "You said no one but you three, Vanguarden, Larissa, and Ruenen's parents knew the truth about Prince Kiernen, correct?"

"There was also a midwife and a few trusted servants, all of whom have since passed away," said Holfast.

"Only the people in this room know Ruenen isn't the real prince. *Rayghast,* himself, believes it to be true. His whole kingdom believes it because they've seen Ruenen. Word has undoubtedly spread across the continent that the lost Prince of Nevandia exists and has escaped Rayghast's dungeons. There's power in that."

"What's your point?" Vorae asked, drumming his fingers on the table.

"You need a king. Your people need hope," said Marai, "so let Ruenen be your king."

The room was so silent, so still, that Marai could almost hear the whispers of the guards in the hallway and the wuthering wind across the valley.

"You cannot be serious," scoffed Vorae. "The throne only passes through the blood of our king. We cannot put someone on the throne who has absolutely no claim to it."

"Ruenen may not be royalty, but he *is* nobility. He's the son of the queen's sister and the king's best friend," continued Marai, stepping closer to the table.

Fenir and Vorae inched away as she approached.

Marai glanced over to the portrait of Vanguarden and Larissa. "He can physically pass for the prince. The monks gave him lessons on governing a kingdom as a boy, and he's a skilled swordsman. Who else is more suited? What other choice do you have?"

"That may all be true, but that hardly gives us incentive to deceive our entire kingdom. That would be considered treason," said Holfast. "Our people's faith in Nevandia hangs by a thread as it is."

Marai glared at them; those powerful, conniving men, who had destroyed a family for the sake of their games. "You've already lied to everyone, but now you have the means to repent. You can give Lady Morwenna's sacrifice, Prince Kiernen's sacrifice, meaning. The only way forward for Nevandia, for the survival of your country, is for it to have a leader. A figure the people can look to for hope, to rally behind. Let Ruenen be that person. Let him lead."

Vorae shook his bald head back and forth, and Fenir grimaced at Marai, arms tightly crossed. Holfast blinked, calculating.

Ruenen appeared at Marai's side, gazing at her as if she was a wonder. She remembered this expression; he'd looked at her this way before, after he'd first seen the lightning.

Marai couldn't tear her eyes away. She hoped he could see how much she believed in him. "You can teach Ruenen everything else he needs to know. He'll learn quickly, and earn the respect of your people. He's a true Nevandian, and they are his people, too. These are his hills and valleys, also. He'll end this war and bring peace back to these lands."

"If this ever got out . . ." began Vorae.

"Are you loyal to Nevandia?" Marai asked, causing the man to jump. She then scrutinized Fenir and Holfast. "Do you care about your country? Well, so do we. I don't believe *anyone* in this room would jeopardize Nevandia. You've kept your own vile secrets for twenty-two years. I think we all can be trusted to keep this secret, as well, if it means saving the kingdom."

Holfast smoothly took his seat again at the table. He gestured for Ruenen and Marai to take theirs. Marai moved first, sitting for the first time, and waited for Ruenen to lower himself into the chair. Marai had stepped out of the role of bodyguard. Here she was, a faerie female, sitting down at a council table, making deals with powerful men.

"*If* we decide to accept Ruenen as our king, there's still a war to be won. How exactly do you plan to end it?" asked Holfast.

Ruenen, stunned into silence, bit his lower lip as he watched Marai think.

Ruen will be our Ruin . . .

Marai knew what must be done. It was obvious, clear as day, because Keshel had already seen it. He'd already given her the answer.

Rayghast had magic. The way to defeat him was *with magic.*

Tacorn was tightly knitted to Varana. At Rayghast's command, Varana would join the war, and their combined forces would easily decimate the Nevandian army. They needed more soldiers. They needed help. But Marai knew the close-minded humans at the Witan table wouldn't be pleased to hear her idea.

"I have powers that will be immensely useful on the battlefield," Marai said. "But I alone am not enough to match the power of Tacorn and Varana . . ."

"Marai—" said Ruenen, reaching for her hand.

She moved out of his reach and met Holfast's gaze. "There are six other part-fae. Several of them are great warriors."

Marai knew the words were a betrayal. She remembered Keshel's warning: Ruenen would be the downfall of their way of life. But that way of life wasn't sustainable, it wasn't *living*. Maybe what Keshel had really seen was for the fae to abandon their solitary life hiding in that cave. Maybe they were *meant* to come to Nevandia, to begin anew somewhere else.

"Why would part-fae want to help us?" asked Holfast. "I cannot imagine they feel too friendly towards any humans, nonetheless Nevandians." But Marai sensed the Steward was genuinely interested in the idea. His eyes were brighter, he sat up straighter. He saw its merits.

"What makes you think we would ever want your help? You're all abominations," said Fenir.

"One more nasty word from you, and my fist will meet your face," snapped Ruenen.

Fenir shrunk down in his chair. There was no one in the room to protect him.

"Marai can kill you all before the guards make it to this table. Perhaps you'd best consider utilizing her skills against Tacorn, and not make us your enemies." Ruenen's face was severe, eyes flaring with fury.

"I think my people would be willing to help in exchange for something," Marai said to Holfast after the room settled.

"What might that be?" The Lord Steward raised an eyebrow, lacing his fingers again.

"A home." If her people were guaranteed a home, a place where they could live and feel safe, Marai knew they would risk coming to Nevandia. "And security. A guarantee that no Nevandians would ever harm them. That they could live on these lands and love them as their own."

"That's preposterous," Fenir huffed.

"*Impossible*," shouted Vorae. "How can we trust that you and your people won't kill us all?"

"We don't want to live in hiding anymore. We want a place to make a home. If you give us that, my people will fight loyally for Nevandia. If you require written assurances, fine, as long as you provide the same for our protection."

Holfast pursed his lips as he thought. "Seven fae will not be enough to break against the tide of Tacorn and Varanese forces."

Marai was aware of this. Magic would certainly help, be an added strength in the army, but the enemy's numbers were too many. The fae would drain their magic before Marai had a chance to square off against Rayghast.

Ruenen sucked in a breath, capturing everyone's attention. "What if we ask the North?"

"Do you have a relationship with King Maes of Grelta?" asked Holfast, face brightening.

"*We* don't, not exactly," Ruenen said with a sideways glance at Marai.

Then it hit her: *Nosficio.* Her mouth twisted cynically. That would be putting a fair amount of trust in a vampire.

"Everyone knows Queen Nieve truly rules the kingdom," continued Ruenen. The color had returned to his face, along with his confidence. "We should arrange a meeting with her."

"Grelta has no reason to ally with us. They've thus far remained neutral," Holfast said.

"Rayghast won't be satisfied once he takes Nevandia. He already has Varana in his pocket, and with Nevandia's combined forces, he'll have the strength to attack any kingdom he chooses. The North, with its proximity to Tacorn, expansive lands and resources, may well be Rayghast's next target. He's been sending troops there for months, scouting and pillaging."

It was a valid point. If *anyone* was to ally itself with Nevandia, Queen Nieve of Grelta might be the best choice: an unconventional female ruler. And her relationship with Nosficio, no matter how bizarre, might help broker the meeting suggested by Ruenen.

"It's worth trying, don't you think?" he asked, leaning back in his chair with casual grace, crossing his arms. There he was again: the Prince of

Nevandia. Holfast saw it too, the potential there, the weight of this discussion, because he regarded both Marai and Ruenen with equal intrigue.

"If you can garner the allegiance of the North and the remaining fae, then I believe we can come to an agreement."

Vorae and Fenir began to protest.

Holfast held up a hand. "I don't take pleasure in any of this, but I'm willing to do what must be done. Our people deserve better. Bring the fae here, let us meet with them all, hash out our concerns. Set up your meeting with King Maes and Queen Nieve. If they accept, we will consider putting Ruenen on the throne."

Marai stood, the relief coursing through her. She placed her hands on the table for stability. "Give us three days and we'll return."

"We cannot welcome magical folk onto our lands, Holfast," Vorae said. "Our people barely have confidence in us as it is. If we let fae live among us here in Kellesar, our people will all defect to Tacorn."

"I'm not comfortable with this either, Vorae, but we're desperate. I will do whatever it takes to save Nevandia." Holfast walked to the side of dais and pulled on a long silk tassel.

A musical bell rang somewhere in the hallway. Avilyard and four guards barreled into the room, hands on their swords. Marai wondered if they heard anything at the door; she was certain they'd tried.

"Please escort our guests safely back outside the city gates," the Steward said.

Avilyard bowed and waited for Ruenen and Marai to join him. For a moment, no one else moved, then Ruenen bowed grandly.

"I look forward to working with you, gentlemen," he said and flashed them a wolfish, toothy grin.

Marai gave Holfast a final, stoic glance, then followed Avilyard from the chambers.

Ruenen's body language was different now as they made their second trip through the city. He strolled confidently behind Avilyard, more so than before, putting on a performance again. People lined the streets; they knew he was someone of importance.

A woman whispered to her friend. "Is *he* our lost prince?"

"Do you really think he exists?"

"You've heard the rumors. Rayghast captured him and he escaped. Who else could that young man be?"

Their mouths fell open as Ruenen passed. He beamed and gave the ladies a friendly wave. One of them blushed and giggled. Marai stopped herself from rolling her eyes. She wanted Ruenen to have this moment.

Avilyard dropped them at the gate. Two guards handed them back their weapons, packs, and Ruenen's lute.

"Thank you for your kindness, Commander Avilyard," said Ruenen. "We shall see you again in three days."

The commander nodded and returned to the office. Marai followed Ruenen, who continued over the bridge, down the road towards the glen. He kept up his confident persona all the way across the valley, past cottages, shepherds, sheep and chickens, and travelers, until they reached the glen's tree line.

Ruenen ducked behind a thick trunk as he disappeared from sight of the city, then took Marai's hand and pulled her to him in a tight embrace. His entire body shook against her. He placed his cheek on top of her head, taking long, stuttering breaths. Marai stayed rigid in his arms.

"I'm sorry, please . . . just let me hold you for a moment," he whispered. His heart pounded against her ear. Her pulse raced in time with his. "Thank you. Thank you for everything you said in there."

"It was nothing," she said. Before, this kind of physical touch brought up those awful memories of Slate, but now she remembered Thora's hands spreading salve across Marai's skin. Keshel's arms embracing her when Marai was at her weakest. Hands could bring comfort. Ruenen's embrace . . . there was nothing *taking* about this moment at all. It was *giving*. It was grateful. Marai needed to be that steady stone wall for him. A wall that would never crumble, even when he did.

His arms tightened around her. "It meant *everything* to me."

Marai shoved aside the thoughts of awkwardness and discomfort, and slid her arms around him, too. She held onto him like he might slip away into that same dark place she knew so well. She wouldn't let him. She could not let him fall.

"I'm sorry." She buried her face into his jacket, taking in the scent of him; tavern smoke, ale, leather, and crisp pine. She held him until his shaking subsided. Until his heartbeat settled, and his grip on her loosened.

When they pulled apart, Marai stared up into his face and what she saw in his brown and gold-flecked eyes took her breath away.

It was affection. Pure, honest, open tenderness. Those were not the eyes of a man looking at his friend.

No, this was a man gazing at someone he lov—

"I hope you didn't do *that* when you met with the Steward," said Nosficio from behind them.

Marai and Ruenen broke apart.

Nosficio leaned nonchalantly against a tree, examining his long talon-like nails. The vampire's mouth tilted into a silky smile. "How did it go? Are you king yet?"

"We have business to attend to first," Ruenen said.

Nosficio slowly pulled on black gloves, covering his gray skin. "They didn't believe you?"

"As a matter of fact, they did," said Ruenen with a rictus grin.

Marai noted Ruenen and Nosficio's casual stances. She wasn't fooled. Both were on high alert in each other's presence. It was noticeable in the way their muscles clenched, their eyes affixed the other in place. After all, Ruenen had stabbed Nosficio with a wooden stake a month ago. Marai doubted the vampire was over that particular wound, despite being fully healed.

Men. She rolled her eyes.

"We need your assistance," she said, stepping between them.

Nosficio's expression flashed with curiosity. He cocked his head to the side and waited for Marai to explain.

"How would you feel about making a trip to see your beloved queen?" she asked.

Nosficio's grin vanished. "Why exactly would I ever want to see her again? Nieve's foolish hunchback hired you to send me a warning, remember? We're not exactly on good terms."

"We'd like you to ask Queen Nieve to ally with Nevandia. To send us her troops so we can rid the continent of Rayghast. We'll send you to Grelta with a letter."

Nosficio bristled. "I'm not a messenger boy."

"A letter from Ruenen means nothing right now. He's newly established and has no reputation with his own people, nonetheless other kingdoms. But *you* know the queen. Intimately."

Nosficio's eyes narrowed. It was a gamble. Marai didn't know the true story of his relationship with Nieve. For all she knew, Nieve and Nosficio hated each other. But the vampire hadn't yet said no. He hadn't disappeared.

"Marai and I believe that you can negotiate with her on Nevandia's behalf," said Ruenen. "You said you wanted to help. Well, here's your first assignment."

"I said I wanted to help kill Rayghast, not participate in politics. There's a good chance that Nieve won't see me, and will refuse your letter."

"She could've had you killed, but instead she merely gave you a warning," Marai said. "I think Queen Nieve still holds some affection for you."

Marai watched her words settle in the vampire. *He's not an entirely heartless monster.*

The corners of his eyes tightened further as he thought. "What message do you want me to convey to the queen?"

Ruenen set down his pack and pulled out a piece of crumpled paper and a slivered stick of charcoal. Marai peered over his shoulder as he hastily scratched out a polite introductory letter to Nieve and Maes. He signed it "Prince Ruenen Avsharian of Nevandia."

Once he finished, he handed Nosficio the letter. The vampire's mouth twitched as he peered at the creases in the parchment and hasty penmanship.

"I know you're new to being a prince, but this isn't the typical way kingdoms request alliances with one another," he drawled, unimpressed. "It's going to take more than childish scribbles to convince her. Why would she help you? Grelta has no part in this war. Nieve won't risk her people's lives merely because Nevandia's weak."

"Rayghast will continue to seize other kingdoms if Nevandia falls," said Ruenen. "I've seen his soldiers on Greltan soil already."

"Tell her about the shadow creatures," Marai added for extra persuasive effect. "They'll continue to multiply as long as Rayghast lives and uses his dark magic. They could become an entirely new army. This isn't only a problem for Nevandia. It's an issue for all of Astye."

Nosficio considered for a moment. He folded the piece of parchment, and tucked it into a pocket within his mauve velvet cloak. "Delivering this letter is a risk on my life, you understand. There's a good chance Nieve will react poorly to my sudden appearance. She's prepared to stake me. If I do this for you, I will require compensation."

Marai snorted. "What do you need with money? If I recall, you take what you need from your victims."

The vampire's nostrils flared. His body tensed. "You should know better than to judge magical folk for their way of life, faerie girl. Don't tempt me to sample that electric blood of yours. Perhaps *that* will be my payment: a taste."

Lightning crackled in the palm of Marai's hand. Thin strands of white light snapped, contained within the confines of her fingers.

"I bested you once before," she warned Nosficio. "I'm not afraid of you." Marai closed her hand, and the lightning disappeared. She flicked off the remains of the sparks on her fingers.

"Getting involved in this war against Tacorn means putting a target on my back, which I'm prepared to do if it means killing Rayghast."

"Why haven't you assassinated Rayghast yourself if you're so desperate to be rid of him?" asked Ruenen. "Couldn't you sneak into his room while he's sleeping?"

Nosficio gave Ruenen a withering look. "I'm not foolish enough to attempt that. I'm no match for the magic he possesses. I've seen it once before . . . That power of yours is why I'm still standing here, Butcher." Nosficio's crimson eyes glowed. "I've followed you for weeks because of it."

"You mean someone has used dark magic before?" asked Marai.

"A long time ago," Nosficio said, glancing away, "and under very different circumstances. Make no mistake, I would've drained you both of blood by now if you didn't possess certain gifts that can defeat Rayghast and his shadow creatures. The minute Rayghast is gone, you and I will go our separate ways."

"Understood." This fragile alliance was temporary, which was good, because Marai didn't want a vampire hanging around her. "We'll be returning in three days from our own mission. We expect you back with a response from Queen Nieve in that time."

"That's a long way for me to travel in three days, then back again."

Marai smirked. "Vampires are exceedingly fast. I'm sure you can do it."

The vampire sighed and brushed back his roped hair. "Fine, but I expect you to follow through with your end of the bargain."

Marai knew this would cost her in some way. Making deals with vampires never amounted to anything good. However, if Nosficio truly sought a place at the table in the war against Tacorn, she figured she could get him that. Marai nodded tersely, accepting.

In a flash of black and mauve shadows, Nosficio was gone.

Ruenen let out a breath. "I never thought I'd ally myself with a vampire."

"He's not an ally," Marai said, "but I think he'll get the message in front of Nieve."

"He's craving your blood." Ruenen grimaced.

"He can try, but I think Nosficio is smarter than that."

She raised her hands, magic flashed, and a portal formed. On the other side, she spotted the red dust and canyons. The stifling desert heat grazed her cheeks through the doorway. She held out her hand and Ruenen took it. She noticed the way his fingers laced through hers automatically. Her hand felt so small in his. Despite knowing she was stronger than him and fully capable of protecting herself, Marai strangely felt safe in that moment. She knew this man would defend her. That he would keep her safe.

They stepped through the portal together. The familiar licks of her magic kissed her cheeks and neck as she passed through. Ruenen let out a surprised giggle. She'd never heard a man make such a sound.

"What?" she asked as he shivered.

"Your magic is tickling me," he replied, smiling. "I can feel it inching up my bare skin under my clothes."

Marai blanched. "I . . . what? It's not doing that to me." Searing heat rose across her face. It had nothing to do with the low sun overhead now that they were on the other side of the portal.

Ruenen winked. "Your magic likes me."

Marai let go of his hand and scowled at him. This made Ruenen grin wider.

"Stop playing around," she snapped. "This isn't going to be easy. Remember, my people are afraid of humans. They hold a lot of anger and resentment towards your kind. I need you to do as I say."

Ruenen swept his arm out in a grand gesture. "After you, my lady."

Marai rolled her eyes and led him down the ravine. The portal had dropped them outside of the borders of the fae territory. She didn't want to magically appear in the cave and scare them all. Marai knew this encounter was not without risk.

"I trekked through the Badlands a few years ago after leaving Chiojan. It's hard to imagine you growing up in this place," said Ruenen, turning around to take in every angle of the canyon. "I always pictured faeries living in the woods amongst lots of green plants."

Marai felt a thrum of magic pulse through her. Keshel's barrier was near. "The deserts of the West aren't our natural habitat, but we've been forced to make do."

There it was—invisible, but Marai caught the slight shimmer in the light. She placed her hand upon the barrier. Her magic met Keshel's and the shield fluctuated and fluttered. Marai dismantled it with minimal force, which meant Keshel was letting her pass through. Ruenen raised an eyebrow. He was unable to see or sense the barrier.

What would her family think of Ruenen and her plan? Marai's stomach twisted into knots. So much was riding on this introduction and discussion. Marai hoped Ruenen wouldn't do anything stupid, and that Leif wouldn't say anything offensive. She didn't know if she trusted either of them.

This is a bad idea . . .

Ruenen stepped closer to Marai as they passed into fae territory. "I can feel it."

"What?"

"The magic," said Ruenen, "it's making the hair on my arms stand on end." He shoved up his sleeve and showed Marai the goose bumps.

A figure leapt from a high rock and landed cat-like in front of them. Raife raised his bow, but lowered it when he recognized the intruder.

"Marai?" he asked, emerald eyes traveling over Ruenen. "Who . . . is that . . . ?"

She nodded. "We're here to talk."

Raife was about the same height as Ruenen. They regarded each other with cautious curiosity. Ruenen's gaze flew to Raife's pointed ears. He wasn't used to the appearance of someone more traditionally fae, unlike Marai whose ears were rounded and human.

Raife's eyes snapped to the knife at Ruenen's hip.

Ruenen raised his hands in submission. "I come as a friend." His voice was light, but wary. "Here, you can take my knife. I have no other weapons on me." He held out the small blade, but Raife didn't take it.

"Are you sure it's a good idea to bring him here?" Raife asked Marai.

"Since she won't introduce me, my name is Ruenen," Ruenen said, and held out his hand.

Marai and Raife stiffened. Raife stared at the outstretched hand as if it was a rattlesnake that had ventured into his bed. But slowly, he reached out and gently took Ruenen's hand.

"Raife," he said and dropped his arm. Out of all of the family to meet first, Marai was glad it was him. "We didn't expect you to come back so soon."

"Plans changed," Marai said and started out towards the cave.

"I should go first . . . to let them all know you're here," Raife said with a glance at Ruenen, then dashed off down the valley. He skidded when he reached the mouth of the cave in the distance and disappeared inside.

"This is exciting," Ruenen said with a mischievous grin, that reckless part of him came shining through. "My first diplomatic mission."

"Let me do most of the talking," said Marai. "Leif and Aresti are as temperamental as I am. They won't hesitate to wring your neck if they deem you a threat."

"I've had plenty of experience with *you*. I think I can handle them. I need to knock them off-balance with my wit and charm."

Marai gave him a look and Ruenen laughed. It was a sound she hadn't realized she had desperately missed. A warm beam of sunshine, it cut straight through to her soul. She let the ghost of a smile appear.

"Alright, I'll sit prettily to the side then," said Ruenen, putting his hands into his pockets and whistled "The Lady Butcher."

Marai huffed, eliciting another peal of laughter from Ruenen. She wanted to take his hand then, to latch onto that merry sound and never let it go.

Instead, she asked, "How are you feeling now?"

Ruenen's jovial whistling stopped. He drew his lips into a thin line. "Still angry. Still horribly sad. I'm trying not to think about it. If I do, I'll end up running away again, and that would make me feel even more of a fraud. I don't know who I am anymore. But maybe I can manage to right these wrongs if I defeat Tacorn."

Marai wished there was a way to ease his pain, but she knew the way to help him was to move forward, ensure his ascension to the throne and defeat Rayghast. She had to start somewhere.

"You're not a fraud," Marai said sternly. "You aren't who you thought you were, but you deserve to be king. You've still earned it."

Ruenen gave her a weak smile, then went back to whistling, with less enthusiasm than before.

They reached the mouth of the cave. Magic wafted out from the cavern, heightened, defensive. Her family was preparing within.

Taking a deep breath, Marai entered the tunnel; Ruenen's arm grazed hers with each step. The tunnel opened wider to reveal the cavern and six extremely perturbed faeries.

All of them stood on the far side, but not in the way they would for a respectful greeting. No, the fae's stances were defensive, faces dubious. Leif and Aresti's hands were full of weapons, while Keshel's faced palm-out, ready to unleash his magic if necessary. Thora and Kadiatu each held a kitchen knife in their fists. Marai saw the fear on their faces, the worry, the bitterness.

Ruenen bowed deeply, opening his arms wide. "Greetings, friends."

None of the fae returned his salutation.

"How *dare* you bring one of them here," snarled Leif, edging forward.

Marai's hand went to her hilt in warning. She didn't want to hurt him, but she'd incapacitate Leif if he attacked Ruenen. "I trust this human," she said, meeting all of their eyes one by one. "Above all others."

Still, no one moved.

"I'm Ruenen, Prince of Nevandia. Please, I truly mean you no harm. I come with the utmost respect." He had not yet straightened from his bow, neck recklessly naked and ready to be chopped. He lifted his head to meet their concerned gaze. "Marai is my dearest friend, and I'm honored to meet her family."

Marai tried not to show any emotion on her face at that remark, but the words coiled themselves around her heart and tightened.

Aresti, however, didn't find Ruenen's statement sweet. She bared her teeth, and pointed one of her swords at Ruenen. "How can we trust that he won't bring his people into our lands and hunt us?"

Ruenen stood up fully, placing a hand to his heart. "You have my word, not as the Prince of Nevandia, but as Marai's friend. I would never dream of hurting you."

Leif scoffed. "Friend? You keep repeating this word like it's supposed to mean something to us. Your kind are not *friends* to us. Your grandfather slaughtered our people. You don't get to come onto our lands and pretend otherwise." His lips curled back into a vicious sneer as he stepped forward, drawing out his blade.

Thora covered her mouth with her hand and emitted a small gasp. Kadiatu latched onto Thora's arm.

Marai crossed in front of Ruenen. "We didn't come here to fight. We came to talk."

"You're an embarrassment, Marai," Leif shot back, not lowering his sword. "You align yourself with human scum!"

Lightning sparked at Marai's fingertips. Flames flickered in Leif's palm.

"That's enough," came Keshel's authoritative voice. He hadn't moved from his defensive pose, and kept his eyes focused on Ruenen.

Leif growled, but extinguished the flames and lowered his sword.

"I don't believe Marai and the human prince mean to harm us," said Keshel to him, then turned his solemn gave to hers. "However, I have to wonder why you thought to break our trust by bringing a human here, Marai. He could run off and tell others where we are."

Marai stared down Keshel. She knew that he was thinking of the vision he'd seen; of Ruen being their Ruin.

"Should we all sit?" asked Thora in the high-pitched voice she used when she was nervous. She gestured jerkily to the stumps and logs around the fire, and sat down first.

Keshel, Raife and Kadiatu followed her cautiously. Marai nodded to Ruenen, who took a seat on a log next to Marai, on the opposite side of the fire. Leif and Aresti remained standing, hovering over the others.

"I'm sorry to surprise you all in this way," Marai said, earning another scoff from Leif. "I would've come on my own, but we unfortunately don't have the luxury of time."

"Why? What's going on?" asked Thora, instantly worried.

Marai was relieved to see that she, at least, was trying, but noted how Raife inched closer to Thora. A small part of her was grateful to Raife for protecting Thora in such a way. Yet, Marai never thought he'd have to shield Thora from *her*.

Marai opened her mouth to speak, but Ruenen cut her off. "What are your names? I think it would make for poor conversation if I don't know whom I'm addressing."

Marai scowled. *Let me do the talking, indeed.*

No one volunteered, so Marai quickly went down the line, pointing as she went. Ruenen nodded with each name and repeated them under his breath. None of the fae took their eyes from him the entire time.

"Excellent, thank you," Ruenen said with a smile. "It truly is an honor to meet you all. I'd lie and say Marai told me all about you, but you know she's not particularly garrulous."

His light chuckle and slight jab at Marai had Raife and Thora relaxing on their log. Marai pursed her lips to stop from retorting.

"You're really a prince?" came the small voice of Kadiatu. Her eyes were as wide as a spooked deer in the woods.

Ruenen smiled his true dimpled grin at Kadiatu and nodded. "I am."

Kadiatu melted a little. Few people were immune to that expression. Marai had pretended for weeks that her heart didn't stutter whenever Ruenen smiled. Kadiatu blushed and flashed him back a small, shy smile.

Keshel remained rigid on his stump. Apparently, Ruenen's dimples didn't work on everyone. "What does the Prince of Nevandia want with us?"

"Besides execution," sneered Leif.

Marai clenched her jaw. When she was younger, she would've leapt out of her seat and pummeled his face to a bruised and bloody pulp, but Marai wasn't that wild child anymore. She was trying to do this right. For Ruenen. She needed to behave like a true courtier. *All* of their lives hovered in the balance.

"I'm sorry," Ruenen said solemnly to Leif, "for what my people have done to yours. For what my ancestors did. My own grandfather."

But it *wasn't* Ruenen's grandfather who had led the charge. He wasn't related to the departed King Talen. Yet Ruenen was willing to shoulder their ire, to apologize for something his family may not have taken part in. He was constantly surprising Marai with his goodness.

"I cannot change their actions," Ruenen continued, "but I'm hoping to make amends. I want to extend my sympathies, and also my friendship to you all."

The fae bristled, but once again, Marai felt the need to clasp Ruenen's hand. She knew he meant every word he spoke. The others didn't know him; they didn't know he was sincere.

"We don't want your friendship," Aresti said. "Leave us in peace. That's the best way to show your sincerity."

"I've actually come to ask for your help," said Ruenen, "and provide mine in exchange."

The room quieted. Eyes blinked. Breaths held. Bodies tensed.

"The end of Nevandia is imminent," Marai stated. "King Rayghast is determined to destroy the kingdom and annex it as part of Tacorn."

"What does that have to do with us?" asked Aresti. Her dark brown eyes blazed with fire. She had always run hot, where her cousin Keshel simmered with ice.

Marai knew there was one way to truly sway the fae. "Rayghast can use magic. He has fae blood."

Kadiatu gasped. The only sign Keshel gave that he was shocked by the revelation was the slight paling of his skin.

"That can't be true," Thora whispered, exchanging looks with Raife.

"There was no mistaking the magic I felt when I met him in the dungeon," Marai said. "It wasn't elemental. It was different. Darker, sinister. I think Rayghast tried to use it on me, but my own magic canceled it out somehow."

"How? How is that possible?" asked Raife, fists tightening on his lap. "He participated in the extermination of magical folk. *He's* the one who destroyed the fae camps. Why would he hunt us if he's one of us?"

"He's kept this hidden his entire life because he knows it would be his downfall," said Marai. "His people would never accept him as king if they knew."

"He resents his faerie blood," said Raife. "Sometimes people look in the mirror and hate who they see staring back." His eyes darted to Marai, as if he knew how many times she avoided her own reflection.

"I must ask again, why does this matter to us?" asked Keshel.

"Those riders we disposed of were merely the beginning," Marai said. "Rayghast won't stop searching for us. It's only a matter of time before he comes here with an army. He'll destroy everything with that dark magic. You know this to be true, Keshel. You've seen it."

"What are you proposing we do?" Keshel asked this slowly, calmly, but the distrust in his eyes told Marai that he already knew what she'd come here to ask.

"Rayghast's army, combined with Varana's, outnumbers Nevandian forces four to one," replied Marai. "Even with my magic, it will be nearly impossible to win—"

"*Your* magic?" spat Aresti.

Marai met her incredulous stare. "I vowed to fight alongside Ruenen and Nevandia."

Aresti shook her head. "You've done many foolish things, Marai, but this is the stupidest of all."

"By using dark magic, Rayghast has also been creating shadow creatures." Marai spoke to Keshel, knowing this, more than anything, might sway him. "We know little about them, but it's clear that every time Rayghast uses his magic, a new beast appears. Their loyalties are unknown, if they fight alongside Rayghast, or if he knows of their existence, but they're an additional complication. One that *we*, fellow magic-users, will be able to stop."

Keshel ran a hand through his long, black hair as he studied Marai's ungloved, stained fingers. The first signs of concern raced across his face.

"Dark magic is a true threat, and Rayghast will continue spreading it across the continent if he isn't stopped." Marai hesitated, knowing now was the time to reveal what she'd been dreading. "I should know. I used dark magic once, myself."

The other fae followed Keshel's gaze and noticed Marai's fingers. She watched their faces shift from confusion to shock. Shame crept up Marai's spine, and traveled all the way down to her guilty fingers. She forced herself to meet their disappointed and terrified eyes. Marai had committed a grievous sin by using dark magic. She had to suffer the consequences.

But no one said a word. Not even Leif berated her. Perhaps the shame was so prominent in her countenance that they knew she already suffered with the ramifications daily.

"We have no choice, but to come here and ask you to fight with us." Marai's words floated in the air like smoke: thick, weighty, and unwanted.

"Us? But we're just . . . *us.*" Kadiatu hugged her knees to her chest. She looked so young sitting there. Asking her to fight in a war must have seemed insane.

"No," said Keshel firmly, "we will not."

"Rayghast won't stop with Nevandia. He'll take over this entire continent with his army and his magic. You'll have nowhere else to run."

"Then we'll run for as long as we can."

"If you join us, there's a chance we can win," Marai said, hearing the plea in her voice and hating it. "Our combined magic can overpower Rayghast and his soldiers. Then you can finally live in peace."

"There's no peace for us, Marai."

"There *is* a place for you," said Ruenen, getting to his feet. "A place where you would no longer need to hide. When I become king, I'll make Nevandia a safe-haven for all magical folk."

Marai blanched. In fact, they all did.

"You'll say anything to get us to do what you want," said Leif with a dismissive gesture.

"The persecution of magical folk is wrong. It's disgusting," Ruenen said, jaw tight. "I thought that before I met Marai. I'll do whatever I can to help end it."

"Your people will make the lives of magical folk so unbearable that none of us will want to live there," Thora said. "Or they'll defect to Tacorn."

"Let them leave, then," said Ruenen. "I want to build a kingdom where humans and magical folk can live in peace together. I want Nevandia to be a place *you* can call home."

Marai's throat burned. Her eyes stung.

Keshel shook his head. "All of us living in one place will make it easy for invading armies to attack us."

"Progress takes time and it will be a difficult path. We'll need to educate the Nevandians and get you to trust each other," said Ruenen, "And I know I need to earn your trust, as well, but I promise I will stand with you. I'll fight for each of you . . . if you will fight for me."

Marai turned to Keshel. "You said that if Ruenen and Nevandia fall, Rayghast will continue his dominance across the continent. He'll come for us. But what if we join Nevandia? What if we fight for our future instead of running from it? Maybe *this* is what you saw in those visions, Keshel. It's the end of *this* way of life. Maybe we can build a new life, a real home somewhere else?"

Raife stared distantly at the fire in the center of the cavern, voice lifting as he said, "End the cycle."

"And what if we all die on this battlefield?" Keshel asked Marai. His face was grim and tight. "What if we leave this cave and none of us survive?"

Ruenen bit his bottom lip.

Marai answered for him. "Then at least we'll die fighting for a cause we believe in. One last stand of the fae, to show them we aren't weak."

A tapestry of silence hung in the air; weighty threads of worry and anger and mistrust woven together.

"You should have time to discuss amongst each other. I'll leave you be," said Ruenen, standing. He gave another bow, flashed an honest smile, and exited the tunnel.

"Do you trust him?" Keshel asked once Ruenen's footsteps were merely distant scratches in the dirt.

"With my life."

Keshel looked away from her, but not before Marai saw the disappointment in his eyes.

"I find it hard to believe that he's worth all this faith," Aresti said. "Even if he's as good as you say, he's one human prince."

"His council has already agreed that if you join us, they'll provide you with shelter. They'll incorporate you into their society."

"You already told other humans about us?" asked Keshel, going rigid once again.

"That's why I'm confident that this will work," Marai challenged back. "If they're willing to overlook their prejudices, so can we. I believe we can work together. I believe we can find common ground."

"I think you're blinded by the prince's charm and smile," said Leif. "He's young. He's new to the throne. He could change his mind in an instant after we help him win the war."

Marai said, "I know it's not easy to trust when we've been so hurt. It took me a long time to trust him, too. But as I've said before, there are many good humans out there. I believe in this future." She looked straight at Thora and Raife. "I want you to have your own families. To see the world outside of this cave. It won't happen overnight, but I *know* it can."

Marai's people exchanged wary glances.

Raife got to his feet. "Give us time to think."

He meant that they didn't want *her* in the room. Marai nodded, not taking offense. She moved to exit the cavern.

"Are you leaving?" asked Kadiatu, appearing at Marai's side. She nervously glanced down at Marai's fingers.

For a moment, Marai held her breath, then Kadiatu latched onto Marai's hand.

"Don't go, please. Stay the night. Eat with us. I . . . want to understand. I want to get to know your prince."

"He's not *my* prince," Marai said, but felt the corners of her mouth twitch. "We would be happy to stay, if you'll have us."

Kadiatu beamed. "Of course, we will. No matter our decision, you're always one of us. You're family. And if the prince is your friend, then he is welcome, too."

Marai gave her a rare smile. "Thank you, Kadi. Let me go tell Ruenen."

Dusk was falling, and she found Ruenen standing by the river, peering up at the rising moon. His whole body was illuminated in a tangerine glow, highlighting the copper strands in his hair. He smiled when he spotted Marai coming towards him.

"That didn't go horribly, did it?"

Marai shook her head. "No, not horribly."

"Did they say no?"

"They want us to stay the night."

Ruenen's smile widened to show his dimples. "Then it went well."

Marai stared up at the sky, too. The desert sunset splashed veins of orange and red through the clouds. "You never told me about your plan to make Nevandia a place for magical folk."

Ruenen pushed his sleeves up, and his bare arm brushed against hers.

"I hadn't thought about it until I met your family," he said with a chuckle. "When I saw them, they reminded me of you when we first met. So rigid, so closed-off. Skeptical of everyone trying to show any ounce of kindness."

"I don't believe I've changed that much," Marai said, but as the words left her mouth, she knew they were a lie. She'd softened in the months she'd known Ruenen.

"Right, of course," Ruenen said, nudging her gently. He gazed back at the dusky sky. "If I'm going to lead, I want to do things that matter. It's not about winning the war. I want to enact change." His eyes opened wider when he glanced back down at her.

"What?" Marai asked, stilling.

"The sunset . . . you look like you're glowing," he said in awe. He raised his hand slowly and took hold of the end of her messy braid. He stroked her hair beneath his fingers, gold-flecked eyes sparkling as they grazed over her face.

Marai's fingers inched towards the other hand at his side. One gentle touch sent a shockwave of warmth through her, fire snaking under her skin.

Ruenen's fingers entwined with hers. At that moment, Marai couldn't imagine any other place she'd rather be. Ruenen dropped her braid and traced one knuckle across her cheek. She leaned into that touch, surprising herself. His face came closer and Marai tilted back her head. It was instinctual; her body wanted to be near him. Nothing else on earth felt more natural than standing with Ruenen by the riverbank.

Scuffling footsteps in the dirt sent Marai jolting backwards, leaving the empty space between her and Ruenen feeling as massive as the ravine.

Keshel stood at the mouth of the cave. His eyes tightened as he took in the scene before him.

"Come in for dinner," he said, then turned on his heel back inside the cave. It wasn't a request.

Ruenen smiled and followed Keshel inside straight away.

The fae congregated around the fire. The typical desert stew bubbled in the large iron pot, steam wafting in twisting strands towards the cavern ceiling. Marai and Ruenen shared a stump, the remaining seat, as Thora doled out the stew. As Ruenen thanked her with a smile, Thora nodded and quickly stared down to her own bowl.

After a moment of weighted silence, Kadiatu's timid voice rose up. "Are you enjoying the stew?"

Ruenen was mid-spoonful. "It's delicious! Thank you all so much for letting me join you tonight."

"I grew the vegetables," said Kadiatu, earning a scowl from Leif, "and Thora's a great cook. But we all help."

"This is the best meal I've had in months," Ruenen said, and Thora's cheeks turned a soft pink. "Honestly, I've been on the run for so long that it's nice to sit down and enjoy a meal with good company for a change."

Marai saw his smile falter. If Nevandia didn't accept him, he would continue to run for the rest of his life. She desperately hoped it wouldn't come to that.

"Thora's also a great healer," Marai told Ruenen.

"Marai—" said Thora, blushing further.

Raife chuckled fondly, making Thora huff.

"Raife, Leif, and Aresti are excellent fighters." Marai inclined her head in their direction.

Leif glared back. Aresti tossed her head, enjoying the compliment.

"What about you, Keshel?" asked Ruenen politely.

Keshel stared at him, face unreadable. "I protect this family."

Ruenen gulped, and returned to slurping his stew.

"Keshel keeps us all safe with his barriers," Kadiatu said, leaning across Marai to speak to Ruenen. "And he's a seer. He saw you in his visions."

"He did?" Ruenen asked, eyes opening wide.

Keshel's grip on his spoon was so tight, his knuckles turned bone white. "Kadiatu." His voice was deep, laced with caution. "The prince doesn't need to know everything about us."

For the first time, Ruenen scowled. "I'm not going to use this information against you."

"We cannot be so certain of that," said Keshel.

Marai nudged Ruenen when he opened his mouth to retort. He pursed his lips into a thin line, and then finished his dinner. Keshel watched the interaction through narrowed eyes.

Ruenen and Marai collected the dirty dishes. They carried the bowls and spoons to the river and set them down in the dirt.

"I can do that," said Thora, hurrying over with a rag. "You're a prince."

Ruenen smiled. "I don't mind. I'm happy to help. I've never felt much like a prince, anyways."

"You can help me collect firewood," said Raife, appearing at the cave entrance with Keshel.

Ruenen nodded and joined Raife, walking slowly up the river, chatting quietly. Keshel watched after them, arms tightly folded across his chest. Those dark eyes turned to Marai. He said not a word, but she could feel *everything* he wanted to say. He was disappointed in her. Angry. Worried. He'd never trust her again. His stare was a hot poker searing into her flesh as she turned to the river and began washing the dishes. After a moment, his footsteps disappeared into the cave.

"Keshel's hardly said a word to me or Ruenen," Marai grumbled, "and he's spent the whole evening scowling as much as Leif."

"Well, can you blame him? You've uprooted everything he created, and you brought a human into our territory," Thora said, drying wooden bowls with her rag. She gave Marai a pointed look. "And he's jealous."

"What?" Marai sputtered, dropping the spoons she'd just cleaned back into the dirt. "What could Keshel possibly be jealous of?"

Thora raised her eyebrows. "He saw you out here alone with the prince."

"Then he saw us talking, that's all."

"Marai," Thora huffed with exasperation, "your feelings for each other are written all over your faces."

Marai felt like something was crawling beneath her clothes. She wriggled away from Thora's knowing stare. "And what does Keshel think of you and Raife?"

Thora drew herself up. "He doesn't know. No one does. Because Raife and I are nothing, as we've already discussed."

Marai raised an eyebrow. She'd been back with the fae for a month, and *she'd* noticed Raife and Thora's affections straight away. She doubted Keshel, a *seer*, didn't know.

"Regardless, why should my friendship with Ruenen bother Keshel?" Marai dipped the spoons into the water a second time and scrubbed away the red dirt.

"He's always cared for you, but since you've come home, I'm not sure, but I think those feelings have changed."

"What do you mean?" Marai didn't like where this conversation was headed. Every part of her cringed. She hastily finished her washing and drying, and gathered everything up in her arms.

Keshel was her *brother*. Not by blood, but he'd raised her. He was seven years older, and had practically been a father to her growing up.

"You've always vexed him, but I know he's never wanted your fire to go out. I think he *admires* it, Marai. You're so different from him. You're free in ways he doesn't know how to be."

Blessedly, Ruenen and Raife returned, their arms laden with sticks and branches from nearby shrubbery.

"We'll set up blankets for you in the cavern," Thora told Ruenen.

"I don't want to be any trouble for you, Thora. I'll sleep outside."

"But it gets cold . . ."

"We'll be fine," Marai said, then Thora returned to the cavern with the clean dishes.

"You don't have to sleep out here with me," Ruenen said, but he grinned, the idea pleasing him.

"I enjoy being outdoors," replied Marai, tilting her face away so he wouldn't see her cheeks redden. "Wait out here. I'll fetch our packs."

Inside, she dumped the clean utensils with the other dishes, then slung the packs over her shoulders.

Ruenen sat on a rock, singing softly to the stars.

"New song?" Marai asked as she approached, handing him his pack and lute. They pulled out their blankets and lay down in the dirt.

"No, I've been working on it for a while," Ruenen said, lying on his back, one arm resting behind his head. "Still can't finish all the lyrics."

"It's nice," said Marai as she closed her eyes, breathing in that bone dry scent of the desert.

After a moment, Ruenen said, "Thora was right. It's cold. Can you make that magical bubble around us?"

Marai snorted, but lifted her hand as she'd done for him every night before Ruenen knew she was fae. Magic spilled out from her fingers, encapsulating them in an invisible barrier, a soft electric haze, like the glow of fireflies.

"Thank you for introducing me to your family, Marai."

She smiled. A warmth spread through her chest. "Thank you for accepting them, Ruen."

CHAPTER 13
Ruenen

Anticipation, stifling and tense, clung to the air.

The next morning, the fae gathered in the cavern. A decision had to be made.

Staring at them all, Ruenen regretted the decision to come here. He hated that he and Marai had asked this of the fae, and brought this war to their doorstep. The fae seemed so fragile standing there against the opposite cave wall, beautiful, ghostly remnants of a once mighty people. Of fae kings and queens with great power and pride.

Are we doing the right thing?

All of a sudden, Ruenen hoped they'd say no. A gush of guilt and fear bubbled up in his stomach, turning his digesting breakfast sour.

Marai, too, appeared hesitant, her lips in a thin line, picking at her blackened cuticles. But she swallowed down whatever feelings had been brewing as she addressed the stoic faces before her.

"We may be fae, but let's not forget that we're also human. Our *families* were human," she said. "Their blood runs in our veins, same as the fae. Every time I look in the mirror, I see my mother. I think of her sacrifice; that she, a human, fell in love with a faerie and left her people behind for him. There are *good people* in this world. Humans who don't hold that hatred and fear in their hearts. People who can accept. But they never will if we refuse to show them that we can also overcome *our* fear."

Ruenen's chest swelled with pride at her words. No longer was Marai the solitary, unfeeling Lady Butcher. Ruenen couldn't stop himself from braiding his fingers with hers. Marai studied their conjoined hands, then met his gaze.

I see you, Marai.

Every eye in the room snapped to their open display of unification.

"I will come with you," said a wavering voice, yanking Ruenen's attention from Marai's face. Kadiatu wrung her hands, as if the announcement pained her.

Leif shook his head. "Don't, Kadi—"

"I want a home. A *real* home," Kadiatu said. "I want to leave this desert. I believe in the future that *could be.* I believe there is more for us." She sent Ruenen and Marai a quavering smile. "My magic is weak and I'm not skilled with a blade, but I'll help you win in whatever way I can, Prince Ruenen."

Kadiatu came to Marai's side, facing the others. Marai took her hand and gave it a grateful squeeze. Ruenen guessed this decision didn't come easily for Kadiatu; she trembled from head to toe.

"I want to make my parents proud," she said, holding her head high as she addressed Ruenen. "My father was a bricklayer from Ain. My mother was part-fae from a camp in Beniel. I was a baby when they died, when Rayghast destroyed our camp. I never knew my parents, but I think this is what they'd want for me. They'd want me to stand with you for a better world."

Ruenen's heart soared as emotion nearly overcame him. He squeezed Marai's hand tighter for stability.

"They would be very proud of you," Marai told Kadiatu with more warmth than Ruenen was used to hearing in her tone. "I know it."

In a strong and determined tone, Raife announced, "I'll come, too."

Panic lit up Thora's face as she bit her lower lip.

"No, brother," said Leif, grabbing Raife's forearm, green eyes shining with alarm. "If you go, you'll be killed."

Raife put a hand on his twin's. "I'm tired of hiding. I'm tired of allowing others to dictate how I live and who I am. This is a half-life."

"Better a half-life than none at all," pressed Leif, urgency in his tone.

"If Prince Ruenen promises to fight for the rights of magical folk, then I will help him usher in this change," said Raife. "For us. For future generations." He stared straight at Thora on that last sentence.

"I do promise." Ruenen placed his hand over his heart. "I swear to you, here and always, that Nevandia will be welcoming to all. We will teach and we will grow together."

Raife stepped out of his brother's reach and approached Ruenen. He held out his calloused hand, and Ruenen smiled, shaking it vigorously.

"*Fuck,*" shouted Leif, kicking at the dust on the floor, issuing a cloud of copper.

Raife had put his twin in a tricky situation. Would this decision split the brothers apart? Leif and Raife stared at each other, silent words traveling through the space between them.

Leif then ran a clawed hand through his curly hair. "You can't go without me, Raife." He crossed his arms, glaring viciously at Marai and Ruenen. "If my brother and I get killed, I'm blaming *you.*"

Ruenen hadn't expected this, and judging from the sharp intake of breath from Marai, she hadn't, either. She'd told Ruenen last night that Leif's hatred of humans was staunch, but it appeared the bond with his brother trumped all.

Three more . . .

Aresti shrugged and cracked her neck back and forth. "Well, I guess I'm in, too."

Keshel tensed, sending his cousin a disappointed, narrow-eyed look.

"What's the point in staying if Kadi, Raife, and Leif are going?" she asked him.

"Because you're safe here," Keshel said.

"And bored," stated Aresti. "I'm not going to stay here with you and Thora. That sounds horrible. Besides, I'm curious about the rest of this continent. I want to see the places where we're from. Our people once lived in the Middle Kingdoms and Grelta. Well, I want to reclaim our homeland."

Thora chewed on her lower lip, her fingers rubbing up and down her brown arms. She and Keshel exchanged glances. Ruenen guessed this was hardest for Thora. Marai said that she'd always been the mother hen, the caretaker. Thora had kept all the fae safe, fed, and clothed for years. Everything she'd done was to protect them. Now, they were all grown and willfully headed into danger. There was nothing more Thora could do for them.

She nodded slowly, staring intently at the floor. Despite her fear, Thora wouldn't be separated from her family. Ruenen didn't miss the shy, darting glance at Raife, either. Perhaps Thora also craved that glorious dream of home and family.

All eyes drifted to Keshel. A deep crease formed between his eyebrows. Ruenen wondered if Keshel might crack a tooth at the tension in his jaw.

"I've witnessed this scene play out many times," Keshel said. "My heart breaks to finally see it come to pass. To lose you all."

"Keshel—" Marai started.

He held up a bony hand. "I cannot stop any of you from leaving. You're adults and responsible for your own choices, but I won't be joining you. I hold no loyalty to humans or Astye. If you all leave, then I, too, will go somewhere else."

Marai scowled. "Where will you go? You're not going to be able to avoid humans, no matter where you are."

"I intend to go abroad. Away from these tainted lands."

The room stilled as the fae gaped at Keshel. *Is he abandoning his people?*

"And what exactly do you intend to do abroad, all by yourself?" Marai asked, crossing her arms. "This is a more absurd idea than fighting against Tacorn."

"I intend to learn more about magic."

Marai didn't like that answer. Her face darkened.

"Why do you need to do that now? Why not come with us first, help us win against Rayghast, *then* go exploring?" asked Marai. "Gods, you could go to Kaishiki and visit the Nine Kingdoms Library and learn a thousand things there. It supposedly houses Laimoen's Book of Knowledge."

"There's far too much we don't know about magic. Its history has all but disappeared, and if dark magic is spreading, I need to know what can be done to stop it," Keshel said.

"You *would* be stopping it," said Aresti, "if we kill Rayghast. Then the dark magic goes away, right?"

"Nothing is that easy," Keshel replied. "Dark magic leaves lingering effects: those shadow creatures, the Nevandian lands . . . and possibly another wielder may emerge. We need to learn how to get rid of it entirely. Only then will we be safe."

Kadiatu came to Keshel's side. She took his hands and held them close to her chest. "We've never done anything without you, Keshel. We need you. We're a family. We need our leader." Her amber doe eyes glistened, pleading.

Keshel thawed under her emotional gaze; the slightest relaxation in his shoulders, in the pinch of his brows.

"It would be an honor to have you on my council, Keshel," Ruenen said slowly. He dangled the carrot, hoping Keshel, a natural leader, would be enticed by the prospect.

Keshel's lips pressed into a fine line. "Your people will not accept a faerie on the council."

"I don't care what my people will or will not accept," said Ruenen. "It's my choice who I place on my Witan. If we're to build a better Nevandia, I want you all by my side, advising me. Who better to lead my initiative than one of the fae?"

Keshel considered, then shifted his intense focus to Marai. It would be a lonely life, traveling abroad. Ruenen knew what it was like to be alone in the world. Keshel, it seemed, had the fortified steel heart to do it, but Ruenen suspected that even *he* wanted to be something more.

Eventually, Keshel closed his eyes, submission written all over the sag in his stance. "I'm a fool to do it, but I'll help you, Marai. Until the war is won. As soon as Tacorn is defeated, I'll leave these shores to begin my research."

The tension eased. Kadiatu wrapped her arms around his torso. Keshel placed a gentle hand on her back, but his eyes flickered to Marai. There was so much Ruenen saw in Keshel's gaze: acceptance, reluctance, fear. This alliance went against everything he believed in.

"When do we leave, Marai? Since you're in charge now," he asked with a bitter bite.

In a strange swap in status, Keshel designated Marai as the new leader, a role Ruenen knew she'd never thought herself capable of playing. But this had all been her idea . . . if she didn't lead her people now, it would fail.

"As soon as possible," Marai replied.

Bags packed and a day later, the fae gazed around the empty cavern. Their lives had been minimized, folded away neatly into sacks and crates, leaving nothing behind. No evidence that this abandoned structure had once housed the last remnants of the faerie race, save for Kadiatu's garden outside. Ruenen tasted their hesitation in the air, sour on his tongue. It was hard to leave the safety and security they'd built for years. Guilt gnawed at him.

"Can you . . . can you really take us all through the portal?" Thora asked Marai, not trying to hide the tears streaming down her face. She wiped her eyes with the back of her hand as she surveyed the empty space.

Kadiatu linked arms with her and leaned her head against Thora's shoulder.

"I've never tried it with so many people, but I think so," Marai said as Raife placed a hand on the cavern wall, saying goodbye.

Ruenen turned away; he wanted to give the faeries these final private moments.

Marai, however, was not so attached to the cave.

She lifted her arms and magic burst forth from her fingers in shimmering multi-colored, electric light. The portal appeared, a solid thing, no longer weak and wobbly as it had been the first time in the Tacorn dungeon. Ruenen smiled, so impressed by how far she'd come. She'd learned to pull deep from the well inside without draining herself, without tapping into that strange, poisonous dark magic.

"This will take us to the glen outside of Kellesar. Let Ruen go first."

He grinned at the nickname and the offhanded way she'd said it. With a deep breath, Ruenen stepped into the portal. He felt the familiar sensation of Marai's power all around him, wrapping him up in the arms of her magic. He swayed, lightheaded, under its potency, addicted to the high of her touch.

Leif appeared next to Ruenen, hands on his weapons. Together, they walked through to the other side. Ruenen's body adjusted to the change in temperature. A soft, cool breeze greeted him as his feet touched the earth, significantly more pleasant than the arid desert air.

Leif scanned the land hawkishly, ensuring its safety. The glen was as vacant as it had been the day before when Ruenen had first seen it. Leif turned back to the portal and gestured to his twin.

Raife took Thora's arm and escorted her through, tossing her heavy bag over his shoulder. Aresti and Kadiatu went next, their eyes widening, mouths falling open, as they felt the magic surrounding them.

On the other side of the portal, Keshel held Marai's gaze before he stepped inside. A twinge of jealousy wormed its way around in Ruenen's stomach when he recognized the emotion in Keshel. Marai didn't respond to it, except stare back with those blazing eyes.

Lastly, Marai entered, and didn't once glance back at the cavern behind her. Her face remained inscrutable as she passed through the portal and came out the other side next to Keshel. The portal closed and shrunk back into nothing.

"*Grass,*" shrieked Kadiatu, falling to her knees and raking her fingers through the brittle plant. She held up her fingers to her nose and inhaled. It was such a strange reaction that Ruenen found himself chuckling. She dashed to an oak tree and traced her fingers across the rough bark, craning her neck up to the sky as two thrushes flew overhead.

"She's never seen any of this before," Raife whispered to Ruenen. "In fact, I can't remember the last time I saw a forest, either."

"Something is wrong with this land," Keshel said as his eyes grazed across the grim dun of the highlands and snarled trees of thicket.

"Rayghast's magic," Marai said. "He's sucking life from Nevandia, killing nature here."

"That's a powerful gift, to cause this much damage," said Keshel with a shiver. "I sense a darkness, something *other.*"

Dark magic. The shadow creatures. Ruenen's skin prickled at the sensation of eyes following them; that something lingered behind the trees, waiting to pounce.

Despite the lackluster sight, the fae gazed around with wonder, taking in the barren trees, the sloping, sepia valleys, the sludgy Nydian River, utterly mesmerized by the world they'd missed.

"Put your head coverings on," Thora said, wrapping a kerchief around her head to hide her pointed ears, then adjusted Raife's wide-brimmed hat.

The others also put on their various hats and scarves, except for Kadiatu, who had rounded, human-shaped ears like Marai. In fact, if Ruenen hadn't already known she had fae blood, Kadiatu would have entirely passed for human.

Once Marai assessed that everyone appeared "human enough," Ruenen led the way down the glen's slanting hill into the barren valley, where the rocky dirt road dropped them at the Kellesar bridge. The fae stayed close together, shoulder to shoulder, hands at their weapons. They sniffed the air, craned their necks at all angles, stared at the cows, pigs, sheep, and their herders, the cottages along the way. It was all so *new* to them, as if they were babes opening their eyes for the first time.

Ruenen tried to relax his breathing, hoping the faeries didn't notice how he kept wiping his sweaty palms on his trousers. Here he was, approaching this kingdom for the second time, with a group of part-fae in tow. Thora sucked in a breath as they stepped onto the moonstone and granite bridge spanning the Nydian River.

"It's enormous," Kadiatu gasped, mouth dropping open as she drank in the sight of such a massive man-made structure as the outer Kellesaran wall.

Kellesar had fortified itself more overnight. The number of guards on the bridge doubled, and Ruenen spotted the archers high up on the stone parapets. They aimed their arrows straight at the clump of advancing visitors. Were they walking into a trap?

This could all go horribly wrong.

Thora seized up, spotting all those weapons pointed at them.

Marai hissed in her ear. "Keep walking."

"Are they going to kill us?" Thora's voice trembled; her whole body shook.

Marai gave her a shove, and they crossed the bridge to stand at the closed iron gate. Dozens of golden-clad soldiers leered at them suspiciously through the bars.

They know. Dread curled in Ruenen's stomach. *The soldiers know who stands at their gate.*

The fae stiffened and clustered closer together as more armed guards appeared on the other side. If Ruenen wasn't so attuned to the rest of his party, he may never have felt the slight shift in the air. Something, *magic,* settled into place around him and the fae.

"Keshel," Marai whispered to him.

A shield. Keshel had created one of his invisible barriers around the group. He wasn't taking any chances with the safety of his people.

The soldiers, it seemed, hadn't noticed the magical shield. They kept their stoic, defensive stances. Ruenen had to make the first move.

He cleared his throat, and plastered on a smile. "Good afternoon, gentlemen. Perhaps you might open the gate to let us in?" No one moved. Ruenen scowled as annoyance bit at his heels. "Your prince gave you a command."

"Don't know who you are," said a soldier, baring his teeth. "You could be a prince or a Tacornian spy, for all we know. Or a group of *faeries.*"

Soldiers raised their weapons higher. Ruenen heard the twanging stretch of bow strings from above on the wall.

"This isn't safe," Raife murmured, "we should leave."

The fae began a slow retreat backwards across the bridge, not taking their eyes off the soldiers. Thora and Kadiatu vibrated with fear.

His plan disintegrating, Ruenen couldn't bring himself to move.

No! I won't let this fail.

He planted his feet and tilted his chin high with all the regality he could muster. "I demand to speak with Commander Avilyard at once."

Ruenen spotted the young guard from the other day amongst the fierce faces of men. The young guard gave Ruenen a brief smile and disappeared from view, back to where the office was located. He returned shortly with Commander Avilyard in tow.

The commander assessed the situation quickly, glancing from his men to Ruenen's entourage.

"I'm surprised to see you back so soon, Master Ruenen. And with guests." The commander's deep voice betrayed no judgment, trepidation, or curiosity.

"Please take us to the Witenagemot, Commander Avilyard. Lord Steward Holfast is expecting *all* of us," Ruenen said.

Avilyard nodded, signaling for his men to stand down.

"But Commander—" a soldier began.

"I have orders. No one will be harmed, by order of the Steward," Avilyard said.

The men backed away, bows lowered, swords sheathed, but most kept their expressions shrouded with distrust and disgust. Avilyard then gestured to someone out of Ruenen's sight. The gate began to rise in loud, screeching sounds.

"Stay calm. Act normal," Marai hissed to the fae once the grate was drawn.

Avilyard called over six guards, the young one among them. "If you'll all follow me, please."

A sea of curious citizens parted as Avilyard, his golden guards, and Ruenen's group passed through Kellesar. Unlike the guards, normal Kellesarans were unaware that faeries were in their city. Ruenen bet all the coin he didn't have in his pockets that rumors had been flying since the moment he'd arrived. Did they know he was the lost prince? Whispers echoed on the wind, but Ruenen couldn't make out any specific words.

The fae remained tense as they walked, avoiding eye contact with the humans, hiding their unusually vibrant eyes and pointed ears. The only one looking up was Leif, who strode forward with confidence, a grimace on his face. It wasn't exactly the first impression Ruenen had hoped for, but Leif had every right to feel resentment. These people, no matter how poor, had more than Leif ever had.

Thank Lirr, they made it through the city unscathed. Inside the castle and away from the crowds, the fae's heads tilted up. Thora and Kadiatu elicited gasps, taking in the windows and vaulted ceilings. Raife's jaw dropped as he spun around, examining the frescoes. Almost as if he were holding his curiosity in check, Keshel took in the details with mild interest.

Marai's face remained stony as Avilyard led them all into the throne room. Guards opened the heavy oak doors to reveal Holfast, Fenir, and Vorae standing at the foot of the dais, dressed again in their black robes. As Ruenen and his company filed into the room, Fenir and Vorae took noticeable steps backwards, but Holfast remained as impassive as he had before.

Triple the number of guards from yesterday were stationed inside the chamber, all with their weaponry raised. Heavy doors closed behind Ruenen and the fae with a booming *thud*; the sound echoing off the marble in a jarring, foreboding way.

Once again, Ruenen found himself questioning if this was all an elaborate trap.

Are we here to die?

Holfast didn't step forward, but opened his arms in greeting.

"Welcome to Kellesar," he announced, but his tone wasn't friendly. It was curt, distant, as if barely holding back his disgust.

The fae slowed to a stop inside the doors. Neither side wanted to get too close to the other. Ruenen sensed Aresti, Leif, and Raife shift into stance. If they were anything similar to Marai, they were counting the number of guards and available exits.

"I'm Lord Holfast, Steward to the throne of Nevandia." He inclined his head, but the gesture wasn't returned by any of the fae.

Vorae wiped sweat from his bald head with a handkerchief as Holfast introduced him and Fenir. Both councilmen stepped closer to the guards standing by the throne.

Holfast focused on Marai. "It appears you weren't lying, Lady Marai. I'm surprised you managed to bring your people here, and right on time."

"We've come ready to negotiate," Marai said, stepping out in front of her family. There was a protectiveness in her stance; her knees were bent and loose, shoulders square.

Ruenen stepped closer to her, showing the Witan and the fae his allegiance. Fenir and Vorae shifted awkwardly on their feet, taking in each member of Ruenen's party. Avilyard and his guards remained nearby at every entrance, every corner, near the table and throne, swords at the ready.

Holfast cleared his throat. "Please, have a seat." No one moved. "Ah, forgive me. Your bags." He tugged on a nearby tassel.

A bell tinkled in the distance, and in an instant, three servants appeared from a corner doorway. They trotted forward, reaching for the sacks and bags belonging to the fae, but their outstretched hands were halted. They couldn't pass Keshel's barrier. It was as if a glass box had been erected around Ruenen and the fae. The servants blanched, turning back to Holfast, confused.

"Lower your shields," Marai scolded from the corner of her mouth.

Ruenen felt the barrier release as if a bed sheet had been lifted off his skin. The servants staggered forward; one bumped into Leif.

"Apologies," he murmured and tried to take Leif's bag.

The fae warrior ripped it from the servant's hands.

"Let them take it," said Marai, receiving a glare from Leif. "They're not stealing them."

Leif slowly handed the male servant his bag, then returned his hands to the sword at his hip. Once the bags were all collected, the servants disappeared back through the door.

No one had yet made a move to sit.

To ease the tension, Ruenen took the first seat at the end of the table across from Holfast. Fenir and Vorae sat on either side of the Steward. Marai walked to Fenir and sat next to him, eyes alight with defiance, as the man trembled.

Raife came next and sat beside Vorae, who stared at the fae male open-mouthed, face mottled with red spots. Ever so slowly, the others took the remaining seats. Kadiatu shrunk low in hers next to Leif, but her eyes still peered up at the portraits on the walls with child-like wonder.

"So here we all are. The rest of the Witan will join us in the next meeting. I thought a smaller gathering might be best at first," said Holfast.

Ruenen nodded in understanding, trying to think of the proper way kings would act at council meetings. He quickly crossed his legs and sat up taller.

"I must say . . . this has never happened in the history of our nation," continued Holfast. "Never before have we shared a table with magical folk."

"That's because you were too busy killing us," snapped Leif.

Everyone at the table stiffened.

Holfast considered Leif, nonplussed. "I suppose you're correct, fae warrior. What may we call you?"

"Leif."

"Do not forget, Master Leif, that your people are also guilty of crimes against humans. We're all at fault, as Lady Marai reminded us yesterday."

"*Lady* Marai?" coughed Aresti across the table, earning a scandalized look from Thora.

Marai ignored her, not taking her eyes from Leif, who seemed ready to pounce across the table at Holfast.

"Both parties are here to come to a peace agreement, not to hash out the past," Ruenen said, voice rising in what he hoped was an authoritative way. "If we all work together, I believe we can create a better Nevandia. That's the goal here, isn't it?"

"As *delightful* as that sounds, that can only happen once we have defeated Tacorn," Vorae droned, still avoiding acknowledging Raife beside him. "What ways do you think you can help Nevandia?"

"First thing's first: we were promised homes and lands of our own in Nevandian territory," said Keshel.

Holfast latched his eyes onto him, sensing Keshel was the leader of the fae.

Keshel *did* give off a courtly presence, with his erect posture, as he said, "This is absolutely paramount. We won't lift a finger unless our safety is guaranteed. The question is, then, Lord Steward, what will *you* do to earn our trust?"

It was a toss-up between Keshel and Holfast on who had the best deadpan expression. The Steward's face remained neutral, but Ruenen sensed the room taking a collective breath.

"I've set aside two cottages on the outskirts of the city. Their previous tenants fled to Tacorn several months ago due to the poor harvests. They've been vacant ever since. The cottages belong to you now. The deeds are here, ready to sign," Holfast said, indicating the papers before him on the table, "but you will need to clean them and make fixes on your own."

"That will do adequately; we don't mind manual labor," said Keshel.

"We need another written agreement; a decree between fae and humans that all citizens must respect," Ruenen said, "stating that any harm or prejudice against the fae will be severely punished."

Fenir and Vorae grimaced, but Holfast nodded. "The agreement must go both ways. It must state that no faerie may harm any citizen of this kingdom. Humans aren't toys for your sport."

"I believe we can agree to that," said Keshel evenly. "And humans never were toys to the fae. Certainly not to us."

Leif leaned back in his chair, crossing his arms with a roll of his eyes in a way that was so *Marai* that Ruenen smirked.

"I'm also appointing Lady Marai and Lord Keshel to be advisors on the Witan," Ruenen added.

Marai shot him a startled look as the table hushed. Ruenen knew she didn't want to take part in politics. She believed herself merely useful on the battlefield, but he couldn't do this without her. He was stronger, steadier with her at his side.

"Faeries on the Witenagemot?" griped Fenir, shaking his head.

Marai's fierce, cold eyes snapped to him. "Do you want to give up your country? Become a Tacornian slave? You of the Witan will be the first Rayghast decapitates. I hope you're ready, because without us, you're doomed."

Fenir ground his teeth, but said nothing back, cowed by Marai's severe tone. The voice of the Lady Butcher sent a thrilling shiver down Ruenen's spine.

"We're quite aware of what will happen to our country if this war drags on any longer," Holfast said. "We're here today out of desperation. Will you agree to help us defeat Tacorn?"

Keshel glanced up and down the table solemnly. All of the fae nodded, expressions so dark that the act was similar to digging their own graves. "Marai, Aresti, Leif, and Raife are skilled warriors. Thora is an expert healer, and Kadiatu can help her tend the wounded."

Ruenen noted that Keshel failed to mention his own gifts.

Holfast nodded, face smoothing over with satisfaction. "We're grateful for your assistance, but I hope you understand that not everyone will be as accepting as we three are." Marai snorted as she glanced at Fenir. "We've already received criticism from the other members of this council who weren't invited here with us today, for that very reason."

"We know prejudices run deep. We hope we'll be able to change people's minds when they see we're here to help them," Thora said quietly, keeping her head bowed.

"Your healing skills will be quite useful and appreciated," said Holfast. The gentleness in his voice caused Thora to raise her head and meet his eyes. "What of Queen Nieve and Grelta? Any news from them?"

"We have a messenger returning soon with her response," Ruenen said. He'd followed through on one end of the deal. He hoped Nosficio would come through with the other. Without Northern forces, there would be no victory. "We're hopeful."

Holfast nodded. "We'll draft up an agreement, then, later today."

"I must be part of the drafting," Keshel said.

"Agreed. Keshel shall serve as the official ambassador of the fae," Ruenen announced, garnering a brief look from Keshel. The faerie male didn't like him; it was clear from his cold behavior, but Ruenen hoped Keshel would see that he was trying.

Holfast's lips twitched. "Very well, then. All members of the Witenagemot and fae should sign this decree."

The room lapsed into silence. Waiting. Ruenen knew what everyone was thinking... *what next?*

Did this mean Holfast, Vorae, and Fenir were going to accept Ruenen as their prince? They hadn't said otherwise, and the agreement was a positive sign.

"You shall all stay here in the castle tonight until the decree is finalized. Tomorrow, you can get settled into your cottages. You'll be quite safe here until then. I'll see to it that you have guards stationed in the corridors," said Holfast, signaling to Avilyard nearby.

Ruenen couldn't see their faces, but he wondered what the guards thought about the news. Could they be trusted?

Holfast then stood and pulled on the tassel bell again. Servants reappeared in the doorway and bowed low. "Please prepare four rooms for our guests, as well as the royal chambers." Holfast said the last line directly to Ruenen.

Acceptance.

The servants and guards stood stock-still, staring at Ruenen, their gazes burning into his skin.

This was it, then: the moment when everything mattered.

Ruenen stood. His legs quivered beneath him as every face watched eagerly.

"Send a message to Rayghast and Tacorn," he stated. His voice bounded off the stone walls, commanding, sounding braver than he felt. "Tell him the Prince has returned to Nevandia, and is ready to meet him on the battlefield."

Murmurs flooded the air. The servants clasped their hands together in grateful prayer, giving thanks to Lirr and Laimoen both. One for blessings and rebirth, one for victorious war. A servant burst into tears. The young, friendly guard beamed at Ruenen from the corner.

But the only pair of eyes that mattered to Ruenen were the amethyst ones at the other end of the table.

"Hail, Prince Ruenen Avsharian of Nevandia," said Holfast.

"*Hail!*" boomed the other voices.

Slowly, and in one grand movement, the Witan, servants, and guards bent low at the waist. Even Marai, Raife, Thora, and Kadiatu bowed.

Ruenen held his breath. It was strange and awkward to be regarded in such a way when Ruenen had spent most of his life being treated as a pauper and lousy bard. With Monks Amsco and Nori, they'd treated him no differently than a normal child. Ruenen may never get used to the opulence, formality, and esteem; for the attention his mere presence now garnered.

The servants crept back into the hallway, whispering excitedly, as another male servant appeared in more formal attire, bowing deeply with flourish.

"This is the Master of the Household, Bassite," Holfast said. "Bassite is in charge of making sure the castle runs smoothly. Any problems with staff, you go to him. This is Prince Ruenen, the heir of King Vanguarden. He has finally come home."

Ruenen could hear the lie in Holfast's voice, but he doubted anyone else could who didn't already know the truth.

"Your Royal Highness, it's an honor and a joy to meet you," said Bassite in a strained tone. Ruenen thought the white-haired man was close to tears.

"Bassite will give you a tour of the castle and escort you to your rooms," said Holfast. "If you excuse me, there's much to be done. I must alert the Witenagemot and our people of your arrival, Your Highness. I'm sure you require time to prepare yourself before addressing the city today."

Ruenen blanched. "So soon?"

"Naturally," Vorae said. "The city is flooded with rumors. We must confirm them, put a face to the name, and allow you to greet the people properly."

"Your Highness, forgive us, but we were not prepared for your arrival. I'm afraid dinner tonight will be an informal affair," Bassite said, then his eyes opened wide in horror. "Unless, of course, you desire a grand feast for you and your guests. We'll do whatever you require, Your Highness."

"Oh, please, not at all. We'll eat in our rooms," Ruenen replied with a casual wave of his hand, in an un-king-like manner. He was overwhelmed enough as it was. A feast that evening was absolutely unnecessary.

Bassite nodded and waited patiently at the main doorway until all seven fae had assembled behind Ruenen. The Master of the Household knew the entire history of the castle. He related which style of architecture was used, why certain colors were chosen, and which rooms were the past ruler's favorites. As they all walked down the grand hallways, Ruenen was too lost in thought, too nervous to take in the beautiful decor and magnificent architecture. Ruenen knew it was rude of him, but the last thing he wanted was a tour and history lesson.

"Ever the student," Raife chuckled, pointing at Keshel, who ate up every word Bassite spoke.

The servant wasn't yet aware he was addressing a group of fae, so he didn't fear Keshel being so close to his side. If anything, Bassite grinned with contentment at Keshel's keen interest.

Ruenen craved a bath and time alone. What was he going to say when he addressed the people? How could he explain to them where he'd been for twenty-two years? How many lies would he have to invent, and how would he keep them all straight?

And perhaps more than all that . . . how would Rayghast react to the news? How quickly would he retaliate?

Bassite came to a long hallway on the second floor. "Here is where your guests will be staying, Your Highness. Their belongings have already been brought up and dispersed amongst the rooms."

"We can organize them," Thora said, and began assigning rooms. Raife and Leif took the first room next to Thora and Kadiatu. Keshel would have his own across from the twins, and Aresti and Marai would share the next chamber.

"No," both Marai and Aresti said defiantly at the same time.

"I'd rather sleep on the floor in Keshel's room," Aresti said, crinkling her nose, then stalked inside and closed the door behind Keshel.

Marai wandered into her own bedchamber through the large oak doors.

"If you'll follow me, Your Highness," Bassite said, beginning to make his way down the hall.

But Ruenen lingered, wanting to see Marai's reaction, to make sure she was pleased. Syrupy warmth spread through him as her jaw dropped.

The room was twice as large as the entirety of the cavern. An enormous four-poster bed stood near a set of large bay windows overlooking a dead garden in the back. A blue settee and two plush golden armchairs were arranged near a grand marble fireplace. A dresser sat against the wall.

Marai trailed her fingers over the silk, embroidered cushions of the settee. "This room is far too big for me." She did appear incredibly small in such a spacious chamber. "I'd prefer the abandoned cottage."

"Don't be silly, Marai, you've earned a night in a comfortable bed," Ruenen said. "How lovely, there's a bath here, too."

Marai followed Ruenen's gesture behind a decorative partition off in the corner, behind which sat a large bronze basin. Ruenen's heart brimmed with light as Marai tried to hide the grin sprouting upon her lips.

For her. He'd done this for her.

A young mousy-haired maid appeared in the main doorway. Her brown eyes widened at the sight of Ruenen, who gave her a smile. She squeaked, and dropped into a deep curtsey.

"I'm here to assist you, Your Highness," she said in a trembling voice.

Marai scowled. "I don't need a maid. I can take care of myself."

"It's her job, my lady," Bassite said from the open doors. "Harmona is here to ensure the comfort of all of the Prince's guests."

"It's a pleasure to meet you, Harmona," Ruenen said, and the young maid blushed. "I'm Prince Ruenen, and this is my very special friend, Marai."

Marai crossed her arms and glared at him. Ruenen nearly laughed when she mouthed *"very special friend"* in annoyance. She then busied herself with staring at an elegant, colorful tapestry of a forest scene on the wall.

"Please let me know if there's anything you need, Lady Marai," said the young maid, still in her deep curtsey.

Marai froze. "It's just Marai."

"Bassite, let's continue to my chambers and leave *Lady Marai* to get acquainted with Harmona."

Marai shot Ruenen a seething look of death, causing him to bark out a laugh. Bassite shut the door behind him as Ruenen exited back out into the hallway.

The royal quarters were more than Ruenen ever imagined: rich colors, plush rugs and furs, blankets, and pillows. A massive fireplace and canopied bed big enough for four grown men, a two-person bathtub. Lofty windows next to gorgeous tapestries and artwork of Nevandian landscapes. It was strange to imagine all of this now belonged to him. Well, at least as long as Nevandia remained independent.

"The previous king and queen preferred living together, as opposed to separate apartments," explained Bassite, watching Ruenen explore the room. "If you'd like us to rearrange or redecorate, please don't hesitate to ask, Your Highness."

"This is perfect," Ruenen said, breaking into a wide grin. He'd never seen such luxury in all his life. In the monastery, he'd slept on a rickety cot in a closet-sized room. Monks were notoriously modest, and lived simplistically. With Master Chongan, Ruenen had spent years lying on a bundle of blankets and straw in the forge's attic, always covered in soot. None of this felt real, as if he'd wandered into a dream that wasn't his. He'd never wanted this life. He would've been content with a cot in a closet as long as he was safe. This room wasn't supposed to be *his*. It belonged to Prince Kiernen, his cousin, but now that Ruenen was here, had *become* the prince . . . a wild, giddy feeling exploded in his chest. His lute sat upon an armchair and Ruenen yearned to compose a song about this moment.

"The Witan apartments are around the corner on this same floor, Your Highness, always close by in case you need them."

Another man materialized at the door. He seemed frazzled, forehead beading with sweat, as if he'd run all the way upstairs. But the man positively radiated joy when he saw Ruenen. Real tears welled up in his brown eyes.

"This is Mayestral, your Groom. He's responsible for taking care of Your Highness' personal wellbeing."

Mayestral bowed, revealing a large bald patch amongst his thin dark hair. "It's an honor, Your Royal Highness, to be at your service. I never again thought I would be Groom to a king. I proudly served your father, His Majesty King Vanguarden."

Ruenen felt a splash of guilt. He wasn't the *rightful* heir, but it didn't seem like anyone so far was second-guessing his claim. The guards and servants appeared genuinely excited and grateful for the return of a royal.

"I regret, Your Highness, that we don't have adequate clothing for a prince in the current style," Bassite said with a shamed shake of his head. "Rest assured, the Royal Tailor is on his way to measure you. He'll be altering His Majesty King Vanguarden's old clothes for you to wear until he's able to produce new ones."

Unsure of what to do and suddenly overheated, Ruenen could merely nod.

Perhaps Bassite sensed the discomfort, because he bowed deeply again. "I shall leave you now, Your Highness, and will return once the Royal Tailor has arrived. You're in excellent hands with Mayestral." He exited the room, ordering the guards at the doors to close them at his heels, leaving Ruenen alone with the Groom.

"Shall I prepare your bath, Your Highness?" asked Mayestral, rolling up his sleeves and heading into the bathing chamber.

"Uh . . . sure," said Ruenen, overwhelmed by the amount of people suddenly at his beck-and-call. He didn't need anyone to prepare his bath. He didn't need servants waiting on him at all times, but Mayestral appeared honored and delighted to assist. Ruenen assumed it would be an insult to send the man away. He let Mayestral prepare the hot water and lay out an exquisite emerald green silk robe on a chair.

"The bath is ready for you. Do you require assistance, Your Highness?"

Ruenen blushed, taking a step away from the Groom. "Uh, no, thank you . . . I can handle things from here."

Steam billowed over the edge of the large tub. He'd never seen a basin so large before. Ruenen caught a whiff of lavender and rosemary.

Mayestral bowed again. "I'll be right outside, Your Highness," then closed the chamber door behind him with a *snap*.

Alone at last, Ruenen let out an overwhelmed breath. He stripped off his leather and linen clothes; each piece tossed aside, never to be worn again. He bet the maids would burn them into cinders. He lowered himself into the hot, lavender-scented water, then let out a long, contented sigh. Ruenen lay there with his eyes closed for a while. The tight muscles in his back relaxed. They were sore from all the proud, princely postures and bowing. It wasn't merely his back that ached; his head and heart pounded. The last few days had felt utterly unbelievable to Ruenen. Honestly, ever since the moment he'd met Marai in Gainesbury, his life had turned topsy-turvy. He never knew what was going to happen. He certainly had never imagined being here.

Do I deserve all this?

He tried not to think about what he was going to say to the citizens of Kellesar. His heart thundered at the mere idea of addressing hundreds of people with a lie. The pressure, the responsibility, threatened to send Ruenen spiraling into one of his frozen moments of fear. Nevandia was counting on him to solve all their problems: to end the war, stop the famine and poor harvests, rebuild and prosper . . . Ruenen didn't know the first thing about fixing them.

After a long while, Ruenen admitted he'd need to leave the bath eventually. Groaning, he stood and stepped onto the polished stone floor, chilly beneath his bare, wet feet. He reached for the fluffy towel and dried himself off. He then slipped his arms through the robe; the silk slid across his skin like water.

He opened the door and nearly choked at the amount of activity in his room. Bassite had returned with two gentlemen who Ruenen guessed were the Royal Tailor and his assistant. Mayestral was ordering a maid to stoke the fire. He'd emptied Ruenen's sack onto the bed and was examining the contents. He gave a disapproving *tsk* at the condition of the shirt and socks inside. Mayestral pointed to the bathroom and the maid scurried inside, collecting Ruenen's discarded clothes.

"Your Royal Highness, it's an honor to meet you," said the Royal Tailor, whose mustache was thin and twirled. Not a single wavy hair on the man's head was out of place. "We'll have you dressed to perfection shortly."

He waved Ruenen over and the tailor's assistant began measuring Ruenen's arm length, chest, waist, leg length, and full height. He scribbled the numbers in a notebook as the tailor studied Ruenen.

"Lots of greens and golds, of course. You have the usual Middle Kingdoms coloring, so darker colors will also do well. But let's stay away from blacks and burgundies for the time being. We want you to appear the opposite of King Rayghast and his menacing Tacorn attire."

Ruenen nodded along as the tailor tossed a long yard of gold fabric across his shoulders.

"You were born to wear gold, Your Highness. It matches the flecks in your eyes. Exquisite!"

Realizing it was best to stay quiet, Ruenen let the tailor work, dressing him like a doll. Mayestral stood off to the side, giving hearty nods and words of affirmation to the tailor. Ruenen was a performer at heart and had no problem with attention, but this was too much for him.

If only I'd had these clothes when I was a bard, I would've finally looked the part.

In a whirlwind of fabrics and colors, the tailor and his assistant left, promising new clothes on the morrow. They'd left behind a pair of form-fitting trousers, a green and white vest overtop a white paisley tunic once belonging to Vanguarden. Mayestral pulled a gorgeous ermine-lined cape from the towering bureau.

"Now, Your Highness, you're the perfect image of a prince."

Ruenen dressed in the bathroom, suddenly shy in front of Mayestral and the servants. The clothing material was soft and comfortable, but the moment Mayestral put the cape around his shoulders, Ruenen felt the weight of the world placed upon him.

"It's time for your speech, Your Highness," the Groom said.

Ruenen gulped. *Already?*

Each step in the hallway was as stiff as an iron rod. Sweat dripped down his temples; the cape was quite stifling in the fair spring weather.

Mayestral led Ruenen to the second-floor balcony. Holfast, Vorae, and Fenir stood with nine other black-robed men: the rest of the Witenagemot. They eyed Ruenen suspiciously, but bowed as he approached. They introduced themselves and their titles, but Ruenen barely heard a word they said. So many people, names, titles, and faces, he didn't know how he'd ever remember them all. Words were muffled in his ears as the roar of a crowd swelled from outside in the courtyard below.

Holfast handed him a piece of paper. "I wrote a short speech for you."

"Thank gods," Ruenen wheezed, and received a warning look from the Steward.

Ruenen tried to read the speech, but the inked words on the page doubled and fractured, turning into nonsense. His head spun.

A councilman edged Ruenen closer to the balcony, granting him a better view of the courtyard. It was packed, body to body. More people stood in the streets, snaking through the city down the hill. Citizens dangled out of windows for a better view. How had so many individuals gathered in such a short amount of time? How had Holfast spread the word so quickly?

Ruenen wasn't ready. He didn't know how to do this. His feet stumbled backwards.

A hand touched his arm. Ruenen glanced down to see Marai standing at his side.

Her face was clean and bright. Her hair had been brushed into a tidy braid. She still wore the same black Butcher clothes, a comforting sight in a swirl of rapidly changing events. The Lady Butcher was at his side, hand on her hilt, posing as his personal bodyguard. She was still there, protecting him from his inner thoughts and doubts.

Marai didn't say anything. She didn't need to. Ruenen merely had to stare into those sharp eyes and a sense of calm settled over him. There was a command in her expression, in her touch.

You can do this, she seemed to say.

This was just another show. Another audience. Another tavern.

Greet them as you would a room full of patrons.

He imagined the lute in his hands. He felt its weight, the strap cutting across his shoulder.

I am the Prince of Bards.

Ruenen stepped forward to the edge where a curling wrought iron railing encompassed the balcony. He spread his arms wide. The crowd hushed instantly; expectant faces turned up to stare.

He heard the lute's clear tone in his head as he mentally strummed its courses; a song danced on the tip of his tongue.

"My good people of Kellesar." His voice rebounded across the courtyard. His heart hammered against his rib cage as he clutched Holfast's speech with steady hands, sensing Marai's gaze at his back. The opening notes of *The Lady Butcher* echoed in his ears. "My honorable, beloved countrymen. I, Prince Ruenen, son and heir of King Vanguarden, have come home!"

CHAPTER 14
Marai

It took everything in her not to go to him.

Ruenen's voice was clear, unwavering, and filled with genuine sincerity. The speech was brief, but it accomplished exactly what the Witan had planned for: hope. The people's desperate need for guidance, for something to believe in, had them clinging to his every word.

When he finished, Nevandians cheered until they were hoarse. Children jumped up and down, clinging to each other. A man fell to his knees, sobbing. He whispered a fervent prayer to the heavens. A woman in all black near the front of the crowd held a man's tattered hat to her breast. Hope was a wildfire and spread through the courtyard.

Ruenen certainly perfected the part of a noble prince, standing above the crowd with his arms wide and welcoming. A diaphanous ray of sun beamed down upon him. He smiled, but Marai saw the strain–no dimples, eyes tight. A mask. So different from the pure joy he radiated when he was onstage playing his lute.

The brief speech Holfast had written outlined Ruenen's absence. The lie concocted outlined his life in the monastery as a child, then how he was sent abroad after Rayghast's destruction of it.

When he stepped away from the balcony, Ruenen was swarmed by council members and richly dressed noblemen. Marai spotted Holfast at

Ruenen's side, whispering directions into his ear. Someone else put their hand on his arm, guiding him away towards the stairs.

"Much work to do," Vorae stated pompously to the nobles.

Marai was shoved back through the cloud of lords and men until she was spit out against the wall.

As the Witan led Ruenen away, his eyes frantically searched until they found Marai's. He mouthed, "I'll find you later," before being dragged down the stairs to the throne room.

The sun cast long shadows across the hallway. There was nothing left for her to do, with Ruenen so occupied. Marai blended in with those shadows, disappeared, and crept to the corridor where the fae were being housed. She heard muffled voices from the gap under Keshel's door. She knocked. The room went silent.

"It's me," she said, pushing the door open.

For a moment, the fae froze, but then activity resumed when they saw it was indeed only Marai.

Keshel sat at his desk scribbling on a large piece of parchment. Raife and Leif hovered over his shoulders. Thora sat on the couch twisting Kadiatu's wet hair into an elegant updo. Kadiatu's feet were curled up under her by the fire. Aresti lounged against the throw pillows, fiddling with the gold hoop in her pointed ear. They all appeared strikingly . . . relaxed. The only sound was the scratching of Keshel's quill on the paper.

"I suppose the prince gave his speech," he said without looking up.

Annoyance flared inside Marai "Why didn't any of you attend?"

"He's not *our* prince," said Leif, snatching a bruised apple from a bowl on the desk. He bit into it, face falling at the taste, then put it back in the bowl.

"He is if you intend to live in this country. Also, that's disgusting," Marai said, indicating the bitten apple. Leif rolled his eyes, removing the fruit from the bowl again, as Marai came to the front of the desk. "Is that the decree?"

Marai recognized Keshel's curly, smooth handwriting, and someone else's tidy scrawl. *Holfast's.*

"I'm making sure nothing is missed or easy to subvert," Keshel said, eyes drafting across the page in hungry strokes. Keshel, despite his reluctance to be in Nevandia, enjoyed the task and jurisdiction he'd been given.

"Have you been treated well so far?" Marai asked.

"The servants and guards have avoided us," said Raife with a shrug. "Keshel's the one who's had any contact with humans since the meeting."

"Holfast, Fenir, and Vorae stayed on the other side of the table. They listened as I spoke," Keshel said, but his voice seemed hollow. "No one made a move to kill me. So it went fine."

"Are you comfortable?" Marai pressed, and Kadiatu whirled around to face her.

"Oh, the rooms are *amazing!* I don't want to move into a gloomy old cottage," she said, scrunching up her face comically.

"I'd rather be in my own space, left alone, than feeling eyes on me at all times," said Thora with a *tsk*. "I swear, the servants have their ears pressed to the doorways and walls. I feel like an attraction in a circus."

"How do you know what a circus is like?" asked Aresti.

Thora waved her off. "Keshel's books."

Raife sat next to her on the couch. "The guards don't trust us at all. It's going to take a long time for everyone to adjust. Us and them."

Marai wished there wasn't an *us* and *them*, but she knew better than to expect that to change instantaneously.

An hour later, a crisp rap came at the door. None of the fae moved; their luminous eyes were as wide as shining moons. Grumbling, Marai opened the door to reveal a group of kitchen servants holding trays of food.

"D-dinner, milady?" asked one girl with a quivering voice.

Marai stepped back to let them in. The fae got to their feet, backing closer to the walls, and watched attentively until the servants hastened out.

Aresti was the first to the trays. She examined a bowl of wilted leafy vegetables that were supposed to be green, but instead were brown and lackluster. She grimaced. "Are they trying to poison us with this?"

"I already told you that Rayghast is corrupting their lands, ruining their harvests," Marai said. "You should be thankful to have any food at all."

"I'm sure this is the best they can do, under the circumstances," said Kadiatu, sticking her finger in a red sauce. Her face lit up with delight. "Doesn't taste poisoned."

"You can't often taste poison, Kadi," Leif said under his breath.

Thora frowned. "I doubt they'd try to off us now." But she still gave the trays a dubious inspection.

Keshel grabbed a porcelain plate and silver utensils, all sporting the Nevandian sunburst crest. He served himself some pork, potatoes, and the wilted greens. The others fell in line behind him and sat around the fire. The food wasn't terrible, but the pork was thin and gangly, potatoes mealy, and the salad bitter. However, the fae weren't the kind of people to turn their noses up at anything. Marai knew they were grateful for the meal and the comfortable rooms, despite their hesitancy to trust humans.

The fae wasted nothing, and once everything was eaten, the group dispersed to their rooms for the night. Marai skulked up and down the dark corridor, hoping to run into Ruenen, but he never showed.

Holfast has him busy.

Something about that made Marai somewhat crestfallen. Why? Why was she feeling so glum when things were going remarkably well?

He's not mine anymore.

Marai closed her eyes and leaned against the wall. Ruenen now had a dozen councilmen to provide him advice. He had hundreds of servants and guards to wait on him, and thousands of subjects to idolize him. He had duties to attend to, people to meet, a war to win. Marai was doomed to blend into the background.

Everything had changed. Their relationship could no longer be what it was . . . whatever it was.

The torches flickered and the castle quieted, settling into slumber. Marai returned to her own room. The refined space was too large for one person. She sat down on the bed, sinking into its plush blankets. Was she worthy of such things? These were the softest sheets she'd ever touched. She had a tended fire in the hearth, warm food in her belly.

Normally, she would have dove under the blankets and fallen straight to sleep, but her mind was awake, tapping against her skull like a child at a windowpane. She paced the rug in front of the fire, her feet bare.

Nosficio would hopefully return tomorrow and bring word from the North. That, at least, was a discussion Marai could participate in. Otherwise, she was completely useless to Ruenen.

She paced and paced until she heard a soft knock, startling her. Marai pulled open the door a crack. Ruenen stood in the hall. The guards patrolled the far end of the hallway, backs turned to Marai's room.

"I'm sorry, were you asleep?" Ruenen asked in a whisper. Marai shook her head. "Can I come in?"

She opened the door wider to let him pass. Ruenen's vest was gone and his shirt was untucked. He bit his lower lip as he stood in the center of the room.

"I . . . I can't sleep."

"Neither can I," Marai said, shutting the door carefully so as not to make a sound. Fae, with their pointed ears, had excellent hearing. She didn't want anyone to know that the prince had come to her room in the middle of the night.

Ruenen raked a hand through his already tousled hair. "Today was . . . it's been a lot of change."

Marai didn't miss the tightness in his voice, the muscles of his shoulders.

"The speech was rousing. You comported yourself with grace and strength. No one else could have done better."

"Marai, life is moving too quickly," he said, breath coming in staccato bursts. "My brain can't keep up. I know I used to joke about being a famous bard, having servants wait on me in my large estate. I wanted loud taverns and crowds. But I . . ." His eyes shimmered. "I wish I was back in the woods, listening to the melody of birds in the trees, the crackling of a campfire, and sitting around it with you. Quiet. Alone."

Marai's stomach clenched. She understood that feeling all too well.

She walked towards him, but kept a space between, a respectful distance. He was the prince now, after all. "I, more than you, don't belong here." She gestured to the room. It was almost laughable that Marai, an ex-pirate mercenary, had been welcomed into this grand space. "But there's a reason we're here. The gods, or fate, what have you . . . we're here because we're supposed to defeat Rayghast. Because he threatens all we hold dear."

Ruenen looked down at the floor. Dark circles had bloomed under his eyes. "What if we don't succeed? What if I'm just . . . a placeholder?"

"Stop that," Marai said. "You know that's not true." She stepped back towards the door. "You need to get some sleep."

"Please—" Ruenen reached out to her with one desperate hand. "I don't want to be in that room all by myself. Would you mind terribly if I . . . stayed here?"

They'd slept in the same room once before in Havenfiord, and they'd slept under the stars together more times than Marai could count. So why did this request bring heat to Marai's cheeks? Why did those words make her body tingle and heart race?

Her tongue felt thick in her mouth. She didn't think she could form a reply, so she nodded. Ruenen's body sagged with relief, and he shucked off his boots. Marai pulled off her tunic, but kept on her undershirt and pants. Ruenen respectfully kept his eyes lowered to the rug, then grabbed a pillow and blanket from the bed and set up on the settee. Marai crawled into bed and watched him fluff up the pillow.

"You're the prince, Ruen. You shouldn't sleep on a couch."

Ruenen gave her a weak smile. "I'm *not* a prince, and I'm not going to kick you out of your bed. I'm the one who asked to be here."

"Then sleep with me."

Ruenen blinked.

The words came out before she'd thought about them. Ruenen waited for her to retract, but when Marai said nothing more he slowly stood and brought the pillow and blanket back to the bed. Marai slid far over under the sheets to the other side as Ruenen slipped in. The bed shifted and sunk. Her whole body went as stiff as a steel blade. She'd never slept next to a man before . . . never once with Slate. He'd never let her stay after he finished . . .

Slowly, the sheets warmed, and Marai's muscles loosened. She wasn't sure if Ruenen was breathing. His hand lay on the top of the blankets. She could reach over and take hold of it. He'd probably placed it there in the hopes that she would.

But his familiar presence was enough to soothe her. He smelled of lavender, but also tavern smoke and damp wood. Her mind began to drift off until she heard the recognizable sound of Ruenen's subtle breathing. She glanced over and saw that the tense planes of his face from earlier had smoothed out; a small smile brimmed on his lips. When she was certain he was fully asleep, Marai softly brushed a strand of chestnut hair from his face, then she curled up next to him and closed her eyes.

She was up at first light, dawn shy on the horizon. Ruenen had stretched out in the night, now sprawled like a starfish across the bed. Marai had woken curled up at his side, fitting against him, a piece to his puzzle. She carefully slithered out of the bed, dressed, and tiptoed across the room to grab her sword and dagger from the table. Once in the hallway, she listened at each door to see if any of the fae were stirring. She was the only one awake.

The castle, however, was alive with a flurry of activity. Servants bustled around cleaning, lighting torches and fireplaces, and carrying baskets full of items. Marai nearly ran into two young pages carrying bundles of wood. The guards remained stationed outside the fae rooms, watching her as she passed.

Marai wove her way through the maze that was the castle halls and stairwells, until she found herself in the back gardens. Or what *should* have been the gardens.

Currently, it was a bunch of dead bushes and trees surrounded by marble walls. Beds that should have housed blossoming flowers sat empty in dusty spoil. Towering hedges that sheltered the garden were wild with black spots of decay on rust-colored leaves. The pond housed sludge and algae instead of swimming fish.

Four well-dressed noblewomen strolled through the garden. The wives of the Witan. Their serene, elegant countenances changed when they spotted Marai in her harsh black attire and weapons. They gasped, averted their eyes, and hurried away, whispering to each other.

Marai wandered out front to the courtyard, grateful to be outdoors and away from prying eyes. Past the main castle entrance, she turned right, following the smell of horses and hay until she came across the stable. Three young groomsmen brushed the mares' slick coats, receiving contented whinnies in return. They stopped when they spotted her.

"Can we help you, ma'am?" the tallest asked.

"Exploring," she replied.

Next to the stable was a large open dirt courtyard. On one side of the square stood a wall of circular targets for archery practice. A few padded wooden posts had been erected on the other. The pads were made from canvas and straw to resemble a figure. Deep gouges and holes had been ripped into the padding. Two benches sat on the farthest end of the square courtyard.

A training ground, most likely built for Vanguarden and Talen, who had both been excellent swordsmen. After the bedraggled garden and confined castle quarters, this place was exactly what she needed. Marai's steps became lighter. The magic in her veins sparked. She unsheathed Dimtoir and focused her breathing, then she unleashed the pent-up energy she'd been gathering for days.

Marai swung and swiped effortlessly. Dimtoir cut into the wooden posts, sending a jarring sensation through her arms. The wood and padding didn't mimic the flesh and bone of bodies, but it felt good when her blade connected with *something*.

She wasn't a lady, like those refined women from the garden. She was the Lady Butcher. Someone who wore death as a scarf; the only perfume she was accustomed to was the smell of blood. She didn't belong to this gilded courtier lifestyle. She desired no servants, no silk. Outside in the fresh air, a sword in her hand, cutting down opponents, was where she thrived.

Marai lost track of time; Dimtoir an extension of her body as she fought her imaginary foe. The whistle of her blade was music all its own. Each stroke seamlessly wove into the next; a commanding dance of metal, speed, and precision. Pivot and chop. Lunge and stab. Spin and feint.

It felt like only a few minutes before a deep voice disturbed her.

"You're quite good with a blade."

Commander Avilyard, without his helmet, leaned against an archery target. Marai recognized him from his voice since she'd never seen his face before. He approached once Marai halted and held her blade to the side in a relaxed stance. How long had he been watching her?

"I can see now why the prince hired you to protect him."

Avilyard had tan skin and dark hair like all Middle Kingdomers, but she noticed his eyes were hazel, lighter than Ruenen's, when he came close enough. He was broad, with gray-speckled stubble across his jaw.

Handsome and sturdy for a man in his late forties. Time had been kind to him; the wrinkles around his eyes added to his rugged quality. Those hazel eyes glanced down to Dimtoir.

He said, "I've never seen a fae blade before."

"It was my father's."

"May I?" he asked.

Marai hesitated. She never let others touch Dimtoir, but she handed it over, and his face alighted with avid interest as he inspected the blade and the foreign words etched into the steel.

"Not a scratch or rolled edge. Amazing. Do your kind . . . do you imbue your blades with magic?"

Marai blinked. Humans never asked about magic. "To make it stronger. I've never seen one forged, but I've been told that's what bladesmiths did. They're all gone now. The craft is lost forever."

"That's a pity." Avilyard handed Dimtoir back to Marai. "I had an aunt who befriended a faerie. She hid her and the faerie's child in her house during the hunt twenty years ago. I remember that she and her son were gentle folk. They never used magic to harm anyone."

Marai almost dropped Dimtoir from shock. People didn't readily share such incriminating facts in Astye. No one wanted to reveal that they had any relations to fae, no matter how distant.

Avilyard frowned and shifted on his feet. "They were discovered, of course. Slain by radicals right here in Nevandia; my aunt alongside them, labeled a traitor." Sorrow flashed across the commander's face.

"Many people confuse magic with evil," Marai said.

"You're brave to come here."

"I'm not one to hide."

"I'm more understanding than most of the citizens, given my aunt's death. You'll need to change a lot of hearts and minds."

"We intend to."

Avilyard nodded, a little unconvincingly. "I dropped your . . . friends off at the cottages. They're getting settled, although they were concerned with where you'd disappeared to."

How long was I out here? Judging by the angle and heat of the sun, it was nearly lunchtime.

"I stationed two of my most sympathetic guards with them," Avilyard continued. "I'll do what I can to keep them protected, but I cannot control everything . . ."

"Thank you." Marai gave him what she hoped was an appreciative look, but she didn't have much practice with that kind of expression.

She sheathed Dimtoir. Marai then noticed the sweat on her temples and back. Hair was plastered to the base of her neck; her hands were coated in brown dust. She needed to gather her things from the room. She'd make final use of the bathtub, then she'd go to the cottages to help.

"His Highness is attending meetings with his advisors, but I know he was searching for you, as well."

Marai nearly snorted at *His Highness,* but she held it in. She'd need to get used to Ruenen's new set of titles. She didn't want to show any disrespect towards the newfound leader when Ruenen needed all of their support.

"I'll find him later."

"If there's anything you and your people need, come to me. I'll ensure you get it," Avilyard said with a courteous incline of his head. "Have a good day, Lady Marai,"

"It's just Marai," she repeated for the millionth time, causing Avilyard to smile, hazel eyes twinkling. He returned his helmet to his head and strode off towards the stables.

Perhaps the Commander was someone the fae might be able to trust.

Once inside the castle, Marai burst through her door to see Harmona laying out something on the bed. The young maid yelped, her whole body recoiling as if she was physically in pain from being in the same space as

Marai. She refused to meet Marai's eyes, keeping her head down at all times.

"I'm simply here for my things and a bath," Marai told her.

Harmona nodded vigorously, then went to work on the bath. After heating water in the ewer over the fire, Harmona quickly dumped the contents into the tub behind the decorative partition, then scooted out of the way. She tried not to ever get too close to Marai.

"Can I assist you in any way?" she asked with a wince, as though it was the last thing she wanted to do.

"No, I can do this myself." Marai yanked off her smelly, black tunic. "And I'll be staying somewhere else from now on, so you don't need to care for me anymore."

Harmona's eyes widened with relief, then she curtsied and disappeared around the other side of the partition.

Marai quickly scrubbed herself down in the basin, enjoying the final moments of pampering. Harmona had left a robe on the chair, so Marai wrapped herself up, then walked out from behind the partition. She was startled to find Harmona still in the room folding Marai's black cloak. Marai blushed; she was entirely naked beneath the sheer robe.

"You can leave that," she told Harmona, who jumped at the strong command.

"Your cloak is dirty, my lady," she squeaked. "I was instructed by Master Bassite to take your clothing down to the laundry."

"That isn't necessary," Marai said, stepping towards the girl.

Harmona shut her eyes tightly and flinched. "I'm sorry, my lady, but I will get in trouble if I—"

Sighing, Marai retreated to grab her clothes. She handed them to Harmona in a bundle, stifling a shiver. It wasn't warm enough to be walking around soaking wet in a robe with the windows wide open. "What am I supposed to wear instead?"

Harmona gestured to the bed where a simple blue and brown wool dress, as well as knee-high cream hose lay. On the floor sat brown slippers. Marai grimaced.

"Ladies in the court wear dresses," Harmona said.

"I'm not a lady, nor am I part of the court. Can't you find a pair of trousers and a tunic?"

"Here in Nevandia, women wear dresses," Harmona pressed, growing paler from Marai's rising irritation. "Lord Holfast and Master Bassite were quite insistent. If you're to be seen in the prince's retinue, you must be presentable."

With a groan, Marai approached the dress. She hadn't worn one since she was a child. The sleeves were too constrictive, length too impractical to move in, nonetheless *fight* in. And it wasn't as if this dress was particularly nice. It was a boxy peasant dress, nothing at all similar to the ones Marai had seen in the store windows in Cleaving Tides years ago, or the fashionable silk dress-robes in Kaishiki.

"Tell Lord Holfast *and* Master Bassite that I'm a member of the Witan now, and they don't control me," Marai snapped, making Harmona gasp.

The girl nodded timidly, then backed out of the chamber, holding Marai's dirty Butcher clothes as if they were infested with fleas.

Marai scowled as she first drew a plain white shift over her head, then the dress. The fabric was itchy and baggy on her, like wearing a sack, and the slippers were too tight. Marai then hastily pulled her dripping hair back in a low ponytail, strapped her weapons to her side, and stormed into the hallway.

Down at the main castle doors, Marai spotted Fenir talking with three other black-robed council members. There was also a bald monk dressed in a plain brown robe.

Probably the same material as this horrid dress.

She stalked over; the men tensed at the sight of her.

"Where are the cottages that Holfast set aside for my family?"

Fenir scowled as the other men stepped away from her. "A greeting would be proper, faerie."

"I'm not here to please you," she bit back, earning a scandalized look from the councilmen. *Be civil*, she reminded herself. *For Ruenen.* "Please tell me where my family is, and I'll leave you in peace."

"Ah, so *you're* one of the fae," said the bald monk, examining her curiously. "I'm Baureo, the Head Monk here at the castle. I hope to see you at our daily worship."

"Doubtful," Marai said. She didn't have time to spend worshiping the gods, especially in a confined space where she'd be surrounded by people who despised her. "My family?"

"They're at the far end of the city, in the area known as Grave's End," said Fenir.

They couldn't have picked a less welcoming name. "Where is that?"

Fenir pointed a shaking hand to the west side of Kellesar, down at the bottom of the hill. In essence, the poorest area. Marai grunted in response, then prowled off towards Grave's End. She heard several appalled gasps and comments from the men as she left.

"She *is* a creature created by Lirr . . ." Monk Baureo mused, although Marai heard the doubt in his voice.

Nevandians gawked at her as she passed through the narrow, winding streets. Marai didn't stand out because of her light skin and hair. No, she stood out with every aspect of her being. The way she glowered, the way she walked awkwardly in that dreaded dress, the weapons strapped to her waist . . . Rumors were already flying about her, the strange woman at the right hand of the prince. Perhaps they knew she was fae. She didn't care if they stared. She didn't care if they whispered. It was the same reaction people gave her as the Lady Butcher.

Grave's End was aptly named. It was the dingiest neighborhood in Kellesar. The streets were covered in rats, trash, and filth, creating a rancid smell in the air. Most of the cottages and buildings were abandoned, in various states of disrepair. Some had caved-in roofs, others had holes in their walls or no doors. They were all made of lime ash and clay, not the sturdier components of stone, brick, and wood in wealthier parts of town nearer to the castle.

The people who remained were thinner and more raggedy than the rest of Kellesar. They ogled at Marai as they cleaned their patched and worn clothes outside their cottages. Dirty children shrieked and ran away as Marai approached the end of the street.

"I think that's another one," murmured a woman to her husband. They glared at Marai as she passed. "Can't believe they'd let those creatures into the city."

"Shh, it will hear you," the husband hissed back.

"Oh, I hope it does. Monstrosities, the whole lot of them," snarled the wife directly at Marai.

Stuffing down the boiling rage inside, Marai shot the woman a saccharine smile. A smile she never gave anyone.

"Hello!" Marai forced a wave.

The woman and her husband blanched, then trotted inside their house and slammed the door.

Marai spotted two golden figures standing outside the worst, most run-down houses at the end of the row, right up against the outer city wall.

"You're Avilyard's men?" she asked.

They bobbed their heads. Beneath their helms, Marai noticed both men were quite young. One she recognized as the friendly guard from the city gate.

"I'm Elmar, and this is Nyle," said the familiar boy.

Nyle sported a thin, patchy beard, while Elmar's chin was speckled with pimples. Mere adolescents now comprised most of the King's Guard. After forty years of war, many of the able-bodied, trained men had already been killed, and now Nevandia only had sons and elderly to defend its people.

Marai gave them a curt nod as she entered the closest one-story cottage, stepping over the door that had been knocked to the dirt floor. Inside, it was a mess of dust and cobwebs, broken furniture, and stray cats. There was a tiny bedroom branching off from the main room, but the fae were used to small spaces.

Her family was already hard at work, covered in dust and sweat. Raife and Thora threw down bundles of rush, a tall grass, to cover the dirt floor and provide insulation in the main room. Keshel swept dead leaves out of the bedroom where they would do the same. Aresti hammered pegs into a big wooden box. Leif carried the unusable furniture outside past Marai and dumped it into the backyard for kindling.

"Nice of you to finally join us," he growled, passing by with a broken shelf. "What are you wearing?"

Marai shot him a withering glare, which he ignored.

"Oh, good, you're here," Thora said. Her apron was covered in dirt. "You can help Aresti repair the grain ark."

The grain ark was a large wooden box used for storing wheat, barley, and other foods. Back in the cave, it often doubled as a prep table for the fae. Aresti seemed to be doing fine on her own, hammering away. Similar to Marai, she was vastly independent. Aresti never asked for help.

Marai frowned, noticing the absence of someone. "Where's Kadi?"

"She's out back, clearing the yard. She thinks she can get a garden growing."

Marai doubted that. Any life that tried to grow here was smothered by Rayghast's magic. She ventured into the yard where Kadiatu was on her hands and knees pulling weeds out of the beds.

"Oh, hello," she said, her bright smile contrasting with the gray dirt smudged across her cheeks and nose. "You look nice in a dress." Marai scowled, making Kadiatu laugh. "Don't be so grumpy."

Marai knelt next to her and yanked more weeds and dead plants from the ground. Once the beds were entirely clear and the soil had been properly turned, Kadiatu reached into the pocket of her apron.

"That nice man, Commander Avilyard, gave me some seeds. I've never planted these vegetables before. They'd never have been able to grow in the desert." Kadiatu excitedly plopped little black and brown seeds into the holes she'd created, then Marai covered them back up with dirt. "This soil doesn't have a lot of minerals. It's dry as a bone, even with water. Not at all healthy."

Rayghast.

"I think I can fix it, though." Kadiatu placed her hands in the dirt, stretching out her fingers. Magic rushed out of her in threads of pinks and purples and greens. It entered the earth and changed the color of the soil into a deep, rich brown. A strong musty scent permeated the air. Kadiatu had returned life to the small plot of land, life that had been sucked away.

Marai gaped at the change in the soil.

Once she was done, Kadiatu lifted her hands and wiped them on her apron. "There! And we'll use our food scraps as compost. I'll have this garden thriving in a few days."

Kadiatu had more power than she let on. To do what she'd done—utterly transform this patch of earth—was more than impressive. Her magic had pushed out Rayghast's darkness to the point where Marai could no longer feel it at all.

The first cottage was entirely ready by the time the sun set. Raife had re-hung two shelves on the walls so they could store their clay pots, bowls and plates. Due to the second room, they decided this larger cottage would be shared by Marai, Thora, Kadiatu, and Aresti. The boys' cottage would be fixed up the next day, but they'd all sleep together tonight.

"I need to return to the castle," Marai told Thora as she stirred a pot of leeks, ground barley, and nettles. A kitchen servant had given Thora a few basic ingredients to start out with. Marai guessed that kindness had more to do with Ruenen than the servant. "I'm expecting news from the North."

"Do you want Raife or Leif to go with you?" Thora asked. "I don't want you traveling alone through the city at night."

Marai's mouth twisted. "I'm a mercenary."

"I know that, Storm Cloud, but I'll worry all the same."

Marai bristled at the nickname. "I'll be back later."

She ventured out into the dark street. Marai was quite used to nighttime escapades as the Lady Butcher. Walking alone in Kellesar at night wasn't as frightening as places like Iniquity in Grelta, but Marai didn't have her black attire to hide amongst the shadows. She missed the weight of her cloak on her shoulders; the anonymity of her scarf. She hurried along, avoiding eye contact with the people in the streets. No one approached her, but she was ready with Dimtoir if they did.

In a dark side street, a breeze lifted the hair on the back of her neck. The air shifted, and Marai scented blood. She halted and placed her hand on her hilt.

"Right on time," she said to the shadows, which moved and came closer, forming the shape of a man. The hood of his cloak was down, revealing his long roped hair. Crimson eyes, two beacons of doom, glowed in the dark.

"You said three days. I keep my promises." Nosficio flashed his fangs, nostrils flaring. "You smell like lavender and summer storms."

"What does Queen Nieve say?"

"Don't you think I should give her response directly to the prince?" Nosficio asked. He removed a letter from within his cloak. Marai spotted the blob of red wax with the royal seal of Grelta: a giant bear wearing a crown.

"You want to enter the castle?" Marai asked. "Not a chance. Give me the letter, and I'll bring it to Ruenen."

Nosficio returned the letter to his cloak. "You're still breathing, aren't you?" The vampire stepped closer, his hair swishing in the breeze, reminding Marai of the ropes binding the bridges of Cleaving Tides. "You had me run to the damned freezing North and back, risking life and limb to get your prince's request to Nieve. I'm fully invested now. And you're going to need me."

Marai scowled. "What are you going to do? Glide through the front door?"

"Where's the prince's chamber? I'll meet you there."

Marai hesitated. Revealing the location of Ruenen's room to a vampire he'd previously staked was a poor decision. However, Nosficio wasn't going to give her the letter voluntarily. She could fight him for it, but he was right . . . they were going to need him again.

She quickly gave him directions to *her* room within the castle. Nosficio promised to meet her there, then disappeared in a dramatic swirl of his cloak.

Marai found Ruenen in the private dining room, eating alone at the table. He sagged in his chair, hand over his eyes. At the sound of her purposefully loud footsteps, he brightened.

"Thank Lirr you're here," he said, pushing out the chair next to him with his foot. "Are you hungry? There's enough here to feed an army." He gestured to the four platters of food surrounding him.

"No," she lied. She'd eaten only a little at the cottage, but the letter couldn't wait. She'd swipe something from the kitchen before returning. "Our friend has returned with a response."

Ruenen's eyes opened wide. "And?"

"He's meeting us in my room."

Ruenen snatched the hunk of bread from his plate and stood. "Let's go, then." In the corridor, Ruenen gave Marai a shifty, nervous glance. "Was last night . . . okay?"

Marai avoided meeting his gaze. "Why wouldn't it be?"

"You were gone before I awoke, and I haven't seen you all day."

"You know I rise early, and I was helping my family fix up the cottage. I wouldn't have let you stay if I was uncomfortable with it."

This seemed to ease some of Ruenen's concerns. Marai's stomach gave a loud growl then, and Ruenen handed her the bread from his dinner without a second thought.

"So . . . why the dress?"

Irritation bubbled under Marai's skin as she bit into the bread. "Why is *everyone* so caught up on this horrid dress?"

Ruenen laughed. "Because it's such a departure from your usual attire." He leaned towards her. "It looks good."

Marai's cheeks burned as she scowled. They reached her room and she pushed open the door, more forcefully than intended. Nosficio leaned against the fireplace mantel with one arm, a silhouette of seductive promises. He'd taken off his cloak, revealing perfectly tailored velvet and brocade silk clothes in gray and black. The window on the far side of the room was open, curtains fluttering. He must've climbed through it somehow . . .

"Ah, Prince, felicitations on your mighty ascension," Nosficio said with a flourishing wave, but didn't bow.

Ruenen crossed his arms. "What does Queen Nieve say?"

"No 'have a seat' or 'can I get you anything?'" Nosficio said, voice lilting with play. "That was a long trip and I'm exhausted. Any youthful servants nearby? I could use a snack."

"*Please*, have a seat," Ruenen replied, jaw tight.

Nosficio sat grandly in an armchair and crossed his legs. Marai and Ruenen sat together on the couch.

Nosficio produced the letter from inside his vest. "The she-demon nearly cut off my head when I appeared before her." But Marai heard the affection tainting all his words. Nosficio *admired* that about the queen. "Once she calmed down, however, Nieve was *very* interested in you, dear prince. She read your letter several times, in fact. She asked me a lot of questions. Then she had several long, tedious meetings with the king and their advisors. And then she wrote you this."

He finally handed Ruenen the letter. Marai tensed as Ruenen's deft fingers broke the wax seal and unfolded the parchment. She leaned closer to Ruenen to read the elegant swirls of Nieve's writing.

His Royal Highness Prince Ruenen,

I never thought I would write those words again to a Nevandian royal. I remember your parents fondly. They were the only two Astyean leaders I could stand. My husband, King Maes, and I were pleasantly surprised to learn of your sudden appearance, let alone existence. You have quite the story, so I'm told. Something about King Rayghast and shadow creatures? I would love to hear all of this from your own lips one day.

In regards to your letter, you have intrigued me with your request for a meeting. This is not typically the first task of a newly seated king. I would imagine you'd have more pressing matters to attend to, what with Tacorn and Rayghast at your doorstep. Perhaps this meeting has something to do with forging an alliance against him. I cannot fathom any other reason you would write to me at such a pressing time. If that is indeed your intention, King Maes and I would consider hearing your plans, but we'd like to speak with you directly, Your Highness. In person.

Well wishes on your successful reign,
Queen Nieve of Grelta

*Postscript: Sending a notorious vampire in your stead was not the wisest way to make friends.

CHAPTER 15
Rayghast

His spies in Nevandia all returned to Dul Tanen with the same news: Prince Ruenen had declared himself.

Rayghast couldn't believe his own failure. He'd had twenty-two years to dispose of that whelp, and he'd failed. His soldiers, his commanders, his mercenaries, *all* failed. Now, Nevandia would rally behind the prince. Perhaps other kingdoms sympathetic to the boy's cause would ally themselves with Nevandia. He had a good sob story. Foolish leaders like Nieve might feel compelled to give support.

Rayghast wouldn't let that happen.

"At least we now know where the boy is," Commander Shaff said. "Nevandia's army is still weak. Their soldiers are the sons of farmers and miners with limited training. I don't believe it will take much to penetrate the walls of Kellesar."

"How do you intend to scale those enormous walls, Commander?" Dobbs asked through narrowed eyes. "It's a fortified keep, as much as ours here in Dul Tanen. And Kellesar, like an island, is surrounded by the Nydian on all sides."

"I suggest a siege. With Varana's numbers, we can surround the city, pummel them with our trebuchets, and starve them out," Shaff said with a wave of his hand, as if his idea was so plain and obvious that everyone at the table should have thought of it already.

"That will take months," Rayghast said, drilling his fingers on the armrest of his throne. "There are far too many opportunities for the prince to escape during the siege. If we take the city, if the boy lives, Nevandia will survive in him. He could take refuge in another kingdom. He could rally another army. No, Commander, it must be one brutal, swift attack that ends it all."

Shaff frowned; his face was permanently set that way behind bushy eyebrows, but Rayghast supposed the man frowned deeper.

"As you wish, Your Grace," said Shaff. "I shall meet with my other commanders to discuss the complete strategy. Once Varana arrives, we should be able to set this plan into action."

"*If* Varana arrives," grumbled Wattling to his neighbor. "Suli has been most difficult of late."

"The queen's latest letter did the trick, at least," said Councilman Verdenian, who was ambassador to Varana. "The Emperor finally replied, and agreed to send his troops."

"He'd better not recant," Dobbs said.

Rayghast snapped his fingers, and a gray-cloaked man, his spy Falien, came out from the corner of the room, and handed him a pile of letters and scraps of paper.

"These rumors are getting out of control. Notes full of lies have been found scattered around the city."

Untidily scrawled on scraps of paper were accusations and conspiracies about Rayghast, himself. One of them claimed he was an illegitimate son of the late King Hershen. Absolute nonsense, of course. His birth had been overseen by Cronhold. Each stage of his life had been documented.

But the "curse" theory had evolved, now stating that Rayghast had killed his three previous wives and his unborn children. That he was losing his mind, or that he'd never had one to begin with.

"My guards found one of these notes in a stable. Five tavern patrons were overheard discussing it, and were arrested, then beheaded publicly as of this morning," Rayghast said with quiet authority. He hadn't taken part in those killings. He'd been alone, kneeling on the moor outside the city, releasing his pent-up aggression and dark magic through the earth by sucking the life from Nevandian lands. This was a weekly ritual for him; an invisible way to expel the dark magic that writhed in his bones, aching for destruction. To anyone watching, it appeared as if Rayghast were praying. "Another note was found by a servant in this castle's own library."

The council murmured and grunted as they passed the notes down the table.

"Are they all written by the same hand?" asked Dobbs, analyzing two letters.

"It's not one individual," said Rayghast's spy, voice rasped like a crackling fire. Rayghast didn't even know the man's name. "It's the same four or five people writing them. We think one hand might belong to the author of those coded messages, as well."

"What is the morale within the barracks, Commander?" asked Cronhold to Shaff. "Are the soldiers hearing these, uh, rumors?"

Shaff's mouth tightened in hesitation before he spoke. "The men are certainly hearing these conspiracies, my lords. Those who repeat them are being punished appropriately."

"We cannot afford to lose the loyalty of our soldiers," stated Dobbs, pounding a fist onto the table. "Doubt among the men could weaken us."

Dark magic and frustration made Rayghast shiver.

Release, that oily, sinister voice demanded inside his head.

Rayghast was about to satiate that need, to prowl down to the dungeons, when a soldier burst into the room.

"Your Grace, Commander, forgive my intrusion, but I have news," he said, tucking his helmet in the crook of his arm. The man's face was splattered with dirt and blood.

Rayghast halted. A vein throbbed in his temple as magic rushed through him, restless and annoyed. He had no desire to stay in this meeting a moment longer. The magic needed to be expelled *now* before he combusted in this very room.

"My unit was attacked on the road last night."

"By Nevandian patrol?" asked Cronhold.

"No, my lords, their bodies were . . . ripped apart," the soldier said with a disgusted grimace. A ripple of concern traveled up and down the council table. "I could hardly see in the darkness, but the attacker used magic, creating strange burn marks on the bodies."

Rayghast tensed. Another magic user?

"Was this the work of that faerie girl? The one who rescued the prince?" asked Wattling, eyes wide in his fleshy face.

No, Rayghast knew this wasn't the Lady Butcher. He'd been obtaining information on her for weeks. Spies discovered her relation to the hidden town of criminals in the Greltan woods. The Nest or Den it was called; a place where magical folk still visited, and mercenaries contracted work. Rayghast tried to gather what information he could on her, and by now, he had a clear picture. The faerie was the first and only being to ever breach the fortress at Dul Tanen by creating a doorway from thin air. Rayghast wanted her dead.

"She doesn't tear people apart," he said. "The Butcher is a skilled swordsman. The cuts from her blade are clean and precise."

As for the scorched flesh, it *was* possible. Dozens of his men had been turned to ash in the Tacornian woods well over a month ago. But still, this recent attack was not the work of the Butcher girl. Why burn the victims and tear them to shreds at all? It was wasted effort. With her magic, the faerie could incinerate them.

"Was it one of those, uh, creatures?" asked Cronhold, voice wavering. Sometimes, it was hard to tell if he shook from nerves or absurd old age.

"I have reason to suspect one, Your Grace," the soldier said. "It made such horrific noises, like a bear or wildcat, but it stood on two legs. I barely escaped with my life, Your Grace."

"It's possibly the same creature that attacked the peasants in the slums," suggested Shaff, and Cronhold's face lit up with recognition.

As if in response, Rayghast's magic leapt, pouncing on Shaff's words. *A new magical creature.*

Rayghast stalked out past the council table; a maelstrom-like sound rushed in his ears as he hastened to the courtyard.

"Your Grace?" called Shaff, armor clanking behind him, the other soldier in tow.

"Take me to the site," Rayghast said, mounting his massive warhorse.

"It's too dangerous, Your Grace."

Dark magic pulsed in his chest. *Use me,* it said. *Yes, use me...*

"Not for me," Rayghast stated, then spurred his horse onwards. The sound of hooves behind him said that Shaff and his men followed.

Night fell by the time Rayghast arrived at the scene of the vicious slaying; only an hour's ride, indeed, far too close to Dul Tanen. The soldier's flickering torches illuminated what was left of the bodies lying scattered across the road. The dead soldiers had been utterly ravaged by claws, bloody gauges pierced their thick armor. However, their bodies hadn't been eaten. This wasn't a normal animal hunting for food. This was a purposeful attack meant for the mere enjoyment of killing.

Rayghast snatched a torch from Shaff and knelt down to examine a body. The blackened flesh on the hands of some soldiers was oddly familiar to him. Dark magic in his veins thrummed in recognition of a similar power.

Whatever these creatures were, they were unlike any others on this continent.

Rayghast stomped into the woods, and was swallowed up by the dense foliage. The torchlight created spectral, snarled shadows from the branches of the trees. An owl hooted, deep and forlorn, a ghost's moan in the darkness. Rayghast followed the footprints of a claw-footed beast with a massive gait. Shaff and his men unsheathed their swords, keeping in close range of their king.

Unnecessary, Rayghast thought. He could handle this creature on his own, whatever it was.

Magic shoved against his skin, trying to break out of its container. Rayghast let it seep through his feet, subtle enough not to draw the attention of the soldiers behind him. Black smoke wove through the leaves and dirt, twigs and grass around him, draining the natural life. Thriving plants shriveled and withered away. He may have given the land this abundance, but the magic could easily take it away.

Heavy footsteps pounded against the earth. Something enormous huffed and sniffed within the dense tree line.

Shaff and his men whirled, chasing shadows, hunting for the source of the sound.

Rayghast's magic lured the beast to him, and he did not quake when two luminescent yellow eyes peered out from the shadows.

The creature materialized, as if from the darkness itself. Its nostrils flared, slitted pupils dilated and then constricted as it honed in on Rayghast in recognition

This was no faerie. No vampire. No werewolf, even. This creature was entirely new.

Part lizard, part wildcat, a hellish mutt with a striking human-esque face: pale cheeks, a human nose, mouth and forehead. A strange indigo half-moon symbol sat between its brows. The torch flames emphasized the shadows across its grotesque visage. Dark magic drifted from its shoulders like a cape.

Shaff and his men gasped and stammered.

"What the fuck *is* that?" one of them squawked.

Rayghast's magic thrashed in response to the creature's similar dark power.

How strange that this beast possesses the same magic. But Rayghast didn't have time to ponder what it was or how it came to be there.

He unsheathed his broadsword. The creature's pale human lips drew back into a sneer, its furred tail thrashed, and dark magic flew from its shoulders directly at Rayghast.

That was one major difference: the creature didn't need to make a physical connection in order to use the magic like Rayghast did. It had *control* over its power.

Rayghast ducked, the force of the magic slamming into two of the soldiers behind him. He knelt, shoving his hands into the dirt. The screams behind him only encouraged the darkness to pour from his fingers. Magic tunneled through the earth and leapt up, surrounding the creature.

For a moment, their powers battled, like two men grappling in a fist fight. Then the creature snarled and broke through Rayghast's magic. Black smoke puffed away into nothing.

The beast charged him. Claws elongated, it pulled its arm back. Ebony flame swirled around each sharp claw.

Rayghast blocked the creature's strike with his sword, but it was larger than him, brawnier. It pushed aside his blade and swiped at his arm.

Those claws dug deep and *burned*, but Rayghast didn't feel pain like a normal human. The magic inside him heightened his tolerance and muted the agony.

The wound was worth it—the creature had left itself wide open.

Rayghast swung, his blade making contact with its strange furred, scaled chest. A deep red gash bloomed. The creature staggered backwards.

It opened its mouth. Words came out in a kind of screeching grunt. It was a language Rayghast didn't know, but he regarded the creature's furious expression, the way it clutched at the wound. The beast was cursing him in its native language.

Its human face turned paler, yellow eyes widened.

Rayghast swung again as dark magic rushed from his feet, underground, and latched itself onto the ankles of the beast, holding it still. Flesh peeled away as Rayghast's power consumed it, climbing up its muscular legs. The creature bellowed again in its guttural language.

The King of Tacorn then beheaded the creature while it was distracted.

"Your Grace," shouted Shaff, coming to his side.

Rayghast's magic receded back inside him.

"My King, are you injured?" Shaff asked, holding a torch up to the gaping gash in Rayghast's arm. In the near pitch-darkness, he hadn't witnessed Rayghast's use of magic.

Rayghast covered the wound with his other hand. "Burn the body."

Only one of Shaff's soldiers remained; the others had been set aflame by the creature's magic. Their bodies lay crumpled in a heap on the forest floor. Black flame had corroded their armor. Rayghast sneered. Scorched flesh and exposed innards smelled atrocious.

He didn't bother with the mess. Shaff could clean it up. Rayghast climbed into his horse's saddle and rode back to Dul Tanen alone in the night. He skulked past the guards, past Cronhold in the hallway who started talking, but was hushed by the aggressive speed of Rayghast's steps.

Once inside his chambers, Rayghast cleansed the wound, a deep gash straight to the bone. The ripped edges of flesh were charred as crispy as fish skin.

Black tendrils of magic oozed from the gash. It dulled the pain as Rayghast sensed a tingle. His blackened flesh stitched itself back together. Like a needle and thread, the magic healed its vessel. It would not be vulnerable.

"Husband?" came Rhia's voice from her doorway.

He'd been seeing too much of her lately. Every night, he bedded her, at the council's urgent requests. It wasn't pleasurable for either of them, but to keep the hounds off the scent of his cursed seed, Rayghast performed his duty.

"Get out," he commanded in a cool, lethal tone. He tried to wrap a bandage around the wound with one hand.

The queen ignored him. "My King, Cronhold said you left to fight one of those beasts." Rhia came closer. "Are you hurt? Shall I call for the healer?"

"I said *get out*." He bit the words, shielding his arm from her view.

Rhia's lips flattened as she bowed her head lower. She turned and made for the door.

Rayghast shifted, too soon. Rhia glanced back over her shoulder. Her almond-shaped eyes widened as she saw black tendrils flickering at the wound.

"What is that?" she asked, paling. She fully faced him now, dropping her usual distant comportment. "Is that—"

"Are you deaf or just stupid?" Rayghast asked with venom. A tsunami of magic rose in him.

Kill her, it called.

Rayghast couldn't do that. How would he explain such a death without revealing his powers? Magic left physical evidence, scorch marks and dead skin. He'd managed to hide it in the forest with the creature thanks to the cover of darkness.

"Leave my room at once."

Rhia gaped as the magic coiled itself around his arm. "You . . . you've been harboring magic!"

Her eyes narrowed, lips twisted into a disgusted, fearful grimace.

There it was: the same hateful expression his father, King Hershen, had bestowed upon him all his life. Rayghast couldn't stand that look.

He prowled towards her. Rhia stumbled backwards into the doorframe, tripping over the train of her gown.

"Do you fear me now, Wife?" he asked with vicious calm. He shoved his arm under her nose, allowing Rhia to fully view his horrific devilry. "Do you see now what power I hold?"

Rhia's throat bobbed as she held her ground, expression clearing of all emotion. "Yes, I see . . ."

He reached out to touch her bare neck, and she flinched delightfully. But his hand hovered above her skin, making no contact. Rhia's breast heaved.

"One touch from me and I could ruin you," he said.

This here was the true test of her loyalty.

Rhia lifted her chin, meeting his gaze. "I won't say a word to anyone about what I've seen. You can trust me to keep your secret, Husband."

She stepped back into her room, then quickly shut the doors. Rayghast locked her in.

I should kill her.

She was a risk. His mind formulated scenarios to dispose of her. He'd never be able to hide the body without someone seeing. Could he ride with her out to the woods and feign an accident? An attack from one of the creatures?

No, his soldiers would never allow both the King and Queen of Tacorn to go anywhere alone. They were watched. Guarded.

He could poison her, but that was a woman's weapon. Cowardly. He wouldn't degrade himself to that level of weakness. Beyond that, he couldn't fuel the rumors further. His soldiers might abandon him, his subjects might rise up if another wife died mysteriously.

Rhia needed to live. For now.

But no more would she be allowed to move about the castle freely. No more stepping into Rayghast's rooms without permission. No more beddings, trying for an heir. She'd be confined to her quarters, kept away from the public and anyone of importance.

He doubted she'd blab. Rhia was smart enough to care about her own self-preservation. No one would believe her, anyways. A woman. Varanese. Rayghast could say she'd gone mad.

But if she *did* speak . . . even if no one truly believed her, there would always be a seed of doubt. The noose of tight-fisted control he'd gained over the years was already loosening. He couldn't afford to have any of his citizens get wind of his magic or soldiers would rebel.

After that . . . he'd take care of Rhia, and it wouldn't matter how.

CHAPTER 16

Ruenen

"She wants me to come there in person?" Ruenen read and re-read the letter. There wasn't time to travel all the way to Grelta and back, especially not for the newly discovered Prince of Nevandia. The trip alone would take at least three weeks, not to mention the days in meetings and negotiations. Ruenen was expected *here*, in his kingdom, preparing for battle against Tacorn. "Does she truly expect me to drop everything and go there?"

"No, she doesn't," Nosficio said, crossing his arms. He frowned at the response from Nieve. "She doesn't play games the way other rulers on the continent do. She writes what she wants; however, Nieve doesn't think you will come."

"Nieve is essentially saying, 'if you want my forces, come take them,'" Marai said with a huff.

"She didn't say no, though," said Ruenen. "Perhaps we *could* go there . . ."

He looked at Marai. She stared back. Then she raised an eyebrow. She understood his meaning; they *could* travel to Grelta and back quickly if they used a portal.

"Your council is already skeptical of me and magic as it is. I'm not comfortable revealing all my secrets so early in this alliance."

Marai picked at her fingernails. It was risky to trust Holfast and the Witan so early on. They could turn on Marai and the fae at any moment. Ruenen didn't want Marai to show how powerful she truly was . . . at least not until the battle with Tacorn.

Fear, sharp and cold, came upon him, when he imagined Marai facing Rayghast on the highlands. Those black, empty eyes still followed him in his nightmares. Blackened hands held a dagger to his face. Leather straps struck his back as warm, sticky blood dripped down his legs, but more often now, Marai knelt next to him, gasping every time the whip bit into her skin.

The real Marai next to him gave Ruenen a quizzical glance. He'd no doubt twisted his face while his brain had wandered.

"I'll show this letter to the Witan in the morning," he said, giving her a swift smile. Ruenen stood, shoulders slumping in exhaustion. It had been another long, tedious day, full of meetings and talking and names and faces.

"I would like to be there," said Nosficio.

Ruenen halted mid-yawn. "Be where?"

"At the Witenagemot meeting tomorrow."

"But . . . it'll be daylight," Ruenen said, staring at the vampire, who wasn't putting on his usual slick charm. His face was as smooth and serious as glass.

"You've seen me many times during the day, Princeling. But that's not your real concern, is it?"

"Can we trust you at this meeting?" Marai asked, tone sharp.

Nosficio's eyes narrowed slightly as he focused on her. "Are you asking if I can control my urge to feed? To kill? In a room full of warm-blooded victims?"

Ruenen stiffened. Yes, that was exactly what he was wondering.

"I'm standing here with you now. I've never once attacked either of you in bloodlust, no matter how much I may have wanted to take a bite."

Nosficio smirked at Marai. "I'm a thousand years old, not some rampant newborn."

"Then why are there so many rumors of your draining habits?" pressed Marai. "Rumors come from truth."

Ruenen's lips twitched. Marai would know; the rumors about the Lady Butcher were similarly sinister to those of Nosficio the vampire.

"I'm old. I've lived a hundred lifetimes." Nosficio's face softened then. For the first time, Ruenen noticed regret in his countenance. "You cannot live for as long as I have and not have shades of gray. I don't have a pristine past, Butcher, but neither do you."

"What about Nieve?" Marai asked, and immediately, the vampire's cold, calculating face snapped back into place. "Why *her*?"

"Because she isn't afraid of anyone," he replied. "You'll see for yourselves, if you manage to meet her." Nosficio faced Ruenen now. "Will you let me attend the meeting tomorrow or not?"

Ruenen pulled at his neck and sighed. "Fine, but if you think about harming anyone, Marai can do whatever she wants with you."

Nosficio's fangs were on full display as he smiled. "She can *try*." Marai rolled her eyes, and Nosficio sauntered to the open window. "Until tomorrow then."

He disappeared in a flash. Ruenen didn't even see him step onto the windowsill.

"Should I have said no?" Ruenen asked in the silence.

Marai made for the door. "I'll keep a close eye on him."

"Are you leaving?" Ruenen blurted before he could stop himself. He had hoped . . . he didn't want to show how much he'd hoped . . .

"I'm returning to the cottage tonight. I don't belong here," Marai said, gesturing to the grand room.

Ruenen's body deflated. He hadn't slept so well in years as he had last night, lying next to Marai in that bed. It had nothing to do with the comfortable blankets and pillows. It had been the sound of her breathing.

The peacefulness upon her face while she slept. The warmth of her. There was a moment when he'd opened an eye, saw her curled up next to him, and his heart had nearly burst. He'd wanted to wrap arms around her and pull her closer, to breathe in the scent of her. To press his lips to her temple.

"I should walk with you—"

"I'll be fine on my own."

Ruenen inwardly cursed himself. Of course Marai would be fine walking alone at night. She'd survived years without him. No one else was more capable.

"Goodnight, then," he said, words coming out clipped. Whatever closeness they'd achieved last night was gone again.

Marai's face betrayed nothing as she turned and placed her pale hand on the door latch. "Goodnight, Ruen."

She glanced back over her shoulder. Her violet eyes scanned him up and down once. Marai smiled, slow and coy, and exited the room.

A fire blazed through his veins. That *look*. Those *eyes*. He'd nearly leapt across the room as fast as Nosficio.

His legs wobbled as he tried to walk back to his own room. The smell of her, woodsy, effervescent, lingered in the hallway. It was a high, enveloping his senses, making his need for her almost unbearable. When he burst into his own chamber, he quickly grabbed his lute from the armchair. Ruenen sat down on the bed, knee bouncing, and let out one long breath. He collapsed backwards onto his pillow, and played the first song that came to his mind, trying not to imagine what it might be like to actually *touch* her again.

Witan meetings were by far Ruenen's least favorite aspect of being a ruler. His body hated sitting still for so long. He had to force his legs not to twitch, his hands to remain calmly on the table and not tap out a rhythm while his brain created a melody. His fingers itched for his lute, so he could strum its strings and take the intensity away from the room.

Especially since Marai and Keshel had walked in the door.

This was the first time all of the privy council sat around the table with fae in the room. Two additional chairs were added, squeezing Marai and Keshel in between two fearful councilmen whose names Ruenen couldn't remember.

But he wasn't worried about Marai and Keshel. His attention flickered from door to window, wondering how the vampire would make his grand entrance.

"Thank you both for joining us today," said Holfast.

Keshel dipped his head in polite greeting, but his face remained shuttered and distant. Marai was the sole woman in the room, and, as usual, she assessed each individual, and every escape route. Both Marai and Keshel's postures were so rigid, Ruenen almost laughed. They were identical in their standoffishness.

"Lord Keshel is the Ambassador for the Fae and Magical Folk," Holfast explained to the wide-eyed Witan, "and Lady Marai is . . . the prince's personal guard."

"Is that not what the King's Guard is for?" Vorae mumbled next to Ruenen.

"There's no one I trust more than Marai," said Ruenen, raising his voice and whetting it sharp as a dagger. Those vibrant eyes flashed to him and pinned him in place. Ruenen swallowed and had to look away.

Stay focused.

He held up the letter from Nieve. "I received a response from the Queen of Grelta."

"So soon?" Holfast asked, taken aback.

"I have a rather fleet-footed messenger," said Ruenen under his breath.

The Witan perked up, straightening in their chairs, leaning closer to the table. Ruenen handed the letter to Holfast, whose dark eyes rapidly read the text with a frown.

"What does she say?" asked Fenir.

"She states that she and King Maes would be interested in discussing an alliance, but only if *I* personally go to Grelta for the meeting."

"Well, that's preposterous," huffed Vorae. "We're not going to send our prince all the way to the North when you've just announced yourself."

"I agree," Holfast said, passing the note to the black robed man next to him. "The journey is too far and too perilous this close to battle. We cannot risk losing you. Rayghast has heightened both his defenses and incursions. There are soldiers stationed along all roads in the Middle Kingdoms, waiting to confront any Nevandians they find."

"Nieve knows this," another councilman said with a grimace. "She knows it's too dangerous for our prince. She's an arrogant bitch."

"That *bitch* has every reason to be cautious," came a lethal, silky voice from behind the throne.

The Witan jumped and flinched at the sound.

Nosficio, covered in his cloak, revealed himself. How long had he been there? *How* had he gotten in without being noticed?

Vorae shot to his feet. "Intruder! Guards!"

Avilyard and his men raised their weapons, sweeping in towards Nosficio.

"*Wait,*" Ruenen jumped from his seat, raising his arms to halt the King's Guard, who'd closed in from all sides.

Nosficio's eyes burned bright. All movement stopped. The guards, weapons raised, stared from Ruenen to Nosficio.

"He's my guest. Please, lower your weapons," said Ruenen.

Avilyard gestured and his guards retreated back a few steps. The Witan, however, remained frozen. Keshel's eyes had widened as understanding clicked into place. He glanced at Marai, who gave him a brief shrug.

"This is . . . Lord Nosficio," said Ruenen as Nosficio stalked forward from behind the throne. "He's my emissary to the North."

"I've heard of him," a councilman said, pointing a shaking finger. "He's that murderous vampire!"

Two members of the Witan shot out of their seats and rushed for the door. Guards raised their swords again. A few people yelled and cursed. Nosficio smirked, showing off his fangs, enjoying this chaos.

"Faeries, and now v-vampires?" another councilman stammered.

Vorae pounded his fist on the table. "We cannot condone this, Your Highness. Nevandia isn't a sideshow spectacle!"

"*Kill him,*" one council member shouted at Avilyard. "Kill them all!"

Ruenen got to his feet. A calm fury rushed through him. "There will be none of that. Nosficio, like the fae, has pledged himself to our cause. He wishes to defeat Rayghast, as we all do. It would be ignorant of us to reject his assistance, not when we're so vastly outnumbered. We need every man."

"He's *not* a man, Your Highness," Fenir said, owlish eyes nearly popping out from his head. "He's a *vampire,* one I've also heard of before. He's Nieve's sanguinary plaything."

Nosficio lifted his chin. "If I am, as you say, Nieve's *plaything,* I would then have tremendous insight into the Queen, the King, and the Glacial Palace. And not to worry, dear Witan, I already ate this morning."

No one moved. The two councilmen hovering near the door behind the guards seemed ready to wet their pants.

Marai released a grumbling sigh. "If he tries anything, I'll kill him."

Nosficio grinned at her, but Marai's statement eased some of the Steward's concern.

Holfast turned to a guard standing protectively at his side. "Please procure another chair for our . . . guest."

The guard hesitated, then grabbed one of the spare wooden chairs lined against the wall. He placed the chair next to Marai, and Nosficio took a slow, purposeful seat.

"Then, Emissary, let us return to the problem at hand," Holfast continued. The two men who stood returned to their seats, but their rears barely touched the cushions, as if ready to bolt again. "We cannot send our prince to Grelta, but we *do* need their soldiers. We shall send an ambassador in the prince's stead."

"I will go," said one of the quieter men at the table. He then addressed Ruenen. "I used to be Ambassador to Grelta, back when Nevandia had better political standing. I still receive friendly correspondence from several Greltan council members."

"Thank you, Lord Goso—" Holfast said.

"Nieve won't accept an ambassador," Nosficio said, and all heads swiveled to him. "For something as major as a wartime alliance, she expects to be treated with respect. She'll only negotiate with Prince Ruenen. She made that clear in her letter."

"Then she's being unreasonable," shouted Vorae. Beads of sweat dappled his brow. "We'll send Lord Goso, and she will negotiate with him. We don't have *time* to send His Highness to Grelta."

"But if Lord Goso fails, what then?" asked Keshel.

Nosficio regarded him with interest; Ruenen watched the vampire sniff the air in Keshel's direction.

"We'll have wasted more valuable time trying to strengthen our forces, to come away with nothing. If a meeting must be held, it must be done immediately, and to the queen's specifications. Rayghast could strike us at any time. We need those soldiers *now*." For someone who was sitting in on his first war council, Keshel certainly knew what to say. A few murmurs traveled up and down the table. "Nevandia is desperate. Sometimes, drastic measures must be taken."

This last sentence was said sharply. Ruenen didn't miss his meaning. Allying with faeries and vampires was certainly a drastic measure for a kingdom who abhorred magical folk. Most of the Witan had taken significant convincing to be in the same room as Marai and Keshel.

"I can take them," said Marai. "I'll take Prince Ruenen and Lord Goso to the Glacial Palace and back."

Vorae scoffed. "That doesn't solve the problem of time–"

"It does if it takes a mere moment to get there."

The table hushed. Next to Marai, Keshel stiffened and shot her a silent warning. The muscles in Ruenen's stomach constricted. She wasn't really going to tell them, was she?

"What do you mean?" Holfast asked.

"I can create a portal between here and Grelta. It's as easy as stepping through a doorway."

"You can . . . create a doorway between two places?" asked Fenir, arching a dark eyebrow. "I wasn't aware faeries had that kind of magic."

"We don't," said Keshel. "Only Marai. She's . . . unusual."

Nosficio stared at Marai openly. Ruenen saw a flash of surprise in the vampire's eyes, but it was gone when Holfast continued to speak.

"You can safely transport multiple people in this portal?"

Marai nodded. "Prince Ruenen and I have crossed the threshold between space several times together." She glanced at him and heat crept across Ruenen's skin. "And I brought all of my people through the door when we arrived here. It's quite safe."

"Sounds unholy, to me . . ." whispered a councilman snidely to another.

"The North will know, then, that we're housing magical creatures," Vorae said. "If we reveal the fae, they may refuse to work with us."

Nosficio cleared his throat. "The queen is more open-minded than you give her credit for. She'll be intrigued by Lady Marai's magic, not disgusted, as many of you so plainly are."

Vorae and Fenir shot the vampire a seething glance, which Nosficio basked in like the sun he never could.

"Lord Goso, you must accompany His Highness," said Holfast. Goso bowed his head in agreement. "Commander Avilyard, we will also require several of your men for added protection."

"Yes, my lord, I shall pick my best in the King's Guard. Since Lady Marai will be present, I'm certain the prince will be well-protected under her watchful eye and skillful hands," Avilyard said.

Ruenen snapped his head towards Avilyard. Since when had the Nevandian commander seen Marai at work? Although, she *did* have very skilled hands...

"Your Highness should compose a response to Queen Nieve, stating you'll be there in a week," said Holfast.

"Tomorrow evening," Nosficio retorted.

"That doesn't give our courier enough time to deliver the letter," Holfast said dryly.

"I'll take it, then," Nosficio said, receiving murmurs and grimaces from the Witan. "I am, after all, *fleet-footed*, as His Highness aptly said. If I leave soon, I can get to Grelta by morning, and Nieve will have time to prepare for your arrival without making too much of a fuss."

"How can we trust you?" asked Vorae through squinted, judgmental eyes.

"You don't have much of a choice, Honorable Councilman," Nosficio said with a slick smile.

Ruenen didn't miss the sarcasm. He glanced at Holfast, who sighed through his nose, then produced a piece of blank paper from the pile on the table. He guided Ruenen through the response, as the rest of the Witan chimed in with suggestions. When finished, he handed Ruenen a stick of green wax and a heavy, royal Nevandian seal. It was a proper letter this time, unlike the note he'd scratched out to Nieve in the woods.

Ruenen stood and walked to Nosficio. He handed over the letter, giving the vampire his most stern expression. "We're trusting you with our lives, Lord Nosficio. Please ensure it arrives safely in Queen Nieve's hands."

Nosficio grinned, showing all his treacherous teeth. "I swear." He tucked the letter into his vest. "I've also come today with news and a warning."

What now? Ruenen rubbed at his temples; a headache began to build. The room was stifling. He needed air.

"You have an unwanted visitor on your lands," Nosficio said, face growing serious. At the confusion from the Witan, Nosficio leaned forward in his chair. "I spotted it last night near the Dale: a creature of darkness."

Vorae waved him off. "Excellent, let's befriend it! We're already doing that with every other unholy creature on this continent. What is it this time?"

Nosficio's intense gaze shot to him. "This creature isn't like the rest of us. I don't know what it is or where it came from, but it's not supposed to be here. It already attacked a farmer's cottage in the Dale. It must be taken care of. Today."

"How do we know it wasn't *you* who killed the family?" asked Fenir, a valid question, Ruenen honestly thought.

"The bodies were . . . ripped apart, charred. Not drained of blood." Genuine concern flitted across Nosficio's face.

Ruenen suddenly felt cold. If the vampire was nervous, the creature was most certainly trouble.

"A werewolf?" asked a councilman, his voice high and tight.

Keshel shook his head. "It wasn't a full moon last night."

"Does it matter what it was?" asked Vorae in annoyance. "It needs to be taken care of."

"I will go to the Dale," Marai said, getting to her feet and adjusting the weapons in the belt strapped around her waist.

"I shall accompany you," Nosficio said. He stood and bowed to the table. "And then I will leave to deliver your letter." His red eyes glistened, making most councilmen cringe.

Here was a chance to get out of this meeting.

"I'll come, too." Ruenen leapt to his feet, but a steady hand on his arm halted him.

"That is unwise, Your Highness," Holfast said, eyes steely. A warning for Ruenen to sit back down and remain in his place.

Ruenen did no such thing. He glared back at Holfast, but the Steward didn't remove his arm.

"You cannot go gallivanting off after this creature," said Vorae with a flippant wave to Marai and Nosficio. "Let *them* take care of it."

Ruenen's teeth ground together. Vorae's blatant insult sent a furious charge through Ruenen's bones. "The safety of all Nevandians is my responsibility. If there is indeed a dangerous, unknown creature loose on my lands, I want to ensure that it's destroyed."

"But there's much more to discuss here, Your Highness," Holfast pressed again.

The warning in his eyes didn't concern Ruenen. He needed to get out of this room. The weight of responsibility began to crush him. The fear of what else was yet to come.

"You can fill me in later. I trust you all to make the proper preparations for the upcoming battle." Ruenen joined Marai and Nosficio by the door.

"Accompany His Highness," Holfast said to Avilyard, resigned.

Ruenen didn't miss the annoyance in the Steward's tone. He glanced at Keshel instinctively. Marai trusted him, possibly more than she trusted anyone else. Ruenen knew he could, too. Keshel's eyes narrowed slightly, still not a fan of Ruenen, but he returned a curt nod. He'd remain and keep things focused. Keshel would ensure the fae's safety during Ruenen's absence.

Nosficio led Marai and Ruenen from the castle and out into the courtyard. Ruenen could barely get out the doors fast enough. He sucked air into his lungs as if he'd been drowning underwater and had just broken the surface. His headache cleared. His anxiety eased. At his side, Marai stared up at him.

"I'm fine . . . a little overwhelmed," he admitted.

Her eyes shimmered like cold flames from distant stars. For a moment, Ruenen got lost in them.

A loud cough brought him back to earth.

Nosficio shook his covered head, a smirk slithering onto his lips. "There's no time for that now, Prince."

The sky was overcast, a dull gray, but it *was* daylight. Nosficio adjusted his cloak and gloves, guaranteeing no skin was exposed to the sun's weak rays. Ruenen couldn't help but gawk at the boldness of this vampire.

"I'll meet you two at the Dale." Nosficio disappeared in a blur. The only indication of where he went were the gasps and staggers of servants in the courtyard that he'd swept past.

Ruenen and Marai were ushered through an archway by Avilyard and a unit of eight soldiers to the nearby stables. Ruenen hadn't spent much time on horseback in his life. Horses were expensive, and he'd never had the money to purchase one. Now, as Prince, he apparently owned several. He struggled into the saddle and held the reins with unconvincing confidence. Marai, however, sat effortlessly erect on the back of a black mare, as if she'd grown up riding across the desert sands. Ruenen had the sneaking suspicion that she could do anything if she tried.

Marai and her many gifts.

"Where did you learn to ride?" he asked.

"Casamere," she said with a shrug. During her time as a pirate.

As they clip-clopped down the winding cobblestone streets of Kellesar, people called his name from their windows. Children waved eagerly, as men and women bowed. Ruenen tried to smile and wave, but the knowledge of where he was going, what he was about to see, curdled the pride in his stomach.

Once out of the city, Ruenen steadied his nerves by focusing on Marai's wild hair. White blonde strands whipped around behind her as she galloped across the rolling highlands. Golden soldiers surrounded Ruenen on all sides, making it nearly impossible to speak with Marai. He wanted to know her thoughts about the creature and Nosficio, about leaving Keshel behind with the Witan alone. About traveling to Grelta. About what she thought Rayghast would do next. *Her* council was what he needed, not a room full of strangers.

But he kept it all inside.

The Dale was a scattered neighborhood in the valley that dipped low between two large craggy hills. A rock path wormed through, leading towards an open, recently-plowed field on the other side. A small thatched cottage stood alone, eerily devoid of life. Marai, Ruenen, and the soldiers slowed their horses to a canter as they approached the silent house.

Nosficio was already there at the door. "It's not a pretty sight."

The scent of blood and death assaulted Ruenen's nose. Marai entered the doorway first and froze. Ruenen walked right into her back—she'd stopped so quickly—and nearly emptied his stomach out onto the floor as he surveyed the carnage.

Bits of torn flesh and blackened bone littered the room, along with shredded clothing. Flies swarmed what was left of the carcasses, *the family*, who had once lived here. Viscera darkened the walls, and in pools on the floor. Furniture had been upturned and scattered across the one-room cottage. Ruenen had never seen such a gruesome sight. Not even the mutilation of the Chongans had been as destructive as this.

"What kind of creature could *do* this?" he asked, barely able to form the words without gagging. *His people* had died here because of dark magic.

Nosficio prowled through the room, calmly taking in the surroundings. He was known across Astye for creating similar scenes of gore and brutality.

The death didn't appear to bother his stony exterior. He sniffed the air. His pupils dilated.

The blood. It was everywhere. It must have been so tempting for Nosficio not to kneel down and lick the floor. Ruenen realized then the restraint Nosficio truly had. Another vampire might have gone crazy in a house full of spilt blood, but Nosficio remained in control. Agitated and tense, yes, but he didn't let the bloodlust, the *hunger*, consume him.

"I've never smelled anything like this before. It doesn't smell *of this world.*" Nosficio's nose crinkled at whatever else he smelled beyond the death.

"What do you mean?" Marai asked.

"I don't know. Sulfur? Like the Underworld . . ."

As a creature who had lived a thousand years, for Nosficio to be so puzzled made a chill skitter down Ruenen's neck. Had these creatures truly materialized from Rayghast's dark magic?

Ruenen leaned over to Marai. "Are you okay?"

She'd gone incredibly white. Her fists clenched at her sides. "I'm used to carnage. I'm used to killing. But this is different. An innocent family . . ." She turned her face so Ruenen wouldn't see how she shuddered.

He reached for her—

Screams from outside shook them all from their daze. Ruenen went rigid. That earlier chill froze his blood to ice at the sound of trained soldiers, grown men, so terrified.

It's here.

Without hesitating, Ruenen, Marai, and Nosficio dashed out the door into a scene of carnage.

One soldier had already been torn in two. His body lay discarded in bloody heaps. A second was currently in the grasp of a massive creature Ruenen knew would haunt his nightmares forever.

It had the head of a canine, but it was scaled in black and brown, with twisted, sharp horns atop its head. Its body was twice the size of the largest man among them, muscular and broad, with a leathery chest surrounded by more scales and bizarre ochre markings and lines, like war paint. Its hands and feet ended in long, thick hawk-talons, able to shred a body in seconds, as it was currently doing to the second soldier. Those talons cut through golden armor like a knife through melting butter.

"Fucking Lirr above . . . what in the Unholy Underworld is that?" Ruenen stammered, mouth going dry.

The creature snarled as it bit off the head of the second soldier and chewed, spitting out the distorted gold helm. Avilyard and the remaining soldiers encircled the creature, but none of them made a move forward. A few trembled.

Ruenen scented Marai's sparkling magic. She thrust out her hand, and a pulse coursed through the air. He'd witnessed Marai use this move multiple times before, but never against something so large. The creature stumbled backwards; its three green, slitted eyes snapped to Marai. Its mouth opened, revealing pieces of flesh and fabric stuck in its teeth.

Nosficio was the next to move. One moment he stood with Ruenen, then he appeared beside the beast, swiping his own sharp nails across its chest.

The creature roared and swatted at Nosficio, who dodged easily, but the vampire's strike barely broke its thick hide. Nosficio tried again, but the creature's skin was impenetrable. In a surprisingly human move, Nosficio punched the creature in the jaw. It barely faltered. Nosficio dodged another lumbering swipe.

Avilyard and his men pressed in. One shot an arrow that bounced off the beasts' scaled back. Avilyard threw a spear that lodged loosely into its shoulder. They were only succeeding in angering the creature more. It roared again and reached for the nearest soldier.

"Stand back," Marai shouted. The soldiers jumped out of the creature's reach as Marai raised both her arms, fingers wide.

White hot streaks of light burst forth from her palms. Magic snaked around the creature as lightning lit up the Dale. Several soldiers fell to the ground, covering their heads. A soldier sobbed out a desperate prayer. Ruenen shielded his eyes, hearing the creature bellow into the sky, a harsh language he'd never heard before. *Speaking,* crying out, as if it was a sentient being.

Through the slimmest opening, Ruenen glimpsed the magic surrounding Marai; magnificent, lethal, more powerful than before. She didn't look fae or human in that moment, surrounded by a white electric halo. This was the power of a goddess. Ruenen's skin tingled, heart raced. It wasn't from fear. It was *her*. Marai caused his adrenaline to spike, the blood to rush to his head, the heat to flush into every pore.

When the magic subsided, Ruenen blinked the white specks from his eyes. The usual smell of Marai's magic was overpowered by the scent of charred flesh.

The creature was a pile of ash on the ground.

A terrified soldier pointed his quivering finger at Marai. "She's . . . she's . . ."

"On your side," Marai said, lowering her arms.

Nosficio stared at Marai with something akin to delight. His eyes glimmered again, and his lips reared back into a grin. He leaned over to Marai's ear and said, "You were holding out on me. I can't wait to learn *what else* you can do."

Marai bristled and stepped away from him. Ruenen let out the breath he'd been holding for what felt like hours. The headache he'd had in the Witan chamber now pounded against his skull. The scent of dead bodies and monster lingered in the air, making him gag again. The elation he'd experienced from watching Marai was gone.

Avilyard approached the pile of ash, removing his helmet and running a hand through his hair. He lifted his gaze to Marai. "Your magic . . . it's the one thing that worked to pierce those scales." His voice didn't waver. His body didn't shake. He regarded Marai, instead, with curiosity. "Are there more of these creatures?"

"Yes," Nosficio said, appearing at Avilyard's side.

That was when the commander flinched. "How many?"

"Dozens? Hundreds? Impossible to know. All across the Middle Kingdoms, darkness is spreading. More of them will continue to venture into your towns and cities."

"But how do we stop them all?" pressed the commander.

"Alert your soldiers to be on the lookout for them," Ruenen said to Avilyard and the others. "Make sure gates and walls across Nevandia are manned at all times."

"But we're no match for them," one of the men shouted, staring at the mutilated corpses of his fellow soldiers.

"Then come find me," Marai said in her dry Butcher voice, "and I will dispose of them."

The man's throat bobbed.

Avilyard continued to stare at Marai. "You're going to be busy, then."

Marai's face hardened. Yet another job to add to her list: Lady Butcher, Bodyguard to the Prince of Nevandia, and now Monster Hunter.

"We must bury the dead," Ruenen said. Not just the soldiers, but the remains of the innocent family inside the cottage. They all deserved to be laid to rest.

He reached for a shovel that was propped up against the outside wall with other farming tools.

"My men will do that, Your Highness," Avilyard said with a stilling hand, his eyes sorrowful. He pointed at the two soldiers who hadn't completely fallen apart in fear. "You two will stay. Don't linger out here too long, in case there are more nearby. Be back by dusk."

The soldiers nodded as the others gathered their mounts, glancing hastily to the ash pile.

Nosficio approached Ruenen and Marai with a wicked smile, and said, "Thanks for the adventure. See you tomorrow," then disappeared.

Marai and Ruenen hoisted themselves up into their saddles and began the ride back to Kellesar. Back to more responsibility, more work and meetings, and most likely, more death if they didn't defeat Tacorn soon. Marai's face, however, was dubious. Something bothered her.

"What?" Ruenen asked, slowing his horse to a trot.

She pulled back on the reins, as well. "Dark magic created that thing. *I* used dark magic in Cleaving Tides. Maybe *I* created it. I might be the reason that family and those soldiers–"

"That wasn't your fault."

Marai stared down at her fingers with loathing. "This monster may not have been mine, but it's out there somewhere, doing the same in another town."

"We'll get them all, one day, I promise. Let's start by dealing with Rayghast. You saved innocent lives today by destroying that creature," Ruenen said gently.

"Did you hear it speak?" she asked, her forehead pinched. "That language . . . it sounded almost like ancient fae, but different. Whatever these creatures are, they're not animals."

Ruenen was wondering the same. "What do you think that means?"

Marai didn't respond. She kept her gaze straight ahead. Her legs tightened on her mare's sides, and she charged forward, leaving Ruenen and the soldiers behind, wondering if he should go after her. With Avilyard and his guards on all sides, Ruenen's movement was limited. Marai was already across the dead-heather-strewn hills near the city entrance. She rode onwards, following the Nydian River towards the horizon.

Ruenen sighed. *She'll ride all night to get away from what haunts her.*

After returning his horse to the stables, Ruenen couldn't bear to go inside, back to that stifling council chamber. The image of the eviscerated family seared his eyeballs. He didn't want to explain what he'd seen to Holfast and the others. He couldn't bring himself to talk about how the creature had slaughtered two of his men.

Mayestral greeted him in the courtyard. "Welcome back, Your Highness!"

"Can someone please bring me my lute?" Ruenen asked in near desperation.

Mayestral bobbed a bow and rushed off into the castle.

Lute finally in hand, Ruenen ventured to find a private place to play outdoors and take away the memories. He entered the training square next door. Wooden practice blades, bows and arrows, sharp spears, and real swords lined the wooden fence.

He wasn't Marai. A training ground wasn't his ideal form of relaxation, but there was nowhere else nearby as secluded. He sat down on a bench, closed his eyes, and his fingers began to strum away. He was conscious of Avilyard and his unit watching along the fence. They'd followed Ruenen from the stables. He could no longer wander freely as a royal. Protective eyes were always on him, but he shut them out as he played. This melody wasn't for them.

One with his music, Ruenen lost track of time. He played for the family. He played for the lost soldiers. He played to Lirr, hoping the goddess would guide their souls to peace.

He was tugged back to reality at the sound of metal.

Ruenen's eyelids fluttered open, revealing Marai railing Dimtoir against one of the wooden scarecrow posts in fierce concentration. Only then did he notice all the spectators around the fences. Avilyard and his unit hadn't left. In fact, more soldiers had joined, along with the stableboys. Even more shocking were the pointed ears and glowing eyes he saw in the crowd.

Marai walked over to Keshel, Raife, Leif, Aresti, Thora, and Kadiatu standing on the far side of the court.

"What are you doing here?" she asked as Ruenen came to her side.

"We came to pick up Keshel from his meeting," Raife said with a shrug, "but we heard music and wanted to see what it was."

"What happened in the Dale?" asked Keshel, lowering his voice.

Marai pursed her lips and glanced at Kadiatu. "I'll tell you about it later."

"This a training court," stated Aresti, surveying the weapons, posts, and archery targets.

"It's yours to use if you should ever want," Ruenen said.

Without wasting a moment, Aresti climbed over the fence with her long legs and strutted over to the wooden posts in the corner.

Ruenen stared after her. "I guess now is fine . . ."

Aresti unsheathed her two short swords and began spinning with the same effortless grace as Marai, plunging her swords into the padded scarecrows. Avilyard and his soldiers watched her with wide, interested eyes. She *was* truly a sight, strength and beauty combined, dressed in form fitting leather and linen.

"I think it's a good idea for these humans to see what we can do," Leif said. He, too, hopped the fence and entered the court. He plucked a bow and a quiver of arrows from against the fence. He nocked an arrow, pulling the string taut to his cheek. Leif let out a breath, and the arrow flew, lodging into the red bullseye.

With a cocky smile, Leif looked back at the soldiers. Marai rolled her eyes, but returned to the court. Raife followed, leaving Ruenen alone with Keshel, Thora and Kadiatu.

"Were you the one playing, Your Highness?" Thora asked, gesturing to his lute on the bench.

Ruenen blinked at her formality, then smiled. "You can call me Ruenen."

"That seems... disrespectful," said Thora, casting her ginger eyes to the dirt. "I don't want to be so informal, especially since your people are still getting to know you."

"I don't mind. Please, Thora, consider me a friend."

She gave Ruenen a smile.

"And yes, I do play," Ruenen continued. "Do you want to hear a secret?"

Kadiatu nodded with vigor, eyes gleaming with anticipation.

"I was a bard before I took up the throne. Marai first met me in a tavern. She called me a *lousy bard*."

Thora gasped as Kadiatu laughed. Keshel's face betrayed no reaction. He probably already knew the whole story.

"That sounds like Marai," Thora said, shaking her head, scandalized.

Ruenen chuckled. "She was right, though. I'm a much better musician now that I write my own songs."

"Will you play for us sometime?" asked Kadiatu.

"Kadi, you can't ask that of the Prince—" began Keshel.

"I'd be delighted to, if it would please you all."

"Oh, yes, please!" Kadiatu then tugged at Thora's arm. "Come, Thora. We can sit on the bench and watch. That nice commander who gave me the seeds, Avilyard, is over there. I want to thank him again."

Thora let herself be dragged away. Avilyard greeted Kadiatu with a warm smile as she approached him. Ruenen walked back onto the dirt where Marai and Raife were sparring. Aresti continued her work amongst the pillars.

Leif swaggered over to Ruenen.

"Let's see what you're capable of, Prince." He twirled a sword in his fingers as Marai always did.

On the sidelines, Avilyard stiffened and made a move to enter the court. Ruenen stopped him with a hand.

He wasn't afraid of Leif.

Ruenen grabbed a sword from the stack and faced his opponent.

Leif charged. Ruenen blocked. They swung, back and forth, on seemingly equal ground. Leif was stronger than Marai, but he didn't have her effortless skill or the ability to anticipate Ruenen's moves the way she always did. Leif hadn't spent years as a mercenary. He'd been sheltered in that desert; his only opponents were his own twin and Aresti.

Ruenen had seen more, *done* more, than the fae male before him. He knocked the blade from Leif's hand. The steel glinted as it flew through the air.

Marai caught the blade in her free hand, suddenly appearing at Leif's side.

Her smile spread. "You're dead, Leif."

CHAPTER 17
Marai

An ember of amusement sparked in the eyes of her fellow fae as they practiced together with Ruenen. Avilyard and his soldiers watched from behind the fence, aghast, as the fae performed with effortless skill. No magic—just weapons. The fae kept their secrets. For now.

Training went better than Marai could've hoped for. Shockingly, Leif seemed to come away from the afternoon without a single snarky thing to say. A gods-honest miracle.

They halted near sundown. The low orange sun cast muted watercolors across the sky as they wiped sweat from their faces.

"How did it go with the creature?" Keshel asked once Marai joined him, Thora, and Kadiatu at the fence.

Avilyard had volunteered to escort them home, but Thora politely refused and Kadiatu blushed at the commander's gentle smile. She stared at Avilyard from across the pitch.

"What creature?" asked Thora.

Marai cringed. She pictured the shadow creature crying out in agony in its native language. The encounter left her feeling uncertain, with more questions than she'd had before. Besides Keshel, none of her family had guessed she'd also created a creature of darkness.

Marai explained to the others what had occurred in the Dale, earning gasps from Thora and Kadiatu, and dark, steely expressions from Keshel and Aresti. She didn't mention her strange guilt.

Aresti jerked her chin haughtily over her shoulder at the remaining soldiers across the ring. "These men had better be grateful we're here. They'd be dead before long without us."

"He's very nice," stated Kadiatu, her voice high. "Commander Avilyard. He has kind eyes." She blushed at Marai's curious eyebrow.

"There's honor in being a knight, I suppose," Aresti said, ignoring Kadiatu's winsome comment and staring at the golden-clad men on the opposite side of the court.

"Yes, but you give up your freedom," said Keshel. "You become duty-bound to protect king and country, many times forsaking your own family."

Aresti continued to watch the soldiers, pondering Keshel's words. "At least they have purpose. Women here live in the shadow of men. They're barely allowed to work, reliant on a husband to survive. And if they *do* have a job, women earn less than their male counterparts. I'd loathe to give up my power that way . . ."

Marai asked Keshel, "How was the rest of the council meeting?"

Keshel sighed through his nose, his face transforming with weariness. "What one might expect of a council meeting in wartime. What towns need aid, how to enlist more soldiers, disagreements about how to handle Queen Nieve and Grelta, then what kind of treaties we might need *after* the battle with Tacorn. Running a country is . . . complicated."

Sounds miserable. Marai hoped she could stay far away from those topics. Ruenen may want her guidance, but she was useless in affairs of state.

"Aresti, those soldiers are staring at you," whispered Kadiatu, eyes wide.

Several soldiers had taken their helmets off and ogled Aresti's back. Perhaps they'd seen her watching them, but got the wrong idea. It wasn't entirely surprising that Aresti would receive such attention.

For her part, Aresti didn't glance back over to them. She huffed, full lips tilted into a smirk. "They can stare all they desire. Men and their attention do not interest me."

Surprise momentarily froze Marai as she met Kadiatu's equally shocked face. Marai also despised unwanted attention, from nearly everyone. But she was as charming as an eel and disliked most people. Aresti wore confidence as a perfume. Each swish of her hips captured men's gaze.

"We should return to the cottages now," Keshel said, exhaustion tugging at his words. "I don't want us traveling through the city at night."

Aresti waved to Leif, Raife, and Ruenen, who were still busy sparring two-against-one, swapping turns every ten minutes. "Time to go!"

The boys paused, wiping sweat from their faces. Was that a grin Marai saw on Leif's lips?

"Feel free to come here whenever you desire," Ruenen said. "What's mine is yours."

Marai couldn't stop the smile. Ruenen spoke to Leif and Raife like a friend, not at all like a human prince. His casual enthusiasm caught both fae males off-guard.

"Thank you." Raife bowed (Leif didn't), then joined Keshel and the girls on the street heading home. Marai watched Raife hurry to Thora's side and instantly begin conversation. Thora's entire face lit up. Marai felt a spurt of envy inside her at their effortless nature, the love they shared.

Ruenen took a long sip of water and wiped his mouth on the back of his hand. Droplets of perspiration glistened across his face and arms. He looked rather un-princely with his untucked shirt and discarded brocade vest in the dirt. Marai doubted Holfast would be pleased with the state of his clothing.

"The invitation is open to you, as well," Ruenen said with a wink. "Will you meet me tomorrow morning for breakfast?"

"I . . ." Marai paused. Was that wise? She *was* an advisor, and his personal guard, but would Holfast scold her for being alone with the prince? "Until tomorrow, then."

Ruenen smiled; his breathtaking, full-faced smile that reached his eyes, making them dance.

Was she worthy of that smile? A prince's attention? Of the home she'd been given? The nagging sensation of "undeserving" rose to the surface.

But in that moment, staring up at Ruenen's shining face, she felt it then: *You are enough. Exactly the way you are.*

"I want to come to Grelta with you," Aresti announced as soon as Marai stirred the next morning. She'd barely blinked the sleep from her eyes before Aresti stood over her bed of rushes, blankets, and one thin pillow.

"Why?" Marai asked, yawning.

Aresti pulled back the sides of her hair with pins. "It's smarter for us to travel in groups. You shouldn't go abroad on your own."

"You just want to see the Glacial Palace," Kadiatu said with a playful grin.

Marai rose to her feet and stretched. "Fine, but we aren't there for fun. We're acting as members of the King's Guard, alongside Commander Avilyard."

"I could be a better knight than them," Aresti replied under her breath, then bent down to lace up her boots.

Marai returned to fixing her braid. "Is that what you want to be? A knight?"

"You and I are better fighters than any of those men. I'd rather not be forced to rely on *them* to win the war."

She offered no further glimpses into her life as she sauntered from the bedroom, feet silently treading across the reeds and out the front door of the cottage. Perhaps Marai had more in common with Aresti than she'd thought...

Kadiatu was already fully dressed and ready for the day. Her round face burst into a smile. "Come and see what I've done with the garden!"

She led Marai out back, revealing the startling transformation. Thick green grass shot out of the ground. A rowan tree sprouted lustrous, red berries. The mineral, musty scent of rich dirt lingered in the air as hearty vegetables grew from tangled vines. Bright wild thyme, buttercups, and honeysuckles swayed in the breeze.

"How far can your power spread?" Marai walked to the farthest corner of the garden and knelt next to a flower bed of merry daffodils. She rubbed dark earth between her fingers, and felt no dark magic at all, no evil presence in the air or the soil.

"Oh, I don't know. I've never tried to do more than this small plot of land."

"Keep experimenting. See how far your magic can reach. Try spreading up the rest of the street."

Kadiatu's smile faltered. "But I don't have the strength you do, Marai. My magic's not so powerful."

Marai put a gentle hand on her shoulder. "None of us ever got to discover the limits of our magic. Give it a try. See what else you can do."

The words became caustic on her tongue. Marai grimaced. She sounded like Nosficio.

"I suppose I can try expanding into the neighbor's gardens... through the earth, of course. I won't go there in person." A pained yell from outside made Kadiatu jump.

Marai rushed to the front door, heart pounding. Was it from Keshel, Leif, and Raife's cottage next door?

Avilyard's two boy-soldiers, Elmar and Nyle, were still stationed outside the fae cottages. Their attention was focused on a commotion two houses up the dirt street.

A man stood outside his home, grasping at his bleeding hand. Marai recognized him from the other night. He and his wife hadn't taken well to having fae neighbors. He spewed a tapestry of curses so impressive Marai briefly thought she should take notes.

"What happened?" his wife asked, running out of their house. More neighbors appeared, also drawn by the noise.

"Hand slipped on the saw," he groaned, indicating the wood and rusted tool lying on the ground.

The wife took his hand and winced. Blood dripped down his arm and clothing.

Thora appeared at Marai's side. "That's a bad wound. Judging by the state of that saw, he could get an infection."

"Or lose the hand entirely," said Nyle.

Marai watched Thora intently. An aggrieved crease formed between her ginger eyes.

"Do you need help?" Marai shouted to the injured man.

Thora blanched and stepped backwards towards the door as the man and wife gawped at them.

"Not from the likes of *you*," the man snapped, then released a gasp of pain as his wife moved his hand.

Marai stepped closer. Thora tugged on her arm as Elmar and Nyle tensed.

"My friend here is a skilled healer. Let her take a look."

The man clutched his bleeding hand to his chest, eyes widening. He stumbled backwards over a piece of cut wood. "Don't touch me, you abominations!"

Marai's fingers twitched in time with the vein in her neck. She grit her teeth, taking another step towards the humans. Nyle and Elmar moved closer, hands on their swords, ready to intervene.

"Marai, stop," Thora said, pulling on her arm again, "let's go back inside."

The man grabbed the saw with his uninjured hand, raising it out in front of him.

Fine, let him suffer. Marai stomped back towards the cottage, then stopped in the doorway. She let out a harsh exhale.

They had to build a bridge. They had to find common ground. Humans and fae had to trust each other. If Ruenen and Leif could do it, so could this man.

Marai pulled her knife from her boot. The man and wife yelped and staggered backwards. With a quick slice, Marai dragged the knife across her own palm. Blood welled instantly, dripping onto the dirt below.

"What are you doing?" Thora asked, appalled.

Marai shoved her injured hand at Thora. "Heal me."

"What?"

"Let them watch."

Thora bit her lower lip, then took Marai's hand in her own. She closed her eyes and a blue light emerged from her gentle touch. Warmth spread over the wound as Marai's skin welded back together. When the pain and blood were gone, Marai and Thora looked up. Everyone was watching; the injured man, his wife, Elmar and Nyle, neighbors from up the street.

Marai raised her hand, revealing no wound, no scar. It was as if the cut had never happened. "We want to help you."

"That's amazing," whispered Elmar in awe, his acne-spotted jaw wide open.

The man swallowed and glanced back down to his shaking hand. "I don't have money for a healer."

There were no healers in Grave's End. And even *if* he did manage to scrounge up enough coin, the wound would most likely fester, and the hand eventually amputated.

"We're not after money." Marai dragged Thora lightly by the arm towards the man. Nyle and Elmar followed. "I'm assuming you'd rather not lose your hand."

"Go inside," the man ordered his wife.

She put a dismayed hand to her mouth, but dashed inside. Her beady eyes peered through the window as Marai and Thora slowly approached her husband.

The man pointed a quivering finger at them. "If you so much as—"

"We won't," Marai snapped back.

"May I... have your hand, please, sir?" Thora asked in a trembling voice.

The man breathed in short, raspy breaths. Ever so slowly, he opened his palm to reveal a nasty, gaping slice. It was hardly visible beneath all the blood and torn flesh. Thora's shaking fingers reached for his hand. The man yanked it back.

"I promise, I won't hurt you. When I was blessed with these healing gifts, I swore I would never use them for harm. Please, I can help you."

The man bit back a comment, glancing to Nyle and Elmar. He unfurled his fingers once again. At Thora's gentle touch, he flinched, but held his hand in place. That same warm, blue magic seeped from Thora's palms into his own. In seconds, the wound vanished, along with the blood. Color returned to the man's pallid face. His jaw dropped as he flexed his fingers, removing his hand from Thora's.

He avoided her eyes as he mumbled a curt thanks, then rushed back inside his cottage. Marai raised her head. The rest of the neighborhood, it seemed, had drawn in closer to watch. Wide eyes and whispers greeted her as Thora bit her lip again. One figure stepped out from the crowd.

"I... have a knee that twinges," said Elmar.

Marai noticed Raife leaning against the doorway of his cottage, arms crossed, watching Thora and the humans.

Thora wasted no time. "I can help with that." She gestured to a stump, and Elmar sat down, jutting out his left leg. Thora knelt and placed her hand over his kneecap. Again, healing light surrounded the guard's knee, and in moments, he got to his feet.

"Incredible," Elmar said with a smile. He bent his knee, back and forth. "The pain is gone!"

Louder murmurs traveled up and down the street. Elmar shook Thora's hand, and she blushed from head to toe.

"We'll soon have a line out the door," Raife said, giving her a grin. Thora's face flushed a deeper pink. Raife turned to Marai. "Can you take Leif to court with you? He can't stand being cooped up in that cottage any longer. He's unbearably irritating."

"That doesn't make me want to take him," Marai said dryly. "What about you?"

Color bloomed on Raife's freckled cheeks. "I think I'll stay here with Thora today. And Kadi. So they can continue their work."

The look that passed between Raife and Thora brought a sudden sadness to Marai. And envy. How glorious it would feel to be so self-aware. To be so in-love. They didn't hide their affection from each other. Maybe they never acted on it, but at least they knew how they felt. Love shimmered between those glances like threads of magic, tethering them to each other.

Keshel marched out of the cottage, Leif and Aresti in tow. Thora stepped away from Raife, who pretended to pick dirt out from under his fingernails.

"Come," Keshel said, sweeping past, long hair fanning out behind him, glossy in the sun's rays.

Marai joined at the end of the pack, leaving Thora, Raife, and Kadiatu behind in the street. They hiked up to the castle, where Keshel and Marai dropped Leif and Aresti off at the training ring fence.

"Don't stay out here too long," Keshel warned them, "It's going to rain."

The sky at that moment was mostly sunny and the air pleasantly tepid. Birds whistled and chirped in the nearby barren trees. The sky didn't exhibit signs of rain, but Keshel *knew*. Leif waved him off and settled into the court with Aresti.

Marai and Keshel parted ways in the entrance hall of the castle. He turned right into the Witenagemot chamber, while Marai headed upstairs to Ruenen's private dining room. She spotted him in the hallway, staring up at a portrait of a young couple.

The handsome man stood behind a chair, where his wife sat demurely. At first, Marai thought the woman was Queen Larissa, but Ruenen stared at the painting in such a sad, wistful way that Marai knew it wasn't her.

"I've walked past this portrait multiple times, and I only now realized who they are," Ruenen said. His fingers traced the wooden frame, but dared not touch the canvas. His face betrayed a hunger and *longing* that made Marai's throat constrict and burn. If anyone saw Ruenen next to this portrait, there would be no doubt as to who his father truly was. Lord Rehan had Ruenen's eyes and strong jaw, and Marai bet that if the man had been posed smiling, he would've had dimples in his cheeks. Lady Morwenna was, indeed, nearly identical to her sister, Queen Larissa, but her hair was the chestnut shade of Ruenen's.

He swallowed. "I would've liked to have known them. She wrote me letters. Dozens of them. I burned all the letters in Holfast's chest, but not hers."

Marai reached for his hand, but Mayestral rounded the corner and she hastily stuffed her hand in her dress pocket. Two guards appeared behind the Groom.

"Breakfast is ready, Your Highness," Mayestral said with a bow, "and for Lady Marai, as well."

"Your shadows are back again, I see," Marai whispered as she and Ruenen followed Mayestral into the dining room, the guards a few paces behind.

Ruenen made a face. "Apparently, I'm not allowed to go anywhere on my own. I swear, Mayestral would come into the privy with me if I didn't forbid it."

Marai had to stop herself from laughing as Mayestral turned, bowing again, after pulling out Ruenen's chair at the same four-person table. Eggs, breads, fragrant sausages and bacon, and buttered scones sat on gold platters. Coffee from Henig steamed in a pot next to a carafe of fruit juice.

"I shall be in the hall, Your Highness," Mayestral said, oblivious to Ruenen's comment. He exited the room, but the guards remained.

Ruenen grabbed two of everything in front of him. "I think this is my favorite part of being royal."

Marai smiled, and started with coffee, a hard-boiled egg, and a piece of oat and seed bread.

"Sleep well?" Ruenen asked lightly, slicing up a juicy sausage. He stuck one in his mouth and moaned with delight.

"I slept on a bed of reeds," Marai said, swiping a pad of butter across her bread. "I'm used to roughing it outdoors. I don't mind."

Ruenen chuckled, a low, warm sound that Marai felt in her chest. "You can always sleep here at the castle. Lirr knows we have the space, and you already have a room set aside."

A glint in his eye made Marai think he *wanted* her to sleep at the castle. Marai didn't answer. Instead, she salted her egg and tried to eat as politely as she could. With the guards watching, she felt strangely self-conscious. Did one use a fork to eat an egg? How do you peel it without making a mess? How many cups of coffee was deemed acceptable? Ruenen dispensed with all decorum and ate mostly with his hands, easing Marai's anxiety slightly.

Upon finishing, Ruenen stood and stretched from side to side. "Ready to whip me into shape?"

Marai nodded, grateful to be outside and away from gold and marble, etiquette and standards.

Aresti and Leif were already sweating by the time Marai and Ruenen met them in the ring.

"Good of you to finally join us," Leif said to Marai. "Did you dine on pheasant or truffles during your fancy breakfast at the castle?"

Marai ignored him. Ruenen discarded his coat and vest, plucking a sword from the weapons rack. Marai unsheathed Dimtoir and pointed it at him. A challenge. Ruenen smirked, devilishly, and his steel met her blade.

After the usual back and forth, Ruenen dropped his blade and caught Marai off-guard, grabbing her from behind. His strong arms wrapped around her, lifting her feet from the ground. She had no leverage to fight him off. There was nothing she could do. But instead of fear coursing through, Marai felt *heat*.

The nearness of him . . . his arms wrapped around her, not possessively, but playful. Ruenen's clothes smelled of fire smoke mixed with the intoxicating clean scents of lavender and coffee.

Marai had the urge to lick the smell right off him.

Ruenen didn't sense that shift in her as he laughed in her ear. He released his hold on her body, setting her back gently to the ground.

"You left yourself wide open. That's the first time I've ever bested you." His smile fell as he took in her expression. Marai hadn't moved. She didn't know what her face betrayed. "I'm sorry . . . I forgot you don't like to be held. Or touched."

Ruenen's eyes flickered down to his hands.

"It's fine," she said. She wanted to trace a finger across his furrowed brow and erase the tension and concern. To speak and show affection with ease the way Thora and Raife did. "I'm fine."

He met her stare, met it and searched for the lie he thought she was telling. But she wasn't lying. She *was* fine. She'd felt no panic when his arms had trapped her. No flashbacks or images of Captain Slate Hemming passed through her mind.

No, now she had a different problem.

Marai wanted Ruenen's hands all over her. She wanted what Thora and Raife had, even if they chose to hide it.

Her nostrils flared as she tried to smother the fire burning in her veins. Marai contorted her face into the steely mask of the Butcher, hoping Ruenen wouldn't find the cracks in her armor.

Ruenen, unaware of Marai's trail of thought, turned back to the fence where the soldiers remained, like gold statues.

"Why don't you all join us?" he asked. The soldiers shifted awkwardly on their feet, glancing at one another. "It must be terribly dull to stand there all day watching."

Slowly, the six soldiers made their way onto the court. They kept their helmets on and distance from the fae.

Leif had been waiting for this opening. A chance to fight the humans. He might go as far as to actually injure his opponent for revenge. Ruenen merely smiled.

"We need to learn to work together if we're going to win this war," Ruenen said, meeting each pair of eyes, glancing between the soldiers and the fae. When no one moved, Ruenen leaned into Marai's ear. "Help me out."

Marai groaned, then pointed her sword at the nearest soldier. "You. Come."

The soldier stammered. Someone shoved him forward. He held up his sword, gathering up his focus and breath. Ruenen paired Leif and Aresti up with soldiers. Marai tried to keep one eye on Leif and Aresti at all times, but despite being more aggressive in their movements than usual, everything seemed to be calm. A ripple of tension pulsated through the air as two sides of a centuries-long animosity trained together. It wasn't friendly, but it *was* progress.

Not long after, cool spring rain splashed across Marai's cheeks. This lasted a moment before the clouds opened up, and a deluge poured down, taking them all by surprise. Keshel, of course, hadn't been wrong.

Ruenen and Marai dashed inside the storage hut nearby. There wasn't room for anyone else in the cramped space, so Leif, Aresti, and the soldiers ran further, ducking inside the stables. Rain pelted the clay shingled roof of the hut as Ruenen and Marai stared at each other, chilled, and soaking wet to the bone.

Ruenen let loose a giddy laugh. And another. And soon, he was laughing like a fool in triumph.

"What are you so pleased about?"

"They were *sparring*, Marai!" Ruenen beamed, swiping wet hair from his eyes. "Fae and humans together. Peace between us is *possible*."

Marai shook her head, chuckling, too, and swung her dripping hair behind her back. She leaned against a crate of tools. It took a moment for Marai to realize that none of the soldiers were around. None of Ruenen's constant shadows.

They were alone.

Their first private moment together since they'd received Nieve's letter two nights ago.

Ruenen didn't seem to notice. He spoke animatedly about the soldiers and fae training together, but as Marai listened, she couldn't stop herself from taking in the sight of the man before her.

The air inside the hut grew closer. Ruenen's white tunic clung to his chest, revealing all the lean muscle underneath. Marai's eyes lingered there, then slowly rose to his face, enjoying every glorious inch of him. Heat flooded her cheeks when her gaze landed on his mouth.

Ruenen cocked his head, noticing the sudden hunger in her gaze.

Dangerous territory. Dangerous to be alone with him, yet not at all afraid.

He didn't blink or breathe.

The need to touch him became too difficult to ignore.

Marai closed the space between them in two strides. She grabbed hold of the collar of his tunic and pulled his mouth to hers.

Ruenen remained stiff as a board as her lips crushed his. His lips remained cautiously soft against her hungry kiss. His hands fisted at his sides, as if he thought his touch would hurt her, would send her reeling back to memories of Slate.

But she was in control. This was *her* choice.

Nothing else mattered except for the feel of his lips on hers, the firmness of his chest under her fingers. She took one of his hands and guided it to her waist. The minute his fingers curled around her, Marai gasped against his mouth.

Ruenen stopped holding back then.

His tongue glided across hers. She sucked on his bottom lip, something she'd been dreaming of doing for far longer than she wanted to admit. She tasted the sweaty-saltiness of him from training. It was intoxicating.

Ruenen let out a surprised moan; the sound of it reverberated through her bones.

Her whispered name on his lips nearly did her in.

Her fingers stroked across his chest and arms. Marai wanted to touch him everywhere. He pushed her backwards up against the crates of tools and supplies, and nibbled at her earlobe. Marai tilted her head backwards, allowing Ruenen to kiss up the column of her throat. She wrapped both arms around him, but there was too much distance between them. She wanted all of him, enveloping her.

Ruenen shuddered and gripped Marai tighter. His fingertips traveled up and down her spine in tortuous, frenzied strokes. Marai's hands found the hem of his shirt, inching beneath to graze his abdomen—

"Your Highness?" came a shout from outside.

Ruenen and Marai leapt apart, panting, faces red and lips swollen. Marai searched Ruenen's face for any sign of regret. There wasn't an ounce of it. If anything, he looked as if he could barely keep himself standing up straight.

The rain outside had calmed to a drizzle. Voices called for the prince again.

"Here," Ruenen shouted, although it was a strained sound. He hadn't taken his eyes off Marai yet. He ran a hand through his wet hair.

Soldiers, including Avilyard, appeared at the hut door. More sloppy feet sounded down the muddy path, and Keshel, Holfast, and Ambassador Goso poked their heads in the door.

"Ah, there you are," Holfast said. "We were hoping you didn't get caught in the rain."

Ruenen hastily adjusted his tunic, turning on his princely swagger. "Briefly. We decided to wait in here until it stopped." He forced his voice to be level, but Marai heard its breathlessness.

Keshel observed Ruenen then Marai. He knew. The bastard could sense it. Or maybe it was so plainly written on their faces.

"Your Highness, it's time to prepare for your visit to Grelta. Councilman Goso has discussion points he needs to go over with you," said Holfast.

Ruenen walked stiffly to his side. Goso chirped advice as he led Ruenen back towards the castle, followed by the retinue of soldiers. Only Keshel remained, staring blankly at Marai.

"Be careful."

"Of what?" she asked, crossing her arms.

"Your heart."

"My heart is none of your business." Marai stalked outside past him into the spritzing rain.

"I don't wish to see you so broken ever again."

Marai bristled. She wouldn't break. Not like she had after leaving Slate, or Cleaving Tides, and certainly not by Ruenen's hands. This time, she was in control. This time, she was safe. Marai focused on her feet, on each step, grounding her to the wet stone beneath her slippers, as she walked into the castle hall.

Guards were stationed outside the doors. Marai was about to enter when she heard the sound of light feet behind her.

Aresti appeared at her side. "I'm coming today, remember?"

"I remember." Although, Marai was hesitant to bring Aresti with her. Splitting up the fae any further would weaken them. Marai knew *she* could handle herself if things went wrong in Grelta, but she couldn't guarantee Aresti's safety. And back here in Nevandia, if anyone rebelled against the new fae agreements in Ruenen's absence, the fae would be vastly outnumbered.

"When do we leave?" Aresti asked, craning her neck upwards to stare at the hall ceiling.

As if in response, the chamber doors open. Avilyard marched out. He spotted Marai and Aresti against the wall.

His deep voice echoed off the marble and granite as he said, "The Witan is ready."

CHAPTER 18
Ruenen

Ruenen wiped sweaty hands on his refined outfit of velvets and silks, as Marai and Aresti followed Avilyard back into the room. Mayestral had dressed Ruenen in gold and forest green to represent Nevandia abroad, as per Holfast's request.

Goso and a younger man, his assistant, who reminded Ruenen of a mosquito, stood with Avilyard and eight King's Guards clumped to the side of the chamber.

"What is *she* doing here?" asked Vorae, gesturing to Aresti.

"*Aresti* wants to help protect His Highness," Marai said quickly before Aresti could retort. "She's a trained fighter. I should think you'd be relieved to have more protection for His Highness."

Vorae grumbled something to Fenir, but said nothing more.

Ruenen approached Aresti and smiled. "I'm glad to have your help."

He expected her usual dismissive shrug, but instead she nodded respectfully, perhaps under the impression that this was some kind of "audition" for her, though Ruenen couldn't imagine what for.

"We should be on our way," Goso said, waving the King's Guard over towards Ruenen.

Marai met Ruenen's gaze. His smile turned cat-like. "After you, Lady Marai."

She shot him a sneer, one Ruenen knew the entire Witan saw, as she raised her hands. Multi-colored magic rushed down her arms and out through gloved fingers. The Witan and guards backed away, tripping over their own feet at the sight of magic. The portal shimmered and crackled into place, revealing glittering snow on the other side. A chill nipped Ruenen's cheeks.

"This will drop us off a short walk from Lirrstrass and the Glacial Palace."

Marai had told Ruenen over breakfast that she didn't want them to simply appear out of thin air in the middle of the unsuspecting capital city of Grelta. That would likely not go well with first impressions.

"I'll check the area," Aresti said, and without waiting for a response, stepped into the portal. Councilmen gasped. Goso's assistant quivered, holding tightly to his briefcase. After a moment, Aresti's face appeared on the other side. "All clear."

Avilyard sent four guards in first, followed closely by Goso and his nervous assistant. Ruenen turned around, meeting Holfast's stern eyes. Every wrinkle was visible in the warning the Steward gave him.

"I'll keep him safe," Marai said, noticing Holfast's serious expression.

Ruenen stepped into the portal, feeling the threads of Marai's magic swirl around him, caressing his skin as the Glacial Palace came into view.

Frigid air ripped through him, biting at his nose and exposed fingers. A layer of snow coated the ground, crunching beneath Ruenen's feet. His breath puffed out in whorls.

Right. Back in the North. Ruenen was begrudgingly grateful that Holfast had forced him to wear the white fur cloak. Already, Ruenen missed the temperate spring weather in the Middle Kingdoms. Grelta was still in the throes of winter; they wouldn't see spring here for several more weeks.

Ruenen had seen the fanciful Glacial Palace before. Something from a storybook, the castle sat before a background of the snow-capped White Ridge Mountains and glistening forests of pine. He'd come to Lirrstrass several times during his travels, before he'd hired Marai. Before they'd begun this insane journey together. Before he'd *kissed* her in the shed a few hours ago...

Don't think about that. Ruenen forced his eyes to focus ahead on the road, and not to Marai at his side. They hadn't returned to Grelta as the Lady Butcher and Ard the Bard.

"Come, Your Highness, we must be quick," Goso said, marching onwards, followed by his assistant.

Guards surrounded Ruenen on all sides, including Marai and Aresti, as they passed over a wide bridge. The frozen stream below cut the castle off from the rest of the capital city of Lirrstrass and the nearby alpine lake and pine forests. Marai's portal had dropped them in the woods up the road, away from the prying eyes of the city. Now, however, people noticed them and the Nevandian banner they carried. Burly Northerners lined the streets in their thick fur coats and boots, watching with curious eyes as Ruenen's retinue passed through.

"Make way, make way," said Goso in a commanding, pompous tone. "Make way for Prince Ruenen of Nevandia."

Then the whispers really started. People flocked to the road, hoping to catch a glimpse of the newest ruler in the Nine Kingdoms.

"Is that truly necessary?" Ruenen asked the ambassador as several women waved.

"Of course, Your Highness. If you want to have a respectful alliance, it starts here with these commoners." Goso continued to shout his commands to citizens crossing the road.

The guards, Marai, and Aresti kept their hands on their weapons, alert, as they approached the metal grate of the Glacial Palace. Constructed from Northern obsidian rock, the castle sparkled in the remaining daylight. Snow caked the turrets, towers, and inclines. Icicles dripped from its many roofs and arched windows. The large Greltan flags on the four tallest towers were frozen stiff from ice. It was a palace from a fairytale.

Except for the nightmare leaning casually against the black gate.

Nosficio's feline grin spread wide, exposing both fangs, as he bowed. "Your Highness, Ambassador . . . Lady Marai." He straightened, focusing now on Ruenen. Nosficio sniffed in his general direction.

Lirr's Bones, could Nosficio smell Marai on him?

The vampire raised a knowing, cocked eyebrow. *Yes, he could.*

"Queen Nieve anxiously awaits your arrival," Nosficio said.

Ruenen swallowed. His palms sweat inside his gloves despite the cold. Nevandian guards blocked Nosficio from getting closer, but the vampire leaned in towards Ruenen.

"She was quite surprised at your sudden arrival, but she is *very* curious." Nosficio looked to Marai, then Aresti. His nostrils flared, scenting her fae blood. "And who, may I ask, are you?"

Aresti regarded Nosficio with caution and skepticism. "None of your concern, vampire."

The silver Greltan soldiers surrounding the castle leered darkly at Nosficio, but they hadn't harmed the vampire, which meant that his appearance wasn't unexpected. Possibly normal. Nosficio turned to the guards at the gate.

"His Royal Highness, Prince Ruenen of Nevandia, has arrived to speak with Her Majesty Queen Nieve. Perhaps you could open the gate," Nosficio said with all the finesse of a practiced courtier.

The guards stiffened, but then proceeded to raise the iron grate. Ruenen and his retinue entered the courtyard. Intricate ice sculptures of the gods surrounded a frozen pond. Ruenen had never seen such craftsmanship before. Lirr twirled, the ice of her dress perfectly capturing the movements, eyes sparkling in joy as a tree sprouted at her feet. Laimoen was mid-stab with his dagger, face set in a fierce gurn. Each of the sculptures were so realistic that if they were not crystal-clear, Ruenen might be convinced the gods were really there, affixed in their poses.

The mighty wooden doors to the palace swung open, and a figure dressed in white emerged. She would have blended in entirely with the snow had it not been for red hair blazing underneath her crown of ice and silver.

Ruenen had never seen a woman hold such command in her posture and stare. Nieve walked with elegance and authority. Strong, steady steps; gown trailing behind her. She was in her forties, Ruenen knew, but her pale face was relatively smooth, save for the black mole by her pointed nose and a few crow's feet. Her blue eyes took in everything around her. A calculating expression Ruenen had seen many times from Marai. The queen's eyes narrowed ever so slightly as Nosficio led the way to the steps leading up the palace.

"Lord Goso, it pleases me to see you again," Nieve said. A courteous smile slid on her face, but it didn't reach those ice blue eyes.

Her husband, the king and rightful ruler of Grelta, was nowhere to be found, but two adolescent children appeared on either side of Nieve, both with equally alarming red hair. The boy was older, whip-thin with none of the imposing presence of his mother. His sister, a head shorter and willowy, hid behind the queen.

Nieve reached out a hand. Several large, glittering jewels graced her slender fingers. Goso kissed her hand with a ceremonious bow.

"You are as beautiful as always, Your Grace," he oozed.

Nieve removed her hand from his grasp, without acknowledging the compliment. Her eyes honed in on Ruenen. Her shoulders shifted, her chin raised, as she beheld him. Her intense eyes grazed him up and down, leaving Ruenen feeling exposed, stripped naked.

"My children," Nieve said, gesturing behind her. "Crown Prince Hiver and Princess Elurra."

Both red-headed young royals bowed and curtsied with effortless grace. They were far more polished than Ruenen was, and they were almost half his age.

"May I present his Royal Highness, Prince Ruenen Avsharian," Goso announced in a bold voice for all to hear, stepping down to allow room for Ruenen.

A man Ruenen hadn't noticed before shifted closer to the queen. He wore a white full-face mask and a gray cloak. Something about his hunched posture was familiar. Ruenen couldn't place it.

"You're a plucky one, aren't you?" Nieve asked; her lilting voice was a seductive caress across his cheeks. This was a woman who had power and knew how to wield it. "Your first note was unconventional. Your second note, even more so. How ever did you manage to arrive here so quickly? And without any of my sentries alerting me to your passage."

Her gaze drifted to Marai and Aresti.

She knows. Nosficio told her about the fae. Her daughter peered at Marai and Aresti from around Nieve's shoulder with round blue eyes.

However, it was the hunched man whom Nieve looked to for confirmation. The white mask bobbed up and down as he nodded. That was when Ruenen recognized him. This was the man who'd hired Marai to give a "warning" to Nosficio in Iniquity.

"This is my Master of Spies," Nieve said, gesturing to the man. The hunchback bowed awkwardly.

"I'm pleased and honored to meet you all," Ruenen said, not trying to hide his shiver as he kissed her bejeweled hand. "Could we continue this inside, in more pleasurable temperatures?"

"My apologies, we of the North have thick skin. Sometimes we forget that not everyone is accustomed to the cold," Nieve said, her smile widening. Then her eyes drifted to Nosficio, standing to the side of the King's Guards. Her face grew serious. The Master of Spies tensed behind his mask. "If you're taking responsibility for the vampire, I must demand that he remain on his best behavior. He claims to be your emissary."

"He'll behave," Nosficio stated. "He ate dinner an hour ago." He licked his lips again.

Nieve watched the movement and didn't shy away from it. Instead, her eyes darkened. The frozen air suddenly felt close and heavy.

Nieve turned and glided inside the castle, her white gown and children trailing. Ruenen and Goso followed first. Marai, Aresti, Nosficio, and the guards hung back, granting space to the lords and royalty as they walked into the nearest chamber. The prince and princess excused themselves, and went up one of the various staircases, followed by a handful of courtiers.

Nieve's council room housed two silver and white bone thrones. Her council, in robes of ivory and robin's-egg blue, were as tall, fair, and broad as most Northerners. They bowed as Nieve took a seat in one of the thrones.

"My husband will join us shortly. He cannot stay for long, but he does want to be cognizant of the discussions."

Curiosity tapped against Ruenen's brain. The King of Grelta was mysterious. No one ever saw him. He didn't make public appearances, at least not for many years.

Nieve crossed one leg over the other and sat back in her throne. "You keep interesting company, Prince Ruenen. Not only women, but faeries and vampires, at that."

Behind him, Ruenen heard the shifting of feet and clothes and armor. He imagined Marai's hand moving to Dimtoir.

"I keep worthy company," he said, sharpening his words with warning. "Everyone standing with me has the same goal to defeat King Rayghast."

"How did you garner such loyalty from a race of people we have been at war with for centuries?" Nieve asked, arching a graceful eyebrow.

Ruenen scowled, spine stiffening. His pulse throbbed in his neck.

"Relax, Prince. I don't fear or despise magical folk the way most people do. If I'm to send my troops to your war, I want to know more about why *you* are so trustworthy."

Pain flared in his jaw as Ruenen clenched his teeth. *Why, indeed . . .*

"Because he views the world through open eyes." Marai's voice, sharp as a blade, sliced through the air.

Ruenen's heart galloped against his ribcage in response.

"Because *he* trusts us." Marai came to Ruenen's side. Her arm grazed his, sending sparks up and down his skin. "He values life, no matter whose it is."

Nieve stared at Marai, unflinching.

"This is Lady Marai," Ruenen said; the words came out hoarse and thick. "She's my personal guard, most honest advisor, and closest friend."

Friend hardly described what Marai was to him. If he looked at her now, Ruenen knew he would damn all the people in the room and sweep Marai into his arms. The memory of Marai's lips nearly brought him to his knees …

Instead, Ruenen focused on Nieve, whose face betrayed nothing. A mask of calm.

A door opened on the side of the chamber, and two figures entered. The smallest of the two leaned on the arm of the broad man at his side. The smaller shook from head to toe; each step was arduous, tentative. His gaunt face was tightly scrunched, as if concentrating hard, but his jaw twitched. His body was hunched, frail, and in constant, uncontrollable motion.

Nieve stood fluidly. "Ah, Husband, please welcome our guests Prince Ruenen of Nevandia, Lord Goso, and Lady Marai of the fae."

The King of Grelta was slowly ushered up the stairs to his throne. The barrel-chested servant at his arm helped him sit gently down upon the cushion. Even sitting, the king jerked, not once calming to stillness.

King Maes stammered something quietly to his wife. She smiled warmly, giving his knee a pat. It was the first time her smile met her eyes. She whispered back to him before she faced the room.

"His Grace, my husband, is happy you're here. He regrets his late arrival. It's difficult for him to get anywhere in a timely fashion," she explained to the Nevandian entourage.

Ruenen tried to hide his shock at the sickly king before him. *This is why Nieve rules the kingdom. Why she welcomes others into her bed.*

Nieve placed a hand on her husband's quivering arm. "You're here to forge an alliance, Prince Ruenen. Your friendship and trust with magical folk is admirable. No other ruler would be so bold. But it's in fact Lady Marai's words that convinces me to grant you the aid you seek." Nieve stood and stepped down the dais. Her blue eyes scoured Ruenen's face, as if searching for his weakness. "We're a non-traditional kingdom here, Prince Ruenen." Nieve gestured behind her to the king, who watched with bright, interested eyes. "Our king is ill, so I, a woman, must rule in his stead. Other kingdoms and empires on Astye doubt us. Scorn us. Consider us *weak*."

Ruenen heard the subtle message. Men doubted *her*, a female ruler, a woman with power on a continent that granted few rights for "the weaker sex."

"I spent many months here in Grelta before I took the throne," Ruenen said. "Only a fool would look at your people and see weakness. They are hearty, determined, and resourceful. The women even more so."

Nieve's eyebrow twitched; she liked his response. "King Rayghast is abhorrent. I've heard how he treats his wives and female subjects. I know what torture he's so fond of in those dungeons." The elegant planes of Nieve's face grew severe and harsh. "He sends his troops onto my land, pillaging my towns and hurting my people, without an ounce of respect for our borders. When his council sought my daughter's hand for marriage, I refused. I wouldn't let her be shackled to such a despicable man. Since then, I've felt Rayghast's resentment breathing down my neck. Because I slighted him, I know Grelta will be the first after Nevandia on his trail of conquest. He doesn't deserve to rule, and I certainly won't allow him to conquer my territory.

"And Nosficio tells me of these so-called *shadow creatures*. He claims Rayghast created these violent beasts using some type of magic." Nieve's chest rose with contempt. In a loud, commanding voice, she continued. "He's despicable, and a threat to all Nine Kingdoms. It is for these reasons, Prince Ruenen, that King Maes and I agree to ally with you."

Ruenen let out an un-princely sigh of relief. Goso murmured his approval, nodding voraciously with his assistant and the Greltan council members.

"Of course, we cannot send all our troops to Nevandia," Nieve said. "Eight hundred mounted cavalry should suffice. We must maintain defenses here along our borders. And our alliance should be forged with steel: treaties and trade guaranteed. And also marriage."

Ruenen froze.

Nieve chuckled. "Oh, don't look so frightened, Prince. Our daughter is but thirteen, and too young for you. I don't believe in giving girls away as brides for political gain. No, we will find proper matches when the time is right between members of our courts. Perhaps when you have an heir of your own."

Ruenen's cheeks warmed and he let loose a weak laugh. Children seemed a long way off in his mind.

"I believe we can come to terms that benefit both of our nations," he said. "Lord Goso is the better man for such details."

Goso puffed out his chest and beamed. A Greltan councilman put a cordial arm around his shoulders, and Goso was soon surrounded in hushed conversation with the men. His assistant bobbed around on the outside of the clump, handing Goso documents and papers and maps.

"We've prepared a feast for tonight in your honor, Your Highness," Nieve said, smiling once again. "I've invited a small number of the court, as well as our council. Let us cast these bonds as we eat and drink."

Goso and the council applauded. King Maes' face stretched into a tight, quaking grin; his eyes crinkled with warmth.

"It would be an honor, Your Grace," Ruenen said with a bow.

Nieve barked orders to servants who'd been standing at attention against the wall. They disappeared as Nieve took Ruenen's arm and guided him through a set of large double doors, into the magnificent banquet hall. Several long tables were decorated with winter greens, holly, candles, and silver runners. Ice sculptures of dancing women and men stood dispersed around the room, dripping slow puddles onto the floor. Splendid savory smells wafted up from the kitchen somewhere. Servants were already at work pouring wine into goblets on the tables.

A group of spritely musicians sat in the corner. They struck up their instruments when Nieve stepped into the room. Ruenen's hands yearned to strum against his lute, and his voice ached to sing along. That corner, with those musicians, was where he'd much rather be.

Instead, the Nevandian guards stationed themselves behind his chair as Ruenen took a seat at the head table. Goso and the Greltan council sat across from him, fully engaged in energetic discussion. Marai moved to stand with Aresti and Nosficio against the nearby wall, away from others, but still within reach of Ruenen. Nieve's Master of Spies blended into a dark corner, but his hawkish eyes watched all movement in the room.

"Would you desire a change of clothes, Lady Marai?" Nieve asked before sitting. With a thoughtful expression, she watched Marai standing against the wall. "There's an empty seat for you next to Lord Goso."

Marai's face remained emotionless. "I'm the prince's guard, Your Grace."

"You're not dressed like a knight of the King's Guard." Nieve regarded Marai's wrinkled, dirt-covered sack dress; the wild flyaways of her hair. "I believe I heard the prince say you were his closest friend and advisor. Should you not attend this feast as a lady of such standing?"

A muscle twitched in Marai's jaw as she picked at her fingernails.

"That's—"

"Very kind of you," Ruenen leapt in. "Lady Marai isn't one for formality, but she *should* attend the feast."

Marai shot him a startled look.

"My daughter, Princess Elurra, is near your size," Nieve said, inspecting Marai up and down again. "I shall have someone bring you up to change."

Ruenen stifled a laugh at the thought that Marai was small enough to fit into the clothes of a thirteen-year-old.

Nieve called over a servant with a snap. Marai's feet didn't move until Ruenen waved her on and Nosficio nudged her. She scowled at them both, but followed the servant from the hall, back rigid. Marai knew better than to disobey the queen's command, not when they needed Nieve's support.

Aresti snickered.

The Queen's penetrating gaze scrutinized her too, but in a different way. "You are not a lady?" The question was direct; her tone sensual.

Aresti's dark eyes brightened at the queen's question, a crooked smile blooming. "Not regularly, Your Grace. And certainly not tonight."

A feline grin slid across Nieve's lips. "What's your name?"

"Aresti."

"Well, Aresti, fae warrior and guard, enjoy the party. Feel free to sample our Northern delicacies."

"It would be my pleasure, Your Grace." Aresti's eyes burned with fire.

The queen's gaze slid from Aresti and landed on Nosficio. Wordless thoughts passed between them in silent conversation. *Nieve certainly does have curious tastes...*

Once seated, food began arriving on massive, shining silver platters. Roast boar, pheasant, steaks, and whole fish were placed before Ruenen and the other guests at the high table. Each dish was heavy with butter and fat, as most Northern dishes were. Delicious, but quite filling for someone used to leaner fare.

Ruenen was pulled into conversations that he understood little about. A wizened Greltan councilman asked him whether certain Nevandian tariffs would be lifted on goods. Another wanted to know more about

Nevandia's strategy in dealing with Varana. Ruenen tried not to appear too inexperienced, like a lamb surrounded by political wolves.

Marai hadn't yet returned. Ruenen's eyes scanned the room for her as more Greltan lords and ladies arrived. Nieve introduced them all to Ruenen. They bowed and curtsied flawlessly to him in deep, rich colored velvets and furs. Ruenen hadn't been properly introduced to his *own* court, yet here he was greeted with pomp and respect.

His knees bounced under the table as he continued waiting for a glimpse of Marai. He downed the contents of his goblet before an attentive servant refilled his wine. Goso, surrounded by his Greltan counterparts, was already red-faced and laughing. The talks must have been going well . . .

Murmurs traveled up and down the tables. The musicians played softer, noticing a new arrival to dinner. Ruenen's eyes lifted to the hall door in time to see her enter.

He blinked multiple times because he wasn't truly sure it *was* her.

Marai was clothed in pale blue silk with long tight sleeves. The bodice dipped low enough to reveal her collarbones and sternum; her skin as white as fresh fallen snow. The gown was tight across her hips, made for a young girl, but it highlighted curves Ruenen never knew Marai had. The blue silk pooled on the floor around her; it was also a little long. Dimtoir was absent, but Ruenen bet Marai's knife and dagger were strapped discreetly beneath her gown.

Ruenen stopped breathing entirely. His knees stilled.

She was no longer the Lady Butcher.

Was it just him, or had the room gone quiet? Had it grown warmer?

Marai tugged at her gown. Shifted on her feet. She carefully walked down the aisle, as if trying not to trip on the fabric's hem. She lowered herself into a seat next to Goso's assistant, who scooted over, giving her a wide berth. Marai was still fae; that fact made obvious by her pristine, ethereal appearance. Her blonde hair billowed down her back like ripples on the water.

Ruenen had never seen anyone more beautiful in his entire life.

"How did you meet your faerie friend?" Nieve asked near his ear, forcing Ruenen to drag his eyes away from Marai.

"I hired her in Gainesbury to protect me from Tacorn. She's a skilled swordsman. One of the best I've ever seen."

"Nosficio claimed she's the most powerful faerie in centuries."

Ruenen nodded. The realization of that fact had his chest swelling with pride. "Her magic is unique by fae standards. I trust her with my life, and the lives of my people."

Nieve glanced to the wall where Nosficio and Aresti were speaking, heads bowed together in intense conversation. Wariness charged through Ruenen as he saw their faces darken with predatory interest.

"I admire your desire to build a kingdom where humans and magical folk can cohabitate," Nieve said. "But I do not envy the challenge."

She lifted her glass. Ruenen did so, as well.

"To new, unexpected friends, and unbreakable bonds," said Nieve, clinking her goblet against his. She took a long sip as Ruenen's eyes flitted back to Marai.

She sat straight-backed in her chair, and ate quietly from her plate, ignoring the stares from the Greltan nobles. Several men gazed upon her with interest. Ruenen gave a chuckle. Marai would never let them touch her.

But she'd let *him* touch her . . .

His fingers fisted the fabric on his thighs to keep himself from sensing the tingles, the aching need to stroke those lovely, sharp collarbones.

"If you will excuse me, Your Highness, I must make the rounds." Nieve stood and wandered across the table to her council and Goso.

Marai was so close, and yet so far away. It would be rude for Ruenen to shout across the table so he could hear her voice. He tried to occupy himself by humming along to the musician's tune, singing under his breath. He imagined the heaviness of his lute in his hands. The illusory taut strings vibrated as he strummed, visualizing musical notes on paper.

It wasn't working. His eyes kept darting to Marai, and he watched while she did everything. Marai nibbling at a piece of venison. Marai taking a sip from her goblet. Marai stiffening as a man accidentally bumped into her back.

Marai's eyes meeting his from across the table.

They blazed, they burned, they simmered. Desire, deep and powerful, flooded through him. He'd never felt anything this intense before. His mouth turned dry.

Ruenen thought then that the heart was the most curious of instruments. How could those luminescent eyes pluck so at his heartstrings? Why did his ears swoon with a melody only she produced? She was the singular song he ever wanted to sing.

The dinner began to wind down, although wine was still pouring. Nobles bid their farewells to Nieve and Ruenen, making their exits, but many remained, ready for what Ruenen assumed was the after-party.

Her plate empty, Marai got to her feet.

"Where are you going?" Ruenen asked loudly over the music. His question drew dozens of eyes his way.

"Upstairs to change out of this," Marai replied. She barely glanced his way as she turned back through the aisle and out into the hall.

Ruenen didn't think. He stood and quickly fought his way through the nobles who stepped into his path, hoping to speak with him. He made his cordial excuses, something about the privy, and reached the hallway. If he didn't get to her *now,* he might very well combust.

He spotted her at the end of the hallway, heading towards the staircase. The gown hugged the slight curves of her body. She wasn't as shapely as Nieve or Aresti, but the dress clung to all the right places. Ruenen made a mental note to buy her a thousand dresses like this one.

At the sound of his harried footsteps, Marai glanced back over her shoulder. Those molten lavender eyes glimmered in the candlelight; eyes that held him and broke him at once. Her current pulled him closer. He couldn't get there fast enough. But running was an undignified thing to do while visiting someone else's castle.

A quizzical look swept across her face. She didn't understand his reaction, why he was *chasing* after her.

Finally, his hand grasped hers, rubbed against the calloused palm, and he pulled Marai into the nearest room to their right.

It was entirely dark. The soft moonlight from the windows illuminated a kind of library or office. Books lined shelves nearby. A desk sat in a corner. All he knew was that the room was *empty*.

He shut the door and pressed Marai against it. Her back touched the wood with a soft *thud*.

"Ruen, what—"

"We left things unfinished earlier," he practically growled as the tenuous hold on his sanity snapped.

Her eyes widened. Her cheeks flushed. She opened her mouth to speak.

His lips were on hers before he knew what he was doing. She let out a small gasp and dove her hand into his hair, yanking slightly as those fingers curled around the strands.

His hand traveled down the bumps of her spine to rest on her hip, feeling every curve, every indentation, every jagged edge, all the strength in her lean muscle. His lips trailed across her collarbones.

Would he *ever* get enough of her?

"Ruen," she whispered in his ear, in a voice she'd never used before. Husky. Desperate.

He wanted to rip the dress right from her body and take her there in the palace library. He wanted to plunge into the wild warmth of her and worship every line, every soft and rigid part of her.

They were fire. They were magic. They were power and need and desire. There was nothing gentle about this. Marai had to know the force she held over him.

But one hand on his chest from her, pushing him backwards, stopped him. He panted, whole body heaving from the need of her. For a moment, he feared they'd gone too far, too fast. Was Marai okay?

But her eyes showed no fear, no regret. They continued to burn with that swirling flame of magic.

"We can't do this right now," she said through equally strained breath. "You must return to the feast."

Feast? What feast? He wanted to feast on *her*.

"Ruenen," Marai said, pressure in her tone. "You cannot be caught here with me."

She was right. Of course she was. Ruenen groaned and sighed and couldn't get his legs to move. He adjusted his shirt, righting himself. Marai pressed her hands against the door, nudging it open.

"Are you coming?" Ruenen asked as his fingers laced through hers.

"They've prepared rooms for us for tonight, though I don't intend to sleep while we're on foreign soil. I'll go upstairs to change, and then patrol the corridors. I'll see you in the morning." Disappointment swept over him. Marai read his expression, the slump in his shoulders. "You have important work here tonight. This alliance must be strong. Nevandia is counting on you."

Always so fucking right.

Ruenen stepped towards the door, but couldn't let go of her hand. He brought it to his lips, gently bestowing a kiss upon the soft skin.

"Goodnight, Lady Marai."

Marai's chest rose against the binding of her bodice.

"Goodnight, Prince."

He slithered through the door and could barely walk back down the hallway. He paced outside the door for a few minutes, sucking in deep breaths, shaking his head back and forth. The taste of her was still on his tongue, sparkling with magic; the scent of her in his nose. He felt the absence of her in his arms like the emptiness of a long, dark winter's eve.

It took all of his self-control to walk back into that banquet hall and not follow Marai up to her bedroom. But when he returned, the party was still in full swing. The musicians continued their upbeat melodies, the remaining nobles roared with laughter, and the wine kept pouring. No one had missed him.

But Nieve, Nosficio, and Aresti were nowhere in sight.

Suspicion brewing, Ruenen walked to the high table where Goso cackled with his Greltan colleagues.

"Have you seen the Queen?"

Goso blinked at him; the focus on his eyes going in and out. "Uh . . . the Queen was . . ." He pointed up at her vacant seat.

His assistant leaned towards Ruenen with a twitch in his shoulders. "I saw Her Majesty leave the room a few minutes ago with the vampire and the other faerie woman."

Icy fear coursed through Ruenen's blood. "Was she taken against her will?"

The assistant shook his head. His face flushed beet red. "No, she . . . led them out, herself."

"Not to worry, Your Highness," came a voice from the shadows. The Master of Spies snorted beneath his mask, leaning against the far wall. "That vampire has been here more times than I should tell you. Our queen can handle herself."

Floored by his nonchalant response, Ruenen bit the inside of his cheek.

Should I go after them? She'd never admit it, but Marai would be furious if anything happened to Aresti.

"There are guards stationed outside her door," the Master of Spies continued, sensing Ruenen's agitation. "If there's any trouble, they will intervene."

That did little to ease Ruenen's mind. If Nieve and Aresti wanted to partake in . . . whatever they were doing with Nosficio, it wasn't his place to stop them.

With a huff, Ruenen sat back down at the high table and poured himself more wine.

CHAPTER 19
Marai

She didn't sleep. Not when the feel of Ruenen's hands and lips across her body kept her mind from settling. Marai patrolled the corridors all night, long after the party ceased and the King's Guard stood at attention in front of Ruenen's door. She climbed into bed in the blue light of early morning, but the bedsheets chafed against her sensitive skin. Even in the cold, Marai kicked them off.

A copper dawn arrived, and Marai dressed back in her boring, shapeless brown sack of a dress. The blue gown she'd been forced into the previous night was beautiful, expertly made, with silver thread. She'd never worn such finery before, but it felt *wrong* on her body. That woman in the banquet hall, who had garnered so many eyes, had been trying to hide her discomfort. Trying not to make a mistake. Trying not to fail Ruenen in this diplomatic mission.

I'd give anything for my Butcher blacks . . .

Marai hastily braided her hair back. Gods, she never wore her hair loose. The castle servant had suggested it, and Marai, too busy staring at the blonde stranger in the mirror, let the woman brush through her tangled locks.

She crept out of the room before any servants came to check on her. Similar to the castle at Kellesar, people already bustled about. Servants and guards didn't look twice at her as she ventured out into the snow. Flurries littered the air, falling faster and faster the longer Marai walked through the frozen gardens. The boughs of trees glittered in white-blue hoarfrost.

"You're an early riser, as well," came Nieve's voice from behind her. Marai spun to see the queen striding towards her, red hair aflame, wrapped in a white fur coat and hat, skins from the notorious white bears of Grelta. Marai had fought one off months ago at the start of her journey with Ruenen.

Marai bowed. "Habit, Your Grace."

"I'm glad to have a moment alone with you. It's a rare opportunity, indeed, to meet any of the fae folk."

"We're both uncommon species," Marai bit out before she could stop herself.

Nieve's eyes widened, then she grinned. "I can see why he likes you."

Marai stilled. "Who?"

"Well, the prince, of course, but I meant Nosficio."

Nosficio? Marai raised an eyebrow.

"When he first appeared in my room after so many months, I was tempted to stake him right then and there," Nieve said, leading Marai leisurely through the glittering frosted garden. "But he mentioned the Prince of Nevandia had surfaced, with a faerie at his side. He spoke of you with genuine awe. Nosficio is a difficult creature to read, but I could see in his eyes that he's interested in you and your well-being." Marai pulled a face, making Nieve chuckle. "No, girl, I don't mean in *that* way. Nosficio said you reminded him of an old friend. A creature like him doesn't have friends, but it was because of *you* that I decided to write back to Prince Ruenen."

"I'm merely a bodyguard," Marai said, but the words felt half-hearted. She *was* someone: Queen Meallán's descendant, the progeny to her power, and perhaps even the faerie throne.

"You're wrong, Lady Marai," said Nieve, giving her that ice-blue stare. "I think you may well be the difference maker in this war. You and Prince

Ruenen are changing the rules. You inspired a vampire to join your cause, for Lirr's sake. He said you may be the only one able to stop Rayghast. I'm sending my troops off to battle because I believe in *you*."

"I could be one of those wild, deviant faeries everyone thinks we are."

Nieve chuckled again. "For better or worse, I trust Nosficio's word."

"Why?" Marai asked, unable to stop herself. "What happened between you and Nosficio?"

Nieve's face shuttered for a moment. The confidence she'd been displaying wilted slightly. "Life is difficult when you have a sick husband who cannot perform his duties. He hasn't for some time . . ." Nieve's eyes glistened, but she shook off whatever emotion she'd been letting in. "I respect my husband. Ours was a friendship before we were ever married; rare in the royal world. He remains my dearest friend, but there was never attraction or passion between us. Maes and I agreed many years ago, after his symptoms first appeared, that I could meet with whomever I wanted."

Shock froze Marai to the spot. Nieve plucked a sharp icicle, long as a dagger, from a branch, twirling it in her gloved fingers. It reminded Marai of a wooden stake.

"I met Nosficio two years ago. At first, it was flirtation. Something forbidden I knew I would not touch. But he was *persistent*. Charming. I'd never known a vampire to be so . . . respectful. Considering the terrible things I'd heard about him, I doubted his intentions. Then, our relationship became strictly physical. And it worked fine for both of us . . . until he bit me in a moment of bloodlust."

Marai couldn't stop the loud gasp from escaping. Nosficio could have killed Nieve, *turned* her into a vampire.

No wonder she hired a mercenary . . .

"Nosficio hadn't eaten in days. I'd refused to allow him to feed on my staff and subjects. I didn't realize that he was starving himself to remain in my company. The bite wasn't bad, especially since I stabbed Nosficio the minute his teeth clamped down on my neck, but my children saw the bite. They'd watched a vampire nearly kill their mother. Nosficio fled, and I barred him from ever entering Lirrstrass again. I hired a mercenary to send him the message to keep away." Nieve looked back at Marai with amusement. "He told me it was *you* who gave him the warning."

Marai dipped her head. "Thank you for the generous payment."

Nieve smiled. "I haven't forgiven him. I don't trust his actions, but I trust his assessment of *you*." Nieve's face grew serious again as she gazed up at the White Ridge Mountains looming in the distance, shrouded in fog and snow. "I've never believed faeries were evil. Certainly not in this lifetime. Your people once ruled these lands before my husband's bloodline took over. War is inevitable when everyone wants power."

"My parents were from the North," Marai said. It was strange to discuss such personal things with the Queen of Grelta, herself. But Nieve didn't seem to have any qualms about intimacy.

"Oh, that's obvious," said Nieve, gesturing to Marai's fair hair and complexion. "I hope that you will not only bring acceptance for your people and other magical folk, but also be a strong force for Nevandian women, as well."

Marai blinked and looked away. No one was less qualified to be a voice for women. Not after Slate. Not after all the lives she'd taken.

"I see the shadow over your heart, Lady Marai," Nieve said softly. "Don't let your past dictate who you are in the future. You're strong. Lead Nevandia to a better place. And I promise I'll do the same here in Grelta."

Nieve held out her bejeweled hand; rubies and sapphires big as walnuts glittered in the morning sun. Marai stared at it. *I am worthy,* she reminded herself. She shook the queen's gloved hand tersely.

"Now, I must go back inside. The council and your prince are already drafting away in there. I always insist on being part of such significant negotiations." Nieve gave Marai one last smile before turning back towards the castle.

Marai stayed outside a while longer, breathing in the crisp winter air. She hadn't thought about her ties to *this* country. The place she was born before her parents moved to the fae camps in the Northwestern part of Tacorn. Before they'd been slaughtered.

Her feet tread through the snow, leaving behind small footprints from her tattered slippers. Eventually, the cold became too great to tolerate, and Marai hurried back inside, shaking the flakes from her clothes in the entry hall. She grumbled to herself, longing for sandy beaches and striking ocean sunsets.

Inside the chamber, Nieve sat on her throne, listening intently to the councilmen and Goso discussing . . . whatever business they had to discuss. Marai wasn't one for politics. The intricacies of treaties and wartime alliances were beyond her.

Ruenen's eyes glazed over as he nodded in his chair, on the dais next to the Greltan thrones. Marai chuckled. It appeared *he* wasn't one for politics, either, but Ruenen perked up when Marai entered. Nosficio, fully covered in his cloak, and Aresti, were also present, standing amongst the other Nevandian guards.

"Enjoy your evening?" Nosficio asked, voice light and casual, as Marai joined them. He plucked a speck of dust from his cloak with a gloved hand.

"Fine. How was yours?" asked Marai, revealing nothing.

Nosficio and Aresti both suddenly avoided Marai's eyes.

"Quite pleasant," said the vampire. "Wouldn't you agree, Aresti?"

Aresti didn't respond. She stared, instead, at Nieve. Suspicion brewed in Marai's stomach, but there were too many people around to ask questions.

Marai crossed her arms. "We need to leave soon. We've been away too long."

After another hour of negotiations, Nieve announced, "Lord Goso can remain here as our guest to further discuss the trade details. You're pressed for time, Your Highness, eager to return home. Rest assured that we will begin preparing our troops immediately."

I hope they arrive in time . . .

Nosficio's heedful glance told Marai he thought the same. Ruenen and Nieve got to their feet, and the chamber fell silent.

"Prince Ruenen, I hope you've had a pleasant stay here in Grelta."

"It was more than I deserved, Your Grace," Ruenen said, kissing her outstretched hand. "Thank you, so very much, for your aid and welcoming arrival. And please give my best to His Majesty, the King. I'm sorry not to say farewell to him in person."

Nieve's eyebrows rose. "You truly mean that, don't you? Most people say such things as courtesy, but the truth is in your honest eyes." She peered out across the room, finding Marai amongst the guards. "You were correct, Lady Marai. He *is* abnormal. I look forward to our partnership, Prince."

Ruenen walked down the dais and shook hands with the entire council of Grelta. After several more pleasantries and goodbyes to Goso and his assistant, Ruenen's Nevandian entourage gathered in the middle of the room.

"As a final show of trust, I ask that you show me the glorious gifts that allowed you to travel to me so quickly." Nieve stared squarely at Marai.

A muscle in the corner of Marai's eye twitched. A display of magic. Nieve wanted to see it for herself.

"You don't have to," Ruenen quickly whispered to her.

Marai wanted to reach out and cup her hand to his cheek for those words, but she raised both arms. The queen had confided in her, and Marai would repay the candor.

Bright, colorful magic burst forth, creating the portal. Nieve's eyes opened wide. She took a small step back. The silver guards along the room moved, their armor clattering, but that was all. Nieve stared into the portal, viewing the Nevandian Witenagemot chamber on the other side. A graceful hand came to her throat.

"It's beautiful," she said, her voice soft in awe. "How extraordinary."

Marai had never thought of her magic as beautiful, but perhaps, when no one was trying to kill you because of it, magic was quite winsome.

Nieve tentatively approached, walking around the portal, examining it from all sides. She turned to Marai, eyes still wide. "Thank you for showing me. I wish you the best of luck. Protect your prince." A vicious smile came to the queen's lips. "May Tacorn and Rayghast burn."

The minute Marai's feet stepped through the portal, chaos swarmed around her. The council chamber was crammed to the brim with soldiers, members of the Witan, and a slew of nobles and servants. All of them shouted and pointed as Marai quickly sealed the portal shut. Apparently, their arrival had taken the counsel by surprise. Several people held their hands to their hearts in breathless alarm.

Marai spotted Keshel off to the side. Aresti was already making her way swiftly there. Nosficio had disappeared as soon as he'd come through the portal. Perhaps the number of people and smell of blood overwhelmed the vampire.

"What's going on?" Aresti asked her cousin.

Keshel's body was closed off, arms crossed tightly, face limed with concern. "We just received word that Tacorn soldiers, one of Rayghast's elite units, attacked Gloaw Crana a few days ago." Gloaw Crana was a town on the Tacorn-Nevandian border, right along the main road. Founded long ago by the fae, its citizens were used to skirmishes in that area, and the occasional death, but this was different. "The entire town up in smoke. Every man, woman, and child dead."

Marai's heart stopped. Aresti cursed, aptly voicing Marai's thoughts.

"Varanese forces are on the move," said Keshel. "Our spies said they're crossing through on the road to Tacorn."

Marai shivered, suddenly as cold as she'd been in the Lirrstrass garden. *How had all of this happened in half a day?*

"Why didn't our army stop them?" Aresti asked.

Keshel knit his brows together. "Because Avilyard is consolidating all Nevandian forces here in the Red Lands. There are hardly any soldiers left in upper Nevandia. Gloaw Crana was completely exposed and unarmed."

Marai glanced over to Ruenen, surrounded by people yelling, talking over each other, waving papers in his face. Lost at sea, his eyes were wide, face paling, as he took in the news of what had occurred while he'd been in Grelta.

But Nieve's forces would come, Marai reminded herself. She hoped Rayghast wouldn't mount a massive attack before they arrived.

Keshel's macabre news wasn't finished yet. "Not only that, but another one of those creatures appeared on the highlands outside the city last night." Marai bolted towards the door, but Keshel grasped her arm, halting her. "Leif, Raife, and I handled it. No one was hurt, but it wasn't easy to kill."

"What did it look like?" asked Aresti, agog.

Keshel shuddered, spooked by the memory. "Two foul heads, six arms, strange markings upon its body—"

"Have you *seen* anything about them?" Marai asked.

Keshel closed his eyes, recalling his visions. "They bloom from the ground like weeds, shrouded in shadow and flame. Dark magic from the earth births them from the Underworld itself."

Aresti's face contorted with disgust.

"*Enough,*" Ruenen shouted, raising his hands in the air in frustration. He made his way up the dais, each step labored and dragging, until he stood before the throne. Chatter drifted off as Ruenen faced a room full of anxious Nevandians. "Tacorn will continue to attack more of our towns. It's time to muster men across Nevandia. All able-bodied men must be ready to fight."

"But many of them don't know how to wield a weapon," a councilman said. "They're peasants, miners, and farmers, Your Highness."

"We have no choice," Ruenen said, voice hoarse with fatigue. "Tacorn and Varana outnumber us. Every man counts. You can teach them the basics while they're gathering in the camps for battle. Commander Avilyard, send out word."

Avilyard bowed. He stood at the long table, gazing over maps spread across its surface. "Yes, Your Highness."

"I believe men ages eleven to seventy-five will have to do," said Holfast, weary face more lined with wrinkles than the day before.

Men? Marai closed her eyes, imagining scrawny, terrified boys standing up against Rayghast's trained killers. Ruenen scowled, probably thinking the same thing. He massaged his temples, squeezing his eyes shut.

"We should retaliate," shouted a golden-clad commander from the crowd. "Sack the city of Elfaygua right over the border!"

Voices rose in agreement.

"I will *not* hurt innocent lives," Ruenen said with cold authority. "Retaliating by killing Tacornian citizens makes us no better than Rayghast. We must strike their army."

"Forgive me, Your Highness, but with our forces spread so thin, we don't have the men to spare to send after the Tacornian unit," Avilyard said.

"Something must be done," said a nobleman. "We cannot allow Tacorn to get away with such an atrocity!"

The room burst into enraged commotion again. Ruenen's face was drawn as Holfast, Vorae, Fenir, and Avilyard launched into discussion with him.

"Send us," Marai shouted.

Ruenen's head snapped to her, along with every pair of eyes. Beside her, Keshel and Aresti went rigid. Marai stalked forward; the crowd parted, letting her pass to the dais. The skeptical, distrustful looks grew with each step she took. Keshel and Aresti didn't follow.

"You cannot spare any men, but you need to attack. Nevandia cannot appear weak. Your citizens need to know you'll protect them," Marai said, speaking solely to Ruenen. "Dispatch the fae, and we'll track down the unit responsible for Gloaw Crana."

"There are only seven of you. What can you possibly hope to accomplish against a unit of Rayghast's most skilled soldiers?" asked Fenir. Next to him, Vorae's red face scrunched in skepticism.

"Five," Marai corrected, thinking of Thora and Kadiatu. "Two of us will not fight."

Marai heard the scoffs and snickers. She ignored them. Her mind was set. No one, not even Ruenen, could change it.

"I say let them go," said a commander next to Avilyard. "Let the creatures prove their worth. If they want to get themselves killed, who cares?"

Anger rushed through Marai. She could turn this entire room to ashes if she wanted. *Shove it down,* she told herself. For Ruenen's sake, for the safety of her people, Marai cooled the fury.

Ruenen's attention snapped to the commander. His eyes narrowed with lethal authority. "You will address Lady Marai with respect, Commander, or you will be removed from your position."

Marai had never heard words uttered from Ruenen's mouth with such strict intensity before. His face darkened with severity. His eyes, usually warm and bright, were as cold and harsh as the Northern Sea. His hands fisted at his sides.

The pitch of his voice lowered further. "If anyone so much as whispers an insult at Lady Marai, Lord Keshel, and their people, you will spend the next several days in a cell. Is that understood?"

Marai's skin prickled. Every single facet of this man: the bard, the flirt, the charming prince, and this new imposing ruler . . . sent pleasurable shivers across her body.

Ruenen returned his focus to her, face softening slightly. "If you believe yourselves capable of handling this, then I trust you."

Marai nodded. The commander *had* been right—it was time for the fae to show what they could do.

Aresti and Keshel followed at Marai's heels as she hastened from the chamber and into the courtyard.

"Are you insane?" Aresti asked. "We can't take down an entire unit of soldiers by ourselves."

"We can," stated Marai, not slowing her steps as they wound their way down towards the cottages. "I've done it before."

"But there will be more soldiers than that time, Marai," Keshel said. She'd told him in the Badlands about the Tacorn woods, when she'd first discovered her power.

"That's why you're coming along."

Keshel's expression grew grim. She knew what he was thinking. *Ruen will be our Ruin.*

Marai burst through the cabin door, startling Thora and Raife. An elderly woman sat in a chair, her foot resting in Thora's lap. The woman's face grew paler as Keshel and Aresti filed into the room behind Marai.

"Can you let me treat Mrs. Whitten's gout first before you all launch into whatever horrific thing happened?" Thora asked with steely eyes.

Mrs. Whitten's mouth opened and closed like a fish. Magic appeared in Thora's hands as she hovered them over the old woman's swollen foot. After a moment, the swelling and redness disappeared, and Mrs. Whitten's face relaxed. She let out a contented moan. When Thora's magic retreated, the old woman cracked a weak smile.

"This is the first time in five years I haven't felt that pain," she said in wonder, rotating her ankle.

Thora smiled. "And you should never feel that pain again. If anything does occur, come back and I'll fix it."

The old woman's rotten-toothed smile widened as she set her foot down, put on her shoe, and stood up. Mrs. Whitten handed Thora a coin, then exited the cottage with a jaunty gait.

Thora's face immediately hardened. "Come to tell us more horrible news?"

Leif and Kadiatu appeared in the back door, arms full of harvested vegetables, hands caked in dark dirt.

"We already dispatched a monster while you were gone," Leif said, puffing up with pride. "Wasn't all that difficult when we used magic."

"Well, now we need to decimate an entire unit of soldiers," said Marai.

Leif's arms and face slackened. A carrot dropped onto the floor.

"You're talking about over thirty trained soldiers, Marai. That's suicide," Raife said, stepping closer to Thora. Their arms grazed slightly, the contact natural and comfortable between them.

"No, it's not," Marai said. "This is our chance to show this continent that the fae should be respected. Because five of us *can* defeat an entire unit of trained Tacornian soldiers. We send a message to Rayghast that Nevandia should be feared."

Raife ran a hand through his unbound curly hair. "You want us to use magic? In front of humans?"

"Humans who will be dead," Aresti chimed in. A slow smirk appeared on her face. "We won't leave anyone alive."

Leif stood taller. "Rayghast killed our families. Here's our chance for justice."

Kadiatu cringed; her body physically shying away from those words. She plopped her vegetables onto the table. "Don't have such joy in taking life. I was too young to remember fleeing the camps, but I'm sure *you* all do. Don't be so quick to experience that horror again."

"It will be different this time," Leif said, coming to Marai's side in a rare show of unity. "It won't be our blood that runs red." He glanced down at the bloodstone ring on Marai's finger. "Let's get going."

Leif grabbed his sword propped up in the corner and handed his twin the bow and quiver.

Someone rapped at the door. Keshel opened it, revealing Avilyard, Elmar, and Nyle. The commander's helmet was off, hair tousled and sweaty. He held a bundle of black cloth in his arms.

"Pardon the intrusion," Avilyard said, staying politely outside. "Are you certain you don't require any of my men? Sir Elmar and Sir Nyle could join you. To take on a whole unit alone—"

"Thank you, Commander, but no," said Marai. "Your men need to rest and prepare for the upcoming battle."

Avilyard gave her a weak nod. There was little more he could do to prepare his young, inexperienced army. The commander held out the black bundle. "Prince Ruenen sent me with these. He said you might want them."

Marai sifted through the clothes: a shirt and trousers in smooth black leather and soft linen, a velvet cloak, all her size. Marai smirked.

"We shall be needing proper battle attire, Commander Avilyard," said Raife, warily watching Marai rub her blackened fingers across her new cloak. "For the next time."

Avilyard nodded again. "I'll see to it that you are properly outfitted. Good luck."

With a quick glance at Kadiatu hovering by the garden door, he turned and walked back up the street. Marai heard his armor clanking from a distance. Soldiers could never sneak up on their enemy.

But phantoms in Butcher blacks could . . .

CHAPTER 20
Rayghast

His army gathered outside Dul Tanen. Rayghast watched the mass of black-armored soldiers train from his position on the sloping, craggy hill. Their swords clashed, arrows aimed true, and their precision within their ranks was unmatched by any other army on Astye.

Satisfaction rippled under Rayghast's skin at his army's display of power, the greatest on all of Astye.

"The men continue to drill rigorously, Your Grace," Shaff said. "And the Varanese forces are close. Many of their commanders are arriving as we speak."

"So we're ready, then?" asked Dobbs. "For the main offensive?"

Several council members had accompanied Rayghast on his visit to the encampment. Cronhold, too doddery to make the trek, stayed behind. Lord Silex was also present. He wore fine velvets and silks, and a flamboyant feathered hat. Rayghast found the lord arrogant and irksome, but he did pay an inordinate amount of money towards the military, and had brought more of his own retainers to join in the cause.

"Yes, my lord. A large Nevandian encampment has sprouted across the moor," said Shaff, pointing out towards the main road.

Rayghast couldn't see the Nevandians from so far away, but he felt them out there. Magic thrummed, snaking around his arteries and veins.

"How many?" Rayghast asked his commander.

"Our numbers far exceed their own. And the men they *do* have are untrained peasants, Your Grace. Nevandia has so few true knights left."

"Are those Nevandian prisoners down there?" asked Silex, peering closely at a cluster of men surrounded by Tacornian guards. His lips spread into a pleased smirk at the sight of the thin, dirty men, in nothing but rags and bare feet.

"Yes, we captured these men on their way to join the Nevandian army. The prince this morning sent out a call for all able-bodied men."

Silex gave a patronizing scoff. "Able-bodied is too polite a term."

The Tacornian guards split up the men, dragging them across the grass to different stations. The prisoners howled and screeched in terror; their fear sent Rayghast's magic aquiver. Archers took aim. Arrows soared. Target practice into real flesh. A giant Tacornian soldier threw a spear straight into the chest of a screaming prisoner trying to run away. One final soldier decapitated the remaining prisoners in a swift, brutal assault. It was an excellent show of skill and might.

Soon, all Nevandians would end up like those prisoners. Even the bravest would be too cowed with fear; they, too, would succumb to his might.

A messenger appeared on horseback. He quickly leapt from his horse and bowed deeply before his king. "Forgive the interruption, Your Grace, but Princess Eriu of Varana's carriage is pulling into the city."

"Ah, finally," said Dobbs, clapping his hands together. "Shall we return to the castle to inspect the girl?"

Rayghast climbed into the saddle of his massive warhorse and galloped back to the fortress; the council and Silex in tow. A blue and gold carriage sat in the courtyard surrounded by six soldiers with Varanese flags. Blue water dragons stitched across the fabric served as the Jade Emperor's insignia.

Rhia knelt in the dirt courtyard hugging a pudgy, little girl, dressed in fine Varanese clothing. His wife had yet to see Rayghast and his entourage approaching. Quite unusual for her, as she was always observing, always aware. Her sister, today, held her full attention.

"Let me look at you," Rhia said, pulling away, squinting back tears. Rayghast had never seen his wife show such emotions.

"The journey took ages," the little girl said in exasperation. "I'm starving. And smelly. Can I eat supper in the bath?"

Rhia then caught sight of Rayghast. Immediately, her warm demeanor shifted. She stood to full height, altered her face into its usual indifference. This was the first he'd seen of her since she'd discovered his magic. There were no new rumors floating around, none of the staff treated Rayghast any differently. It appeared Rhia was keeping to her word. Now that her sister was here, Rayghast had even more leverage to keep her silent.

Rhia addressed her little sister with a stern, regal voice. "You are a princess, Eriu. You must behave. I'm glad to see you left your dolls behind."

Rayghast was mildly pleased to hear her scolding the obnoxious child.

"Because Mother forced me to," Eriu said, twisting her mouth. "Do you know who I'm to marry? Is he old? Is he grumpy? Does he smell like moldy cheese and sour milk? Where's the king? Can I meet him?"

"The king is here, child," Dobbs said in a commanding tone.

Rhia dropped into a curtsey. Eriu spun around, staring at Rayghast like a largemouth bass. The child, despite being a princess, was physically unimpressive and had a nasal, irritating voice Rayghast wouldn't be able to tolerate.

Rhia quickly yanked her sister down into a curtsey. Rayghast ignored Eriu's lack of immediate respect. She was clearly dim-witted.

"She's arrived, then," Rayghast said.

"Yes, Your Grace," Rhia replied, frozen in her curtsey.

Rayghast's gaze didn't linger on Eriu long. His attention strayed to within the castle where the door to the dungeon opened. A soldier and Wattling appeared as a wretched female scream from below pierced the air. Eriu jumped, eyes opening wide.

"What's down there?" Eriu whispered.

"The dungeons," said Rayghast. "For people who disobey."

Eriu shrunk back towards Rhia.

Dobbs frowned as he stared down at the girl. "Your sister didn't inherit your beauty, I see."

"She looks as I did as a girl. Princess Eriu will grow into herself," Rhia said evenly, although Rayghast detected a spark of anger.

Dobbs replied with a skeptical *hmmm*. Lord Silex's nose wrinkled in distaste as Cronhold hobbled down the steps towards them; Wattling followed behind with a sour expression.

"Good, good," Cronhold said. "She's here. I trust you had a pleasant, uh, journey, Princess?"

Eriu rolled her eyes. "Oh, yes, a nice, *long*, trip."

Spoiled brat.

Cronhold's sniff echoed around the courtyard. He gave one hacking, phlegmy cough. Eriu made a face, receiving a nudge from Rhia, and the girl cleared her expression.

Cronhold swept a careless hand in the air. "The wedding will be in five days' time. You may go settle in your rooms."

"Forgive me, Husband," said Rhia before Rayghast had even taken a step, "but who will Princess Eriu be married to?"

Rayghast said nothing, but gestured to the nobleman beside him.

Silex prowled forward with formidable hauteur, and pointed at Eriu. "Let me see you."

Eriu's eyes darted between all the men, fingers fidgeting with the bell sleeves of her dress. Silex circled her twice, no doubt noticing every flaw.

Rhia's sister was Rayghast's gift. An encouragement for Silex to continue supplying coin, men, and support for the war. It was the highest reward Rayghast could offer. A princess would bring Silex power and esteem.

Silex frowned and sighed dramatically. "I suppose she'll have to do. Her dowry is significant, and that's the most important matter." He stared pointedly at Eriu with disdain. "You'd better give me sons."

Rhia's eyes tightened as she said, "Come, Eriu, let's get you settled," then ushered her sister inside the castle.

"I don't want to marry that man," Eriu said in a loud whisper. She used that bratty, childish tone Rayghast hated. "Please, don't make me marry him!"

"Women don't dissent here," Rhia replied, matter-of-fact, taking one last glance at Rayghast. "You will do whatever the council and Lord Silex demand."

Once the sisters were out of sight, Wattling pulled Rayghast aside in a conspiratorial manner. "Your Grace, I would speak with you." Checking over his shoulder to see that Cronhold and Dobbs had Silex engaged in conversation, Wattling produced a small vial from his pocket. "While conducting the search on Queen Rhia's rooms, as requested, we uncovered this in her bedside drawer."

Rayghast took the small bottle of plum-colored liquid in his fingers. "What is it?"

"We summoned an apothecary, who said this is some sort of tonic that women use to . . ." Wattling's voice dropped to a low murmur. "To rid themselves of a child. We're questioning one of the queen's servants right now—"

Taking the stairs three at a time, Rayghast burst through Rhia's bedroom doors, fury blazing inside him. Eriu was lying on the chaise, crying into a pillow. Rayghast's wife sat at her vanity as one of her ladies brushed her long, straight hair. Rhia vaulted from her stool and into a low curtsey. Eriu, her ladies, and servants froze in place.

"Take the girl and get out," Rayghast growled to the nearest maid. The woman quickly escorted Eriu from the room, closing the doors behind her. Rayghast pulled the vial from his pocket. "Recognize this?"

Rhia glanced from the vial to the floor. "No, My King."

"I had men search your room this morning while you ate breakfast with your ladies."

Rayghast prowled closer to Rhia. She tensed; the other ladies and servants in the room stared guilty at the floor.

"Apparently, this is a concoction that prevents pregnancy."

"What are you implying, Husband?" asked Rhia, drawing herself up. "That I purchased that bottle? That I purposefully drank its contents to avoid having your child?"

"That is *exactly* what I'm implying," he snarled. "Although, I'm sure you had one of your loyal ladies purchase it for you."

His jaw ticked as he shot the women a glower. One of the servants bit her lower trembling lip.

Rhia screwed up her face into an expression of pity and heartbreak. She collapsed to her knees dramatically. "I was afraid, my dearest! Afraid of those rumors. Can you blame me for not wanting to die like your other wives?"

She should have been an actress instead of a wife.

"You went behind my back."

"I meant no harm, Husband—"

"And I heard your wretched sister. She begged you to break off the betrothal with Lord Silex."

"She's too young," Rhia said in desperation, body shaking with sobs, though Rayghast saw no tears. "She's not ready to be a wife. Lord Silex would be quite disappointed in her. If we delay a year or so, she will—"

He had no time for this distraction, for her lies and deception, for her weakness and folly.

"Lord Silex doesn't care how young she is. He cares that he's getting a princess in exchange for his loyalty to the crown."

Rayghast crushed the vial in his fist. The fragile glass pulverized to dust, as plum liquid dripped through his fingers and onto the rug.

"How dare you undermine me. This is treason. I should have you and all your ladies hanged for this."

The servants and ladies-in-waiting gasped and shuddered. One cried silent tears. Another wet herself; the odor of urine assaulting Rayghast's nostrils.

Yes, yes, urged the darkness within. It lapped at their fear like flames in a pyre. *Kill them all.*

Rhia, however, didn't flinch. She got fluidly to her feet; her face wiped of emotion. "Do what you feel you must, Your Grace."

The whirlpool of magic in his chest ceased. It fed on fear and hysteria, but Rhia's voice, as cool and steady as stagnant water, doused the flames in his veins. The magic was once again *bored* by her.

Rayghast rolled his shoulders back with a crack.

"You're fortunate I have a war to win. I don't have *time* to deal with you," Rayghast said through gritted teeth. "You won't leave this room. You speak to no one. Your ladies and servants won't be allowed entry." He glanced up, and the other women scattered like mice into the hallway. "You may be the Queen of Tacorn, but I am your master. Your king. You belong to *me.*"

Rhia didn't move. She didn't shiver. She was done playing the innocent doll.

Rayghast stalked out the door and slammed it behind him.

CHAPTER 21
Marai

The Tacornian unit, dressed in their matte black armor, marched along the dirt road between Gloaw Crana and what seemed to be their next intended target of Dal Riata, a small mining town. Marai and the fae hid amongst the trees on the side of the road. She smelled the blood and fire on those thirty soldiers, who laughed, sharing tales of the slaughter. How many they'd killed, which Nevandians screamed and begged for their lives. How many women they'd raped.

Aresti ground her teeth. Raife nocked his bow. Leif's fingers tightened around the hilt of his sword.

These soldiers were the embodiment of the wickedness of humans. The type of people who relished in hunting down the fae, who delighted in the massacre. Not all humans were reprehensible, but these ones were.

Marai and the fae had first portaled to Gloaw Crana, a quaint town now in smoldering cinders, civilian bodies strewn about, lying in puddles of dried blood. The other fae had gone quiet at the sight of such violence. Leif had squeezed his eyes shut, overcome by anguish, unwilling to look any longer.

They'd tracked these soldiers in silence for several hours, spurred on by incandescent vengeance. Marai would have portaled them directly to the unit's location, but she'd summoned a lot of magic in the past few days; enough that her well would have previously been depleted. Thanks to her work with Keshel in the Badlands, she was stronger than before, but Marai had to be careful how much more she used.

They caught up to the unit quickly, however; five agile faeries moved faster than thirty heavily armed soldiers.

Keshel flicked his long, thin fingers. An invisible barrier surrounded the soldiers and the fae, trapping them in a confined space. Easy targets with nowhere to run.

For a moment, the unit kept walking, unaware, until the front of the line bumped into the barrier, a solid creation from Keshel's magic. Confusion and curses traveled up and down the ranks.

"What's the fucking hold up?" called one soldier to the front.

A man put out a hand. It lay flat against an invisible wall.

The Lady Butcher charged from the tree line and severed the soldier's arm. Marai proceeded to swipe across his neck. He didn't have time to scream.

The phantom of death was upon them.

Her sword sailed, whistling in the air, slicing through anything in her path. Tacorn soldiers leapt into action. Like a swarm of furious bees, they surrounded Marai. Swords chopped and jabbed. Marai danced away from the blades, all too slow to make contact.

As the soldiers closed in, she gathered her magic into a ball of burning light inside her. A wave of magic burst from Marai's hands, spewing dust into the air. Marai's ears popped at the concussive sound as the impact knocked soldiers off their feet.

She'd transformed Keshel's defensive barrier into a weapon.

The other fae joined. Silver blades cleaved through the mass of black. Marai heard the *whoosh* and *thunk* of Raife's arrows sinking into flesh. Orange flames engulfed soldiers. Their screams echoed through the trees, causing birds to screech and fly off. Leif's fire ravaged a whole row of men.

A blur appeared at Marai's side. Nosficio's face grinned back at her.

"I couldn't let you have all the fun, could I?" he asked, then grabbed hold of a soldier and brought his teeth to his neck. A moment later, Nosficio ripped off the man's head. Crimson blood poured from his mouth, down his chin, and onto his velvet cape.

Marai didn't bat an eyelash at the savagery.

Keshel erected more barriers, sectioning off the soldiers into smaller groups. Aresti called forth a wind, blowing a line of soldiers over onto their backs. Down the line she went, plunging her short swords into the gaps in their armor as they struggled to rise. Wind fed Leif's flames, spreading them across the road, engulfing men in a whirlwind of fire.

It felt *good* to be the Butcher again. There was a sense of rightness to this moment. Marai's breath was as calm as still water. Her mind wholly focused on this one task. For the first time in a day, Marai wasn't thinking about Ruenen's mouth or his body or his hands. It was just her and death and gore.

She became their nightmare.

The bloodstone ring pulsed, tightening around her finger, urging her onwards. *This is your purpose,* it seemed to say. The cursed object savored every drop of human blood spilt.

More soldiers, another thirty or so men, came barreling up the road. A second unit. Reinforcements.

Damn.

"Lower the barrier and pull back," Marai shouted to Keshel.

He stared at her, at the carnage on the road. Keshel's face was emotionless, but his eyes betrayed him. They simmered with terror and regret and repulsion. For a moment, Marai thought he'd frozen, but then she felt his magic disappear around her. "Fall back!"

Leif, Raife, Aresti, and Nosficio leapt into the safety of the woods where Keshel still remained. Body parts littered the ground; men lay bleeding, screaming, like those innocent children in Glow Crana had. The surviving soldiers were scattered about, trying to reform their ranks as the new unit joined them. Horses reared and ran from the fray. Pandemonium.

Now vastly outnumbered, Marai had no choice but to unleash everything she had.

The charge vibrated through her body, electric and wild. The ring glowed, sensing her power and purpose. She didn't repress it, nor did she shy away. Marai let the magic rush as she pulled from the deep well inside her.

The road came alive with bright white light. Streaks of lightning snaked across the path. Marai closed her eyes, letting magic do its work. She heard the screams, the curses, the crackling of lightning as it whipped past her ears.

Soon, the only sound she heard was a long whistle from Nosficio in the woods. She opened her eyes, revealing the devastation before her: piles of ash, trees in flame, thick burning scars etched into their bark, and black scorch marks across the dirt.

"Fucking Unholy Underworld, Marai," Aresti said as Marai fell to a knee, lightheaded.

Not a single soldier remained alive.

Aresti swallowed; her bloody hands trembled. Raife's freckles turned white as they observed the aftermath of Marai's calamitous power, and Leif gagged, then vomited into the dirt. Marai breathed deeply until she found the strength to stand again.

The only one unaffected was Nosficio, who stepped over an ash pile with a chuckle. "I *told* you, didn't I? You're stronger than I thought."

Keshel remained in the tree line. He stared and stared at Marai. Then back to the ash and pools of blood.

"Kadi was right... I remember the slaughter from when I was a child, but I don't know if I'll ever get used to it," said Raife, his voice hoarse.

I hope you never have to, Marai thought sadly, watching the others deal with this death. *Gentle hearts. That makes you all better people than me.*

"How did you do this for eight years, Marai?" Raife asked, staring at her with questions and anguish and revulsion in his face.

She hated that expression, especially from someone she cared about. It made her feel unworthy. Dirty. "I killed for survival before. But this is different, *I* am different. I do what must be done, because I have people I need to protect."

Marai remembered Kadiatu's words back in the Badlands.

"Because even when you're afraid, you stand up for what you believe in. Because you make the hard decisions, even if it means others judge you for them. You chose to stay here and protect us. If that doesn't show true strength, I don't know what does."

Maybe Marai should have felt guilty for not feeling guilty, but this carnage altered nothing inside her. She did her duty for her new kingdom. She'd saved lives by taking lives. But maybe once this war was done, when Ruenen and her people were safe, she could become something *more* . . . someone worthy.

Leif dropped his sword and stumbled over to a nearby tree, the bark still smoldering. He crouched down and took several sporadic, deep breaths, covering his face with his hands.

"I guess this is why you're Meallán's heir," said Raife after clearing his throat. He wiped the horror from his face. Perhaps he could understand her motivations, perhaps he forgave her a little. Raife gestured to the road, and glanced at his sullied hand. He quickly wiped the blood on his pants with a pained cringe.

Nosficio's head snapped to Marai. "You're Meallán's heir?"

"Supposedly." Marai shot Raife a look, but he was too busy hovering over his brother, who still hadn't moved from his crouch. Raife held out his hand, whispering words of encouragement. Leif swatted him away.

"No wonder your blood smells so familiar," Nosficio said, coming closer. He sniffed around Marai like a dog, pupils dilating. "I . . . I didn't know her line survived."

The vampire's face changed. The usual devilish grin replaced by a hunger Marai didn't understand.

"You said you knew her," she stated. "Were you her lover?"

Nosficio's red eyes blazed, then softened. "No. Meallán was my friend. My *first* friend. Never my lover. Aras was—"

He stopped and shut his mouth. His hands clenched at his sides. Marai had never seen Nosficio hold himself back before, at a loss for words.

"*King* Aras," Keshel said. He still hadn't moved, but no matter the trauma, he couldn't pass up a history lesson. "Meallán's husband?"

Nosficio stared further up the road, to where the riderless horses whinnied and pranced. He said nothing for a moment.

"You remind me of her sometimes... Meallán. And you have Aras' eyes."

Marai's heart clenched at the grief in Nosficio's voice when he said the fairy king's name. Her father's eyes, passed down through the generations, from King Aras.

Nosficio turned, gazing at Marai with sharp intensity. "It's fate that brought us together. Or strings set in motion by Meallán from the Underworld. But I think deep down I knew, the day I met you, that you were theirs. Perhaps that, more than anything else, is why I'm helping you. To repay Meallán for her kindness. To protect the last piece of Aras that still survives."

Nosficio's throat bobbed. Marai had no response for him, but she saw the pain in his eyes. Pain that had lingered for centuries. Pain that he'd tried to shove aside by allowing those dark, shameful parts of himself to take over. Marai wished she could tell him she understood, but her mouth was dry and wouldn't form the words.

"We should return to Kellesar now," Keshel said.

Marai raised her arms, beginning to tug on the remaining embers of magic inside.

Keshel placed a hand on her bicep. "No portals. You've used a lot of magic the past few days. I can see that you're exhausted."

"I can get us back to Nevandia."

Keshel shook his head, countenance still haunted as he studied at her, as if he was looking at a stranger again. "You must conserve your magic. We all must from this point on, until the battle. We'll need every ounce of our strength."

Had Keshel *seen* something? Something Marai needed to be ready for?

"Then how do you suggest we get back to Kellesar? It'll take us a couple days to walk there," Aresti said, crossing her arms.

"We'll take the horses," Raife said, as he walked towards them, so light on his feet Marai barely heard the scrape of his boots across dirt and pebbles, so as not to startle the horses.

"We should take them all back to Kellesar," Leif said, finally finding his voice. He got to his feet with a wobble, and spit on the grass. "I'm sure Avilyard will appreciate the unexpected Tacornian gift."

Marai felt no satisfaction in seeing her kin's reaction to death. Leif's anger was a front. She was beginning to understand that he'd always been more affected by the events of his past than the others. Perhaps he felt *too* much.

Raife calmed the traumatized horses, easing closer, clicking his tongue. Marai counted ten that hadn't entirely run off. He grabbed hold of the reins, still issuing hushed commands and gentle encouragement as he stroked the long nose of a sleek, muscular brown one.

"I'll meet you there," Nosficio said quietly to Marai. "I've no need for horses." He stalked off into the woods.

The fae awkwardly climbed into their saddles. None of them but Marai had ever ridden a horse, but after some brief instruction, the other riderless horses were tied off, and the fae galloped back towards Kellesar. The journey took the rest of the day, and well into the night. Marai blandly thought that it was far easier to portal.

They came across a city of tents and bonfires lighting up the night, flags waving in the breeze. A Nevandian encampment of men Ruenen had mustered. Marai trotted up, the others behind, and raised her arms in submission as the sentries blocked their entry with long spears.

"State your name and purpose."

"Councilman Keshel of Nevandia. We're friends of His Highness Prince Ruenen." Keshel used his most authoritative voice. "We're returning from our mission to dispatch the unit of Tacornian soldiers who sacked the town of Gloaw Crana."

"We've brought their mounts," Raife said. "We hope you can make use of them."

The sentries' eyes raked over their pointed ears, bloody clothes, Tacorn emblems on the horses' coats. They didn't lower their weapons; hesitation drawing their faces.

Several golden-clad commanders exited a nearby tent, and Marai recognized two of them from the Witenagemot meetings.

"Stand down," one of the commanders said to the guards. The soldiers lowered their spears, but didn't step aside to let Marai through. "They are who they say they are. The girl in black has the Nevandian pin."

Marai glanced down. Sure enough, a gold and green brooch was pinned to her black cloak. She hadn't noticed it before.

Always trying to protect me, Ruen.

"He said they'd come from dispatching Tacorn soldiers," one of the guards said, leering at Keshel.

"You defeated the entire unit yourselves?" asked a commander Marai didn't recognize.

Leif, back to his haughty self, replied, "Two units, actually. You should be thanking us. You'd be engaged in battle tomorrow if we hadn't intercepted them."

The commander's eyes narrowed. "People have heard that Nevandia is harboring magical folk. A few weres came here searching for you."

"Weres?" repeated Raife, blanching as if the commander had asked him to strip naked and perform a little dance. "You mean werewolves?"

"We'll take the horses, but you lot have to take the weres with you. They're in the way here."

Marai understood his meaning. No magical folk would be welcome in their encampment.

"Where are they?" Marai asked the commander.

He pointed to a large boulder on the outskirts of the encampment. Six muscular figures paced back and forth, weapons in hand. Two shaggy horses stood next to a small wooden cart carrying sacks and boxes.

Marai and the fae approached. The werewolves, in their human forms, raised their weapons defensively. Marai noticed their hairy arms, low-set ears, and various scars across their faces and exposed skin; all distinguishing marks of a werewolf. Sturdy blades and axes were clutched in their hands.

"We aren't leaving," said the tallest and brawniest of the six. His skin was as dark as the coal in the back of his wagon; his head shaved on both sides. "You can keep trying to intimidate us all you want. We have just as much right as you to be here."

"We heard you were looking for us," Marai said.

The tallest werewolf, most likely the leader, squinted his eyes as he looked from Marai to Keshel, spotting his pointed ears. Keshel and the others regarded the werewolves with equal interest. They'd never seen them before.

"You're the fae, then."

"We are. How can we help you?"

The leader snorted. "Funny, 'cause we came to help *you*."

The other weres lowered their weapons and nodded along. The leader held out his hand to Marai. "Name's Tarik."

Marai shook his scarred, calloused hand. A laborer's hand. A warrior's hand. "Marai."

"We were coming through the Middle Kingdoms, trading our goods up from Ain." There were several secluded pockets of werewolf communities across Astye. These ones, it seemed, were coal miners. "We met up with another faerie on the road. He told us the rumors about the new prince and his faerie band."

Keshel stepped closer, face alight with intrigue. "Another faerie? Is he still here?"

Marai's mind whirled. *Maybe it's him . . . the part-fae from Cleaving Tides.*

"Nah, he left when we arrived. Said he didn't want to go into the camp. I think he got spooked by all the soldiers," said Tarik with a shrug.

"People up and down the road are talking about you all now, saying the prince is allowing magical folk to live here," said another werewolf, with dyed red hair sheared close to his scalp. A tiny sword earring dangled from his earlobe. Marai caught Aresti regarding it with envy. "We thought we'd lend him our skills."

"That's quite generous of you," Raife said, "but why would you risk your life here when you live in the South?"

"We're tired of how poorly we're treated," Tarik replied. "Tired of being denied work or basic rights 'cause we turn into wolves once a month. So what? Doesn't make us any less feeling or trustworthy."

Leif muttered, "Damn right."

"Is it true?" the shortest werewolf asked, with eyes as wide and blue as the ocean on a clear day. He had long hair and a bushy beard. "Is the prince really so . . . unusual?"

Marai smiled. "He is. I know Prince Ruenen would be happy to meet you all."

There it was again—hope. Hope in the faces of all six werewolves, and such a powerful thing it was, too.

"Well, then let's go," Tarik said. "We're not doing anything useful around here. Those bastards won't let us set foot inside the camp."

"Progress is slow," Keshel said dryly to Tarik as the weres climbed into their wagon.

Tarik sat upon the saddle of the shaggy horse with a smile. "But at least it's *something*."

Back on her own horse, Marai's body drooped as the fae and werewolves made haste towards Kellesar. The effects of using so much magic the past few days began to take its toll. Her mind dragged, body ached, and she struggled to keep her eyes open in the saddle.

Finally, at daybreak, Kellesar rose from the valley. A wan sunrise illuminated its white stone, painting the city in a golden hue.

A strange feeling brewed inside Marai as her horse galloped steadily towards the gate, the werewolf wagon clattering behind her. She was *happy* to see the city. She was *excited* to bring the werewolves in to meet Ruenen.

Because change was coming.

Change was here.

CHAPTER 22
Ruenen

An immense battle brewed like bubbling lava beneath the earth, waiting to burst from the crater of a volcano.

Ruenen's constant headache felt much the same.

Events escalated once the fae returned from their mission in Gloaw Crana. Days went by in a blur. Avilyard and his commanders spent hours analyzing maps and strategy. The Witan chattered for hours in the hallways after meetings, seemingly afraid of wasting a single moment of planning in order to rest. Weapons in the armory were sharpened. Blacksmiths hammered away, forging new blades. A drum of war, Ruenen heard the steady, rhythmic beat of mallets on steel every time he went outside.

"Rayghast is furious," Avilyard explained to Ruenen and the Witan. "His attacks are more consistent and aggressive, retaliating after the loss of those two elite units in Gloaw Crana. There's now a massive congregation of Tacornian soldiers encamping opposite our troops on the moor."

"There've been two skirmishes in the past three days," said another commander, whose name Ruenen couldn't remember. His arm was in a sling and there was a cut across his eyebrow. He'd been involved in both skirmishes. "We've lost around seventy men and four of our top battlefield commanders, not to mention civilians."

Ruenen swore under his breath.

"Not only that, but Varana is marching through the Red Lands as we speak, pillaging our towns along the way," said Avilyard. "Half of their troops have already joined up with Rayghast's."

"Is there nothing we can do to stop them?" asked Fenir.

Avilyard and the other commanders exchanged glances.

"There are too many of them," he replied solemnly. "We don't have the men. We need to consolidate our forces in one place if we're going to make a stand."

Ruenen watched the citizens of Kellesar from his bedroom window whenever he had the chance. People huddled together, whispering, faces lined with worry. Citizens from nearby villages and towns flocked to the capital city. Kellesar's walls were high, and with the Nydian River surrounding it, quite difficult to penetrate. It was the safest place in Nevandia.

Boys no older than eleven, and old men well past their prime marched from the city with their heads held high, knowing the fate that awaited them on the moor. They'd give their lives for Nevandia. Many of them had never held a weapon, let alone taken a life. Each tearful goodbye to a loved one was a nail to Ruenen's heart as he watched from the castle balcony.

"These people are far braver than me," Ruenen said to Holfast, standing behind him. "I've hid from this place my entire life, and yet they all sacrifice for Nevandia, knowing they may not ever come home."

A woman in the street kissed her adolescent son as a golden soldier pulled the boy away.

"Make Nevandia proud," she shouted after him. The mother only let fear take her after her son was out of sight. She sobbed into her hands.

It was enough to make Ruenen want to tear his hair out. Only women, young children, and the few men deemed unfit to fight, lingered in the city streets. Everyone else had been sent to the army camps on the moor between the two countries.

The one silver lining was the arrival of the six werewolves. *Men*, strong, gritty, and hardened. Ruenen could hardly believe his eyes when Marai brought them into the Witenagemot. Tarik, their leader, had a no-nonsense way about him, which Ruenen admired. Along with the fae, the weres joined in on every strategy meeting in the Witan chamber.

The Commander of the Nevandian Army was as bone-weary as Ruenen felt. Dark circles and deep lines formed around Avilyard's eyes; creases across his forehead and between his eyebrows. Ruenen recognized an achingly familiar question in his eyes. How could they possibly win?

"We don't have the numbers to siege the castle at Dul Tanen. It's too well fortified. We're better off having a battle on our terms—here, Your Highness," Avilyard said, pointing to the highlands between Nevandia and Tacorn. The same heather-strewn moor Marai and Ruenen had careened through two months ago trying to outrun Commander Boone. "It's far enough away from our major towns, but close enough to Kellesar for us to flee should . . . should the worst happen."

Ruenen chewed bitterly on his lip. Kellesar could protect them for only so long. Eventually, Rayghast's forces would batter down the gates and flood the city.

"Let's hope it doesn't come to that. Where are the Varanese forces?"

"A day out of Dul Tanen, Your Highness, but they're congregating on the moor." The commander's deep rumble of a voice grew quieter. "And there's no word yet of Greltan soldiers. We've recalled nearly all of our own forces stationed along the border. It's possible the Greltans are closer than we know."

"How do we know that Grelta hasn't tricked us, gone behind our backs, and allied with Rayghast?" asked Commander Gasparian.

"Rayghast would never ally with a woman," Marai said curtly from the back of the room. "And I don't believe Queen Nieve would ever parlay with a man who disrespects her and her people."

"Their alliances wouldn't last long. Nieve has a vast army, herself. Tacorn doesn't have the numbers to hold Nevandia, Varana, *and* Grelta at bay. Not yet, at least," added Ruenen.

But he will if he annexes Nevandia.

"Grelta will come," Holfast said, but Ruenen heard the doubt in the Steward's voice. Holfast had sustained the kingdom for nine years. He was skilled at spinning fear into hope.

"Sure, but how quickly?" Ruenen asked.

"It takes time for a large force to move from country to country, even cavalry," Avilyard said, but he, too, sounded unsure.

Ruenen rubbed his temples. The two cups of coffee he'd already had did nothing to energize him. Sleep escaped Ruenen, night after night. His mind wouldn't slow. He hadn't had time to play his lute; the one sanctuary where he could shut out the noise and rising panic inside.

But each night, Ruenen wondered if Marai would appear at his door. He ached for the subtle spark when he traced his fingers across her skin. He pined for her presence, to hear her voice, to know her thoughts. But she never came. As their eyes locked from across the Witan chamber, a rope taut between them, Ruenen still couldn't be sure how she felt. There was attraction and affection, but could Marai sense how deeply Ruenen's emotions ran? Did she know that his heart burned and twisted for her every second of the day?

Marai was smarter than him. She knew what they faced. Marai had the ability to compartmentalize in ways Ruenen could only imagine. If there *was* ever to be something more . . . she would do nothing until this upcoming battle was finished. She wouldn't get distracted. Ruenen supposed he should follow her example.

Which brought Ruenen's mind back to Rayghast.

There was no doubt the King of Tacorn would be there on those sloping hills.

How much dark magic had he used since the last time they'd met? Ruenen wondered if the black stains had appeared elsewhere on his body. How much of himself had the king given over to the darkness? And what would that power do to Ruenen's army? To Marai?

There was no watching from the sidelines. No safety at the back. Rayghast wouldn't settle for mere defeat. It would be death or nothing, for both of them. The question was . . . whose body would be swinging from the castle walls?

I can't hide from this any longer. He swallowed down the fear and the sensation of ruination.

"I will meet him there," Ruenen said to the room.

A collective breath was held.

"Your Highness—" Holfast began.

"This has been my destiny since the day I was born. If I don't stand against Rayghast, how can I expect my own countrymen to do so?" Ruenen wasn't of royal blood. He wasn't *supposed* to be king, but fate or the gods had guided Ruenen here. This was how it was supposed to be. "If we take down Rayghast, this war will end. Let's make this the final battle. Let's bring our people peace."

Solemn nods circled the room. Vorae's hand pulled at the back of his neck. Fenir's chest rose and fell quickly. They wouldn't be on the battlefield. It was decided that the Witenagemot would remain, ready to govern with Holfast at the helm, should Ruenen fall. Or rather, ready to submit and bow down to Rayghast. Ruenen doubted any of the Witan would keep their heads should Tacorn win.

"Then we should ride out today, Your Highness," Avilyard said. "Join the men already camped on the moor. I'm sure seeing you will raise their spirits."

Ruenen nodded, scrubbing his hand over his unshaven jaw. "We'll leave by midday."

Avilyard and his fellow soldiers tramped from the chamber in steady, powerful steps. Other members of the Witan left in a hurry, chatting animatedly with each other. Holfast, Vorae, Fenir, Keshel, and Marai remained. Holfast regarded the two faeries, standing aloof in the corner. He seemed to be holding back a thought, jaw working.

"Whatever happens in this battle . . . we appreciate that you came to our aid," Holfast said to them. "For as long as Nevandia remains, you will have a home here."

Holfast held out his hand. Keshel didn't move at first. Then, slowly, he clasped the Steward's hand. It wasn't exactly a shake, but it was as friendly as either man would be.

"We must go gather the others," said Keshel, releasing Holfast's hand. "There's much to do before we leave."

"I believe you requested some armor," Holfast said. "I'll have it delivered to your cottages within the hour, although we don't have much to go around."

"Thank you, Lord Steward. Any pieces will do," Keshel said. His expression remained stoic as he swept from the room.

"We'll meet you at the gate," Marai said to Ruenen, then followed Keshel out.

Holfast placed a hand on the desk. A single, steady hand. Ruenen stared at it—it was easier than looking into Holfast's anxious and tired face.

"You've done well, Your Highness," Holfast said, a flicker of emotion in his voice. "Far better than any of us could have hoped for."

"Glad to hear you're not yet regretting your decision," replied Ruenen. His joke fell flat. He had no energy for humor. Fenir and Vorae's eyes, however, shimmered with hope.

"We'll pray for good news," Fenir said. "Good luck, Your Highness."

In one synchronized move, the three lords placed their hands to their heart and bowed. The deepest show of respect they'd ever offered Ruenen. His throat closed. He couldn't swallow. His eyes spasmed, fighting back the sting.

"I expect things in good working order for when I return," he managed to stammer out. "And please handle those land disputes . . . I don't want to come back to all that."

"We'll also make plans for your coronation, Your Highness," Holfast said with a weak smile.

Ruenen nearly laughed. That future was so dim, so improbable, it was a fool's hope.

As servants strapped golden armor around his chest, arms, and legs, Ruenen stared at himself in his bedroom mirror. He'd never felt much like anybody. He *tried* so hard to hide. But the man standing before him in gleaming armor, green cape fanning out behind him, helmet crooked under his arm... this was who Ruenen was always meant to be. Even if he'd not been born the true Prince of Nevandia, this was his destiny, designed by Lirr. And for once, he felt proud. Exhausted, but proud.

If he was to die, it would be for something meaningful.

He couldn't let this country down.

Midday arrived, and he and Mayestral sat on their horses outside the Kellesar gate, surrounded by soldiers, flags, and spears. Ruenen looked back at the city that had become his home. His responsibility.

I will make this country better, he vowed. *I'll stop the pain and suffering. I'll empower those who have been mistreated. I will create a land of acceptance.*

He could feel them with him; ghosts wrapping cold, translucent arms around him. Monks Amsco and Nori. Master Chongan, the Mistress, Yuki, and the boys. Every soul who had ever helped him and lost their lives.

This was for them.

Tarik and his werewolves appeared through the gates on horseback, dozens of knives and axes strapped to their bodies, faces covered with elaborate warpaint. More intimidating in appearance than Tacorn soldiers, Ruenen pitied any man who had to face the brawny weres on the battlefield.

"Your Highness," Tarik said in a cheerful voice, coming to Ruenen's side. "It's an honor to be included in this momentous occasion."

Ruenen smiled. "The honor is mine. Nevandia is stronger with you at our side."

Marai and the fae came into view. Keshel, Leif, Raife, and Aresti wore pieces of armor and chainmail, sitting erect upon their mounts, appearing the part of regal warriors. Thora, sitting in front of Raife, had a large pack stuffed to the brim slung over her shoulder. Medical supplies, Ruenen wagered. She wore a jacket and pants made of thickly padded beige gambeson. Kadiatu, clinging to Leif's waist, wore the same in green. She carried nothing with her. Ruenen had never seen either female without a dress. They appeared as frightened and uncomfortable as they were the day they first entered Kellesar. Now, they were going off to war. A war they never had cause to fight in, if Marai and Ruenen hadn't plucked them from their safety.

Marai, however, had no armor or padding. She wore her traditional Butcher blacks, Dimtoir and dagger strapped to her belt. Her horse trotted over to Ruenen's side.

He leaned over. "You should be wearing armor."

"I don't want anything to get in my way."

Ruenen scowled, grabbing hold of the reins of her horse. "You'll be entirely too exposed and vulnerable, Marai. Please—"

"I'm the Lady Butcher, Your Highness. Let me do my job as I see fit." Her voice was as crisp as the mist hanging in the air. Her legs nudged the sides of her horse, walking it back behind Ruenen where the fae and werewolves remained.

Avilyard and two flag-bearers took her place. "Ready, Your Highness?" he asked.

Ruenen had no choice. He *must* be ready. He slammed his helmet onto his head. It severely limited his vision, but he heard the sonorous call of a horn echoing off the craggy hills. Gripping the reins as tightly as he could through thick gloves, Ruenen galloped across the moor. Thundering hooves pounded the earth behind him.

The encampment was a massive city of tents and people and horses. Weapons of all kinds were in piles near a large boulder, guarded by soldiers. But despite the overwhelming size of the camp, Ruenen knew it wasn't enough. Even with the mustered men, his army was only three thousand-strong. Across the gray, cloudy moor, flames flickered from large fires in the distance. The fog covered the view of the Tacornian troops encamped on the other side of the road across the valley. Three times Nevandia's numbers, not counting the near one thousand Varanese.

Ruenen came across a group of adolescent boys hovering close together, sharing a loaf of bread by a campfire. They shot to their feet as Ruenen approached and bowed low.

"Your Highness," they said in chorus. The boys were younger than Elmar and Nyle. Only one of them had shoes on.

"You boys bring honor to Nevandia," Avilyard said roughly at Ruenen's side.

"Where are your weapons?" asked Ruenen, noticing their empty belts.

"We don't have any, Your Highness," one replied, keeping his eyes low.

Ruenen looked to Avilyard.

"There aren't enough to go around right now," the commander said. "You boys stay in the back tomorrow at the beginning of the fight. Weapons will become available to you after a short while."

When Nevandians died.

Ruenen put a hand on the bony shoulder of the nearest boy. "Fight hard tomorrow. Together, we'll defeat Tacorn and bring peace to our lands."

The boys nodded; their youthful, dirty faces brimming with nervous courage.

"All hail, Prince Ruenen," one of them shouted.

Ruenen's breath caught as the chant echoed throughout the camp.

Avilyard led Ruenen to his own tent. Ruenen brushed aside the canvas flap, revealing accommodations fit for a king. Fur rugs lined the ground and walls, along with small tapestries depicting the Nevandian coat of arms. A table and two chairs had been placed in the center. A cot with lavish pillows and blankets sat on the other side. Food and wine were readily available in the hands of servants stationed inside. It was far warmer and more comfortable than any of the other tents. Guilt sliced through Ruenen as he thought of those boys outside with their stale bread.

"Bring some of this outside to the men. We don't need all of this food," he said to Mayestral, who conveyed the order to a duo of servants.

"Our spies spotted Varanese flags across the moor," said Commander Gasparian as the servants loaded up trays with half of the spread. "The armies have joined. A thousand more men. All the players in place."

Thora and Kadiatu huddled near Raife, eyes wide. Their shaking fingers entwined. They looked so small in a room full of armor and weapons. Neither of them carried a blade. They didn't examine the maps that highlighted the overwhelming odds of failure. Their brows furrowed in confusion at the language of war.

They shouldn't be here, Ruenen thought savagely. It was wrong of him to uproot two gentle souls with hands that had never killed and simply wanted to heal and nurture. Thora and Kadiatu didn't belong on that field, never mind the war tent.

Another commander shook his shaggy head. "With those numbers, Tacorn outnumbers us nearly four to one."

Avilyard's eyes raked over the maps. Miniature wooden flags indicated different units; green for Nevandia, black for Tacorn, and blue for Varana. They'd been positioned like pieces on a chess board. The number of black and blue flags on the other side of the road overwhelmed the green. White flags for Grelta sat off to the side of the map.

"Rayghast stationed Varana on the far left side, and assembled Tacorn's cavalry and main infantry along the middle." Avilyard pointed to the thicket of black flags. "This is where we should focus our strength."

"But then you're leaving the left and right flanks entirely open," Ruenen said. He wasn't used to strategy. War was something he never imagined taking part in, but he wasn't blind. Varanese forces would shatter the left side of the Nevandian army, then come around behind and swallow Ruenen's troops whole.

"We're already spread too thin as it is," said Avilyard, a hint of resignation in his eyes. "Our priority should be Rayghast. Get to him, and we win it all. Varanese forces will fall back if Rayghast is no longer in charge. They have no stake in this, other than their deal with Tacorn. Without Rayghast, the deal is off."

"Put us on the left flank," said a voice of cold steel.

Ruenen's eyes bolted across the table. Blood rushed to his ears. Marai's gaze pinned him in place.

"*Marai,*" Thora gasped, yanking on Marai's arm to no avail.

The room was silent, other than a small whimper from a trembling Kadiatu. Keshel's face was unreadable.

"That's generous of you, Lady Marai, but seven faeries are no match for an army," Avilyard said, looking from Marai to Kadiatu, who was hugging Keshel's arm to her torso.

"Not just seven faeries," Tarik said with gusto from the back of the packed tent, "but six wolves, as well."

The werewolves thumped their weapons against their chests in a show of strength and pride.

"While I admire your bravery, I don't see how this will work without all thirteen of you getting slaughtered," Avilyard said. "I may not know much about werewolves, but I do know that in your human forms, you're no stronger than the average man."

"Yeah, but we've each got more grit than twenty of you," Tarik said, holding his head high with a smirk.

Grit could only account for so much. Fear like nothing Ruenen had ever known pierced his lungs, driving a shard of ice through his heart. But Ruenen knew that Marai would never suggest this plan if she didn't wholly believe it. He met Marai's stare, and read her resolve.

"Can you do it?" Ruenen asked. His heart was fracturing. He shouldn't be encouraging this idea. As Prince, he could tell her no.

Raife stepped forward, clapping a hand on Tarik's shoulder. "We can hold the line. We'll be the rock that breaks the wave."

Thora gaped up at him, one tear streaking down her cheek.

"We'll pull out all the stops, at least until Grelta arrives," Leif said with a roguish shrug.

Avilyard stared from fae to werewolf. "How do you intend to do this?" Skepticism laced every word.

Marai cocked her head, looking up at Keshel. He stepped up to the table. "Shields. Magical barriers. I'll place one around the entire Nevandian army."

Jaws dropped.

"What exactly do you mean?" asked Commander Filitto next to Ruenen. Swords and arrows were one thing humans could understand, but magic was an entirely different entity.

"After our army is in place, I'll erect an invisible shield. Let Tacorn and Varana waste their arrows. They won't penetrate the barrier."

"You cannot hold that shield forever," Ruenen said, knowing that all magic had limits.

"I'll slowly pull back, unit by unit, until I no longer have the power." He would use it all. Keshel would spend every ounce of his magic to create and hold that shield. "Once my shield comes down, the rest of the fae will use their magic." His eyes went strangely blank for a moment, gazing at something far off in the distance. "Except for Marai. She'll be our last line of defense."

The look that passed between Keshel and Marai was deep and filled with so much meaning. Ruenen stiffened. What had Keshel seen? An ominous feeling crept up Ruenen's spine.

"Count me in on the left," came Nosficio's silky voice from the tent entrance. Bodies shifted and recoiled as Nosficio strode to Marai's side, eating up the attention and shocked expressions. "Magical folk fight together."

Marai crookedly smirked.

"A vampire?" asked Tarik. A few of the werewolves raised their weapons higher. "You certainly *are* a welcoming country."

Nosficio replied with a fanged grin.

"Fine, I'll lead the middle—" Avilyard began.

"No, I need you commanding the right side," said Ruenen, fighting back the tremors that inhabited him, all the way to the tips of his fingers. He wouldn't let them see his fear. "I'll lead the main offensive, with Commander Filitto."

"Your Highness—" multiple commanders said at once.

"Rayghast wants *me*. It must be *me* who meets him on the field in the center of everything. Might as well make myself easy to find," Ruenen said.

"And who will lead the left—"

"I will," Marai stated in a voice so clear and strong, Ruenen felt she'd been born for this moment. Laimoen's creature, she'd once called herself. The God of Death, Destruction, and War. If Lirr had indeed sculpted Marai from her partner's darkness, Ruenen knew she would lead, and never accept defeat.

"Trust her," said Nosficio with a devious leer around the tent, "she *is* Queen of the Fae, after all."

It was as if Nosficio had unleashed a giant slap across the tent, cracking across the faces of each commander and all the werewolves. The fae didn't appear surprised, although Leif scowled, less than pleased. Marai, however, sent a vicious, blazing glare at the vampire, who ignored it by sweeping his dreadlocks over his shoulder. The air pulsed once with a power Ruenen knew belonged to Marai. If she had looked daggers at *him* in that way, Ruenen would've cowered. Any other human would've pissed themselves.

Questions sizzled on Ruenen's tongue. So many questions. But the revelation had to wait.

I don't have time to unpack that *statement.*

"I trust you to hold the left flank alone," Ruenen said. Scorching eyes softened, and Marai nodded once. "You and your unit are dismissed."

Marai signaled with a jerk of her head to the magical folk, and they all exited the tent. Nosficio glided out after them, not at all like someone marching off to war.

The commanders slumped, loosening the tension they'd been holding at the presence of magical folk.

"Let's continue," Avilyard said, placing his hands on the map.

Ruenen's feet moved before his mind had made the choice. "Excuse me for one moment, Gentlemen. Continue without me."

He brushed aside the tent flap and found the fae, werewolves, and Nosficio huddled away from the soldiers. Raife pointed, stone-faced, assigning tasks to each of them. As Ruenen approached, Raife stopped.

"I want to know what your plan is."

"We don't use any magic until Keshel's shields go down," Raife explained. "Until then, we shall use our physical weapons. Leif, Aresti, and I will then deplete our magic reservoirs. Thora will remain in the rear to offer medical assistance."

Thora bit her lower lip; red bloomed, but she didn't notice. Her lips were already chapped and bruised.

That left Marai and Kadiatu, who stared at each other from across the huddle. Kadiatu, usually brimming with life, radiating joy, had her face set in steely determination.

"Do you think you can combat his magic through the earth?" Marai asked her.

Kadiatu's lips pursed.

"What do you mean?" asked Ruenen. "Like . . . through a tunnel?"

"Kadi's been returning balance, taking back what Rayghast stole from Nevandia," Marai said. "She's already been battling him through the earth for days."

Ruenen's eyebrows nearly shot off his face. "You can do that? Reverse the effects of his magic?"

Kadiatu swallowed. "He makes the ground heave and fluctuate, like an earthquake. It cracks, and I mend it."

"But *can* you fight him?" Marai pressed, stepping closer. Kadiatu was taller than Marai by a head—Marai had to tilt her chin up—but she stood like a seasoned general commanding her soldiers.

"For a short while."

"Your main task is to distract him, provoke him. Force him to deplete his well," Raife said, putting a hand on Kadiatu's shoulder.

"Rayghast uses dark magic," Marai explained to the werewolves. "His well doesn't empty the way ours does. Dark magic will continue to replenish him."

"Won't Keshel's shields prevent him from using magic until they're down?" Aresti asked.

"My shields only work above ground. I've no way to stop him underneath," said Keshel, brow furrowed. It was the first time Ruenen had seen his impassive mask crack. "That will be up to Kadi."

Kadiatu squared her shoulders, but her eyes betrayed the fear inside. Anguish bolted through Ruenen. This girl was not meant for gore and death. She wasn't supposed to *battle* anyone. The usual glowing radiance of her skin had dimmed, the light gone from her heart. Ruenen had taken that from her this day.

"That leaves you, Marai," Keshel said, his dark eyes landing on Marai's face. "You save your magic for the end."

"Why? She's the most powerful of us. Let her go first," Leif said. It wasn't spoken with his usual tone of contempt.

"I don't have the power to defeat two armies. I've never tested my magic against a force so large. Whittle down the numbers for me, and then I'll finish it," said Marai, "and hopefully stall long enough for Greltan forces to arrive."

Ruenen didn't like the dark glint in Marai's eyes. Bells pealed in his head in wariness and warning. Marai was the last resort. Once she unleashed her power, Ruenen knew she wouldn't stop. Gods, she might even call upon the dark magic, herself, if she had to. Ruenen felt it right down to the marrow in his bones: she'd give all of herself and more. But if they reduced the numbers, broke the ranks of the Tacorn and Varanese lines *before* she reached into her well of power, then she wouldn't have to go so far.

Maybe she could give *enough*.

The tent emptied sometime in the evening. Ruenen was left alone to stare at his untouched dinner plate and wine goblet. Then to toss and turn in his lavish cot. There would be no rest for him tonight. Not with the battle looming, racing through his consciousness on horseback. Rayghast's dark, murderous, miasmic rage crept across the moor, worming its way through the encampment, seeping in through the seams of the canvas tent.

A figure paced outside the canvas. He watched the shadow prowl back and forth, illuminated by the nearby campfires. Eventually, the shadow decided to enter, whispering curtly to the guards at the flap. A pale hand pushed aside the tarp and peered inside. Ruenen bolted upwards, lowering his feet onto the sheepskin rug.

"You should be asleep." Marai stepped inside, flap closing shut behind her.

"I've watched you pace around outside for five minutes deciding whether to come in or not."

The corners of her mouth twitched. "I didn't want to disturb you, in case you were resting."

"Why aren't *you* sleeping?" he asked.

"Leif snores."

Ruenen snickered. He smelled the lie. He saw it in the way her eyes simmered in the dark tent; two beacons of purple flame.

"Are you really a faerie queen?"

Marai glowered. "Nosficio shouldn't have said that."

"But are you?"

Her jaw clenched. "I'm Queen Meallán's descendant. Progeny to her power. Nosficio seems to think this makes me heir to her nonexistent throne, as well."

An ember glowed deep within Ruenen. Something bloomed and spread, and brought him warmth. He began to laugh.

Marai stared at him as if he'd gone mad. "Why is that funny?"

"Because it's ironic. I have no royal blood at all, yet I'm Prince—"

"Not so loud," she hissed at him, stepping closer.

"—While *you*, the Lady Butcher, are actually heir to an ancient throne."

"I have no intention of taking action on it, though," Marai said, crossing her arms.

"You could. You're already the leader of the fae—"

"Keshel's leader of the fae—"

"No, he's not. They look to *you* now, Sassafras. The moment they stepped foot in these lands, you became their leader."

"I don't want it. A throne. Power. None of the responsibility."

"You sound like someone else I know," Ruenen said with a snarky grin.

Marai's lips twitched again. They quieted. He couldn't look away from her. His heart hurt so deep it felt like it might devour itself. If this was the last night he would gaze upon her face, he'd savor every single second.

"We could die tomorrow," he said, sucking the air right from the tent. He couldn't help but voice the growing fear that had ravaged his mind all day. They didn't have enough men. Even with Nosficio's strength and speed, and the magic of the fae, it wasn't enough.

Marai's face shuttered. "Don't say such things, Ruen." Her voice was as soft as the silken petals of a flower, ones Ruenen had rubbed between his fingers in the garden at the monastery, distracting him from Amsco's lessons.

"Why are you here?" he asked.

"I didn't want you to be alone."

Another lie. Ruenen knew it was also because *she* didn't want to be alone that night.

He gulped down the unspoken things. Words that were too heavy to say out loud. Not when they could both die in mere hours. Three words stayed on his tongue, sweet and sour at once, twisting his gut into knots.

"Stay with me, then."

He reached out his hand. Four steps and she'd crossed the tent. Her calloused fingers closed around his own. He laid back onto the cot, scooting to make room. Marai curled around him, holding his hand to her chest. Ruenen draped his other arm over her small body and pressed his forehead to hers.

Their breath synchronized. Their hearts beat in tandem, a music so pure and potent. He'd never truly appreciated those sounds before. That music could be a person. A feeling. A moment suspended in time. A song in his blood. Ruenen breathed in the leather and verdant smell of her. A crackling fire in his lungs.

And slowly, over the course of the night, their eyelids drifted closed. Her soft breath, a whispered kiss against his cheek, lulled him to a sleep he didn't believe possible.

All through the night, they held each other. The Butcher and the Bard.

CHAPTER 23
Rayghast

The city of Dul Tanen was electric with preparation for battle.

Hundreds of soldiers vacated the barracks and the city. Rayghast had been worried about the morale of the men with all the nasty rumors, but his concerns were swept away by the evening's appearance of several blue-armored Varanese commanders through the castle's portcullis.

Varana's forces had finally arrived.

"King Rayghast." A stoic Varanese commander bowed to him, his voice heavily accented. "I'm Commander Chul, head of Emperor Suli's forces."

"Good of you to finally join us," Silex said snidely from Rayghast's side. "We half-believed you wouldn't show, or that we'd need to start the battle without you."

Silex had joined Rayghast, Commander Shaff, and members of the council as they rode in and out of Dul Tanen to the war camp on the moor all day.

"Queen Rhia was quite convincing in her letter to the Emperor," Chul replied, giving Silex an unsavory grimace, hinting at the threat the letter had contained. With both of his daughters trapped within Dul Tanen, Emperor Suli had no choice but to send his men.

A second Varanese commander craned his neck, searching the courtyard in the waning light. Servants were already lighting the torches for the evening. "We were hoping to see Her Grace and Her Highness while we're in the city. Are Queen Rhia and Princess Eriu available?"

"I'm afraid both are indisposed," Rayghast stated. Chul and his Varanese commanders exchanged dubious glances. "Between the battle and wedding preparations, they've worn themselves out."

Silex sniggered. "Women are so fragile. How tiring could it be to plan a wedding?"

In two days, Eriu was to wed Silex. Rayghast hadn't allowed Rhia to see her sister since he'd locked her away. The only times Rhia spoke to another soul was when a servant showed up at her door with a tray of food twice a day. Even then, Rayghast made sure the servant never stayed long enough for true conversation, and the door was always guarded by two of his men.

"We should like to see the young princess, at least," Commander Chul pressed. "Express wishes from the Emperor and Empress."

Relenting, Rayghast gestured to a servant who exited into the castle.

"Would you be interested in some, uh, dinner before you head over to the camp?" asked Cronhold. "You pressed your army hard to make the journey so, uh, quickly."

The commander's dark eyes slid to Rayghast. "We did not have much of a choice."

"While we wait for the princess, we can enjoy a brief dinner, and then we'll ride with you to the moor," Shaff said.

The five Varanese men reluctantly agreed, and followed the council and Shaff inside to the dim, stone dining room, lit by a massive chandelier and roaring fire. For half an hour, Rayghast suffered forced, pleasant conversation with the uptight Varanese commanders, exuberant Cronhold, and unimpressed Silex while they dined.

Princess Eriu still hadn't come down.

Is the brat refusing? Rayghast impatiently drilled his fingers on the armrests of his chair.

A servant entered the room and tiptoed to Rayghast's side. He whispered in a low bow, hovering at Rayghast's ear, "Your Grace, we're searching the castle, but Princess Eriu is missing."

Rayghast stood, without making his excuses to the table, and dragged the servant into the hallway by the arm.

"Don't tell me she's missing," Rayhast growled to the trembling man. "I don't want to hear about more failures. The girl has been locked in her room for days. How could you buffoons lose one stupid child?"

"I'm sorry, Your Grace, we're not sure, we're continuing to look, but another servant is also missing. One who regularly tends Queen Rhia."

"Find her, or it will be your head." Rayghast shoved the man away and returned to the dining room. The Varanese commanders watched his agitated, heavy gait. Even Shaff recognized that the expression on Rayghast's face was one to be concerned about. "The princess won't come down. She's experiencing wedding jitters, and has upset her stomach. She's a dramatic child, as I'm sure you know."

Rayghast doubted a single soul in the room believed his terse lie. Commander Chul appeared ready to argue, but Shaff and Silex were already ushering him and his men from the dining room; servants swept in to clear their plates and goblets.

"You'll be wanting to see the men. Shall we travel to the camp?" asked Shaff, overly loud and enthusiastic.

Rayghast waited until his commander and the Varanese disappeared into the city, then he turned on his heel and bounded up the dark, chilly staircase.

His guards hastened to unlock Rhia's door. With a roar, Rayghast kicked it open.

She'd been sitting at her desk, writing by candlelight, fingers splotched with ink. The Queen of Tacorn rose slowly to her feet, eyes wild, face resolute.

She already knew why he was there.

Rayghast's eyes narrowed on her as he prowled further into the room. "Where is she?"

"I wasn't expecting a visit from you, Husband," Rhia said, dipping her eyes down, voice cold as murder. "You haven't visited my bed for several days. I assumed you were distracted with your war."

"Where is your sister?" Red, searing anger crept up Rayghast's neck.

Rhia didn't even flinch at the animal rage in his voice. "I haven't left this room, Your Grace. I haven't seen Eriu in two days."

Rayghast pulled Rhia forward by her wrist so their faces were inches apart. The fabric of her nightgown's sleeve was the only thing between his blackened hand and her skin. One touch, and his magic would consume her.

"You did something," he growled in her face. "You arranged an escape for her."

"Why would I do such a thing? I've been an obedient wife, as you demanded. I've told no one of your . . . abnormality. I've kept your secret."

Rayghast stared at her defiant, beautiful face. Gone was the mask of demure compliance; her eyes now two flints of fury. *Finally, an honest reaction.*

Magic awakened inside him, stretching out like a cat.

Rayghast let go of the queen's wrist and continued to examine her with his dark gaze. "My father, the late King Hershen, believed I was an atrocity, as well. A prince of royal blood displaying magic? Unacceptable. He thought my powers were a weakness. He thought he could remove them." Rayghast lifted his hand and stared at the blackened flesh. "How wrong he was."

Rage rushed through him as he remembered the pain and torture he received from King Hershen's hand. How the magic had only grown and festered within him; his father's hatred a rich, fertile soil.

"My father experienced the magic firsthand. One strike too many. One insult piled on top of the other. I could no longer allow him to treat me as if I was nothing more than a worthless Nevandian convict. The magic made quick work of him."

Rayghast remembered the moment, burned forever into his brain: black smoke had crawled up Hershen's nose and squeezed his heart to a pulp. Hershen, once so powerful, a villain in Rayghast's childhood, crumbled to the ground like a marionette whose strings had been cut. The healers had blamed it on a heart attack. No one was any the wiser to Rayghast's regicide, a treasonous act alone, but with *magic* . . . if the rest of Tacorn knew the truth, they'd rise up and refuse to fight in the upcoming battle.

Rhia gaped at him, horrified, backing away against the wall.

"I can hear the thoughts inside your head. You think me a monster," Rayghast said with vicious pleasure. One glance at her desk, however, had Rayghast distracted from her paling face.

Papers were scattered across the polished mahogany. Rayghast recognized the strange foreign writing, coded messages amongst the clutter. Tattered and ripped parchment regurgitated rumors, the same ones heard amongst the citizens, copied dozens of times.

Rayghast's mind went black with fury. "It was you. *You* created the false rumors."

Emotions and thoughts flashed across Rhia's face. *She can't talk her way out of this one.*

"False? Hardly," Rhia snapped back, gathering her courage. "You think I didn't feel it the minute I first stepped foot in this castle? Darkness surrounds you. You *breed* evil."

"And the coded messages?"

Rhia's lips curved into a sinister smile. "Ancient Varanese, a language no longer practiced in our country, save for members of the royal line. Your alliance with my people stands on a razor's edge. I've sowed enough discord and doubt that at the first sign of trouble, they'll turn to Dul Tanen and sack this city instead."

He could have been impressed with his wife. She was far smarter, far braver, than he ever gave women credit for.

But she was a traitor. Disloyal and dishonorable.

His teeth ground together. "You used your ladies and servants to distribute the messages."

Rhia sneered. "Oh, yes, the women of this city were more than happy to assist me. Abused servants, mistreated wives . . . and you, with your obsession with Nevandia, never once suspected your network of traitors was run by women."

Rayghast stepped closer to her, reaching out with his stained fingers.

Rhia leapt to the side; her legs collided with the bed. "Don't touch me," she snarled.

"Tell me where your sister is."

"Gone. Away from you and Silex." Rhia swallowed, but kept her composure, tossing her glossy hair from her painted face. Even in confinement, she chose to look her best. Rhia didn't cower as she said, "Kill me and be done with it."

The magic in his veins flared at the thought.

No, that's too easy, too painless.

"You are a beautiful woman, Rhia. But that's all you are. So let me take that from you as well."

His fingers stroked the flesh of her soft cheek as she struggled and reared. Black smog encompassed her. It seared deep within the tissues and tendons and muscles of her face, eating away from the inside out. She bleated a cry, tried to wrench herself away, but magic had wrapped around her waist, tethering her to Rayghast. She screamed and screamed.

Then Rayghast stepped back to admire his handiwork.

Rhia put a hand to her blazing cheek and gagged at what came away in her hand. Black flakes of skin, like the ash on a burnt log. She swerved around to look in her mirror.

She screamed again.

And again.

From jaw to forehead on the right side was entirely charred. Dead flesh blistered away, peeling back to reveal bone and teeth.

Behind her, Rayghast burned with pleasure and black flames.

"You should be grateful that I didn't take your head. Next time, I will. And when I find Eriu, you can be sure she will be similarly punished for running away."

Rhia abandoned all fear and decorum, turning to him in a reckless frenzy. "You will *never* touch Eriu. I pray Nevandia wins. I pray to Laimoen that you and this entire country go up in flames. I *curse* you. I may not have the powers you do, but for this one act, I wish I did. I curse you to the fiery depths of the Underworld!"

Rayghast turned without another word, no flicker of emotion at all in response to her words, leaving her to rage. His last image of his wife was of Rhia smashing her beloved mirror to the floor, letting the image of her ruined face break into hundreds of shards.

He locked her room and left to kill a prince.

CHAPTER 24
Marai

Black, hazy tendrils brushed across the recesses of her mind. Tiny pinpricks, like a spider's feet, crawled up her arms.

Marai... Marai... called a voice wan and haunting, gossamer as smoke.

Her magic rushed and spiraled, spinning and whirring, pulsating within the confines of her body. But there was another presence, magic that wasn't her own. A dark shadow slunk up her legs. Filmy hands made of cobwebs inched over her hips, her torso...

Use me, it seemed to say.

The pull was so great, the tug on her magic so strong, it jolted Marai awake. She bolted upright, unsheathing the dagger at her waist.

But all she saw was Ruenen asleep at her side. No other presence lingered in the tent. Nothing sinister. Outside, she heard the low mumbles of guards and soldiers, the crackling of campfires, wuthering of wind through bushes, early-morning chirps of birds. Nothing out of the ordinary.

A nightmare, she told herself.

She'd imagined Slate's vicious hands clawing at her before. She was used to these kinds of nightmares, but this one had been different. Never before had she heard that voice, seen hands like *that*. Nothing about them said *human*. Or even magic.

Her black fingertips tingled, almost needle-sharp.

Would dark magic consume her if she went back to sleep? Marai laid down next to Ruenen, who continued to breathe evenly, face peaceful. She burrowed into the crook of his neck, every part of her alert. Her eyelids never shut. Her hand never left her dagger.

Ruenen stirred before the horn sounded. Marai watched his eyes flutter open, blinking away the sleep. She counted the gold flecks–a dozen or so in each brown eye. He stared back, perhaps doing the same with her own eyes. Memorizing them. Losing herself in them.

But at the horn, she and Ruenen sat up. Any second, Mayestral and soldiers would burst into the tent. They couldn't see Marai and the Prince of Nevandia lying together. She climbed off the cot and strode towards the tent flap.

A hand grabbed hers. In an instant, Ruenen's arms encompassed her, clinging to her body like a lifeline. Marai raised up on her toes, hooking her hand behind his neck, and pulled his face to hers. Their lips met, sweet and gentle. She felt no hunger, no desire. Her fingers laced through the strands of his hair, savoring the final silken touch against her skin.

Marai counted down from five. Four more seconds of this safety. Three more seconds of his soft lips. Two more seconds of his hands gripping her to his solid chest. One more second of *him*.

She pulled away, unable to meet his eyes again. She rushed from the tent before she could change her mind. If Marai didn't leave then, she never would.

Out into the misty, gray morning, the air was static with tension and unease. The guards on duty outside Ruenen's tent peered at her through their visors. They knew she'd been there all night.

"Protecting the prince," she grunted, indicating the sword and dagger at her hip.

The guards said nothing as a group of commanders stomping towards them caught their attention. Marai ducked behind another tent, not wanting to explain herself to anyone else. The commanders had two other figures in tow: a woman in a brown cape, and a girl in a deep blue one.

"What's this?" asked Avilyard, appearing from the opposite side of camp.

"Tacorn defectors," Commander Gasparian said. "Found them crossing the moor a bit ago in the pitch dark."

"Please, we seek refuge, sir. We walked all night," said the woman with breathless desperation. "I'm Queen Rhia's servant from the fortress at Dul Tanen. I come with Princess Eriu of Varana."

Marai peeked around the edge of the tent. The girl dropped the hood of her cloak, revealing her round face and long black hair, her nose red from the early morning chill.

"Why exactly is the princess here?" Avilyard asked.

"My sister sent me," Eriu said in youthful boldness. "It wasn't safe for me in Tacorn. King Rayghast was forcing me to marry a bad man."

Marai's stomach curdled. *She's just a child.*

"Please, sir, we're hoping you'll allow us to remain. We women in Tacorn have heard of your prince's merciful nature," the woman said, practically groveling, she was bent so low before the commanders. "We risked our lives to cross the border, and our queen uncovered a heinous secret about our king. He has *magic*, sir!"

None of the commanders or soldiers flinched at the news. They were already aware of Rayghast's power, thanks to Marai.

Avilyard studied the girl. "Your sister is the Queen of Tacorn. Your father is the Jade Emperor of Varana. Their forces stand opposite ours on the field. Don't you think you're safer with them?"

"Don't send me back," Princess Eriu yelped. "King Rayghast will hurt me if he finds me! He'll hurt Rhia, too. He already locked her in her room."

"If he discovers you missing, he'll hurt your sister, regardless," Avilyard said in a gentle voice, as if he were a father speaking with his own daughter. "I'll not send you back, but you cannot stay here. A battlefield is no place for a child. I'll find someone to escort you to Kellesar. Once the battle is over, we'll figure out what to do."

If Nevandia fell, the girl would be returned to Rayghast and her betrothed. They'd punish her in some brutish way, and the servant woman would be executed for treason.

The princess' face brightened through her tears. "Thank you!" She wrapped her arms around Avilyard's middle, startling the commander.

He hesitantly patted her on the back, then Avilyard called Nyle over. "Take two horses. Come back as soon as they're safe behind Kellesar walls. We may already be engaged in battle by then."

Nyle nodded and shoved his helm onto his head.

"Tell Prince Ruenen . . . I hope he wins," Eriu said. Her young face grew resolute.

Once Nyle ushered Princess Eriu and her servant away, Avilyard turned to his other commanders.

"We can use the princess as leverage over Varana," Gasparian said.

"No harm will come to that child," Avilyard ordered severely, "but we should send a messenger with a white flag over to Varana's lines, let them know we have her, and tell them about the magic. I doubt they're aware."

"Brave of them all, don't you think?" asked Fillito. "Queen Rhia, the little princess, and the servant? To defy Rayghast on the eve of battle . . . takes balls."

Marai smirked to herself, then wove through the city of tents to the outskirts of the encampment, far from the others. There, she parted the canvas flap to enter the ratty tent that housed the fae.

Inside, they were already awake and dressed, faces etched with fear. Thora clung to Raife's hand, squeezing so hard his fingers turned purple.

All Marai could do was stare at them. Stare and stare, and wonder why in the Unholy Underworld she'd brought them to this place; ushered them to their likely deaths. How could she ever forgive herself if one of them perished?

Unworthy. Ruined. Tainted, that nasty voice echoed in her ears. The voice she'd managed to turn off for days.

Marai combatted the voice with her own. *Don't let them see your fear. You're the Lady Butcher. You're Meallán's heir. You're their leader, and you do what you must.*

It took all of her inner fortitude she had to speak.

"We're here to fight for all magical folk." Her throat burned. A quiver began in her left leg. "Our future. Nevandia can be our home. We can find peace here, shape a future for so many others."

"Home will wait for every one of us," said Kadiatu softly, taking Marai's hand. "It will wait."

Marai let out a shuddering breath as Kadiatu's fingers tightened around hers. "Let's win this battle. Let's claim victory for ourselves and for our parents. For those we lost, who sacrificed themselves so we could live. Let's bring honor to the fae."

The bloodstone ring thrummed, sending a shiver of magic through her. Meallán's magic, beckoning, beseeching, a shade darker than Marai's own.

I will, Marai told the ring. *We shall have our revenge against Tacorn and Rayghast.*

The jewel quieted. It purred like a curled-up cat against Marai's finger. She hadn't used its magic before, but it was now time to find out what kind of power was in a faerie queen's curse.

For too long Marai had hid in the shadows. Now was the time to step into the light.

"For the fae," Raife said, putting his fist to his heart. He let go of Thora's hand to do so.

Leif and Aresti followed with vigor, echoing his words. They'd become warriors; their parents would be proud. One by one, Keshel, Thora, and Kadiatu all did the same.

Marai was last. She whispered the words, remembering her father's eyes. Her mother's face. The moment she was ripped away from them and thrust into this life of hardship. Alone, except for the people in this tent. Love washed over Marai with staggering strength. Her knees wobbled, barely keeping her standing. Her family.

"The last march of the fae," Leif said with a grin.

They all watched her again. Their leader. Their unintended queen.

Marai dismissed them with a nod, throat too constricted to make a sound. Leif and Aresti slammed their helmets on their heads, clattering outside in their golden Nevandian armor. Thora adjusted the pack strapped across her body, took a sputtering breath, grabbed Kadiatu's hand, and walked after them.

Before Marai could follow, Keshel took her arm and pulled her close. His fingers didn't hold; they were light upon her forearm. His warm breath caressed the shell of her ear as he bent down. "Don't use it, Marai. No matter what happens, do not touch the dark magic."

She glanced up into his eyes, shimmering with emotions he always kept hidden behind a veil of detachment. How Keshel had not broken . . . how he'd managed to save the lives of so many, how he always stayed calm in the face of so much fear . . .

"Of course," Marai lied. "I'd never let that happen."

They exited the tent together. The others were speaking with the fully-armed weres and Nosficio. He'd discarded his velvet cape in favor of black gambeson and a full hood over his head. His whole body was covered, except for his red eyes and fanged mouth, which quirked at the sight of Marai.

"Envious of my hood, Butcher?" he asked with amusement. "It doesn't fall down when I fight."

Marai snorted. "If only I'd come to you for fashion advice."

Nosficio grinned, revealing all his teeth. The sky was overcast. There'd be limited direct sunlight, but the vampire still risked his life twice over by being out on a battlefield with no shelter.

He must truly believe in this, she thought.

No, you are *the one he believes in.* It wasn't Nevandia. Nosficio hated Rayghast, but he was there because of *her*.

Horns sounded. A call to arms. Soldiers rushed about, abandoning their breakfasts and watery coffees by the campfires. They mounted horses, grabbed weapons, adjusted their armor. The poorer Nevandians had no coverage in their thin and ragged clothing. They held pitchforks and scythes with freezing fingers in the early spring morning. But they marched towards battle with honor and courage, bracing themselves for the inevitable.

Tarik held out his massive hand to Marai. "It's an honor to fight with you."

Marai gave the werewolf a rare smile. "The honor is mine, Master Wolf."

Tarik grinned, then turned to bellow orders to his men.

Thora latched on to Raife's arm, yanking him back towards her. In a breath, Thora pulled his face to hers. Marai pretended not to watch. The desperation in their kiss, the love and longing, regret and unspoken promises seized Marai. Raife and Thora clung to each other like two merging souls.

"I've loved no one but you," Raife whispered into her pointed ear. "My whole life, I've loved you."

Thora choked back a sob; tears glistened on her bronze cheeks. "I'm sorry. We should have . . . I shouldn't have said no. Because now all I want, Raife, is the life we could have had."

Raife held her to his chest. "We will have that life. We'll have years and years ahead of us."

Thora kissed his palms as Raife went to cup her cheeks. She uttered "I love you," those three small words over and over again like a prayer.

Marai finally turned away, eyes burning, throat tightening. If they both made it out alive, it would be a miracle from Lirr.

Side by side, fae, werewolf, and vampire marched onwards.

Marai searched for Ruenen. She couldn't spot him in the mist and masses.

Hold the left.

Marai led her small unit to the far side of the sprawling army, feeling as if she were a tiny rowboat lost in an endless sea. Avilyard had sectioned the units into blocks. It was easy to spot the rows of gold armored mounted cavalry—Nevandia's most skilled knights. Their horses were bedecked in Nevandian colors; the sunburst symbol sewed onto their caparison cloths. The cavalry had been relegated to the outer edges, surrounding the infantry, except for a small grouping in the center. Marai's chest tightened. Ruenen was in that grouping.

Infantry surrounded the mounted knights. They gripped lances, javelins, swords, and shields, while the archers were dispersed in clumps amongst them. The most experienced soldiers were spread across the front lines, forming the shield wall. Green and gold shields overlapped, edge-to-edge, across the infantry ranks, back and back until the final row.

Sunburst flags billowed in the breeze as the army marched onwards, leaving the camp behind. They marched towards the dirt road cleaving the Red Lands in two. The only sound was the stomping of the marching army, moving as one. No one spoke. All their concentration was focused on the battle before them.

Across the moor, black shapes gathered through the thick fog, like a massive flock of crows. Rows and rows of infantry soldiers, a tight, long line of black shields stretching across the horizon. Marai couldn't see where the far right side ended.

Rayghast's army was assembled.

Nevandia stood ready for its finale.

As the enemy neared, Marai spotted details amongst the black cloud of soldiers: their crossed-sword emblem pins, red feather plumes in their commander's helmets, their painted shields. They were in range now for the archers.

The air fluctuated and flexed as Keshel's shield snapped into place around the entire Nevandian army. The scent of decadent wine, leather, and old parchment wafted through the fog; the distinctive scent of Keshel's magic. Marai reached out her power and gently pushed against his barrier, sensing its oscillating boundaries. Next to her, Keshel shivered and sucked in a deep breath as her magic skimmed across his.

The shield stretched farther and farther, all the way to the far right side of the Nevandian army where Commander Avilyard sat on his horse, bellowing orders. No one besides the fae, weres, and Nosficio had registered the appearance of Keshel's shield. Marai didn't know how long Keshel's magic would last, being stretched so far.

The heavy beat of war drums reverberated through the ground at Marai's feet. The sound echoed in the cavities of her chest, instilling a strength and steadiness there. Horns blazed again.

One lone golden figure on the back of a white horse broke the ranks in the center of the Nevandian army.

Marai watched the figure raise his sword. She couldn't hear the words he shouted. So instead, she imagined him up on a stage, singing; deft fingers strumming on his lute.

He'll write a song about this day.

It began from the center of the army. A mighty roar rippled through the ranks. Marai's lips reared back and she echoed the courageous sound, thrusting Dimtoir into the air.

Tacorn and Varana unleashed a volley of arrows. Shooting stars in the daytime sky, they arched through the air and collided with Keshel's shield. Nevandians flinched, raising shields over their heads to protect themselves, but they watched, aghast, as the arrows bounced off the invisible barrier and fell to the ground.

Then Nevandia returned fire. Keshel allowed anything on his side to travel through freely. Raife and Leif pulled back on the string of their longbows. Arrows whizzed through the air. Raife's arrow expertly cleaved through space, finding its mark in the neck of a Tacornian, where the armor was weakest. The arrow penetrated deep.

Another volley of flaming arrows from Tacorn ricocheted off the shield. Then another from the Nevandians.

A third from Tacorn, but this time, the arrows came with rocks.

Tacorn had brought their trebuchets.

As each rock collided with Keshel's shields, the barrier flickered. The area of impact burst with color and light, but didn't crack. At Marai's side, standing with his arms spread high and wide, Keshel winced with each strike of stone.

The barrage became more persistent throughout the hour. More rocks, more arrows. The sun climbed higher, shrouded by thick clouds. The fog lifted, granting a clear view of the black wall of Tacorn. To the left, facing down Marai's unit, were the blue-armored Varanese. Their cobalt and white flags billowed in the breeze. A water dragon was their symbol, and their blue armor was scaled like the mythical creatures with a line of spikes across their spines.

Giant rocks, pieces of highland boulders, crashed against the shield. Keshel swayed. His barrier spasmed in a sea of iridescent color, but he didn't lower his arms. Raife grabbed hold of him, dropping his bow to keep Keshel on his feet.

"Time to shrink the barrier," Raife said. Keshel nodded, gritting his teeth.

Like a retreating tide, the shield withdrew from the right flank. Avilyard's side was entirely exposed now. Then slowly, the shield peeled away from the center.

Ruenen, on his white stallion, must've noticed the magic receding as Tacornian arrows finally hit their marks. He shouted something and men raised their weapons. They began to run; Ruenen's horse leading the charge. Horns sounded. Then the right side followed and Avilyard galloped onwards. Next to Marai, Tarik and the werewolves shouted words of encouragement to the Nevandians.

Tacorn forces charged to meet them. Marai cringed as the black and golden walls collided. The sound of clattering, clashing metal would live in Marai's ears forever, along with their immediate screams. Heads and arms were lopped off. The sight was gruesome, even to Marai who was used to such carnage.

Leif shut his eyes. He covered his pointed ears with his hands, and dropped to the ground in a squat. His labored breath heaved his whole upper body.

"You have to see in order to fight," Marai said, kneeling next to him.

Leif shook his head, squeezing his eyes tighter. "I still see them . . . my parents and sister. All I can hear are their screams."

Marai placed her hands on his arm. *I wish I could spare him from this.* But Marai was a unit commander now. She couldn't let any of her troops break.

"You are vengeance, Leif. A warrior. Unleash your anger upon Rayghast. Do it for your family. Remember what you're fighting for."

Leif met her unyielding stare. "How do you do it, Marai? How do you see these things and keep going?"

For a moment, Marai couldn't speak. She didn't know the answer. But Leif's eyes swum with questions and pleadings and fear.

"Defeat is not in my blood," she said, as magic and courage swirled around in her chest, "nor is it in yours. We will not be conquered." Marai allowed her lips to curl into a vicious grin. "I'm a nightmare."

Leif's emerald eyes widened, then his face hardened as he said, "Let's make Rayghast rue the day he killed our people."

Marai lifted Leif to his feet.

He arched an eyebrow. "My Queen."

For the first time ever, they shared a smile.

The Varanese charged forward now, too, but Keshel's shield remained in place around the left side of the Nevandian forces. Varanese smashed their weapons upon the shield, but couldn't penetrate it. Weapons broke and shattered against the forcefield.

Marai hadn't realized she'd walked to the edge of Keshel's barrier. She hadn't noticed her feet guiding her towards Ruenen. She watched him cut down a Tacornian soldier, but she was trapped within the glass box of duty.

Hold the left.

"You've done enough, Keshel," came Thora's pleading voice, making Marai turn. "Drop the shield."

Keshel knelt on the ground, dripping with sweat, panting as he continued to hold up his arms. His entire body shook from the effort, as if the pressure was pinning him down to the ground. Keshel shook his head viciously, face scrunched up in concentration. Marai sensed he still had power. His well wasn't empty yet.

Then the earth rumbled.

CHAPTER 25
Rayghast

He'd expected the Butcher. He knew the faerie would join her beloved prince on the battlefield.

But Rayghast hadn't anticipated others.

Tacorn's arrows and trebuchets couldn't penetrate the invisible shield. His army couldn't move forward. Nothing but magic could have created such a strong barrier. It was almost impossible to believe that Nevandia had employed other fae. A kingdom seeped in deep prejudice, not unlike Tacorn, gladly accepted the help of magical folk?

The young prince was bold, indeed; dangerous for both the continent and humanity to grant those creatures such power.

"How is this possible?" Dobbs asked, face paling as he stared open-mouthed at the stagnant scene before him. Until the barrier came down, there was no point in sounding the charge. "I thought the faerie girl could only open doorways?"

"The units leaving Gloaw Crana were entirely decimated by fire and other savage things. That couldn't have been the work of one faerie," said Commander Shaff.

Rayghast watched from his position on a mound of earth next to Shaff, Dobbs, Silex, Chul and another Varanese commander, and flag bearers from both countries.

"It wasn't," Rayghast said. "Nevandia has several."

Chul sent Rayghast a bitter glare. "You never said anything about *faeries* in Nevandia—"

Silex blanched, cutting off the Varanese commander. "I thought we rid the world of them years ago!"

Chul and the other commander bowed their heads together in serious conversation.

"It appears we weren't as thorough as we thought," Dobbs said with a sneer. His face then went taut with concern as he beheld Rayghast upon his horse. "Your Grace, are you certain you don't wish to don your armor?"

Rayghast sat in his saddle wearing nothing but black pants and tall boots. He'd left his crown in the fortress, not that he ever wore that heavy ornament, except during important state events.

"I'm sure we'd all feel much better if you'd at least wear a gambeson, My King," Silex said, glancing down to Rayghast's bare, black torso. "Any injury to you, our most sovereign and powerful king, would be a great blow to Tacorn. Not that I believe that will happen, of course. You are a superior warrior to any of them."

Rayghast ignored their comments. Why would he need armor when he had all the protection he'd require within his own body? His eyes narrowed as he scanned the field.

They were wasting arrows. It was quite clear that until the barrier fell, their assault was pointless.

Magic rushed to Rayghast's fingers. It seared behind his eyes, blazed in the wiring of his brain. It sped up the beat of his heart to a frantic gallop. The mere sight of battle, and Rayghast could scarcely contain it. The dark beast paced back and forth through his veins, whispering thoughts of murder.

"How do we fight against *magic*?" asked the other Varanese commander with wisp-thin hair and an equally slim mustache.

A rider appeared, carrying a message with the Nevandian seal. He cantered to Chul and handed him the folded letter. "This was given to me by a Nevandian envoy, Sir." The rider, mussed and harried, then bolted back down the hill and into line with the other cavalry.

Chul read the letter, crumpling it in his fist when he finished. "They have Princess Eriu."

The other Varanese commander swore under his breath. Rayghast had had a feeling that was where the little imp had run off to.

"Did they threaten to harm her?" asked Silex, but Rayghast heard no true concern in the lord's voice for his young bride-to-be.

"This Commander Avilyard says that he'll return the girl to us if Varana retreats and returns home. He also rambles on about *magic*—"

"You will do no such thing," spat Silex, taking the note from Chul and reading it himself.

The other Varanese commander gaped. "But, my lord, she's to be your wife. We cannot let harm befall her—"

"If they kill her, then I'll get another wife. There are other princesses in Astye," Silex said imperiously, facing Rayghast and chucking the message over his shoulder. "The important thing is to win this battle."

Rayghast, bored by the conversation, drawled, "Princess Eriu is of no concern to us now. Once we win the day, we'll take her back, if she still lives."

The two Varanese men glared at him, mouths jerking in anger and withheld comments.

A shimmer in the gray sky caught Rayghast's attention. A filmy shield peeled away from the right side of the Nevandian army. It pulled back and back towards the left.

Suddenly, Tacornian arrows hit their marks. Golden soldiers and peasants fell after a Varanese volley.

The shield was down.

"Go. Send the men in *now*," Rayghast ordered sharply to Shaff.

The commander bowed his head, then hastened down the hill towards the lesser-ranked commanders on the field. Horns blared and the troops, en masse, marched forward to cross the dirt road.

Nevandia had already begun their charge. A golden-clad man on a white horse barreled straight down the center.

The prince.

Rayghast could still see the slight gloss of the magical shield in place over the left side of the Nevandian army.

That's where they are.

As long as the fae remained, Nevandia had a chance to win. Rayghast didn't know what kind of powers they had in their arsenal, nor how many of them there truly were, but the one person capable of eliminating them, fighting against them, was him.

Rayghast jumped from the saddle; his boots slammed into the grass. He knelt down and put his hands on the earth, resulting in gasps of concern from Dobbs and Silex.

"Your Grace, is something wrong?" asked Dobbs. The fool thought Rayghast was ill.

Magic swirled within him. It burst from his hands in dark, mirthful release. He could almost feel the magic *smiling* as it tunneled underground.

Finally, we're free, it cooed as it fled from his body and into the soil, heading towards the left Nevandian side. Black flames rose from the Underworld, encircling Rayghast in blazing, cold darkness.

"Your Grace, what . . . what is that?" asked Silex, pointing to the writhing flames surrounding Rayghast. The smell of sulfur permeated the air. Rayghast tasted the familiar scratch of pepper in his pharynx. "Is that . . . ?"

Everyone backed away. Their horses reared with shrieking neighs. Dobbs and Silex's skin went ashen. By revealing his magic, Rayghast had done something unconscionable, something horrific. Silly, considering how many people Dobbs and Silex had seen killed and tortured in the dungeons.

With terror in their faces, the two men galloped away back towards Dul Tanen.

"The rumors *are* true," a flag bearer bellowed and ran down the hill to spread the word amongst the soldiers.

"Queen Rhia wasn't lying," Chul shouted, pointing a finger at Rayghast. "She told us you were a monster, and the Nevandian commander said the same. We're calling off our men. We won't fight alongside a monster!"

The second Varanese commander snarled. *"Abomination!"*

He unsheathed his sword and swung down towards Rayghast's back. Magic reared, engulfing the commander in darkness. When it dissipated, all that was left of him was his sword, melted into searing-hot iron.

Chul shrieked, and made to flee on horseback towards the Varanese ranks. "Withdraw! Varana withdraw!"

But the magic ran him down, consuming both him and his mount, before anyone heard him.

There was no point in hiding any longer. He'd need to use the magic inside of him in order to combat the fae. Besides, his power was too robust, too difficult to contain. Rayghast no longer worried about retaliation. Once Nevandia was destroyed, no one on Astye would dare challenge him, not when people were this scared of his dark abilities.

City after city would fall to him. Dark magic was limitless. He could call and pull forever, and it would always grant him more. And more. And more. Rayghast was unstoppable.

But then, across the moor, someone began pushing back.

CHAPTER 26
Marai

A tremor crossed the field, causing soldiers on both sides to stumble. The air shifted again. This time, Marai caught the unmistakable scent and sensation of dark magic: pungent sulfur, decay, icy darkness, and burning logs. Gray clouds above darkened. The sun all but disappeared from the sky. Fog swirled as magic rumbled through the ground.

Rayghast had unleashed.

"Kadi," Marai shouted. In an instant, Kadiatu appeared at her side, hands clenching the thick fabric of her pants. "See what you can do."

Kadiatu's chin dipped once as she steeled herself. She dropped to her knees and placed her hands on the brittle grass. Fingers became claws as they dug into the earth. Kadiatu closed her eyes.

White and viridescent light seeped from her hands. It burrowed into the dirt and grass. The shockwaves under Marai's feet suddenly stalled; the earth had been frozen. Green bloomed around Kadiatu. Sprigs of purple heather popped open, flaxen gorse burst to life, and broom flowers blossomed.

Across the moor, a wave of earth rose like an ocean from the ground, knocking Varanese soldiers off their feet. It rushed, plowing through people, as if coming ashore, spewing gravel in its wake.

Kadiatu met the swell with a burst of her own power. The ground before her rose up and crashed into Rayghast's attack. Rocks and dirt went flying.

Keshel's shield protected Marai and the others from the debris, but several soldiers to the right were struck and injured.

Kadiatu's body shook, covered in sweat.

"Excellent, Kadi," Marai urged, breathlessly, putting a hand on her shoulder.

"I'm not sure how long I can do this," said Kadiatu, turning her round, anxious face towards Marai. "He's strong... so much stronger than me!"

Marai squeezed her shoulder. "You're stronger than you think. Stop for nothing."

A dutiful soldier, Kadiatu nodded, focusing once again on her magic beneath the ground. The ground shuddered as Kadiatu *pushed* against the darkness. Marai felt the verdant magic shove the darkness back and back across the moor. With a massive thrust, Kadiatu let out a yell, as her pure magic ran down Rayghast's. The ground went still.

"I knocked him down," Kadiatu said with an air of surprise. She stared down at her dirty hands, a smile growing across her face. "I overpowered him. I pummeled him with rocks, Marai. I hit him in the face!"

Marai clapped Kadiatu on the shoulder. "Great work!"

But the compliment was short-lived. Kadiatu's magic had weakened with such a strong attack, and Rayghast would be on his feet again in moments. His supply of dark magic was seemingly endless.

"Back to work now," Marai said as the earth began to rumble again.

Kadiatu laced her fingers in the grass, and submerged herself in the battle.

Marai caught the snippets of an argument from behind. She glanced over her shoulder.

"But people are dying over there!" Thora twisted out of Raife's grasp. "Let me tend to the nearest ones—"

"It isn't safe—"

"Then why am I here, Raife?" Thora snapped, backing farther away from him and closer to the barrier's edge. "What's the point of standing here watching all those men suffer? I can hear them *screaming,* Raife! They need me."

"You can't heal them all," said Raife, voice softening. He stepped towards her. "You'll run empty of magic too quickly. There are other healers in the encampment and on the field. We need you for the end."

"But none of them have *magic,"* pressed Thora. Silver lined her eyes.

"Let her go," Marai said, causing both of them to halt. "But stay close by, Thora. We're going to need you soon."

Marai's eyes flashed between Keshel and Kadiatu on their knees, bodies trembling with the effort to sustain their magic.

Thora tugged on the strap of her bag, and stepped straight through the barrier. Marai tried not to linger on the sight of Thora rushing towards a bleeding man on the ground, feet away from Varanese soldiers.

Marai turned in time to watch soldiers in black swarm around Ruenen and Commander Filitto at the front. Ruenen hacked at the enemy forces with his sword, but Filitto was pushed backwards, away from his prince, by the Tacornians.

In one horrifying moment, Ruenen's horse reared up on its hindlegs, and he toppled backwards from his saddle.

He was lost in a sea of black.

CHAPTER 27

Ruenen

The impact knocked the breath from his lungs. His teeth slammed together. His helm toppled from his head.

Ruenen lay on his back, too stunned to move. A jagged rock underneath him broke one of his ribs. He'd narrowly missed the hooves of his horse. Two combating soldiers tripped over him, stepping on his arm.

Ruenen was surrounded by Tacorn soldiers. Panic flooded through him. He saw no light, no gold. He reached for his fallen sword, inches away.

"Kill him," shouted a gruff voice.

One of the black-armored men who'd stepped on him raised his sword. "Nevandian scum!"

"Protect the prince," shouted another, someone not so hostile.

Ruenen's fingers grasped his sword. Arms linked under his own and yanked him to his feet. Two men dressed in rags pulled Ruenen to safety as others blocked the Tacornians with their longshields.

"Thank you, friends," Ruenen said in breathless relief.

The men spun, raising their pitchforks into the air. Soon enough, a wave of gold swept the cluster of Tacornians back, led by Commander Filitto.

Sharp pain shot through his side as Ruenen tried to breathe. He lifted his sword, ignoring the rib the best he could before he sliced into Tacornian flesh. Blood spurted across his golden chest plate. The soldier keeled over, and Ruenen moved on to the next.

There were too many. When one trained killer fell, three more took his place. The ground was covered in bloody viscera. Bodies stacked on top of bodies from both sides.

And the *screaming* . . .

The sounds brought Ruenen back to the day Chiojan collapsed. The screams he'd heard then, cowering in that alley . . .

Well, Ruenen wasn't cowering now.

As his men began to lose steam, as black soldiers battered down the line, Ruenen kept his courage. He kept swinging and tried to rally his exhausted army.

"Come on, men! Push forward!" He thrust his sword high into the air. "For Nevandia!"

His soldiers released a mighty yell, gathering their strength. Ruenen led the charge back into the fray, but it didn't last long.

One of the farmers who'd saved Ruenen's life was cut down in a ravaging slice across his torso. The man's face froze, dropping his pitchfork, falling to the ground.

"*No!*" Ruenen rushed to his side, killing his Tacornian opponent, and held the farmer's hand as he drifted off to the Underworld. He didn't know the man's name, but he whispered a silent prayer for him before leaping to his feet and striking down another Tacorn soldier.

The weight of the farmer's death and heroism pressed against Ruenen's breastplate. Another son of Nevandia lost.

Anger fueled Ruenen, mixing with adrenaline, becoming a mighty force inside him.

He hadn't spotted the mad king yet, but Ruenen had seen the earth move and roll. He'd felt it rumbling beneath his feet. Black clouds gathered and roiled in the dark sky.

I won't die until I fight Rayghast.

CHAPTER 28

Rayghast

Rocks and dirt and dust bombarded him.

The faerie battling him beneath the earth had sent a mighty pulse of magic his way. The black smoke that had been tunneling underground was vaporized as lush, green power shattered his magic. Rayghast hadn't had time to dodge before the ground pounced.

Pebbles and stones assaulted his face. One may have knocked out a tooth. Grit and dirt worked its way into his eyes and mouth. A heavy rock landed on his leg.

Rayghast hissed at the pain and shouted curses from his prone position on the ground.

Why was this weak little creature able to use his own technique against him? Rayghast seethed. *Only I control the earth!*

Thankfully, no one had seen him falter. No one had seen him be overcome by such frangible, soft elemental magic. He was alone on the hill. His army and Varana's were entirely engrossed in the battle below. Reserve troops waited patiently in the valley, surveying the slaughter of Nevandia.

They'll get their turn soon. He wouldn't leave a single Nevandian son alive on the field. Not one faerie would remain.

Rayghast stumbled to his feet. His knee was swelling; he could feel the contusion, but it wasn't a break. Blood from small lesions dripped down his face and chest. The pain was minor, but humiliating. Rayghast couldn't let anyone see him in such a state. Any sign of weakness was his death sentence, now that he'd revealed his magic.

"Heal me," he ordered the darkness, wiping a trickle of blood from his nose. It appeared so starkly crimson against the black stain of his skin.

In response, a sensation of *disappointment* rose in him.

You're failing me, it replied, sounding so much like Rayghast's father that it made him, a grown man, wince. *You let a weakling overpower you.*

"I can kill the faerie. It used up all its strength. One more push is all I need. Just give me your power," he said.

Magic flooded through him, but it seemed *reluctant,* as if it was giving him one final chance to end things. If he failed again, Rayghast wondered if it would abandon him.

"I'm not a disappointment," he growled to the magic and the memory of his father.

In an act of punishment, the darkness didn't heal his injuries. Rayghast grit his teeth and kneeled in the grass once more, leg smarting as he did so. He dug his fingers into the ground, dark power snaking and tunneling beneath the earth, and began again.

CHAPTER 29
Marai

Keshel's shield gave out.

Marai watched as he got to his feet, exhausted, and lifted his sword. He could barely hold it, never mind fight, but as the Varanese finally crossed over the threshold, Keshel held his ground.

Seven fae, six werewolves, and one vampire now stood before the Varanese army, blocking them from overtaking the Nevandians. But the Varanese had no idea who they were encountering . . .

Wind rushed around Aresti, stirring the bushes and Marai's hair. With a swipe of her arm, five Varanese were thrown backwards across the battlefield.

Fire burst from Leif and Raife's palms, engulfing dozens. Men screamed, their armor ablaze.

The weres barreled into the Varanese lines, slashing axes and swords through bodies.

Dimtoir sang as it sliced through the air. The Protector. Her father's sword passed down through the generations. Marai stayed by Kadiatu's side as the youngest fae continued her terrestrial battle below the surface.

"He won't stop," Kadiatu said through gritted teeth. "No matter how hard I push, he still presses back. There's no end to his magic!"

Marai cleaved the head from the shoulders of a man. "You don't need to beat him, Kadi. Keep Rayghast occupied. That's all you need to do."

She stabbed upwards through the stomach of another. She moved from soldier to soldier; they dropped like rotten apples from a tree around her.

The Lady Butcher was in her element.

The bloodstone ring hummed with each drop of blood spilt, filling Marai with strength. Magic cascaded up through her chest as a need to destroy sent heat to her fingers.

Revenge, it goaded.

"Not yet," Keshel shouted from behind her. He'd sensed the spark of her power, saw it flicker at her fingertips. He cut down a Varanese man with a bludgeon-like swing.

Marai shoved the magic back down, sealed it off again. *Wait,* she told it. The ring bucked against her bones with impatience.

The others still had power. Through magic and sword, might and nerves, Aresti, Leif, and Raife cut three bloody paths through the Varanese ranks. The weres were too entrenched within the mass of chaos to see, but Marai hoped they were still holding on.

Nosficio's path was marked by decapitated bodies, eviscerated throats, and gaping chest wounds. Darkening skies allowed Nosficio to ditch his gloves, granting him full access to his long nails. Every part of him was covered in red. He didn't slow, his movements a blur. The more he killed, the more blood he drank, and the more overcome he became by bloodlust. Only a stake through the heart would stop him now . . .

Marai made certain to keep Kadiatu, Keshel, and Thora in her line of sight at all times. Despite being at the back of the fray, Thora was still in the thick of things. She wrapped bandages around injured, wailing men, poured liquid down their throats. Her hands and wrists were soaked with blood as she pressed down on a mortal stomach wound.

Thora wasn't paying attention when a Varanese soldier ran straight for her.

But Marai was.

She launched into the air, knocking the soldier to the ground. She sliced across his throat, then stood in time to take down another.

"You need to pay attention," Marai snapped at her.

Blood-red stripes smeared across Thora's face. "I'm trying," she yelled back, wiping away strands of sweaty hair with her sullied hand.

"*Marai,*" came a desperate scream.

The sound wrenched through the nerves in Marai's body.

Kadiatu collapsed, prone on the ground, weak and shaking. "I'm empty!"

She clawed at the earth, trying to drag herself to Marai and Thora, away from the front lines.

"Stay there—I'm coming!"

The earth leapt into the air before Marai had the chance to take a step. Rocks and dirt towered like a colossal wave, a rearing snake, as it sped towards Kadiatu. It knew. Rayghast's dark magic knew she was empty.

Marai's feet barely touched the ground, as if she truly was a phantom. She careened to Kadiatu's side, shoving through combating soldiers. She hurdled over bodies.

But she wasn't fast enough.

The terrestrial wave pounced. In one horrific move, earth engulfed Kadiatu. Her scream was swallowed by grass, dirt, and rock. One dark arm protruded from the mass, clawing, reaching out to Marai.

Marai latched on to Kadiatu's delicate hand. It didn't grasp hers back.

An agonized screech seized Marai from the terror.

Thora appeared at Marai's side. She scratched and pulled with despairing hands at the heap of crumpled earth. "Get her out, Marai," she cried, tears staining her blood-streaked face. "Help me!"

Numbness settled over her. Marai stared at the scene as if she watched it from a distance. Detached. A spectator.

She can't be gone. She can't...

Thora didn't notice that she'd ripped off several fingernails as she continued to frantically dig. She threw rocks aside, enough to reveal Kadiatu's battered, bleeding face. Her body limp, eyes closed, as if she was merely sleeping. But no breath expanded Kadiatu's lungs. No pulse beat in her thin wrist.

A million screams caught in Marai's throat. Pressure building; tightening, tightening in her chest. Her mind struggled to catch up.

"*Kadi,*" shrieked Thora. "I can heal her!"

His name is Ruin, Keshel had said. *I see a great battle. I see death and carnage.*

Marai cursed Keshel's cryptic vision.

"She's gone, Thora," Marai said, but the sound came from someone else's mouth, said in someone else's world. Sensation returned to her body. The lens she'd been staring through widened, bringing the world back into view. Marai pulled Thora from Kadiatu's body and into a tight embrace. Thora struggled against Marai's strong grip, sobbing. "There's nothing you can do for her."

Is this what it meant to be a leader? A queen? Soldiering on even when your heart was breaking?

"*No!*" Thora thrashed, forcing Marai to cling tighter. "I can save her—I can!"

Thora let out a mighty wail as her body, wracked with heaving sobs, gave up. She collapsed against Marai; fingers clenching the fabric of Marai's shirt.

Fury like nothing Marai had ever known flooded her veins and bones as molten lava.

"Go back to work, Thora," she said. Fiery anger hissed from her mouth. "Heal those who have a chance."

Shoulders slumped, Thora didn't meet Marai's eyes as she staggered back to the soldiers she'd been tending. All the fight had gone from her.

And all the joy and light in the world vanished with Kadiatu.

CHAPTER 30
Ruenen

Where was Rayghast?

The king was known to be a hellhound on the battlefield. A vicious warrior who led his own men through the charge. He should've found Ruenen by now, especially since the earth had stopped rumbling. But the king was nowhere in sight.

"Come on, Rayghast," Ruenen growled as he cut down another soldier. "Come and get me!"

Filitto was dead. His body lay near Ruenen's feet, amongst the rivers of blood. Hundreds of dead on both sides. Boys with decades left of their lives to live, lying prostrate in the muck, getting trampled. Old men, too frail to lift a sword, lay broken and ravaged amongst the heather.

The dents and cracks across Ruenen's armor served as proof of how close he'd come to death. So many strikes, so many blades hit the armor instead of flesh. He'd be dead a dozen times over without it, but now it was barely clinging to him, damaged beyond use. Ruenen peeled the armor from his body. Now nothing stood between him and the edge of a blade.

He shouldn't have looked, but Ruenen couldn't stop his eyes from darting across the moor, searching for Marai.

There were too many bodies around him. Too much chaos. He couldn't see past the circle of black and gold encompassing him.

But a glint of orange flame sputtered in the corner of his vision. A swirling tornado of wind flung rocks, grass and soldiers across the moor.

Marai hadn't yet unleashed her mighty power, which either meant the other fae were still fighting, or she was . . .

No, there's still hope.

A dark shape caught Ruenen's attention. It rose from the moor on the Tacornian side straight into the sky. Ruenen's head snapped upwards and his jaw dropped.

A *man* with large, hawk-ish wings *flew* overhead. Or at least, the creature had the physique of a man. He soared above the battlefield; a vulture, searching for prey. Hip-length silver-white hair fanned out around it in the breeze.

"What in the Unholy Underworld *is* that?" Ruenen uttered to no one as the hair on the back of his neck prickled.

"*Demon*," a man yelled, but they weren't pointing at the creature in the sky. The Tacorn soldier gaped as a massive bull-like beast materialized from swirling black flame and smoke, as if it had been birthed from earth and magic itself right before their eyes.

Two more. Rayghast had just created two more shadow creatures from this battle alone.

The creature cracked its neck to the side, flexed its muscular arms and long humanoid fingers. Its blunt snout sniffed at the scent of blood. Then it turned and stabbed straight through the armor of the nearest Tacornian soldier with its thick, towering, twisted horns.

Demon, indeed.

The beast shook the dead soldier off its horns, tossing the body unceremoniously to the ground. With frantic yells, soldiers on both sides retreated from the creature; the Tacornians appeared as terrified as the Nevandians.

"Bring it down," a Tacorn commander shouted to everyone in the vicinity.

So these beasts weren't allies of Tacorn, then, although they'd been created by their king's usage of dark magic, directly from the Underworld.

Men hurled axes, spears, mallets, and knives at the horned devil. It blocked with its muscular arms, knocking aside the weapons.

Faeries, vampires, werewolves, and now shadow creatures . . . *who else* was going to join the fray?

CHAPTER 31
Marai

Marai lost track of how many soldiers she'd killed. Dimtoir's blade was so slick with blood Marai could hardly grasp its hilt. White hot rage consumed her. All thoughts but revenge evaporated from her mind, hissing like steam.

She didn't register the slice of a blade across her cheek as it narrowly missed removing her head. Nor the gash on her right bicep. Marai's body was numb, fueled by the ring's desire for more blood, more death; if only to hide the aching sorrow and guilt that threatened to swallow her whole.

Across the sloping valley, Nevandian forces began to fall back and back, until their ranks had dissolved. Until golden bodies and men in rags gave up any sense of order. They turned and ran towards Kellesar in the distance. Tacorn rushed forward, a tidal wave of black, spurred on by the Nevandian's weakening strength.

"Fall back," Keshel shouted to Marai and the others, following the army's lead.

Tarik and two other weres, one severely wounded, withdrew behind Keshel. Soon, the fae would be the only Nevandians left on the field. Aresti, Leif, and Raife were surrounded by blue scaled armor. Their movements slowed down. Their strikes became less precise, less frequent, magic all but spent.

Keshel rallied a brief spurt of power. He sent a flame into the masses of Varanese, granting enough time for Aresti, Leif, and Raife to dash back to his side. Nosficio appeared in a blur next to them, wild-eyed and drenched in blood. He snarled, but wasn't too lost in his bloodlust to know friend from foe.

A hushed, spine-chilling voice stroked against her skin. *Marai . . . Marai . . .*

She slashed through the Varanese soldiers, fighting her way to Rayghast. She had to kill him. She must protect Ruenen and her people. She had to silence the voice and its magical allure.

As if it knew, dark magic raised the earth again. Without Kadiatu to stop it, a rolling, moving hill careened towards Marai. She dodged, but the dark magic wouldn't relent. It wanted *her*. Its eerie call echoed inside her head.

Instead of rock and dirt, black smokey flames burst from the ground. Marai met the magic with Dimtoir, hoping to slice through or extinguish those flames.

But the magic was as solid as stone.

Marai watched in horror as cracks splintered up her father's blade.

Dimtoir shattered into fragmented pieces, and Marai was knocked backwards. As her body slammed into the ground, air abandoned her lungs and anguish took over.

Dark magic chuckled in her ears in victory as it receded. She stared at the broken shards of Dimtoir, now bones of a once-great sword to be buried like the last remains of her own father. Dimtoir had been her trusted companion, a friend in the darkness, since the day her father had thrust it into her small hands.

Now, her hands were empty. Who was she without that sword?

Marai felt the sting in her eyes, the tightness of her heart, but she had to let it all go. As with Kadiatu, there was no time to mourn.

More Tacornians were moving to the left flank. They saw the opening. They knew they could rout the Nevandians; encircle them, cutting them off from their retreat.

She clambered back to her feet, and Marai stared down at the broken shards of steel as she tossed aside the worthless hilt of her beloved sword.

"Thora," she heard Leif call. "Leave them, and get over here!"

Marai didn't know if Thora did as Leif told. She didn't turn. Instead, her fingers latched onto the handle of a sword from a nearby fallen Tacornian. It felt foreign in her hand, bulky and inelegant. But a weapon was a weapon—they all killed the same.

She rejoined the fray.

"Marai, fall back and regroup," Keshel yelled.

The panic in his voice should have made her turn, but Marai wouldn't listen. He didn't *order* her on the battlefield. She wouldn't fall back. She would not stop.

Not until I reach Rayghast and chop off his head.

She would have kept cutting through, a straight line right to Rayghast on the other side, if it weren't for the cries behind her.

Cries of pain. Screams of shock.

Marai finally whipped around. She assessed the tableau before her as the world shut down.

A sword plunged into Leif's chest. A black-armored hand was its owner. Leif's arms stretched out wide, a protective stance. Behind him lay several unarmed, injured Nevandian men. Thora's small body shielded a wounded man on the ground.

The Tacornian soldier twisted the blade and cut downwards.

Leif was skewered and mauled as the sword cut through his stomach.

Protecting Thora. Protecting *humans.*

Marai staggered over as Tacornians began to flood the area. Nevandians rushed past, knocking into Marai as they fled towards Kellesar.

Not another. No, please, not another.

Leif's legs crumpled. Raife was there to catch him.

"Brother . . ." whispered Leif through a cracked, far-away voice. He stared those vibrant emerald eyes up into his twin's face. Marai watched the life leave them, a vacantness there, snuffing out Leif's internal fire.

The last march of the fae, he'd said.

Aresti collapsed to her knees next to Raife. She took Leif's hand and squeezed, bringing it to her heart.

In a mad frenzy, Thora leapt from the wounded Nevandian on the ground. With a simple paring knife, she roared and stabbed the Tacornian murderer in the neck, over and over again, with a feral scream to rival Marai's. As blood gurgled from the soldier's mouth, he fell, eyes wide with shock.

Thora stepped away from the body, heaving with adrenaline. Then she dropped the knife and flung her arms around Raife's neck, breaking into a sob.

As Raife clung white-knuckled to his brother's body, Marai met Keshel's pale and frightened face.

Ruen is our Ruin . . .

"It's up to you now, Marai," he uttered. The wall of impenetrable stone had shattered. A ghost, Keshel wandered to Raife's side with the others. Keshel closed Leif's open eyes with two gentle fingers, then mumbled a prayer to Lirr.

But it wasn't Lirr he should be praying to.

Laimoen, God of Destruction, was who Marai called upon. She dug deep inside the well. She pulled and felt the charge travel up her spine, igniting her.

Let them burn. Let them all *burn!*

As the air came alive with electric, volatile power, Thora looked up at Marai. Her tear-lined eyes blazed with ferocity.

"Do it."

Marai unshackled her magic.

She became the storm. She became the nightmare. She released a primal scream that came from deep within; the place where she tucked away all the anger, all the sorrow, guilt, shame, and hatred.

The bloodstone ring rattled and sung. *At last! At last!* It cried with joy.

Marai raised her hands and unleashed.

CHAPTER 32
Ruenen

It was impossible to miss the tower of blinding white light.

It shot straight up into the sky. A beam of pure lethal power with the crack of a whip, amplified a thousand fold.

Lightning, a blazing scar across the black sky. Clouds flashed and shimmered. The earth shuddered. Vibrations, more powerful than Rayghast's dark magic, knocked the armies off their feet. Ruenen stumbled, lowering to a knee, as he and everyone else gaped at the left flank of the Nevandian army.

Like a geyser, the column of lightning collapsed and expanded outwards. Snaking strands of lightning snapped across the moor in the direction of the enemy, engulfing blue and black soldiers into swirling terror. Long, white fingers reached out, ensnaring all within their path. Bodies disappeared in blinding light and splintered electric bursts.

The screams of torture were unlike anything Ruenen had ever heard.

His heart stopped. His gut clenched.

Marai.

Her power was unreal. Something improbable. Something Ruenen assumed belonged to the gods . . .

The majority of that terrifying magic was focused on Tacorn forces. Several hundred Varanese took one look at that magic, turned, and ran. Ruenen watched their blue and white flags travel farther and farther away. Varana abandoned Tacorn on the battlefield and headed towards the woods, out of the valley.

Ruenen's palpitating heart nearly burst forth from his rib cage.

Marai could destroy everyone with that kind of power. She could take over *the world* if she wanted. But she had control... the magic didn't touch a single golden-clad soldier, no one on the Nevandian side, no boy or wilted old man.

Nevandia had a chance.

Ruenen stepped forward, breaking ranks with the astounded Nevandian army. Both armies had frozen, goggling at the power displayed before them. Ruenen helped an injured man, not much older than himself, to his feet. His leg wound was deep, and hand sticky with blood.

"I don't want to die," the man moaned, face as pale as death. "My wife... my babies..."

"You won't," stated Ruenen, clinging tightly to his hand. "Not today, my friend. You will see your family again soon."

Ruenen wouldn't let this man die. Not one more Nevandian would perish.

"Thank you, Your Highness," the injured man croaked, face shining with gratitude and tears.

Ruenen called two soldiers to help the man to the back of the line, then continued walking as he gazed up. The flying shadow creature had paused, wings beating in midair, as it, too, stared at Marai's magic. The other horned beast was gone, vaporized by Marai's power or brought down by soldiers.

As lightning turned bodies to ash, Ruenen shouted across the moor.

"Rayghast! Let's end this now!"

I will kill you today. The thought was a sunburst, bright and explosive within him. If Marai could defy the odds, so could he.

Ruenen had been sacrificed for this kingdom, for this war. His mother had sacrificed her newborn son. He'd been ripped right from her arms.

He would never know that love. It was a life he'd not been allowed to live. Ruenen had been hunted, tortured, and wrecked for a lie.

But he would no longer be a pawn in anyone else's game.

Nevandia was *his* kingdom. He was King. And he would destroy anyone who tried to hurt him and his people.

"Rayghast," he yelled again, wrenching open his arms wide. A clear and easy target. "Come and get me, you fucking coward!"

Across the moor, a black shape emerged through the lightning and mist.

It wore no armor. Its chest was bare, striped with bright red blood, dirt, and bruises. Battered.

Perhaps the terrestrial battle with Kadiatu actually had weakened the mighty king.

The figure stalked towards Ruenen, each step deliberate, as it bent down and ran its fingers through a pile of ash. The ash of a body that had once stood there. The figure then wiped the ash across his chest in a slow, purposeful move.

Disgust wormed through Ruenen, fueling his anger, emboldening him.

Dark magic had claimed more of the enemy king since Ruenen had previously seen him in the dungeon. His arms were fully black from tip to shoulder, as was his abdomen. Ruenen could see the toxic magic, a necrotic poison, inching upwards.

The king held out his broadsword, continuing his steady stride. Ruenen felt each step reverberate through the earth. Powerful. Commanding. Confident.

Rayghast, King of Tacorn, crossed over the dirt road bisecting Tacorn and Nevandia, and finally met Ruenen on the battlefield.

CHAPTER 33
Marai

This was power.

This was vengeance.

Magic flowed from her hands in steady, controlled chaos. Lightning scorched everything it touched. It turned rows of soldiers to dust. Battalions and regiments were annihilated. Marai wiped one third of Rayghast's remaining army off the chess board.

I must kill as many as I can. Marai urged her magic onwards. Nevandia had been utterly shattered, its paltry cavalry and infantry torn apart. Around four hundred men remained of the original three thousand. Although Varana had turned-tail, Tacorn still had the numbers to win.

More, more!

The bloodstone ring shimmered; its curse finally being fulfilled after centuries of waiting. Marai, Meallán's progeny, had unleashed its revenge. The ring's magic shuddered through her arms, giving itself over to her cause. The curse, a different, darker kind of magic, strained against her direction. It wanted to take every human soul on the field, including Ruenen.

Human prince, it said into her bones as it surged towards him, target acquired.

Marai bullied the curse's power away from Ruenen and the Nevandians. She had to stay in control. Marai channeled the magic into her own, using every drop. Her well emptied. The ring grew silent on her finger, all but a cinder of power remained, now nothing more than a jasper stone and a symbol.

Marai's body shook as she continued tugging at the depleted reservoir within.

You've reached the limit.

But there were at least two thousand Tacorn soldiers still on the field. Another thousand in reserve. If Marai stopped now, Tacorn would regroup. Varana might return. Nevandia had nothing left to defend itself.

Her magic shuddered out. Lightning snapped and crackled as it retreated within her. She collapsed to all fours in the grass, gasping for breath as if she'd run a hundred leagues.

In the settling dust and aftermath of her magic, the world quieted.

She raised her head. Through the smoldering ash across the moor, Tacorn's reserves were already taking advantage of the reprieve. They charged forward, passing their retreating comrades. As Marai predicted, Tacorn's lines were reforming. They'd perform one final charge and win it all. Then they'd storm the walls of Kellesar, and spare no innocent Nevandian.

Marai forced herself to her feet. There was no one coming to save them. It was all up to her, but she had nothing left to give.

Marai . . . Marai.

A beckoning finger of smoke flickered across her brain. Tendrils of black gossamer flames crept up through the earth like weeds licking at her feet. Marai had never before seen that kind of magic.

Use me, the smoke said.

It was tempting. The magic was *there,* accessible all around her. She could save Ruenen and her people. She could save Nevandia. All she had to do was let dark magic in . . . then it could finish Tacorn and Rayghast forever.

Dip into the darkness, my darling, it purred, a lover's breath in her ear.

Darkness had always been her candle. Its power didn't frighten her.

Time to make a choice between your devils and your demons, love, and take the outstretched hand of darkness.

Its allure was strong. Enticing. Great, god-like power at her fingertips.

But then Marai thought of Ruenen, her family, and that intoxicating feeling curdled.

If Marai listened—if she tugged on that power—she'd become no better than Rayghast. She'd taint herself further, create more despicable, unnatural shadow creatures, and then she'd truly be unworthy. Black stains would spread across her body, marking her forever as undeserving and shameful. Marai would never be able to face those she loved ever again, nor herself.

Piss off. She mentally sent the darkness a rude gesture.

Marai gathered herself up, raised her arms, and tugged deep within. Weak strands of lightning sputtered from her fingers. Her well was bone dry, but she kept pulling from within herself. From her life force, Lirr's seed of glowing energy. Keshel had warned that tapping into this seed would drain her of life entirely, but Marai would use it all if it meant the others would live.

I can buy Nevandia time.

She stumbled sideways. Her body contorted, as if she was shriveling away from the inside out.

Perhaps this was her purpose. The reason Lirr had stayed her hand years ago in that forest near Cleaving Tides. When Marai had once been so ready to end her own life, wondering why she was ever born, Lirr had stopped her. Since then, Marai often pondered why the goddess wanted her to live. Perhaps it was for this moment. Marai was supposed to give her life on this battlefield to ensure Nevandia's victory. To put Ruenen on the throne so he could make Astye a better place.

"That's enough, Marai," someone shouted behind her. Their voice was muffled, as if she were hearing it through thick ice under water.

Someone tugged on her shoulders. She ignored those hands. She ignored the cries in her ears.

"*Stop,*" they yelled.

"Marai, *look,*" said another voice.

Her stinging, blurry eyes dared a glance to the right.

There, cresting over a craggy hill—eight hundred mounted riders in gleaming silver armor appeared. At the helm, a figure with billowing bright red hair thrust a sword towards the sky. Horns blared. Cheers resounded across the moor.

Grelta had come.

Black-armored soldiers scattered as Queen Nieve led the grand charge down the hill. Tacorn's organized ranks dissolved and the battlefield erupted into chaos. Nevandian infantry men gathered up their remaining strength and charged forwards to join the fray again. Nieve and Greltan forces swept the Tacornian reserve infantry back across the road, out of Nevandian territory, then back further, towards far off Dul Tanen.

Tarik and his remaining weres let out a howl of victory as they rushed forward to help the Greltans.

It's finished.

The last remaining embers of Marai's magic fizzled and snuffed out. Her body wrung dry, arid as the Badlands, she felt the pressure of hands on her shoulder, trying to guide her.

Her body gave out. She plunged forward, crashing to the ground.

Darkness crept in from the corners of her vision. Numbness spread.

She managed to turn her head, one slight, painful movement to watch Nieve galloping onwards, overtaking Tacornian troops with aid from the remaining mounted Nevandian cavalry and infantry. Nieve was a force to behold. A true queen.

But one shadow stood tall amidst the ash and mist.

One shadow stalked towards its prey.

Opposite this shadow, stood a man in broken gold armor. One single beam of sunlight poked through the clouds. It blessed him, illuminating him in radiance. Lirr, herself, smiling down on him . . .

Ruenen.

He was the ruin of Tacorn, of the Middle Kingdoms as they'd been. Ruenen would bring about meaningful change. Even though he was also Marai's ruin, she'd happily given it all for him.

She watched as he faced down his enemy, his hunter, his demon, with unfathomable courage.

It would all end now, and there was nothing more Marai could do to help.

CHAPTER 34
Ruenen

The king was coming, but Ruenen didn't care. Not when he'd watched the lightning disappear and Marai collapse twice across the nearly vacant field.

She used too much.

Ruenen's feet ached to rush to her side, but he kept them frozen in place. Marai would never forgive him if he wasted this chance, if he didn't finish this war now.

Although his heart splintered into frightened fragments, he stared down the King of Tacorn. Behind him, Grelta's mounted forces corralled Tacornian soldiers into small groups. Many more of Rayghast's men escaped over the hills. They'd remain a danger if they organized, but that was a fight for another day.

Avilyard and the one hundred Nevandian cavalry rode out to meet Nieve. They'd take Tacornian soldiers as prisoners. That was something Ruenen ordered—not every man need be slaughtered, show mercy whenever possible.

He'd be a better ruler than the twisted king in front of him.

"The boy who would be prince," said Rayghast. He was merely feet away. Too far to reach by sword, but close enough for his raised voice to be heard, he'd clearly been battered by Kadiatu's terrestrial assault. Rayghast was covered in scrapes and bruises, dirt and blood, and black stained flesh. He favored one of his legs slightly.

Still, the sight of this imposing figure made Ruenen flinch. The memory of the dungeon, what had almost happened, sent Ruenen's heart thumping.

"It's over, Rayghast," Ruenen said. "You've lost."

The king's soulless eyes sharpened like daggers. "You think you've *won?*"

"Your army has been routed. Varana has fled. You've nothing left. You're king of *nothing*." Ruenen let the words bite and snarl, but they never made an impact against the bare chest of Rayghast.

"You think I cannot rise again?" Rayghast questioned. "You think one lost battle means I still cannot destroy your pitiful country? Your lands, your castle, your people belong to *me*."

"My people will no longer cower to your cruelty," said Ruenen, holding his head high, despite the unnerving manic gleam in the dark pools of Rayghast's eyes.

"I need no army. I have all the power at my fingertips," he said, raising his blackened hands. "Your faerie is dead."

Ruenen's pulse stuttered. *No, she's not dead. That can't be true.*

"The Butcher was a formidable enemy. She had powerful magic, but all abominations must die eventually."

Fury flared within Ruenen. "*You* use dark magic. If anyone is an abomination, it's *you*."

Rayghast stepped closer, drawing his broadsword into both hands. "Today is the day you finally die, Prince."

He flung himself at Ruenen, who barely had time to block the blade crashing down upon him. With another mighty swing, Rayghast nearly took off Ruenen's arm.

The king pummeled him, unleashing a barrage of strikes so vehemently Ruenen didn't have time to counterattack. Rayghast was stronger; his muscles rippled, flexed, and heaved as he struck again and again, pushing

Ruenen to his knees. Dark magic leaked out from his pores in wafting black threads.

Ruenen had no time, no space, no way to move. He curled into a ball and rolled away from Rayghast's lethal, ending blow. He scrambled to his knees as Rayghast ruthlessly attacked again. The man barely breathed, didn't hesitate. His black, void-like eyes glinted with a power-obsessed lunacy. Was it the magic keeping Rayghast going like a wild, desperate beast?

No, Ruenen couldn't blame magic. Rayghast was the better swordsman. He was stronger. Unafraid. He'd been killing on battlefields before Ruenen was born. He, like his army, had trained for this.

His feet turned, upper body twisted, and Ruenen finally swung his sword at Rayghast. Their blades crashed together, the vibrations jarring through his arms and teeth. Ruenen found his rhythm. Blow for blow, block for block, he fought the King of Tacorn.

And then Ruenen missed a step.

Rayghast's sword slashed through Ruenen's exposed side.

Searing flames of pain ripped through him. Stinging, burning, aching—a gaping, bloody hole in his side. Ruenen staggered, collapsing to his knee, keeping himself upright by leaning on his sword in the dirt. Blood poured from the wound onto the grass and heather. A mortal blow.

The king towered over Ruenen. His emotionless face brimmed with hunger and victory.

Cold undulated through Ruenen like lapping water. Darkness crept in. Ruenen clutched at the fatal wound in his side. Blood dripped through his fingers.

Rayghast sneered, an ugly, twisted expression, as he pulled back on his sword and aimed for Ruenen's neck.

"Goodbye, Prince."

CHAPTER 35
Marai

Gentle hands stroked her back.

Warmth spread through her dying, cold body. Marai's vision lightened. Darkness bled away. Muffled voices became more distinct.

"Hold on, Marai. Stay with me."

But Marai saw the distant shadows of Ruenen and Rayghast. She watched the golden prince fall to his knees. The wicked king now stood ready to end Ruenen's life. The wound was deep. She didn't need to be close to know that. Marai had delivered enough death blows to know when a strike hit its mark.

Keshel had seen the wound. He'd warned Marai that this would happen to Ruenen.

It was all over if Rayghast lived. Even without an army, he could destroy Nevandia. Ruenen would die. *She* would die. Her people, her family. All dead.

But then the golden prince dodged with a tortured yell, and rolled away from the final strike. Ruenen rallied his strength, staggered to his feet. His sword arm shook in relentless effort.

"Stop," Marai murmured thickly to the hands on her back.

"What? No, Marai, stay still," said Thora, pouring healing magic into Marai's wasted body.

"You're running low," Marai replied, and reached up to grasp Thora's hand. "Heal Ruenen."

"I can't . . ." Thora's lip trembled. Tears dripped down her cheeks. Her glossy brown hair was tangled and matted with blood. "I can't lose anyone else, Marai. Please, let me heal you."

"I'll be fine," Marai said. The lie tasted true and sweet on her tongue. She'd used it all. By all accounts, she should be dead, but Thora had pulled her back from the majestic, soothing light of beyond. A small amount of Thora's magic tethered Marai to this world. "Save your magic for Ruen. He must live."

"I want *you* to live, Marai!"

Too tired to hold on any longer, Marai dropped Thora's hand and said, "Heal Ruen. Consider that my dying wish."

Thora swallowed. She bit her scabbed lower lip. Then she stood in one fluid movement and grabbed Raife's hand.

"Come with me," she said.

Raife nodded, and ran with Thora towards the final battle.

Their conjoined hands and Ruenen's defiant stance were the last things Marai saw before her eyelids drifted shut.

CHAPTER 36
Ruenen

As Ruenen struggled to remain standing, Rayghast reached out a stained hand. Dark magic twirled around his fingers. Ruenen spun, avoiding Rayghast's outstretched arm, but stumbled into the grass. Searing pain burst through his side. He gasped and wheezed, but he had to stay alive long enough to kill Rayghast.

However, the brutal king showed no weakness. He stomped towards Ruenen, reaching, reaching those blackened fingers out.

Brilliant flames charged towards Rayghast from the left. Sweat droplets formed on Ruenen's upper lip from the heat. The king barely had time to kneel. His hands pressed into the ground, and a wave of earth leapt up from the spot, blocking the fire before it singed him.

Ruenen peered around the mass of terrain and spotted Raife, flaming arrow raised.

"You killed my brother," Raife said in a steady, unyielding tone. "You killed Kadiatu and my family."

Raife shot that arrow at Rayghast, who used another terrestrial wave to block it. Rayghast then sent a pulse through the earth. Dirt and rock rippled at Raife's feet, wrapping around his ankles, shackling him there.

Ruenen used the momentary distraction to attack, swinging downwards. Rayghast was quick, though. He blocked, and Ruenen swung again. Rayghast parried, then swung, but winced as his injured leg twisted beneath him.

A flaming arrow pierced straight through Rayghast's right shoulder. The black, necrotic flesh burned. Dark magic and black blood bled from the hole.

For the briefest of moments, Rayghast froze. A flicker of surprise crossed his face. Then he tore the arrow from his shoulder with a snarl. Ruenen took advantage of the pause and flung himself recklessly at the king.

Rayghast grabbed Ruenen by the throat. His fingers tightened.

Ruenen expected black flames to burn him, encompass him, but he felt nothing besides the desperate need to breathe.

Concern flashed across Rayghast's face. Whatever was supposed to happen when he touched Ruenen's flesh hadn't occurred.

Dark magic abandoned him. It bled from the king's body, dripping, slick as oil, onto the grass, and disappeared back beneath the soil.

With his final ounce of strength, Ruenen kicked Rayghast's injured knee.

The king stumbled; fingers loosened their grip.

Ruenen shoved his sword into Rayghast's stomach.

The king's eyes flared open. He growled into Ruenen's face. Ruenen pushed the blade deeper. He twisted it, hoping to catch all the internal organs.

Rayghast staggered backwards; the sword dislodged from his wound. He fell to the ground, lacing his fingers amongst the grass.

"Come to me," he ordered through clenched teeth.

But the magic didn't come.

"*Heal me,*" Rayghast bellowed at the dirt. Desperation and sweat glistened on his face. The king roared, tearing blades of grass from the ground with his blackened fingers. Now he was just a man.

Ruenen's throat burned. He could barely suck down air. Blurry white dots popped into his vision. His knuckles stalled, hovering before knocking at death's door.

Finish it, Master Chongan's voice told him.

Dragging his sword across the ground, Ruenen went to Rayghast's side. The king glared up at him with a sneer.

"I win," Ruenen whispered, then promptly cut off Rayghast's head.

As Rayghast's head rolled one direction, and his body keeled to the other, Ruenen's sword clattered to the ground.

The odds had always been stacked against him, but he'd won. No more running. No more bloodshed. No monster to haunt his nightmares. Ruenen had finally vanquished his predator.

The ominous, dark clouds parted above him, and sunlight dappled the landscape of his Nevandia. Strength left him, and Ruenen fell backwards.

He could die now. He'd saved his people. He'd done what he set out to do. He'd avenged Amsco and Nori, the Chongan family . . . his parents.

He could happily join Marai in the Underworld.

He closed his eyes and saw her.

She stood on the precipice of light, surrounded by a halo of radiance. White blonde hair flowed around her in the temperate breeze. She extended her pale hand and smiled.

Ruenen was ready. He reached out his hand, expecting to feel those callused, strong fingers entwine with his. But instead, he felt warmth. Light, yes, but warmth that sucked away the pain from his side. He could almost feel the organs, tissues, veins, and skin meld back together.

Then Marai grew farther and farther away. She was leaving him . . . or he was leaving her.

No! I want to stay with you!

But Marai smiled with pride as Ruenen returned to earth.

CHAPTER 37
Marai

She was dead.

Marai lay somewhere between worlds, bathed in golden-white light.

Her body was leaden. Unmovable. Her voice trapped within. It mattered not—she couldn't open her jaw, anyways.

Sometimes, she felt hands; warm and gentle. They lifted her head and poured liquid down her throat. A wet cloth was draped across her forehead. Her limbs were sponged off.

Sometimes, she heard voices. Muffled, distant, quiet. They sounded familiar, but she couldn't place them.

Her mind was full of cotton. Or sludge too difficult to traverse.

If she gathered her strength to crack open an eyelid, she saw slivers of blurry shapes and outlines. Nothing recognizable. But the effort was unsustainable and costly. The world was too bright. Too colorful. Her eyes burned. Sounds scraped against her eardrums. Feet on stone. The shuffle of clothing against skin. Water being poured into a cup. All as loud as a thunderstorm.

She'd then lapse back into an endless sleep.

Ruenen.

The name shot through Marai like a lightning bolt.

She jolted upwards, waking as her body sat upright in bed. She was in her room in the castle at Kellesar. Plush blankets and pillows surrounded her.

Thora, Raife, and Aresti all jumped in alarm at her sudden movement.

"Where's Ruenen?" Marai asked. His name sent an electric current beneath her skin. The last time she'd seen him, he'd been mortally wounded by Rayghast. It had appeared as if the King of Tacorn would claim victory, as well as Ruenen's life.

Marai hadn't heard Ruenen's voice once during her momentary bouts of consciousness.

"Is he alive? Did he win? What happened? How long was I asleep?" The questions tumbled from her mouth.

For a moment, the others gaped at her. Marai was more alert than they'd expected her to be. In fact, she felt tolerable, other than a general tiredness in her bones, but her mind was wide awake.

Thora chewed on her lower lip. It was cracked and scabbed over, as if she'd been doing that a lot lately. "You've been unconscious for ten days."

So long . . . no wonder Marai's body felt like she'd been trampled by two dozen horses.

"Prince Ruenen is downstairs in a meeting with Queen Nieve," Raife said.

Relief eased out of her with a sigh and slump of her shoulders. It was then that Marai noticed the golden armor Raife and Aresti wore. "Why are you wearing that? Are we still at war?"

Strangely, Raife smiled. "The war is over."

Over. Marai's breath hitched. And Raife's smile . . . Ruenen was alive . . . it had to mean . . .

"We won?"

Raife nodded. Marai nearly burst into tears, but she held them back by squeezing her hands into fists within the bedsheets.

"Those Tacornian soldiers are real bastards, though," said Aresti. "We've been constantly engaged in skirmishes with the soldiers we haven't managed to wrangle yet. They set fire to some cottages outside the city last night, and we barely have the manpower to fight them off. Oh, Raife and I are officially part of the King's Guard." Aresti gave Marai a smug grin. That expression normally would have annoyed Marai, but instead, she found herself returning it. "Avilyard, himself, appointed us."

"And Thora has been promoted to Royal Healer," Raife said, then planted a kiss on the top of her head. Thora blushed a pretty rose, and took Raife's hand.

Marai's eyes and ears couldn't gobble up the news fast enough. Raife and Arest—King's Guard, honored positions in the Nevandian army. Thora—Royal Healer, a title reserved for the best.

Nevandia had *won,* and her people were granted titles of prestige and respect. Faeries who had defied the odds and served Nevandia loyally in battle. Marai's heart soared. It was more than she could have hoped for.

And Ruenen was *alive.*

This was the second time Marai had thought she'd lost him, but unlike the first, she hadn't given up on him. She'd believed in him and the future he wanted to create.

"Not all the commanders and soldiers are happy about it, to be honest," Raife said, running a hand through his curls. "Just because Avilyard, Holfast, and Prince Ruenen agree, doesn't mean others do. We're largely ignored by the rest of the Guard. We have a long way to go before fae are recognized as equals by everyone . . ."

"Keshel's trying, though," said Aresti. "He's been working with Prince Ruenen, Holfast, and Tarik on new laws regarding magical folk. Nieve's working with him to establish sanctuary in the North for our kind, as well." Aresti then frowned, exchanging a look with Thora. "We barely see Keshel these days. And he's been acting strange. When he's not busy with the Witenagemot, he's out wandering around somewhere."

Keshel acting strange? Had something happened to him during the battle?

"I'm surprised Keshel's still here. I thought he'd be long gone by now," said Marai.

Aresti, Raife, and Thora's faces fell. A somberness settled around the room. Marai didn't like the weightiness.

Thora's eyes shimmered. "He's trying to ensure our safety before he goes . . . so we don't lose anyone else."

The words slammed into Marai.

She'd forgotten.

She'd forgotten about their deaths.

Kadiatu and Leif.

"I'm sorry," she said, squeezing her eyes tightly, trying to block out the images of their lifeless bodies on the moor. "I'm so sorry."

"It wasn't your fault, Marai," Raife said softly.

Marai shook her head. "Yes, it was. I brought you all here. Their deaths are *my* fault."

"No," stated Raife with such fortitude that Marai opened her eyes. "Rayghast is to blame for their deaths. Leif and Kadiatu fought to avenge our families and make the world a better place for our people. You didn't force them to come, Marai. Leif and Kadi made the choice to fight for Nevandia. They came because they believed in a better future."

"But I could've stopped it. If I'd used my magic sooner—"

Raife sent her a stern look. "If you'd used your magic sooner, you still wouldn't have killed enough soldiers to stop the attack, and we'd have been defeated before Grelta arrived. We'd be burying your body alongside Kadi and Leif. They died honorable deaths, believing in a just cause. That's a far greater outcome than my brother ever expected for his life."

"And they will be remembered in history across Astye," Aresti added. "Leif and Kadi's names will never be forgotten, especially by the magical folk whose lives they're changing."

Marai gulped back tears. "And Nosficio?"

Aresti let out a snort and crossed her arms across her plated chest. "Oh, he's been hiding out in the glen. He needed to stay away to quell the bloodlust. He also got severe burns from sun exposure, but he's healing. I've been taking care of Queen Nieve in his stead."

"What does *that* mean?" Marai sensed it was something she didn't want to know in full detail.

Aresti grinned devilishly. "She's needed *someone* to entertain her while she's here."

Marai rolled her eyes; this definitely wasn't something she wanted to question further.

"Once Rayghast died, the life force he'd sucked from Nevandia returned. The lands are healing, as are the people. They see the change as a sign from Lirr," Thora said. "I think some of Kadi's magic still lingers in the ground. You should see the flowers blooming, Marai, so vibrant and beautiful . . ."

Like Kadi.

A tear fell down Thora's cheek.

Raife wiped it away with a gentle finger. "And Thora's worked night and day on healing those she can." Raife gave Thora his sweetest, most loving smile. The open tenderness there filled Marai with gratitude and a deep, forlorn ache. "She's saved a lot of lives. If there's anyone the people trust amongst us fae, it's Thora."

Dark circles had formed under Thora's eyes. How had she had the time? As far as Marai was aware, she'd hardly left her side. Each time Marai had awakened, Thora had been there.

"It's a healer's duty," said Thora, blushing again.

"The war may be over, but there are still battles to be won. We've taken some Tacornian commanders and soldiers prisoner in our dungeons. They're being questioned and tried fairly, but many are still at large," Aresti explained. "Dul Tanen is currently occupied by Grelta to maintain order there, since the loyalists are rather persistent. A curfew is in effect for the whole city. Queen Rhia and the Tacorn privy council were escorted here to Kellesar. A few escaped, but we'll find them eventually."

Queen Rhia... what would happen to the woman who'd been bartered to an evil king by her own father? She'd protected her younger sister from a similar fate, and most likely suffered tremendous consequences for that betrayal.

"Varana's also a problem," said Raife with a sigh. "Ruenen's still contemplating what to do with them. They're begging for forgiveness, saying they had no other choice, that Queen Rhia was passing Varana information for weeks. We aren't sure we can trust them."

"Your prince already wrote a ballad about the battle," said Aresti with a rare smile for Marai, "and he sang it on the moor to honor the fallen heroes of Nevandia. He... he sang it next to Kadi and Leif's graves."

Aresti turned away, shielding her face as she rubbed her wet cheek on her shoulder.

Ruenen.

Marai could barely contain the overwhelming emotions. "I need to see him."

Thora frowned. "After his meetings, he'll come to see you. He's been busy, but he comes every night."

Marai flung her legs over the side of the bed. She placed her bare feet on the fur rug and stood for the first time in days. Her whole body shook. The weight on her legs was too much; Marai staggered, and Raife came to her aid.

"Maybe this isn't a good idea..." he said as Marai took a wobbly step forward.

"I *must* see him."

Raife sighed through his nose, but grabbed hold of her arm as Thora took Marai's other hand. Without another word, they slowly led Marai to the bedroom door; Aresti followed behind. As they stepped out into the hallway, the temperature dropped. The early spring chill still lingered in the air. Marai became acutely aware of her bare legs and feet, and thin nightgown.

Buttery soft sunlight beamed through the windows. It seemed brighter than before. Servants in the hallway buzzed with activity. Some smiled, others gaped, not in fear, but in awe, as Marai approached. They stopped their tasks to watch the fae pass. One of the servants bowed her head in respect.

Marai nearly fainted on the stairs. There were so many stone steps, and her body was too weak, but she willed herself to go on, leaning her full weight against Thora and Raife. Eventually, her toes touched the cold tiled floor of the main hall.

The Witenagemot chamber doors were wide open. Four golden guards stood outside, along with three Greltan soldiers.

Marai shrugged off Raife and Thora as she stumbled forward. She couldn't get her legs to move fast enough. She pushed too hard and fell against one of the oak doors, causing a *thump* to echo throughout the chamber.

All heads turned to her. The Nevandian Witan and Keshel stood around the table, mid-argument. Several chairs had been added for Nieve and her ambassadors, as well as a few timid Tacornian councilmen who had obviously turned coat already (one of them was quite old). Marai had interrupted something important, but she didn't care at all.

The only person she saw was *him*.

Ruenen's eyes opened wide. Dressed in all his finery, he stood from his throne and raced down the dais, discarding royal airs.

Marai rushed forward to meet him. She barely made it halfway across the room before collapsing.

But Ruenen caught her. As he always did.

He lowered her gently to the floor as she broke into wracking sobs. She couldn't contain them anymore. She didn't try.

Ruenen's arms enveloped her as he gently rocked her back and forth. She clung to him, the way one does when coming up for air after being underwater. Like a freezing woman to a warm hearth. Flesh to bone.

He held her close, stroking fingers through her hair, kissing her brow. Rain drops from his eyes fell upon her already damp cheeks. They'd been so close to losing each other again. Only Thora's magic and pure grit had kept them tethered to this world.

I will never leave him, Marai vowed, eliminating the old oath she'd made after Slate. That had been made in anger and fear. This new vow was stronger; stronger because it was forged in something more powerful than hate.

"You're shivering," Ruenen whispered against the shell of her ear. He wrapped his cape around her, shielding her small body from the cold, but also from the impropriety of it all. There she was, in merely a sheer nightgown, embracing the Prince of Nevandia before the entire privy council and the Queen of Grelta. "You should go back upstairs and rest. I'll have food brought to your room and a bath prepared."

Marai clutched him tighter. She didn't want to leave his arms. She wanted to bury herself in his warmth for the rest of eternity. His affectionate chuckle reverberated through her body.

"I'll come to you tonight. I promise." His whispered pledge and the kiss he planted in her hair was the main reason she was able to unlatch from him.

Elmar arrived at the door, breathless. "Your Highness, there's a group of Tacorn loyalists with weapons headed towards the city."

Ruenen sighed, then raised Marai to her feet. He resumed his earlier princely stance, but his eyes danced with affection. He didn't look away from her, not even as he addressed Raife. "Please escort Lady Marai to her chambers, and return once she's settled. I need your immediate assistance with these loyalists."

"I can help," Marai said.

"You can barely stand," said Raife.

"But what if—"

Raife led Marai from the room, the chill once again taking hold, her arms empty without Ruenen. She couldn't make it back up the stairs, so Raife's arm slid under her legs and lifted her off the floor. He carried her all the way up, and back to her room.

Strength abandoned her by the time she made it to the bed. Marai flopped into the sheets. Thora pulled the blankets up to Marai's chin, then stroked a strand of wild hair out of Marai's face.

"Sleep, Storm Cloud. I'll wake you if there's any trouble."

Marai was about to protest, but Thora's healing cobalt magic seeped into her pores, and sleep pulled Marai under.

CHAPTER 38
Marai

Harmona drew Marai a bath. The young maid avoided her gaze, staring modestly at the floor, bobbing up and down in frenetic curtsies. Harmona had sprinkled orange peels and flower petals in the water, along with lavender oil. It was deliciously fragrant and warm, and the water soothed the aches and pains in Marai's rundown body. No bath had ever felt better. She soaked until her fingers and toes shriveled like dried apricots.

For the first time in many years, Marai felt optimistic. Hopeful. Anticipation tickled her skin and throbbed in her veins. There was a life worth living here. Maybe Marai could become someone different, too.

A soft rap sounded at the door. Harmona scuttled over and pulled it open, revealing Keshel. Marai had barely given him a second glance earlier in the Witan chamber, but now she could clearly see the scratches and bruises across his face from the battle; an indigo shadow encircled one eye. His long hair was draped in such a way to hide it.

Keshel noticed her gaze flicker from injury to injury. "These are but small wounds. Thora needs to be helping others."

He looked her over then, and Marai knew he was observing the prominence of her bone structure, the hollowness of her face, after days of not eating. Her body still craved food, but Thora had warned that Marai needed to eat slowly and in small amounts for a while.

"You look well," he said. "When you didn't wake, I thought I'd—we'd—lost you." A pink tinge came to his cheeks. He then produced a smooth wooden cane from behind his back. "Do you want to take a walk with me?"

Marai grimaced at the stick, but knew she'd never make it on her own two feet with legs as unsteady as a newborn foal. She snatched the cane from Keshel's grasp and hobbled into the hallway.

"I heard you've been hard at work," she said after several minutes of silence. "And that you've been wandering off alone for hours."

They'd made it down the main stairs and into the garden. It was awash with color and beauty, so opposite of what the garden had been before. Marai breathed heavily as her pace slowed, taking in the strong floral scent of gardenias. She stumbled to a bench underneath a blooming trellis of vines and wisteria.

Keshel gazed around the garden, staring at everything *but* her. "The wandering is . . . sometimes, I need some space to think, is all."

He was being cagey. *What is he hiding?* Had he had another vision?

"And I'm busy because I must do my part while I'm here, so that when I leave, you're protected." Keshel's fingers stroked the soft petal of a pink rose bush next to him, perhaps reminding him of Kadiatu. Marai couldn't help but see her face in every bloom and bud.

"Why must you leave at all?" she asked. "You're needed here. Respected. Why leave somewhere you can finally call home?"

Keshel's eyes slid to hers. "I cannot call Nevandia home, Marai, not until I see more of this world, and learn what I can."

Marai's anger flared. "What else do you need to learn, Keshel? There are hundreds of books in the library here. It'll take you months to get through them all. And you've created a sanctuary for magical folk, and convinced another kingdom to open their hearts and minds. Stay, and continue to lead this growth."

"Are you asking because *you* want me to stay? Or because Ruenen and Nevandia need me?"

The question caught Marai off guard as Keshel's dark eyes searched hers.

"Of course I want you to stay. You're my family, one of the few people I trust. I don't want you to leave."

Keshel's face hardened briefly. That wasn't the answer he wanted to hear, but he'd already known, or he wouldn't have asked.

"I've had recent visions. Dark magic isn't gone. This land may be free of it, but elsewhere in the world, others are using its power. The shadow creatures Rayghast created survive. Darkness will keep spreading, but we cannot stop it if we don't know how. *Something* is coming. A war is brewing between light and dark. How can we prevent someone else from tapping into that power again?"

Another war. Dark magic didn't die with Rayghast. Its power slunk beneath the earth, lying in wait for the next zealous, destructive soul to tap into it. Someday soon, Marai would face it again.

"There's something important we're missing. I need to know why I can *see*," said Keshel. "Why *you* are so powerful, despite being half-fae. When I'm satisfied, I'll return here. To you."

Marai knew she had a part to play in this decision. If she'd asked him to stay, promised him something, he would have agreed, but Marai could promise Keshel nothing. Because she'd already given her heart away so thoroughly that there was never any coming back. Marai could never belong to another. She knew that now.

"Then I expect letters. Frequently. Detailing your findings."

Keshel's lips twitched. His eyes softened. "Yes."

"You should look into Andara."

Keshel froze. "Why?"

"Other fae escaped the massacres. The weres traveled to Nevandia with one, remember? And I met another on the docks in Cleaving Tides, and he told me that Andara might hold answers. Perhaps they've all been hiding over there."

Keshel's lips formed a thin line, as if holding back a remark. Instead, he nodded. "Maybe."

Marai narrowed her eyes in suspicion. *Cagey again,* but she decided not to question him further. Perhaps this was merely Keshel's way of dealing with grief. A melancholy washed over Marai as she heard a duo of thrushes chirp in a nearby tree.

"Can you take me to their graves?" she asked quietly, staring at the flowers surrounding the pond. "Please."

Keshel stood, offering Marai his hand. Together, they walked back through the garden, into the entry hall, and through the portcullis. Slowly, they made their way through the streets of Kellesar and out the main gate. People stared and pointed at them openly, not all in malice and judgment.

Mounds of earth appeared across the moor; rows and rows of recently dug graves in this newly-erected cemetery. Nevandia had lost hundreds of lives. The sight seemed astronomical to Marai. Staggering. Keshel ushered her past a solemn woman and her two young girls placing flowers upon a grave. Marai turned her head away. She couldn't watch them grieve.

Finally, Keshel stopped at two mounds of brown earth dug side-by-side. Their headstones had their first names etched crudely, permanently, into the gray rock. Marai knelt between them, placing one hand on each gravestone, allowing her fingers to trace the letters.

She remembered what Raife had said: they'd died with honor, fighting for what they believed in. Perhaps that was true, but Marai knew she'd never look at another fiery sunset, another blossoming flower, without thinking of Leif and Kadiatu.

She and Keshel stayed, for how long, Marai couldn't tell. Until the tears dried on their cheeks. Until her hands stopped shaking.

"I'd like to see Queen Rhia," Marai said, changing the subject before grief entirely overcame her. Keshel frowned in response. "There are things I want to speak with her about."

An hour later, Marai and Keshel walked down into the depths of the dungeons below the castle.

"Why is she down here?" Marai asked. This dungeon was nothing like the ominous prison of Dul Tanen. There were no sounds of torture. No rivers of blood on the floor. No nasty instruments and weapons. Only soldiers locked in clean cells.

"She was offered more fitting accommodations, but she kept cursing and screaming at Raife and Aresti, accusing them of using dark magic, too. She caused such a ruckus that Prince Ruenen worried she might convince others into thinking the same. We locked her down here two days ago; she's been much calmer since."

Keshel led Marai to the farthest cell from the stairs, passing a group of finely dressed Tacornian nobles. A woman sat in a chair wearing a red and black robe-dress in the Varanese style. Her black hair was lank and lackluster over her face, hands pale in her lap. She sat subdued, dark eyes unfeeling as she gazed out the small barred window above her.

"Your Grace," Marai said as she approached the cell bars.

Rhia didn't move. "I was wondering when you'd come to interrogate me . . . the *monstrosity* my husband feared so." Her voice was cold, harsh.

"I think you know your husband was more of a monster than I."

"You turned hundreds of men to ash with your magic," the queen seethed. "You're no better than Rayghast."

Marai scowled. "You sent your sister to us for safety. Clearly, you feared Rayghast and trusted Prince Ruenen to take care of her. Did you know that he'd corrupted Nevandian lands with dark magic? That he created creatures of shadow that have attacked both Tacornians and Nevandians?"

"Are you asking if I was complicit in his atrocities?" Rhia turned slightly. Her hair fell away from her face, revealing black, necrotic, flaking skin upon her cheeks, forehead, and neck. Her teeth and jaw were visible through her cheek; the flesh burned away.

Marai held back her horror. She wouldn't insult this woman, not when dark magic had done this to her.

"I found out when it was already too late. I couldn't stop my father from sending his troops, from sending Eriu, although I tried. I sowed the seeds of doubt in Dul Tanen, and he would have had me and my ladies killed for it. I'm *glad* Rayghast is dead," Rhia said, voice as sharp as a shard of ice. "All those with magic in their blood should be punished."

"We've been nothing but kind to you and your sister—" Keshel began, but Marai put a hand on his arm.

"Don't bother. You won't persuade her," she said dryly.

"What will happen to Eriu?" asked the queen.

"She'll be sent back to Varana after the coronation," Keshel said, scowling.

Coronation? Marai had forgotten . . . Ruenen still needed to be crowned king.

"And myself?" Rhia posed. "The people of Tacorn have no love for me, I assure you. I held no power there under my husband's rule."

"Prince Ruenen is debating what to do," said Keshel. "Your home country of Varana allied itself with Tacorn. We cannot send you back there for fear of you striking up another war."

Rhia laughed darkly, shaking her head. "Men crave war. We women must deal with the aftereffects. I don't expect a pardon. I'm the Queen of Tacorn, Princess of Varana. You have every reason to hold me hostage. Besides, my father will not accept me back, not with this face. I'm no longer his problem. Spoiled goods."

Marai regarded the queen, so rigid in her chair. She was a performer, like Ruenen. There was no doubt Rhia was strong and intelligent. She played her part well, and kept her true feelings always hidden. Marai understood what it had cost Rhia . . . she did what was necessary to survive in a world that treated women as objects. How had she endured Rayghast when three other wives had perished before her? What daily fear she must have felt.

"I'll send the Royal Healer to see what she can do for your face," Marai said.

Rhia hadn't asked for this life, and now she would be forever marked by Rayghast.

However, Rhia's eyes narrowed. "I won't let that faerie's dirty hands touch me. *No one* will touch me ever again."

The queen's words had a familiar ring; words Marai, herself, had echoed for years.

"Thora can possibly heal the effects of magic on your skin. But if you'd rather look like *that* for the rest of your days than be touched by a faerie, so be it."

Rhia stared back at the wall, ignoring Marai's comment. That earlier compassion and empathy dwindled away. Clearly, one could be a victim, but also blinded by deep-seated prejudice.

Best give her time to cool down. I needed time before I met Ruen.

Marai marched back to the main entry hall with Keshel behind her.

"Not all minds can be swayed," he said. "Some prejudices run too deep."

"That may be true, but does she deserve to spend the rest of her life in a cell, merely because she was forced to marry a madman?"

"That will be Prince Ruenen's decision."

Marai grew suddenly weary and closed her eyes. The weight of all the work that still needed to be done was inordinate. She swayed, using the cane for support.

Keshel's hands steadied her. "Come, let me take you to your room."

Someone was always knocking on her door.

Marai had nestled herself on the couch by the fire, covered in a thick blanket. She was contentedly cozy and enjoying a few moments of quiet alone. She'd dismissed Harmona for the night, and had practically shoved Thora out the door to stop her fussing.

Then the knock came, and Marai knew who it would be. Before she could pull back the blanket, the door creaked open and Ruenen's face peered in.

He smiled, those boyish dimples on full display. "Am I disturbing you?"

"Not at all."

Marai stood up too quickly—blood rushed to her head. Her body was still weak. Her stomach rumbled loud enough for Ruenen to hear at the door.

"Good thing I have a cure for all that," he said, pushing the door wider. He carried a silver tray stacked with bowls and plates and wine. He'd left his princely finery behind; all he wore were trousers and a shirt. He waltzed in, kicking the door shut behind him, and set the tray down on the rug before the fireplace. "And I also brought entertainment."

He grinned as he removed the lute strapped to his back. Marai snorted, stuffing a piece of cheese into her mouth. The assortment of food Ruenen had brought wasn't a grand feast, more akin to picnic fare, but it was perfect for Marai's still-rocky stomach. Ruenen poured her a cup of burgundy wine, then frowned.

"I'm sorry, I forgot you don't like to drink," he said. His hand with the cup hovered in midair. "I'll get you some water."

Marai took the cup from him. "I'll have a glass tonight."

She took a sip. The wine wasn't bad, probably from somewhere South, since the Middle Kingdoms weren't known for their vineyards. "What happened with the loyalists?"

Ruenen leaned back on his hands. "No casualties this time. Captured a few of them, but others managed to escape. They're not very organized, but they *are* persistent. Every single day it feels like someone's coming for my head." He let loose a nervous laugh. "I thought I had meetings and paperwork before, but *now* . . ." He raked a hand through his hair with a sigh. Those sparkling brown eyes met Marai's. "Tomorrow is my coronation."

Surprise slammed into Marai. They were still burying bodies from the battle; she'd watched them on the moor earlier. "So soon?"

"The Witan wants to do it while Nieve and the Varanese princess are present. Apparently, having royalty from other kingdoms at our court makes it more official. Holfast invited all sorts of other people from across Astye, including nobles and ambassadors from the other kingdoms. I swear, Fenir's about ready to have a nervous attack. He's been so jittery."

Marai saw his confidence slip as his face fell. "Are *you* nervous?"

"Absolutely, but this is what I agreed to when I came to Kellesar. I'm lucky to be alive right now. I'll do whatever I have to do."

Even if that meant more performing. King was a role he'd need to play for the rest of his life. Every moment of every day, he would need to be the person they all expected.

But for tonight, Marai could let him be the bard.

"Play something for me," she said, gesturing to the lute. She popped a grape into her mouth which burst in tart sweetness and bright colors.

Ruenen lifted the instrument into his lap. "I have so many new songs in my head, but I don't have time to write them all."

"I heard you wrote a ballad, and sang it for the fallen as a memorial."

Ruenen's fingers paused on the strings. "It was the least I could do . . . to give their families peace and closure."

"You sang at Kadi and Leif's graves," Marai said with a swallow.

"Kadiatu once asked me if I'd play for her. I never got the chance. I hoped she'd hear it, even from beyond . . ." His voice broke, and he sniffed, shaking his head.

"Thank you." Marai swept away her tears with the back of her hand.

Ruenen nodded, cleared his throat, then strummed back and forth, setting his face into a cocky smirk. Marai laughed, grateful for the distraction from her sorrow. He sang "Road to the Red Lands" with an ironic swagger, then "The Lady Butcher," making Marai narrow her eyes, for show. She'd long since stopped caring about the song depicting her. Now, she genuinely enjoyed its epic and boisterous tune. The mysterious mercenary he sang of was no longer her identity. The Lady Butcher had indeed become a mere legend.

"There's no reason why you cannot perform regularly for your court," Marai said as Ruenen took a pause to swig his wine. "You'll be known as the Bard King. All royalty will want to visit, then. Meetings will boast politics *and* music."

Ruenen rolled his eyes. "If I find the time. I'd love to have an hour to play every day."

"You need to make time for the things you love, Ruen. That's what will make this life sustainable."

"Since when did you become so wise, Sassafras?" Ruenen asked, and Marai snorted, making him laugh. "I love when you snort like that. Like an angry boar. It's endearing."

"Are you making fun of me?"

"I wouldn't dare."

It was so easy to be around him. To sit on the rug in front of the hearth, laughing and playing. Marai ate the moment up like a tart grape, bursting with brightness in her heart. She savored the affection in his gaze, the sincerity in his voice, the soothing nature of his presence.

"Will you come tomorrow? To the coronation?" he asked while plucking out another song. Marai remembered Ruenen playing this song before. The ballad didn't have words, but it sounded melancholy, wistful, and romantic.

"Why wouldn't I?"

"It's a big day—ceremony, then a feast with dancing . . . I don't want to wear you out."

Before Ruenen, Marai wouldn't have dared to attend such an opulent, crowded event. Yet sitting there on the rug in her white nightgown, hair billowing down her back, she didn't feel the same. Certainly not at all like the woman who had recently turned hundreds of men to dust, and slit so many throats . . .

"I'm fine. A little tired, but growing stronger every minute. I'll be there," she said. Marai *had* to be there. For him.

The smile that Ruenen gave her then took her breath away. It was so achingly beautiful and raw and real that Marai knew. She *knew* that even though she was terrified, there was no place else she'd rather be. No one else she'd rather open her heart to and reveal all those dark, twisted, shameful things. Because he saw those parts of her and embraced them. Cherished them. Because he also saw the good in her, too. Good that no one else before him had dared to search for.

Marai took another sip of wine. Better that than crawl into his lap and lick the corners of that dimpled smile, which is what she wanted to do. "What about your wounds? Have they healed?" She'd noticed the slight winces he made whenever he moved too jerkily.

"Getting there. Thora healed me well enough on the field, but she emptied of magic before she could finish. I've been letting the rest of the wound heal on its own. I can manage the pain, but I keep making it worse when I fight off the Tacornians."

Always sacrificing.

The food and wine had been consumed. There were no other distractions. It was just them, staring at each other in the twilight blue of night.

The room suddenly grew airless and close. Marai couldn't find her breath. She stood and padded to the open window. Shining beams of silver light illuminated her face as she stared up at the full moon. The stars were out in full, dotting the inky blackness like burning diamonds, making her feel small and one, both at once.

"If I could gaze upon you for the rest of my life, that would be a life well-lived," came Ruenen's breathy voice from the fireplace.

Marai glanced back to see him watching her, eyes shimmering pools of starlight.

A blush seared her face as Ruenen stood and walked to her. With aching tenderness, he swept aside her hair. His gentle thumb stroked her cheek, sending an electric tingle across her skin. She couldn't tear her eyes away. An old fear bubbled up inside, shouting that she was unworthy of this affection, of this *love*. But once his lips brushed against hers, the voice was silenced. Her arms became vines as they wrapped around his neck. Up on her tiptoes, she kissed him so freely she thought she might fall into everlasting oblivion from the joy of it.

"I don't want to hurt you," he whispered against her lips, hands stalling on her hips.

She reassured him by kissing him again.

Ruenen's fingers untied the string at the top of her nightgown. He pushed the sleeves down to her forearms, exposing her pale sternum, razor-edged collarbones, and the slight swell of her breasts.

Marai pulled him away from the window and towards the bed. He planted soft kisses on her shoulders, and down her back to the sharp wings of bone. Marai let out a gasp before clamping her lips on his neck.

Her fingers did what they'd been aching to do for weeks. They untucked his tunic and inched up the muscle beneath. Ruenen shivered against the calloused pads of her fingers as they traced his abdominals and pectorals, mapping out the landscape of his body. He yanked his shirt over his head, tossing it on the ground. Marai's eyes dipped to the lean, defined torso, and the jagged red scar on his side.

Immediately, horror filled her to see the wound that nearly took his life up close. Her fingers hovered over it. She was afraid she might hurt *him*.

"I'm alright," he said against her ear. "You could never hurt me."

Then he pulled Marai's nightgown down farther, revealing her breasts, the smooth planes of her stomach. The nightgown fell to the floor in a pool around Marai's feet. She stood, wholly exposed to him, vulnerable.

"Lirr's bones," he uttered, shaking his head, gazing at her as if he could hardly believe she was real. He caressed a hand down the length of her side, taking in her curves and edges. All the things she tried to hide.

She kissed him again, needy and desperate for the taste of him.

Ruenen gently pressed her backwards until her legs hit the mattress. Without a second thought, Marai lifted her hips onto the bed and lay back. Ruenen climbed over her, planting kisses along the way, starting at her stomach and working up to her mouth.

I could die from this. Her heart could give out right now and Marai wouldn't care, so long as he kept touching her in this reverent way.

Her fingers fumbled with the buttons on his trousers, but soon she guided them down over his hips and Ruenen quickly stepped out of them.

The sight of him, all lean, smooth muscle. He placed a hand on either side of her, steadying himself. She couldn't stop her body's reaction to him. She was lightning waiting to strike. Marai knew that the moment he was inside her, she would explode with power and light.

Ruenen hesitated, watching her expression for any sign of discomfort. He still relived the moment in the alley when she'd run from his touch.

Not this time.

"I want you inside me," she whispered, she begged.

Ruenen didn't hesitate again.

One thrust and Marai shouted with pleasure. He filled her so perfectly; she'd never known this kind of intimacy could feel so *good*.

Slowly, his hips undulated and circled, making Marai writhe with pleasure beneath him. Ruenen was *giving*. He studied her reactions, noticed what she responded to, worshiped her with kisses and caresses in places that made her moan and gasp.

Her body was on fire, heart thundering. White and gold and starlight and sunlight and crashing waves . . .

The world exploded around her in a cosmic display of colors and stars. The sound that escaped her throat was one she'd never made before—guttural ecstasy and joy.

Ruenen called out her name.

And Marai swore then that she'd never heard a more heavenly sound than her name upon his lips.

CHAPTER 39
Marai

A symphony of birds sung in the birch tree outside the window. Golden sunbeams splayed across white sheets.

Strong arms tugged her closer with a groan-like sigh. He tossed a leg over her. His stubbly chin burrowed into the crook of her neck.

I don't want this to end.

"You're not going to like this, but I have to go," Ruenen whispered.

Marai's heart sunk, but she knew why he needed to leave. His coronation was in a few hours. Already, Marai heard servants dashing back and forth outside in the hallway. They were probably searching for him . . .

What would happen if they were discovered? Kings often did whatever they wanted with women, but Marai was different. This whole situation was different. Marai could already hear the scolding from Holfast, Fenir, and Vorae: the king shouldn't *dally* with a faerie.

Ruenen groaned as he turned over onto his back. Marai felt immediately chilled from the absence of his body.

"I need coffee," he said with a rasp, scrubbing a hand across his jaw.

They hadn't gotten much sleep, spending hours exploring each other. It had been a night Marai would never forget. She traced a finger across his lips. Ruenen closed his eyes at the touch. When he opened them again, he tucked her wild hair behind her ear, as Marai so often watched Raife do with Thora.

"I'm in love with you, you know," he whispered. "I have been since the moment you told me your name. I think even before that, when I saw you single-handedly take down those thieves in Grelta."

Ruenen's confession swirled around in the chambers of her heart. The words burst within her, warm and rosy and bright; Marai was surprised she wasn't glowing.

Those words shattered the last hurdle between this new Marai and the Lady Butcher. She'd said those words before to Slate, and they'd been a lie, something forced upon her.

"You don't have to say anything," continued Ruenen, "but I wanted you to know—"

"I do, too," Marai blurted, then felt her cheeks flush. "Love you, that is."

Ruenen beamed as if he'd eaten the sun. His lips met hers. Marai was where she always wanted to be—home in his arms. Lost and found again in his kiss.

The birds outside the window chirped with more persistence. Ruenen groaned.

"Time's up, I'm afraid," he said with a pout.

Ruenen clamored out of bed with all the grace of a toddler, and Marai studied his glorious form in the morning sun. The red scar was more prominent in daylight. A symbol of his bravery. A symbol of his sacrifice. She hoped it never faded, like the sunburst mark on his wrist.

As he bent over to fetch his trousers, she admired the taut muscles in his rear and thighs.

"Careful, Lady Marai. You're drooling," Ruenen said, winking. She threw a pillow at him. He caught it with an expression of mock alarm. "Pardon me, but I think it's bad form to abuse the king on his coronation day." He then released a melodic laugh as Marai made a face.

"I don't have anything to wear."

"Oh, I'll have something sent up for you," Ruenen replied lightly with an air of playfulness that made Marai instantly suspicious. "As long as you leave the black cloak behind for the day." Fully dressed, Ruenen leaned across the bed and smacked her lips with an unabashed kiss. "Duty calls."

Marai trailed her fingers once more through his soft hair. Ruenen closed his eyes, leaning into her hand, and shivered a sigh. Then, he strode with peacock swagger from the room.

Insufferable, she thought with a laugh, remaining wrapped within the warm sheets that smelled of Ruenen.

Not long after his exit, Harmona appeared. Horrified, Marai realized she was completely naked underneath the sheets—her nightgown still on the floor. If Harmona noticed, she didn't show any sign. Instead, she placed a bowl of porridge on the table and scampered into the hallway. Marai quickly stepped into her nightgown and tied the string at the top. She wolfed down her porridge as Harmona came back into the room with another servant carrying green fabric in her arms.

The servant draped a dress across the bed, and as Marai approached, she fought back a gasp.

The bodice was rich forest green velvet that plunged to a low v, trimmed with braided gold and aureate jewels. The back was bare, save for gold necklace-like strands that hung from one side to the other. On each shoulder, green gauzy fabric floated down like a cape, but didn't cover the low open back. The dress had no sleeves, save for a sliver. The green silk skirt hugged a body's curves, ending in a long train smattered with gold ivy vines.

It was a gown made for presentation, for highlighting the beauty of a woman's figure. It was the most arresting, most beautiful dress Marai had ever seen.

How could she wear this? It didn't suit her. The dress would show off too much skin. It was too eye-catching. Too rich. Marai had hoped to blend in with the crowd during the celebrations, another face . . . this gown wouldn't allow for that.

"Where did this come from?" she asked Harmona, fingers gliding over the fine fabric.

"His Grace had it altered for you days ago. It belonged to the late Queen Larissa."

Marai's hand stilled. This was a *queen's* gown?

Before she'd even recovered, Ruenen had picked this gown for *her* specifically for his coronation. If Marai wasn't already overcome with love for him, she would've fallen for him right then and there.

I should at least try it on. It probably won't fit, anyways...

Harmona helped Marai into the delicate, complex dress. If Marai pulled or twisted the wrong way, one of the gold chains could snap. Then Harmona sat her on the stool at the vanity, and wove green and gold ribbon through Marai's hair in an elegant updo which accentuated the back of the dress. Harmona topped off the hairstyle with a gold jeweled headpiece that matched the chains on the gown, obviously also from Queen Larissa's personal effects.

Without asking, Harmona quickly dabbed rouge upon Marai's cheeks. She swiped red paint across her lips and lined Marai's eyes lightly with kohl. Lastly, Harmona handed Marai two gold-chained pieces that slid onto Marai's hands like gloves. They latched at the wrists and draped across the top of her hands.

"Why go through all this trouble?" Marai asked, staring at the stranger in the mirror.

Who was this woman? She looked powerful. Feminine. *Royal.* A part deep inside of Marai delighted in gazing upon this woman. She was so different from the surly face she usually saw in the mirror. For once, Marai saw her human mother, and she didn't shy away from the reflection. But this woman was a stronger version, not so delicate and docile. *This* woman was flame and magic. Marai's body changed—she held her head higher, shoulders back, in a regal stance.

I suppose I am *Queen of the Fae* . . . for the first time, Marai felt the rightness in knowing her ancestry.

"His Grace and Lord Holfast agreed that you must dress your best. There are noblemen from all across Astye here, and you are an honored guest." Harmona said all this to the floor, as usual.

"Thank you, Harmona."

For the first time, Harmona looked up and met Marai's eyes. There was still fear shining in them, but the maid gave a weak nod in return, a small tight-lipped smile. Perhaps Marai might win her over yet.

"It's time, my lady."

Marai was aware of every single pair of eyes that tracked her.

She stood at the doorway to the vast hall of the monastery, a place in the castle she'd yet to explore. It was a sparse room, as most monasteries were. No gilded colors in sight. No jewels. Enormous windows lined the walls. Vaulted ceilings displayed paintings of Lirr and Laimoen. Hundreds of candles covered the front of the hall on wrought-iron pillars and stands. The only decorations were the large, vivid bouquets of native flowers lining the aisle, and the Nevandian sunburst banners and flags hanging from the walls.

Hundreds of people lined the rows within. Thousands more stood outside in the courtyard behind her, and in the Kellesar streets. Through the open archways, Marai spotted children tossing flower petals into the air, coating the cobblestones in pink, purple, and yellow. Women jingled belled bracelets to drive away evil spirits. Music floated on the breeze. People danced in the streets. A city alive with celebration.

Heads followed Marai as she ventured down the green carpeted aisle. Representatives from most of the Nine Kingdoms were there: dark skinned nobles from the Southern countries of Ain and Henig, shorter tanned diplomats from Ehle and Beniel in the West. Marai spotted fashionable men and women from the Empire of Syoto. Princess Eriu, Rhia's sister and the singular representative of Varana, stood demurely near the front of the hall with the servant who'd rescued her.

Then there was Nieve with her retinue, taking up the majority of the front right side of the hall. The Northern Queen was the most prominent person in the room. If people weren't staring at Marai, they were gawking at Nieve, who preened at the attention. She shot Marai a slow, arrogant smile, one of the few in the room to actually hold her gaze.

Heads leaned together to whisper, not too quietly, about the faerie who had single-handedly destroyed a third of the Tacornian army. Many regarded her with genuine terror as she passed. Others grimaced and scowled. Others avoided eye contact at all costs. Marai tried to ignore them, and kept her focus centered.

Halfway up the aisle, Thora waved to Marai from the end of a row. She wore a nice, simple blue dress; nothing near as flashy as Marai, but clearly new for the occasion. Her hair had been styled prettily atop her head with sprigs of heather and gorse. Tarik and the other two surviving werewolves, Brass and Yovel, stood next to her in the row. Hazel-eyed Yovel lost his arm in the battle.

"Good to see you, Lady Marai," Tarik said.

"I'm glad to see you all well." A heaviness settled within her. Three of Tarik's compatriots had not survived. "I'm sorry for your loss."

Tarik's face fell. "The fact that three of us still stand here to see this day, when humans and magical folk can share the same room, is joy enough for us." He gave her a swift nod, then returned to chatting with the other two weres.

"You look gorgeous," Thora said, taking Marai's sweaty hand. "Where did this dress come from?"

"It was Queen Larissa's," said Marai. "Ruenen had it fixed up for me."

Thora quirked a playful eyebrow, making Marai flush.

Keshel entered, looking harried and winded. He walked briskly down the aisle and came to Marai's side. He was dressed in a conservative dark vest and pants with a deep blue cloak, but his hair was unusually messy and cheeks were wind-blown, as if he'd run a long way to make it in time.

"Where have you *been*?" Thora hissed at him. "You never came home to the cottages last night."

"Busy. Witan meetings. Walking in town . . ." Keshel tried to fix his tangled hair.

"You're hiding something," said Marai, narrowing her eyes at him.

"Nonsense. Where are Raife and Aresti?" he asked.

Keshel was good at keeping secrets, but something wasn't sitting well with her. It wasn't a secret lover, Marai guessed, not with the way Keshel's eyes traveled up and down her dress. What was Keshel keeping from both her and Thora?

"The King's Guard is walking in behind Prince Ruenen," said Thora, clearly not as concerned by Keshel's odd behavior as Marai.

Head Monk Baureo entered in his brown robes, and the massive, echoing chamber quieted. Slowly, he walked down the aisle, chanting the ancient language of the gods. Everyone bowed as he passed.

Then two brown-robed priestesses entered; each wore a headdress adorned with lit candles. They joined hands and walked, chanting, down the aisle after the Head Monk. Once they reached the dais, all three religious leaders raised their chins to the ceiling and reached up to the gods painted there. They swayed, reeds in the wind, and the priestesses' candle flames flickered.

Avilyard, his armor polished to gleaming perfection, appeared next at the door, followed by two flag bearers. The steady clank of their boots down the aisle thumped in rhythm with Marai's heart.

Then Ruenen stepped into the room.

Heads bowed, knees bent low; no gaze could fall upon him until he reached the dais where the Head Priestesses now twirled around themselves, chanting.

From her curtsey, Marai watched Ruenen's feet pass. Tall black boots. The white fur cape dragged heavily behind. His steps hitched a moment when his feet approached Marai, but he passed without a word, heading towards the dais.

The King's Guard followed, rattling down the aisle. Raife and Aresti were at the rear, behind Elmar and Nyle, as was expected for newer members of the guard. Marai dared a glance up; they both marched with poise and honor. Aresti, in particular, seemed to be in her element.

Who would've thought this would be the life she chose?

Aresti and Raife met Marai's eyes and smiled as they passed. *Kadi would have loved this.*

The Witenagemot entered last. Holfast, Fenir, and Vorae were at the front, black robes recently pressed, not a wrinkle in sight. Shining gold livery collars hung around their necks, and Nevandian emblem pins sparkled against the black robes. This was an important day for them, as well. Holfast had somehow held this country together for nine years. He had every reason to celebrate his accomplishments.

But Fenir looked jumpy, as Ruenen had said earlier. He twisted his hands in the fabric of his robe as he walked. His owlish eyes darted around the room, as if he expected Rayghast to pop up from the Underworld at any moment. Or like he was expecting some kind of attack . . .

Finally, Head Monk Baureo spoke. "You may rise, my children."

Hundreds of bodies shifted, standing to full height. Marai could scarcely see anything over their heads. A particularly statuesque group of Henigis in their turbans stood in front of Marai. Peering between two bodies, Marai finally caught a full glimpse of Ruenen. His outfit was almost entirely gold brocade, except for the trimmings and lacings in forest green.

Marai's heart swelled with pride and eyes stung with tears as Ruenen knelt to one knee. The priestesses blessed Ruenen with holy words and marked his forehead with a smudge of brown dirt. Dirt of Nevandia, his home and duty.

Monk Baureo droned on in boring words about Ruenen's courage. His leadership. Marai's ears tuned him out as she focused on Ruenen's expression.

He kept himself composed and regal, but she saw the twitch of his mouth. The tightness of his eyes. This was an emotional moment for him. She knew he was thinking about the monks who raised him. They'd be proud of the man he had become. And the Chongan family . . . while they hadn't known Ruenen's secret, they would be standing amongst the crowd now, too, if they'd lived.

Ruenen agreed to the duties set before him in a strong baritone voice. Head Monk Baureo lifted a golden crown, each pointed bedecked with emeralds, high into the air.

"With this crown, we name you King Ruenen, of the House Avsharian, Sovereign of the great country of Nevandia."

Slowly, the crown was placed upon Ruenen's wavy chestnut hair. He stood with grace, a commanding presence.

"All hail the King," shouted the priestesses and Monk Baureo.

"*Hail!*" The word echoed through the hall, loud as thunder.

Ruenen faced the room, swimming in sunlight. The recessional began with the Witan, then King's Guard. Every guest bowed deeply once again. Marai could only tell what was happening based on the shoes of the people passing.

Then black boots stopped right in front of her. A green suede-gloved hand reached out.

Marai lifted her gaze to Ruenen's twinkling eyes.

"Lady Marai, you must *never* bow to me."

Her heart completely stopped. Ruenen smiled with both dimples and waited until Marai finally placed her hand in his.

He shouldn't be doing this...

As Ruenen led her down the aisle, Marai trembled. She was acutely aware of her sweaty palms, how every eye was on her; this faerie girl the King of Nevandia had plucked from the crowd and paraded before them all.

The matching regal clothes, the walk, the words...

It was a statement.

Ruenen was announcing his intentions loud and clear.

Judging by the disgruntled and shocked looks on the Witan's faces, they had no idea their king would be making such a statement. Fenir appeared like he was choking on his own tongue. Holfast frowned deeply, but said not a word, though Marai knew there were many on his tongue.

They headed towards the banquet hall, but Ruenen quickly pulled Marai into a hallway nearby as the cavalcade of feet marched past.

"What are you doing?" she asked, breathless. Was it because the dress was tight against her ribs? Or was it from her proximity to Ruenen? To his obvious choice...

Holy gods, that cannot be right.

"I wanted a moment alone with you," he uttered, taking her in. "I knew you'd be resplendent in gold."

Marai's face and chest heated. "People will see us. Isn't this rather improper for a newly crowned king?"

"I don't care," Ruenen said, running fingers down her uncovered arms. "Sit beside me at dinner." Marai could do nothing but nod stupidly as he pressed his forehead to hers. Their noses touched. "I know this is all overwhelming and uncomfortable for you. But please trust me."

"I do," she whispered.

"There's something I want to discuss with you. And I have a gift. May I come to your rooms later tonight?"

Marai went hot and cold all over. Her body didn't know if it should feel pleasure and excitement, or shock and fear. He couldn't mean ... was he going to ... *her?*

She never thought she'd be one ... a wife. It was a dream she never dared imagine, because it was too improbable. She was too wild and untamable. But Ruenen had seen through those defenses. He'd shattered her walls with kindness.

But could she be a wife? *A queen?*

The country would never accept her. It was madness.

But she loved him. She *loved* him, and he loved her.

Ruenen stared down at her with starlight and gold in his eyes, then led her into the banquet hall where guests were already seated and eating. The room roared with life and laughter and music. Young couples danced, twirling around each other with abandon and joy. It was as if Nevandia had been reborn. Nothing remained of that gray, desolate country.

As Ruenen passed tables with Marai on his arm, men and women raised their glasses to him. They shouted his name, wished him a long and healthy reign.

Holfast and Nieve sat at the high table, two vacant seats between them. As Ruenen and Marai sat down, Nieve gave her a knowing smile.

"Why, Lady Marai, I hardly recognize you," the Queen said. "Nevandian colors suit you."

To Ruenen's right, Holfast frowned.

"Your Grace is too kind," Marai said. "It's an honor to be seated at this table in such mighty company."

"Don't be silly. If *anyone* deserves to sit next to King Ruenen, it's you. Many are aware that it's due to your power that he lives at all."

Marai coughed into her wine. Beneath the table, Ruenen squeezed her hand. Nieve's smile widened, ice-blue eyes gleamed.

"You honor me, Your Grace," said Marai.

Behind them, Raife and Aresti lingered, standing guard over Ruenen. It was a place of honor, to stand at the high table with the king. It was clear Ruenen had stationed them there as yet another statement to his guests: *magical folk are respected here.* He turned, smiling, and waved them off.

"Thank you both, but you should go and enjoy the celebration," he said.

"Is that wise, Your Grace?" asked Fenir, who'd grown paler and sweatier since the ceremony. "You never know if a Tacornian assassin—"

Ruenen shot Marai a wink. "With Lady Marai at my side, I'm well protected."

Raife bowed and dashed off to sit next to Thora, Keshel, Tarik, Brass, and Yovel. Aresti, however, inched closer towards Nieve. Marai swore she heard the queen mumble something to Aresti before she joined Raife at the table in the far corner of the room.

Ruenen offered Marai his hand. "May I interest you in a dance?"

Marai's eyes widened. "I don't know how."

He laughed, clear as a bell, and lifted her to her feet. "Neither do I, but it looks like fun. We'll make it up as we go along."

Without giving her a moment more to protest, Ruenen swept Marai to the center of the room where the young couples continued their caper. Ruenen's face was alight with boyish charm and mischief as he followed the dance moves of the young noble from one of the Nevandian houses next to him. Marai tripped over her own feet trying to keep up with the steps.

But then Ruenen grabbed her hands and twirled her. They spun and galloped, completely disregarding the obviously practiced dance steps of the others. Marai let out a laugh, a free, girlish sound she never made. She'd never *felt* so free before.

After their rambunctious dance, the music slowed. Couples changed out, but Ruenen held onto Marai's hand. This dance was quite different, languorous, with a sweeping instrumental. The couples encircled each other, arms moving in elegant strokes. Marai let Ruenen guide her. Men twirled their partners inwards. Marai's back hit Ruenen's chest as he pulled her closer. His nose grazed her temple. Her breathing quickened.

"My restraint is hanging by a very loose and tenuous thread right now," he whispered in a husky, sinful voice that roused searing heat across Marai's skin.

They swayed, the rest of the dance forgotten. Marai drowned out everything except the sound of his beating heart, the air in his lungs. She didn't hear the room applaud at the end of the song. She didn't see the couples swap places for the next dance.

Eventually, it was Ruenen who came to his senses. He swallowed, cleared his throat, and stepped away from her.

"As much as it pains me, I must go speak with the ambassadors from Syoto and Ain. They've been trying to catch my attention across the room, and Holfast was relentless in his urges that we create a trade deal with them, since they are two of our closest neighbors."

"Go, I'm fine," Marai said, but the moment he turned away from her, someone else approached.

"Have fun last night?" Nosficio's seductive voice asked. He grinned toothily at her. The dancers gasped, and immediately returned to their tables at the sudden appearance of a vampire. "Looked as if things were heating up."

"It's rude to spy," Marai said, trying to hide the heating of her cheeks with a scowl.

"Not my fault you were standing in front of a window, darling. Honestly, I'm surprised you and the king didn't rip each other's clothes off right here." Nosficio offered her his hand. "Your dancing skills could use practice."

"I've no use for dancing."

"You will if the king asks you what I think he's going to ask."

"Stop giving me that look."

Nosficio's eyes opened wide in innocence. "What look?"

"That *knowing* look."

Nosficio's grin turned vexatious. "My dear, I've been alive a long time. I cannot help if I *know* things."

Marai's glare deepened. "Tell me you're leaving tomorrow."

"I am, indeed," Nosficio said with a laugh. "Vampires are natural nomads, and I've stayed in one place far too long. But I'll be back, Butcher, so don't be too sad upon my departure. I've decided to keep an eye on you—make sure Aras and Meallán's heir fulfills her duty."

His eyes then pinned onto Nieve, who was making her own rounds at various tables. Her hand was currently being kissed by a nobleman from Ehle.

"Are you suggesting that we're friends now?" Marai asked him.

"I don't have friends anymore," Nosficio said, "but if I did . . . I suppose you'd be acceptable."

Marai smirked and marched back to the high table. She was loathe to admit it, but Nosficio was right. She'd developed some kind of feeling for the vampire. It wasn't friendship, exactly, but she would be sorry to see him go. He'd stayed true to their alliance. He'd been a valuable asset. She knew he would keep returning to claim his place in the Witan.

She smiled to herself as she sat down at the nearly vacant table. Holfast was the only one who remained; Vorae was laughing with a group of noblemen, and Fenir was standing against the wall, wringing his hands, as if frightened someone might ask him to dance. Holfast regarded Marai with his usual serious expression.

"You seem quite happy, Lady Marai."

"I suppose I am. It's a good night."

Holfast watched her take a long sip from her wine. *Here comes the scolding . . .*

"We owe you a great deal, and I want to thank you," he said.

Surprise washed over Marai as the wine warmed her throat.

"I will never forget what you did for us. Nevandia would be lost now if it weren't for your bravery, your magic, and for the alliances you helped forge." Holfast was a guarded man, but honesty and respect shown in his gaze. "I'm truly grateful, Lady Marai. The power you wielded on that battlefield . . . I watched from afar. I *saw* the things you can do. You could have used that power on us at any time. You could have wiped Nevandia off the map and taken it for your own."

"How do you know I still won't?" she challenged, raising an eyebrow.

The wine was making her bold. *Don't be reckless, Storm Cloud,* Thora's voice warned. She, Thora, was currently on the dance floor with Raife, brimming with irrepressible glee (and also doing the steps far better than Marai and Ruenen had).

"Because you love him." Holfast's eyes snapped to Ruenen, who was surrounded by a group of noblewomen and their pretty daughters, tossing their hair and batting their eyelashes. "I know you'd never do anything to harm him."

The young ladies around Ruenen giggled. He smiled and nodded politely, but his eyes wandered to Marai at the high table.

Those women wouldn't be paying Ruen any notice if they knew he wasn't truly of royal blood.

If he'd remained a bard . . .

"Nevandia is heading towards a tremendous period of rebuilding," Holfast continued. "There's much we need to fix, and to do that, we will need strong alliances. I've no desire to break the bond between you and the king, but I have Nevandia's future to consider. Most advisors would try to run you off, tell you that you shouldn't marry him, that you're nothing but a faerie and a commoner."

The warmth she'd received from the wine chilled within her. Marai hardened her expression, trying to reveal nothing of how those words affected her. "So you're saying I *should* marry him?"

"I'm saying that my hands are tied," Holfast said. His tone wasn't harsh. It was matter-of-fact.

Those beautiful, refined ladies standing with Ruenen, with their money and powerful families . . . They were the type of women he was expected to marry, to bring strength and wealth back to Nevandia. He would be betrothed to the Greltan or Syoton princess. Hells, maybe young Princess Eriu of Varana. Binding himself to Marai would only bring Ruenen contempt.

"However, I believe I have an alternative for you, Lady Marai," Holfast said, now focusing his stoic brown eyes back on her. "I'd like for you to continue your role as his personal guard. Perhaps even be a permanent advisor on the Witan. You will always have his best interests and safety at heart. There's no one who will serve him with more vigor. Ruenen must marry the appropriate queen, however that doesn't mean you cannot become his mistress."

"What?" Marai spat the word.

"We can come to an appropriate arrangement," the Steward continued. "His queen can be situated in a suite on the opposite side of the castle. As long as she produces a royal heir or two, you can still be adored by the king, love him, have your fun. Even have a few children of your own, if you so desire."

The acidic words burned. The food and wine she'd consumed turned rancid within her stomach.

Could she become Ruenen's mistress? Watch as he married another, knowing that he'd be forced to perform his husbandly duties and sire an heir? Did Marai have the strength to see another woman bear his children?

Marai had barely begun thinking of her future, but she'd never imagined being the *other woman*. She steeled herself, sharpened her features like a blade. Holfast wasn't trying to hurt her—he was trying to open her eyes.

"Whatever you decide to do, make certain it's a life you can live with," he said, not unkindly. "Someone with your spark should never feel confined to a cage."

Marai couldn't bear to watch those girls flirt with Ruenen any longer. She hated how Vorae was already hard at work in talks with ambassadors from different kingdoms around the room, probably discussing which princess had the highest fortune.

Air. I need air.

Marai practically ran from the hall into the courtyard. She leapt out into the night and gulped down the cool spring breeze, the smell of wisteria filling her nose.

Holfast was right, of course. It wasn't as if Marai hadn't known or expected . . . she'd gotten swept up in the fantasy of it all.

But what would Ruenen think? She knew he wouldn't accept Holfast's words. Ruenen would fight against any betrothal, but eventually, he'd have no choice. He had a duty, as all kings did before him.

There was a part of Marai that wanted to run. To grab her black cloak and disappear into the night, so she could shut out the breaking of her heart. But she couldn't become the Butcher again. She couldn't erect the walls and hide from the world anymore.

I'll talk to him. Tonight, when we're alone, we'll discuss this together.

That was the right thing to do. They'd started this journey together. They would find an answer.

"Marai, are you alright?"

Marai whipped around. Keshel strode towards her, pack slung over his shoulder. Another larger one was strapped to his back.

"I'm fine," she blurted, then her mind began to comprehend Keshel's appearance. "Are you leaving?"

"It's time, I think."

"You don't want to stay until the end of the feast? Did you say goodbye to the others?"

"Yes, during dinner. I thought it was best to slip away," he said, studying Marai's face. He clearly didn't believe she was fine. "Will you remain here in Nevandia?"

"I have no intention of leaving Ruenen," she stated firmly. "I suppose I need to decide what kind of life I want to lead, as Holfast so aptly reminded me . . ."

Keshel stepped closer. "You could become Queen of the Fae. You could leave, take up your birthright, and unite the magical folk of this continent."

"Leave and go where? I have no kingdom, Keshel," said Marai with a shake of her head. "I don't even know if I *want* to be Queen of the Fae."

There was an eagerness in Keshel's voice as he said, "I think the gods are telling us something. You're *meant* to lead your people, Marai. I've had visions recently. Visions of you, of the future. You don't need to stay here. You owe Ruenen nothing. You saved his kingdom. You can come with us."

"I won't leave Ruenen. This is where I choose to be," Marai said, then halted. "What do you mean 'us'?"

Keshel's face burned with excitement. "I didn't want to say before when you were still healing: I met another faerie."

Keshel's words punched Marai in the stomach. "How?"

"Well, actually, he found *us*. He's the one who traveled here with Tarik's group." Keshel grinned.

This was why he'd been acting so strange. He'd been sneaking off to talk to another faerie!

"Oh, here he is now—"

Footsteps approached from the courtyard entrance. A man, with a small pack slung over his shoulder, strolled across the cobblestones. He had dark skin and bright silvery eyes. His knit cap covered shiny black hair and pointed fae ears. He was strikingly handsome . . . and also *familiar.*

"Marai, this is Koda," Keshel said, gesturing to the stranger.

Koda grinned and bowed to Marai. "We meet again."

The man on the docks in Cleaving Tides who'd bought her fish, had urged Marai to come to Andara.

"I remember you," Marai said in disbelief.

Koda's grin widened. "I'm honored. I've been hoping to run into you again."

A strange, wary feeling crept under her skin. Koda seemed *too* eager. Although, Marai supposed that a solitary fae *would* be excited to meet more of his kind . . .

"I've been tracking you ever since Cleaving Tides, when I helped free your prince, or rather, *king,* from Rayghast's hunters," he said.

"I thought perhaps you were behind his escape," Marai replied.

"I watched the battle from afar. I saw your powers." Koda's eyes glistened in the moonlight. "You're something special, Marai. Truly magnificent! And Keshel told me that you're Meallán's descendant."

Unease slithered along her spine. Marai didn't like the way Koda was moving towards her; how he knew so many things about her, and she didn't know a thing about him.

"Weren't you going to Andara?" She took one step backwards towards the castle doors.

"Yes, that's where Lord Keshel and I are headed now. There are more of us there. I told you—Andara is a *fascinating* place, full of magic. Many magical folk took up residence there to escape the massacres, not to mention the native-borns." Koda animatedly told his story with gestures and gleaming eyes. Next to him, Keshel was enraptured with each word. "We get along with our human compatriots."

It sounded too good to be true. Whatever secrets isolated Andara housed, Marai wasn't interested in seeing first-hand at the moment.

"Come with us," Koda continued. "My fellow fae will be thrilled to have a faerie queen leading us once again. We'd welcome you with open arms. What's there for you here? Nevandia may be trying to usher in change, but it'll be slow and dangerous."

"All the more reason for me to stay," Marai said, trying to keep her tone polite.

Koda's smile disappeared. "There's much you don't know. Besides, there's someone very important who wants to meet you."

Keshel was frowning now, glancing between Marai and Koda.

"Whoever they are, they can come here and meet me, if they so desire," said Marai, sharpening her words into a spear. She no longer feigned politeness. "I'm not going to Andara."

"That's fine, Marai," Keshel began, sensing the rising tension. "I'll let you know what I discover."

Koda sighed. "What a shame."

He raised a hand, and Marai reached for Dimtoir.

But then she remembered it wasn't there, at her hip. It had been broken by dark magic on the battlefield. In fact, Marai had *no* weapons strapped to her that night. A careless move. She reached for her magic, but she was already too late...

Magic slammed into her body. Cold seeped in, paralyzing every muscle. She couldn't move. She couldn't breathe or blink.

But she *could* see.

People in the courtyard had frozen in place. All the Nevandian and Greltan guards stationed at each entrance, several citizens dancing in the streets. Even Keshel hadn't been able to produce a shield fast enough.

Marai reached once again for her magic, but it was frozen, too; a giant block of ice sitting within the depths of her.

The only thing moving was Koda.

Through her stationary eyes, Marai watched Koda pull out a small tin box from his coat pocket. He lifted the lid, revealing a kind of metallic powder the color of charcoal. He took a pinch, silver eyes gleaming in the night as he faced Marai.

"This would have been much easier if you'd come willingly."

He blew the pinch of powder into her face. Marai wanted to cough, but her paralyzed lungs wouldn't contract. The powder settled in her eyes and up her nose. It burned on contact, and smelled chemical, sulfuric.

Her vision dimmed. A buzzing hummed in her ears.

Koda performed the same routine on Keshel as Marai's world went dark, the powder knocking her unconscious.

Someone see us! Please! She tried to shout, but everything was growing faint.

Suddenly, Koda's magic released her. She dropped, boneless, to the ground.

"Open your portal," Koda ordered, voice coming from above her.

"*Fuck you,*" Marai snarled with the remaining strength she had. The powder made her weak, sucking all the energy from her.

"Open it, or I kill Keshel," said Koda.

Marai heard the scrape of metal as Koda unsheathed a small blade. Keshel grunted from a physical impact.

"My knife is at his neck. Do it now, or I slit Keshel's throat."

Lie. Unleash the lightning instead.

But she couldn't see. She couldn't direct her magic. What if she hit Keshel or the guards?

"Or should I announce to the entire party inside that your king is a *fake*?"

How Koda knew, Marai was unsure, but it didn't matter—she had no choice.

"Where?" she asked through gritted teeth.

"The Syoton port of Baatgai."

Marai lifted one arm, heavy as lead, and pulled from deep within, remembering details of the Baatgai port she'd visited in her travels. She felt the magic leave her fingers, but couldn't tell if she'd truly formed the portal.

"Good girl," said Koda. Strong arms looped around her stomach and heaved her to her feet.

Ruen... come find me...

CHAPTER 40
Ruenen

He finally created a polite way to escape the cloud of young ladies and mothers. There was only so much giggling and fawning he could take. A few months ago he would have enjoyed such company, but now he was used to all the mysteries and complexities of Marai. She made those girls seem dull, lackluster.

Ruenen returned to the high table and took a sip of sparkling wine, scanning the room for Marai.

"Where has Lady Marai gone?" he asked Holfast, who stood nearby with Fenir and several noblemen in conversation.

"I'm not certain, Your Grace," said Holfast, with an air of avoidance, as Fenir's eyes widened.

"I saw you talking to her moments ago. She didn't seem particularly pleased."

Holfast pursed his lips. He made a quick excuse to the nobles and pulled Ruenen aside. "I merely told her what she needed to hear, Your Grace."

"Which was?"

"That Nevandia must come first, and that you'll do what's right by your kingdom."

Ruenen's eyes narrowed. "By marrying someone you choose for me, correct?"

"A woman whom the Witan deems the most beneficial and suitable, yes."

Irritation ignited in his blood. "You had no right to discuss those matters with Lady Marai, especially before talking with me."

No wonder Marai had looked so upset. Did she truly believe Ruenen would listen to those orders? He had to tell Marai that she was the only woman he wanted to be with. Perhaps she'd gone upstairs to her room . . .

Ruenen stormed off through the reveling hall, past crowing nobles and inebriated dancers. Thora and Raife were nose to nose, laughing on the dance floor, effortlessly, freely in love. Aresti and Nosficio were engaged in a flirtatious conversation with Nieve, all coy smiles and steamy eyes, their heads bowed together in a corner of the hall.

Once in the entryway, Ruenen turned to the guards by the main hall doors.

"Have you seen Lady Marai?"

"She went outside, Your Grace," said Elmar.

Ruenen thanked the young guard, and ventured into the courtyard.

All the air left his lungs at the sight.

Ten soldiers, Nevandian and Greltan, lay motionless on the ground. Four bodies lay outside the portcullis. Two packs of belongings had been left in the middle of the courtyard. It was completely silent. An eerie chill, far too cold for spring, hovered in the air; Ruenen's fur cape couldn't block the chill from seeping into his bones.

Ruenen rushed to the nearest soldier, placing his fingers on the man's neck. A heartbeat, sure and steady.

He checked the next one. Unconscious, but alive. Relief washed over him, pushing aside the chill.

"*Guards*," shouted Ruenen inside the castle. "Call Commander Avilyard!"

Within minutes, Avilyard and a slew of guards burst into the courtyard from the feast. Raife and Aresti were with them; Thora trailed nervously behind.

"What happened?" Avilyard asked, trying to rouse one of the unconscious guards. It was Nyle.

Thora rushed forward and took Nyle's hand. "He's ice cold."

Magic spilled from her hands onto Nyle. The boy's eyes fluttered open. He bolted upright, gasping for air as if he'd been drowning.

"You're alright," Thora said, rubbing his back. She then moved on to the next one. "I can feel the residue of magic on their skin."

Magic? Dread rose the hair on Ruenen's arms. Why was it so bloody cold?

Someone sniffed the air, loud as a wolf. Ruenen nearly jumped to see Nosficio standing in the middle of the courtyard, having appeared out of nowhere.

"She's right," the vampire said, eyes darkening. "I smell strange magic. And something else . . . something chemical."

Chemical? What the fuck is going on?

"What happened, Sir Nyle?" Ruenen asked the only conscious man.

Avilyard handed him a flask. Nyle took a long drink, then his body heaved with a hacking cough.

"I can't remember . . ." the young knight said weakly. He chugged more of whatever was in Avilyard's flask.

"I can smell the Butcher," Nosficio said, prowling around the courtyard as Thora continued waking the other guards and revelers outside the portcullis. "And the fae councilman, Keshel. And someone else."

"Marai *was* out here?" pressed Ruenen.

"Yes," came a new, weak voice. Ruenen turned to another conscious guard; this one in silver Greltan armor. "She was speaking with the long haired fae on the council."

"What were they discussing?"

"Leaving."

Leaving? The pit in Ruenen's stomach grew larger. Had Marai and Keshel left together? But why knock out the guards?

"Then a man arrived."

The stranger Nosficio smelled. It had to be.

"He wasn't from here, and he wasn't dressed as a noble guest," continued the guard.

"What do you mean?" Avilyard asked.

"He had dark skin and wore peasant clothes. I think the faeries knew him," the guard said, holding his head and grimacing, as if the remembering hurt.

Marai had never mentioned this stranger before. Of course, there were plenty of things Ruenen still didn't know about her, but who was this man?

Nyle's eyes opened wide. "Something happened. The air grew cold and I couldn't move. As if I'd been turned to stone. The next thing I knew, Your Grace, I was waking up here on the ground."

Raife and Aresti exchanged dark, nervous looks.

"Do you know who this man could be?" Ruenen asked them.

"If Marai and Keshel truly knew him, they never introduced him to us," said Raife, jaw tensing.

"Or *mention* him," Aresti added as Holfast, Fenir, and Vorae appeared at the door. "Although Keshel *had* been acting odd since the battle..."

Fenir gasped, Vorae went slack-jawed and pale. Holfast stood and stared at the scene before him in disbelief.

Ruenen turned his attention back to Nyle. "You didn't hear any of their conversation?"

"I believe the man wanted Lady Marai to come with him somewhere."

"Where?"

"I'm sorry, Your Grace, but I was speaking with another guard, so I didn't hear them."

"Maybe she portaled Keshel and this stranger somewhere. She could be right back. Keshel did intend to leave tonight," suggested Thora, returning to Raife's side. All the attacked guards were now conscious and receiving water.

"And leave his precious books behind? Absolutely not," Aresti scoffed, lifting the packs. There was worry in her eyes. "How long ago did this happen?"

"I spoke with Lady Marai not twenty minutes ago," said Holfast.

"Then they may still be in the city," Raife said, turning to Avilyard.

The commander turned to his men. "Search the streets. I'll send out riders, as well."

Raife, Aresti, and the rest of the King's Guard rushed through the portcullis and into the Kellesar streets.

Nosficio's red eyes flashed. "I'll join them." He disappeared in a haze.

Ruenen made to follow, but someone grabbed his arm.

"No, Your Grace, you must stay here where it's safe," Holfast said. Ruenen glared back at him. "This could be an attack on *you*. Stay inside and let Commander Avilyard do his work."

"I cannot sit by and do nothing while Marai is missing," yelled Ruenen, fists clenching at his side.

Calmly, Holfast turned to Fenir and Vorae. "Go back inside and ensure our guests know nothing about this. Tell the guards to lock down the room, just in case."

Vorae nodded, and had to usher the visibly shaken Fenir back towards the main hall.

Ruenen stepped further into the courtyard, eyes darting around for a missed sign, some hidden clue. His heart raced as a sense of desperation took hold of him.

"I'm sure she's fine, Your Grace," Holfast said. "Lady Marai can take care of herself. Please, come back inside where it's safe."

No.

No, something was wrong.

Marai wouldn't vanish without a word again. Not after last night. Not after she'd told him she *loved* him. This wasn't like the last time ...

She'd been taken against her will somehow. Keshel, too. By this stranger ... someone else who had magic and could incapacitate not only an entire group of soldiers, but two powerful fae.

Ruenen stared into the night, lips reared back in a growl. His fingernails dug deep crescent moons into his palms.

But all the while, his heart was splintering.

"Marai!" He called her name into the eerily still night. His voice echoed off the cobblestones and marble castle walls. He shouted her name again and again, voice breaking as the fear began to take hold.

But Ruenen refused to lose her again.

I will find you.

Gods grant me this, I will find you.

CHAPTER 41
Marai

The world rocked back and forth.

Her stomach roiled. Her eyelids and limbs were leaden. When she tried to move, something held her down.

She'd been drugged. She could feel the substance flowing through her body. She could still smell it in her nostrils.

A man groaned next to her.

Slowly, she cracked open her eyes.

It was dark. It smelled of musty wood and salt water. Crates were stacked against the walls. Ocean crashed against the hull of the ship.

Marai was below deck; her ankles chained to the ground, and her arms were raised above her head, shackled to the wooden wall. Something heavy was latched around her neck. Another chain.

Think, Marai, get out of this!

She tried to pull on her magic, but the weight around her neck shocked her. A spark of foreign magic coursed through her, stifling her own.

She tried again—the zap that went through was a thousand daggers stabbing her at once.

Marai's heart plummeted as her magic cowed to this new, unknown power. Her eyes traveled hopelessly to her side, searching for anything to help, and landed on Keshel chained up next to her. His head lolled to the side, unconscious. An iron collar ensconced his neck.

Footsteps approached. Marai turned her stinging eyes to the stairs leading to the upper decks.

Koda knelt before her, opening his tin box. "Magic won't help you, Marai. Don't worry, the trip to Andara will pass in the blink of an eye."

"Ruenen will find us . . ." Marai slurred through a broken, tired throat.

Koda grinned from ear to ear. "You mean your human king? Even if he *did* somehow know where we're going, he'd never make it past the docks. I told you, Andara is a land of magic. Only those who've seen it, or are accompanied by a native may enter. My employer cannot *wait* to meet you, Marai. He'll put you to good use as the crown jewel of his collection."

He blew a pinch of powder into Marai's face. She gasped and hacked to no avail; the powder began to do its job.

"Sleep now, Marai. Your horrors aren't over yet."

Koda stepped aside, that same vicious grin plastered on his face, disappearing back above deck.

As darkness crept in around her, a new figure stalked towards her.

His blond, patchy hair stuck up at odd angles. His face was covered in thin, branch-like lines. On one side of his mouth, a nasty, abrasive scar sliced from lip to cheek. Leathery-red burns crawled up his arms, erasing the blue, green and black tattoos that had been there.

But his eyes were as strikingly blue as they'd always been.

Marai squirmed, shrinking backwards, though the chains kept her stationary. Her heart threatened to explode. Panic seized her.

No! No, please!

The severely scarred man smiled. It was crooked. Frightening. Wrong.

As Marai's strength failed her, her head fell to the side. The last thing she felt before disappearing into the void was hot breath against her ear, and a finger caressing the exposed skin of her arm.

"Hello again, Marai, my love," purred Slate.

THE STORY CONTINUES...

The story continues in . . .
"Queen of the Shadow Menagerie"
Dark Magic Series Book 3
Coming 2024

Please consider leaving a review—this indie author would really appreciate it!
Never miss a release day, cover reveal, or giveaway–sign up for J. E. Harter's monthly mailing list on her website:
https://jeharterauthor.wixsite.com/j--e--harter-author

GLOSSARY

AIN - Kingdom in the Southwest on the coast of Astye

ANDARA - Far away, mysterious country

ASTYE - The largest continent, home to The Nine Kingdoms

BAUREAN SEA - Body of water in the South

BENIEL - Kingdom in the Northwest of Astye

CASAMERE - Large country off the continent

CHIOJAN - Capital city of the Kingdom of Varana

CLEAVING TIDES - Prosperous port city in Henig, the Southernmost point of Astye, wealthy area above in the hills called High Tides, harbor and beaches called Low Tides

CLIFFS OF UNMYN - On the Northern Coastline, part of the White Ridge Mountains

DAL RIATA - Small Nevandian mining town

DUL TANEN - Capital city of the Kingdom of Tacorn

DWALINGULF - Large logging town in the lower North

EHLE - Kingdom in the Southwest of Astye, known for its deserts and canyons of red dirt

ELFAYGUA - Town in Tacorn

FENSMUIR - City in the Kingdom of Ain

GAINESBURY - Small village in the Northern White Ridge Mountains

GELANON -   Holiest day in the entire year, a winter holiday known for fasting, throwing minerals into fire to show colors for gods to see for blessings

GLOAW CRANA -   Town in Nevandia on the Tacornian border

GRAVE'S END -   Poorest neighborhood in Kellesar

GRELTA -   The Northernmost and largest kingdom on Astye, cold and snowy most of the year

HAVENFIORD -   Large town on the border of Grelta and Tacorn

HENIG -   Kingdom in the Southeast, busy harbors and port cities

INIQUITY -   Town of criminals, also known as the Den, the Nest, Vice, etc.

KAISHIKI - Capital city of the Kingdom of Syoto, home to the Nine Kingdom's Library

KELLESAR -   Capital city of the Kingdom of Nevandia

LAIMOEN -   God of Destruction and War, Lirr's partner

LIRR -   Goddess of Creation and All Living Things & Fertility

LIRRSTRASS -   Capital city of the Kingdom of Grelta

LISTAN -   Small, sandy country off the continent

MIDDLE KINGDOMS - Name for the two middle countries on Astye–Tacorn and Nevandia

MOUNT ERA -   Highest peak on the White Ridge Mountains

NEVANDIA -   Kingdom in the middle of Astye, in a bitter forty-year war with Tacorn

NYDIAN RIVER -   River that stretches East to South on Astye

OSTARA -   Holiday honoring Lirr and the welcoming of Spring, offerings of flowers and food, candles cleanse away the dark and usher in the light

PARACASO -   Town in Ehle

PEVEAR -   Town on the outskirts of Tacorn, once the site of a bloody battle

RED LANDS - Nickname for the Middle Kingdoms–a land so covered in blood

SILKEHAVEN - Small town in the Northern White Ridge Mountains

SYOTO - Empire in the Southeast of Astye

TACORN - Kingdom in the middle of Astye, in a bitter forty-year war with Nevandia

THE BOGGS - Slum town in Tacorn

THE DALE - Farming neighborhood in Nevandia, outside Kellesar walls

UKRA - Country off the continent

VARANA - Empire in the Northeast of Astye

WHITE RIDGE MOUNTAINS - Large Northern mountain range made of obsidian rock

YEHZIG - Small, tropical isle off the continent

Acknowledgements

I can't believe I'm writing one of these again. I'm so utterly grateful and lucky that I actually get to fulfill this life-long dream of telling stories. Publishing two books in one year is an insane amount of work, and I would never have been able to do it all if it weren't for my supportive team of fabulous individuals.

I must begin again with my amazing editor Erin Young. Your advice is essential, and I thank you profusely for your detailed notes and genuine enthusiasm for the Dark Magic Series and my writing style. Thank you for pointing out my addiction to the em dash.

Thank you, Miblart, for yet another fantastic cover design. You always seem to know exactly what my vision is, and I appreciate your patience as I tweak things a thousand times.

Alec McK for the world map of Astye.

My critique partner Addison—you are a literal STAR! Thank you for reading "RL&BF" *twice,* editing with care, and believing in my story. Sometimes, I think you know my characters better than I do. You have a real talent for editing and writing, and I learn a lot from you every single time.

Kelsey, Kinsey & Timm, my fabulous beta readers—thank you for reading/editing both Books 1 & 2! I really appreciate the time you put into your feedback, and you all had such fabulous ideas to make the story better. It matters more than I can say.

Kate & Molly—thank you both for your constant years of friendship. I so appreciate your willingness to provide opinions on book titles and covers, and to cheer me on as I continue to pursue this strange career. Much love to you both!

To my family and friends for reading and reviewing Book 1, and now doing it all over again with Book 2. One day, you will be really tired of reading my books, but I appreciate that you haven't yet reached that point. Your support means everything!

Lastly, thanks again to you, dear reader, for falling in love with Marai and Ruenen. I wouldn't be publishing "RL&BF" so quickly after "B&B" if you all weren't begging for Book 2 as soon as you finished Book 1. Your beautiful review comments make me tear up, and my heart genuinely wants to burst with joy. I'm so touched that people are connecting to these characters and their stories. Thanks for supporting this indie author!

Also by J. E. Harter

See where it all began in...
"The Butcher and the Bard"
Book 1 in the Dark Magic Series

About the Author

J. E. Harter is a lover of music, theatre, beaches, cats, and books (obviously). "The Butcher and the Bard" was her debut novel. She lives in NYC with two fluffy children Simon Catfunkel and Ziggy Starcat. When not authoring, she is (hopefully) inspiring young performers as a youth theatre director. Visit her website to sign up for her monthly newsletter:

https://jeharterauthor.wixsite.com/j--e--harter-author
Instagram: @j.e.harter
TikTok: @j.e.harterauthor
Facebook: J. E. Harter Fantasy Author

Printed in Great Britain
by Amazon